Advance Praise for Deeds of Darkness

"This guy has a wonderfully twisted mind! Buckle up for a scary ride."—Peter James, International bestselling crime thriller author

"William Burton McCormick is one of the most inventive and original writers currently working in the mystery short story field. He excels at everything from flash fiction to 20,000-word-plus novellas, employs settings ranging from Ancient Rome to contemporary Latvia, and incorporates ingenious clues in his stories based on everything from ancient engineering to the most up to date high-tech. One thing is certain: You won't be bored by a story collection from this American-born author who has lived in North-Eastern Europe for many years, and the stories will stay with you for a long time." —Janet Hutchings, Editor-in-Chief, *Ellery Queen's Mystery Magazine*

"William Burton McCormick's *Deeds of Darkness* showcases a rare talent. With lyrically evocative prose and astonishingly original plots, McCormick weaves an omnibus of tales that are a sheer pleasure to read. This collection belongs in your home library."—David Dean, two-time winner of the *Ellery Queen Mystery Magazine's* Readers Award.

"*Deeds of Darkness* was a good reminder to me of why I've always been a fan of McCormick's fiction. These twenty-four stories are not just suspenseful, entertaining tales—most are international thrillers, with settings that range from Ukraine to Latvia to Scotland to Ancient Rome. I loved every one of them!"—John M. Floyd, Shamus Award-winning author of *The Barrens*

"William Burton McCormick's *Deeds of Darkness* is a delight for those who, like me, enjoy twisted tales of suspense and bad behavior. A compendium of human nature's darkness, it's a shame Alfred Hitchcock isn't around to adapt some of these into film or television. "—John Harrison, Writer/Director of *Tales From The Darkside: The Movie*, the *Dune* miniseries, and *Clive Barker's Book of Blood*. He is also the author of the paranormal thriller novel, *Passing Through Veils*.

'If you are a fan of the mystery short story you owe yourself a big dose of McCormick. Suspense, comedy, history, intrigue – the man runs the gamut, whatever a gamut may be."—Robert Lopresti, prize-winning author of *Shanks On Crime*

"If Alfred Hitchcock was alive today, he'd be making movies based on William Burton McCormick's short fiction. In *Deeds of Darkness*, he takes readers on a whirlwind tour across time and space, with compelling suspense stories set from Rome in AD 50 to nineteenth and early twentieth-century Russia to Latvia in 1910 to small-town America in the 1940s and '50s to the Isle of Skye in 1989. Make sure your passport is up-to-date and enjoy the journey!"—Josh Pachter (author, editor, translator)

"William Burton McCormick's genius knows no bounds. Rich historical detail, vast international scope, and a lively array of reversals, surprises, and twists—the stories in *Deeds of Darkness* always dazzle and delight."—Art Taylor, Edgar Award-winning author of *The Adventure of The Castle Thief And Other Expeditions And Indiscretions*

DEEDS
OF
DARKNESS

STORIES

DEEDS
OF
DARKNESS

STORIES

WILLIAM BURTON MCCORMICK

LEVEL
SHORT

First published by Level Short 2024

Copyright © 2024 by William Burton McCormick

All rights reserved. No part of this publication may be reproduced, stored or transmitted in any form or by any means, electronic, mechanical, photocopying, recording, scanning, or otherwise without written permission from the publisher. It is illegal to copy this book, post it to a website, or distribute it by any other means without permission.

This novel is entirely a work of fiction. The names, characters and incidents portrayed in it are the work of the author's imagination. Any resemblance to actual persons, living or dead, events or localities is entirely coincidental.

William Burton McCormick asserts the moral right to be identified as the author of this work.

Author Photo Credit: Nika Popova

First edition

ISBN: 978-1-68512-790-9

Cover art by Level Best Designs

This book was professionally typeset on Reedsy.
Find out more at reedsy.com

To my mother, Susan, thanks for your love and support
AND
To Shirley Bozic, who read and gave me her thoughts on these tales.

This collection wouldn't exist without them

Foreword

The potential value of setting in a short story is both a commonplace and profoundly true. A beautifully evoked sense of place and time can efficiently and effectively inform both plot and character. In a form defined by constraints of length, every element must carry the greatest possible storytelling load, and thus a mastery of setting is an important article in the writer's toolbox. When it is well used, we often speak of the setting as the equivalent of a character unto itself.

As a writer, William Burton McCormick is adept with all the tools in his box, but his skill with setting is the aspect that comes first to my mind when I consider his work. I'm proud to say that *Alfred Hitchcock's Mystery Magazine* published Bill's first short story, "Blue Amber," in 2011, and this facility with place and time were already apparent. A historical mystery, "Blue Amber" is set in Latvia in the early years of the twentieth century, and the landscape, the political passions of the era, and the hope and desperation of the central character combined to produce an impressive debut.

Indeed, Latvia and Eastern Europe are territories that Bill has particularly staked out as a writer. Several of these stories, beginning with "Hagiophobia," feature a modern-day journalist, Santa Ezeriņa, who is based in Latvia and whose reporting takes her not only around that country, but even as far afield as Ukraine and the Svalbard Archipelago. Bill's command of setting enriches these stories immeasurably.

But Bill, of course, is also a writer of tremendous range, not only in time and place but also in tone and genre, as this collection in its entirety demonstrates. The stories in another series, for instance, feature mysteries that border on horror, as the twins Tasia and Eleni find themselves constantly welcoming dark and disturbing strangers into the boarding house they run in early twentieth-century Odessa. In another series, a Roman tavern thief called Quintus operates in the early years of the Common Era, repeatedly over-reaching himself with amusing but dangerous results, and needing to rely on his wits to extricate himself.

Likewise, his standalone stories also demonstrate wonderful variety, ranging from ironic humor to psychological horror. His terrific, Edgar-nominated story "Locked-In," for instance, starts from a quotidian domestic mishap and steadily ratchets up the suspense notch by notch to its incendiary climax.

I'm thrilled these stories have been brought together to reach new readers. William Burton McCormick is a writer to watch.

—Linda Landrigan, Editor-in-Chief, *Alfred Hitchcock's Mystery Magazine*
  February 2024

Introduction

Shortly after I left Russia to move to Ukraine in the Summer of 2007, I encountered an old man in some nameless Kharkiv cafe who, with great earnestness, wished to converse with an American writer so far from home. I spoke no Ukrainian; he no English, so we communicated through my broken Russian. What I remember most about that discussion was his warning, unheeded by me, that Ukraine was a live grenade. (We did not muster the vocabulary for "grenade," so he illustrated it on a napkin.) This puzzled me at the time. Only two years after the pro-democracy Orange Revolution, Ukraine shared the aspirations, if not feel, of Latvia and Estonia, two post-Soviet countries I'd already lived in, nations that were stepping towards democracy. In our limited communication, I didn't fully understand what combustive threat terrified the old man. It seemed to be the Kremlin's response to the Revolution and its ability to stoke unrest and violence. But Russia had little support nationwide. Only twenty percent of Ukrainians supported unification with Russia in 2007.

Still, if you seek democracy, dissenting views are not only allowed, but encouraged. Putin was a scary guy, but he was admired by some in the Russian-speaking part of Ukraine. My Kharkiv laundry lady, a sweet middle-aged woman, who always gave me tea and often gifts, had a poster of Putin in her office. It was startling even then. I disagreed with her admiration of such a terrible man, a killer ever since his wars on Chechnya, but as a foreigner, who was I to tell her whose picture she could hang on her wall?

Russia attacked Georgia the next year. I was on a payphone with my mother when Kharkiv's air raid alarms went off, Ukrainian defense forces believing Russian aggression had spread to their country. They weren't wrong, just premature by six years. In 2014, Putin illegally seized the Crimea, that old man's metaphorical grenade lobbed into Ukraine.

My laundry lady took her poster down.

In February 2022, the grenade exploded. Russia invaded Ukraine from East, North, and South. My laundry lady fled to Romania. Never having any affinity for dictators, Russian or otherwise, I returned to Latvia, where I volunteered, helping Ukrainian refugees in Rīga.

Less than one percent of Ukrainians now want unification with Russia. As my laundry lady adroitly said: "It's impossible to support someone who bombs you."

All the stories in this collection were written while living in Ukraine or Latvia. Even those tales with settings in America, Scotland, Siberia, the Svalbard Archipelago, or Classical Rome were conceived, drafted, and finished while living in Kharkiv, Rīga, Kyiv or during lengthy sojourns in Odesa. My time in Kharkiv was the longest and most productive. Some of the places I wrote in are now gone, wiped from the Earth by Russian aggression. Weeks before the drafting of this introduction, the Kharkiv Palace Hotel, whose lobby café with comfortable chairs and soothing live jazz bands made it the perfect place to write, was ravaged by multiple missile attacks. The open market one hundred yards from my apartment appeared on CNN—burning. Another café that I often wrote in was damaged by an adjacent strike. The café owner, a friend of mine, has remained in Kharkiv, sleeping every night in his basement with his wife and pets. He remains defiant with a cheerfulness and optimism I admire and doubt I could match. This sixty-ish man smiles as he serves cappuccino. He also owns a grenade belt to be used on the invaders "if they should reach Kharkiv's streets."

Many of my Ukrainian friends have fled to other countries. Others remain and fight on the frontlines. Others are dead. Meanwhile, a Trump supporter on Nevada television during the 2024 Republican caucus claimed the war was fiction, and the ten million refugees were actors hired by Zelensky to fool America. Surreal. Ronald Reagan must be turning over in his grave. But who am I to cast stones? I didn't believe the old man and his clumsily drawn grenade. I wonder where he is now. But I wonder where many Ukrainian friends are now.

The war is not fiction, but the stories in this collection are. The more modern stories set in Eastern or Northern Europe were written when the 2010s version of the Cold War was still cool before Russia brought war to Ukraine and threatened so many neighbors. Like Alfred Hitchcock's *The 39 Steps* and *Foreign Correspondent*, the days before war are fertile grounds for thrillers. I have preserved these more innocent times in this volume, where fighting the bad guys was "fun" and leaving many place names as they were with Russian-influenced spellings as a postcard of the times ("Kyiv" is spelled old-style "Kiev," "Kharkiv" is "Kharkov," "Odessa" instead of the more modern "Odesa" etc.). I would not write them the same now.

Despite all this talk of Europe, the first entry in this collection is a historical suspense tale set in America called "Locked-In," which appeared in the January/February 2022 issue of *Alfred Hitchcock's Mystery Magazine*. It was nominated for an Edgar, the most prestigious award in all of mystery fiction, so it has earned its pole position. It reflects many of my influences: 40s noir, Old Time radio, and most of all Hitchcock, Hitchcock, Hitchcock...

After "Locked-In," the stories are something of a greatest hits collection, proceeding in publication order from the beginning of my career. The Latvian setting of "Blue Amber," the oldest story in the book, was my first work of published fiction appearing in *Alfred Hitchcock's Mystery Magazine* June 2011 issue. I was encouraged by the Historical Novel Society, who, in reviewing the story, wrote "The sense of time and place is so strong I felt I was there on the Baltic coast. I can't fault the writing, which is equally strong and tight. There isn't a word out of place. The writer's knowledge of and authority over his subject matter meant that I remained gripped to the page from beginning to end and forgot I was reading 'professionally' rather than for pleasure. Stunning."

"The Antiquary's Wife," my homage to M.R. James with a Ukrainian setting, appeared in the March 2013 issue of *Alfred Hitchcock's Mystery*

Magazine. That story introduces sisters Tasia and Eleni, who would feature in several other stories, including the award-winning novella *A Stranger from the Storm*. "Killing Sam Clemens" followed in a 2014 edition of *Sherlock Holmes Mystery Magazine*. This story was a personal favorite of the late Senator Harry Reid of Nevada. I broke into *Ellery Queen's Mystery Magazine* with "Pompo's Disguise" in their March/April 2015 issue. This story introduced another series character, the ancient Roman thief Quintus. (I was an Ancient Studies major in college and, surely to my parents' relief, finally put that degree to use). Each of the above-mentioned stories was nominated for a Derringer Award from the Short Mystery Fiction Society, though none won.

Other notable stories in the collection include *The Saturday Evening Post's* "On Record," a murder story set in 1950s Brooklyn that amazingly became a student reading assignment in English-as-a-foreign language class at *MIKC "Nacionālā Mākslu vidusskola,"* the Latvian national ballet high school in Rīga where Baryshnikov once trained. "Myrna Loy Versus the Third Reich" was added to the archives of *The Myrna Loy*, a theater and arts center in Helena, Montana, named after the actress and dedicated to her activist work.

"Locked-In," "Voices in the Cistern," "The Three Camillas," and "Night Train for Berlin" all made to Robert Lopresti's "Best of the Year" list at *Sleuthsayers* while "Murder in the Second Act" was Lopresti's *Little Big Crimes* "Story of the Week" for March 11, 2019. For the eagle-eyed among you, "The Last Walk of Filips Finks" includes a cameo by Otomars Rooks, a major character in my historical novel *Lenin's Harem*.

I wear my writing influences proudly in *Deeds of Darkness*. Within the thriller stories prowls the presence of the old masters like Alistair MacLean, Frederick Forsyth, and Graham Greene, or more modern authors who write in retro settings like Alan Furst and the late Philip Kerr. In horror tales, I'm a strict classicist: Poe, Sheridan Le Fanu, M.R. James, Ambrose Bierce, Robert Aickman, Oliver Onions, H.P. Lovecraft, and the radio programs of Wyllis Cooper. My travels and twenty years living in foreign countries impact my writing considerably, as does the copious amount of nonfiction I read, both historical and scientific. One lengthy story in this collection was inspired by a documentary on terrifying and mysterious wounds found on arctic seals. Another tale transports a real-life Scottish writers' retreat I attended from the outskirts of Edinburgh to the wondrous Isle of Skye.

The most frequent character in this collection is investigative reporter Santa Ezeriņa. She merges aspects of real-life journalists like Julia Ioffe with a loveable duplicitousness and down-on-her-luck life reminiscent of a foreign and female version of Jim Rockford or Carl Kolchak. Her given name was stolen from a Rīga librarian I knew who could magically unearth any hidden information, her last name taken from Latvian model Zane Ezeriņa, and her physical appearance influenced by the art of Budd Root. The character debuted in "Agoraphobic Alibi," a You-Solve-It puzzle mystery in the ezine *Over My Dead Body* in 2014. (The non-traditional format of You-Solve-It stories has necessitated its omission from this collection.) Santa first arrived in a traditional formatted story in "Hagiophobia" from *Alfred Hitchcock's Mystery Magazine in* November 2015. Since she has appeared in many award-nominated stories, including the Derringer-nominated story "Matricide and Ice Cream," the Shamus Award finalist "The Dunes of Saulkrasti" (a favorite of *Atomic Blonde* creator Antony Johnston), and the novel *KGB Banker* written with whistleblower John Christmas which won Best Conspiracy Thriller of 2022 from BestThrillers.com.

Santa also features in two complete novellas towards the end of this collection. The first is "Demon in the Depths," a finalist for a 2022 Thriller Award and voted 2nd on Ellery Queen's Reader's Poll for best story of the year. "Demon in the Depths" is my personal favorite in *Deeds of Darkness*, though I would likely change the denouncement if writing it today. Some aspects make me uncomfortable with current events, but I leave it unchanged to preserve its time (written in late 2018 to early 2019, revised in the summer of 2020, and published in late 2021) and out of respect to editor Janet Hutchings and the readers of *Ellery Queen's Mystery Magazine* who treated it so kindly in their poll.

The last novella and youngest story in this collection is "House of Tigers," which was an Honorable Mention for the Black Orchid Novella Award and made the honor roll for Mysterious Bookshop's Best Mystery Stories of 2023 (though published in 2022). It mixes the motifs of Agatha Christie and John W. Campbell with an eco-apocalyptic bent.

I would like to thank Linda Landrigan, editor of *Alfred Hitchcock's Mystery Magazine*, for many things. For making me a paid, professional author by publishing "Blue Amber" in 2011, for continuing to publish me in the years since, and for being kind enough to write the foreword to this edition. She, and the wonderful Jackie Sherbow, who works on both *Alfred Hitchcock's Mystery Magazine* and *Ellery Queen's Mystery Magazine*, have been a joy to know for more than a decade.

Currently, I split my time between Latvia and my native Nevada. A few weeks from this writing, I will return to Ukraine for the first time since this war began, working in a caravan convoy driving vehicles and humanitarian supplies from Latvia through Lithuania and Poland to Ukraine.

We all must help in some small way. Evil is usually defeated in fiction, but reality is less certain. Our borders are not as far from the conflict as some may think.

Slava Ukraini.

—William Burton McCormick
March 2024

I

LOCKED-IN

Originally published in Alfred Hitchcock's Mystery Magazine

Locked-In

August 1943

The whoosh of a swinging door, the click of a latch, and instantly I know I've locked myself in the cellar.

Idiot.

I try the handle. The door rests firmly in basement brick, its iron face like a battleship hatch, gray and riveted with flecks of red paint clinging to the edges and beneath the bolts. It does not budge at my tugs, not a quarter of an inch, even as the wrenching turns violent and my words profane.

Trapped.

I caress my brow with dirty, housework fingers. How could I do this? So much to do today and I strand myself in here? So typical. *Moron.* Mr. Watkins warned me about it on taking the house.

That cellar door swings, Jeffrey. Bad hinges. Bad construction. Damn treacherous thing. Always prop it open. June locked herself in twice our first year.

I'm well on pace to eclipse his ex-wife's record, not three days into my rental. Watkins will find that amusing when he comes to collect the rent in ... Jesus, twenty-eight days?

I release a long pensive sigh. Better get him on the telephone when I'm out, insist he remove the locks altogether. Solve the problem once and for all.

But as for today?

My wristwatch says quarter to three. Let's somehow salvage the afternoon.

With no obvious tool in this filthy, mice-infested basement to break down an iron door, I move to the far wall, stand beneath the two narrow street-level windows just below the ceiling. Their dusty panes rest nine feet above the floor, looking out over lonely Jasper Lane, a dead-end side street enameled in black brick and shadowed under dying trees. Little more than an alley between two rows of small dingy houses, seldom trafficked even in the heart of the great city.

I consider my predicament. A deep cellar, the windows are too high and too small to crawl through. And even if I could get up there, why compound the day's folly by breaking the pane? Pain in the ass to replace the glass. And I'd lacerate my skin poking an arm through to signal someone.

The musty air tickling my nostrils. I stifle a sneeze and opt for patience. Not such a tragedy, really. Nothing scheduled today that I can't do tomorrow if necessary. I'm my own boss. A stranger, new in town. No one's expecting me.

I wait.

And wait some more.

Damn isolated lane. They should plant some living trees, give people a reason to come here.

At five after four in the afternoon, the first pedestrian strolls by outside. Tan pant legs and black loafers are all I can see through the high windows. He walks at a leisurely pace, the man exiting Jasper for the open avenue nearby.

"Hey!" I shout, rising on my toes and instinctively waving. "Mister! Hey! Can you help me? Down! Down here!"

He passes the first window, the second, and then out of frame. Not slowing a step.

Can't even hear me in this pit.

I rummage through the cellar's sparse storage shelves, find a handful of old bolts and lug nuts. I'll toss a few against the window, hard enough to be heard, yet hopefully not enough to damage the glass.

More waiting. At four twenty, a woman in a navy blue dress walks by. I cast the bolts against the windows as she passes. No reaction.

I throw again, a bit harder, when a man walks his terrier at five o'clock sharp. The dog woofs, smudges the window with a curious black nose, but the master drags his pooch away without a downward glance.

May have to break the glass.

At five twelve, a handful of lug nuts rattle the pane hard enough to gain the attention of a woman in bright yellow heels. She kneels down, stares at me through the window.

"Help me, please, miss!" I shout. "I've locked myself in this basement. Can you come inside and unfasten the door?"

Her stare is icy cold. "If you think I'm coming in there alone with you, fellah, you're crazy!"

"But—"

"No. Not with all the odd things and killings happening in this part of town. Sorry."

She stands and her yellow heels are quickly lost from view inside the darkening street.

Good God, what a day. Mary told me to stay in Nebraska.

I crush the next lug in my palm, wind back for maximum effort. Poised to throw, pent energy in every muscle as I wait. *Come on.*

I am lucky. Seconds after the woman, another pedestrian nears, a man wearing spectator shoes with reddish brown toes and heels. I cast, moxie in the motion. The nut punctures a hole in the glass, a spider web pattern over the pane. Propelled like missiles, a few shards lodge in the fabric of the stranger's trouser legs.

He stops. A white-gloved hand brushes off the glass, the face still too high to be seen.

"Sorry about that, mister. I needed your attention," I say. "Look, can you help me, please? I've inadvertently locked myself in this basement. The front door is open. The keys are hung on a chain at the base of the stairs, by the curtain. Would you come in and unlock the cellar? I'd be really grateful. I've been here over two hours."

He clears his pants of glass, pulls his gloved hand up out of view.

I continue: "I'm new in the area. No one else really to help, you know. An insurance man, lonely business. Hell of a way to meet the neighbors, right?"

He stands silently, one shoe toe grinding glass into the pavement. A gritty sound that somehow births unease in me.

"I'd be happy to give you a Lincoln for your trouble. Anything to get out of this situation... If you're worried about being in the home of a stranger—someone said something about killings in the vicinity—go get friends. Or your wife. Or call Peter Watkins. He's my landlord; he's in the book. Tell him Jeff Hartley is trapped in his cellar."

The man walks off.

Lord, what is the matter with people in this neighborhood? I may have to spend half the—

The creak of hinges above! My front door opening? Is it?

Yes. Footsteps overhead confirm a presence in the apartment. *Thank God.* The spectator-wearing stranger to the rescue.

"Oh, thank you, buddy! Down the steps on your left. The keys are right at the bottom, on the hook. Behind the drapes. You'll see 'em."

But he is ahead of me. Footfalls on the steps descend to the cellar. Then, a swish as the velour curtain at the base of the stairs is pulled aside; a tapestry likely hung by the absent June Watkins to camouflage this ugly iron door from guests.

The jingling of a keychain pulled from its hanger. His footsteps cross the narrow alcove between curtain and cellar door. The keys rattle again.

"It's one of the bigger keys," I say, flipping the switch to light the cellar's single lamp, a naked bulb directly above the door. "Find it?"

I see a key tip enter the upper lock.

"No, not the upper. That's the original bolt. It's always unlocked. You need the key for the lower lock. That's the one that catches. Try a—"

The upper bolt turns.

Come on fellow, now both locks are set.

"Yeah, turn that back, please. You need to unlock that top one now and use the other key for the lower. Understand?"

No reply. Only a thick rasping, like a lifetime smoker, just audible through the door.

"Are you still looking? Take your time…" Has he ever spoken? Even a grunt? Maybe he's some foreigner unfamiliar with English? If I weren't so new here, knew the neighborhood ethnicities.

"Is English your native tongue, by the way? ¿Hablas inglés? Parlez-vous anglais? *Lei parl* or is it *parla*, can't remember my damn Italian. Heh. Maybe, a good thing with the war goin' on, right, fella?"

Silence. A minute passes. Maybe two. All key rattling ceases. I press my ear to the coldness of the door's iron skin, his moist breathing beyond.

Calm, Jeffrey. Calm. "You know what might be easier, pal? If you slide the keychain under the door. I think there's room. It's got a full inch at least."

I get down onto my stomach, press a cheek to the floor, and peer with one eye under the door, past dust bunnies and mouse droppings to where those spectators stand as if rooted in place. The reddish-brown shoe toes six inches from my nose.

"Okay. Just slide 'em under here. We'll laugh over a beer. They drink beer where you come from, buddy?"

The shoes pivot from the door, stepping out into the alcove. That curtain swishes back cutting off my view. His footsteps rise up the stairs.

What the hell?

"Hey, where are you going? No need to look elsewhere! Those were the right keys!"

I wait for minutes, unheeded as he bustles about upstairs. In the kitchen and hall. In the bedroom, his footsteps directly above me. Doors slamming. Drawers opening, closing.

He's robbing me. The bastard is robbing me.

"Look, take what you want," I shout. "But leave the keys, okay? It's my only hope of getting out of here tonight."

Something weighty crashes overhead. A piece of furniture overturned?
Christ. What is he doing?

At last, I hear the front door slam, see his familiar spectator shoes pass the windows under the streetlamps.

Good riddance.

"Could this day get any worse?" I mumble aloud. "Yeah, you could sleep the night in this cellar. Talking yourself nuts."

Insanity. God making me appreciate the open skies I left behind, locking me in this forsaken basement. *Joke's over, Lord. I feel the walls closing in already.*

With little alternative, I focus on manufacturing a way out, no matter how unlikely.

I consider taking a pipe, smashing the windows if I can reach 'em, then shouting for help. A network of plumbing passes along one wall and over a portion of the ceiling. But there are no valves to cut the flow. Take one piece out and I flood the basement with water or sewage. Not an appealing option.

We'll call that Plan C.

Instead, I catalog what else is down here to work with:

Gas and electric meters.

Fuse box.

Furnace (no coal or wood, as it's summer). Igniter doesn't function.

Assorted bolts and nuts.

A box of dusty Christmas ornaments

A turpentine can, the interior dry, the contents long since used, and now a nest for young mice.

A suitcase containing four wire coat hangers and filled with women's intimates: scarves, ribbons, underwear, tampons, perfumes, lipstick, false eyelashes, dried-out makeup cases. Poor Pete Watkins must have stuffed all his wife's things in the bag when she ran off with that chiropractor to Connecticut. Hoping against hope she'd walk back through the front door someday. (Now would be the perfect time. Mrs. Watkins!)

I rub my temple with grimy fingers. A disaster. Not even a wrench or hammer amongst the rubbish. What can I do? I go back to Plan A, hailing passersby on the street. But no one comes to this dreary alley at night. It's forty minutes before I hear approaching footsteps.

I ready a lug nut. My morale spikes with hope of rescue, then plunges into despair. Those familiar spectator shoes step into view, a paper sack hanging low in one gloved hand.

He drops the bag. "MacDougal Hardware and Lumber" printed on the side.

A shop I know. Only six blocks away.

A wooden plank, one he must've carried over his shoulder, is lowered over the glass, eclipsing the first windowpane. A moment later, the second window suffers the same fate. Not a ray of street light seeping through.

As I attempt in vain to scale the wall, to interrupt the boarding up of the cellar, I hear the bag's paper rustle, something weighty withdrawn.

Over my pleas for mercy, a heavy hammering seals me inside as a corpse is sealed within a tomb.

* * *

Time passes with nothing to do but sit in the cellar and listen to the rhythms of a modern home: the floor creaks, the electric hums, the water flowing through the pipes, and the occasional ringing of an unanswered telephone. Without conscious effort, I become attuned to the footsteps of the stranger, the claps of his spectator heels climbing the stairs or on the pavement beyond the boarded windows. In a way, their rhythm keeps me sane in my solitude, allows the mind to focus on something, other than the questions of coming fate.

I note the details of his paces. If I ever get this squatter in a police lineup, I'll demand they make him walk before us. March an army by me, and I'd still identify that gait with ease.

Your day is coming, Jack.

He shows no signs of leaving, bustling about the house, the scent of burning oil in the air as he cooks something on the stove. He eats while my stomach growls. I'm not quite ready to devour raw mouse meat. I abate my thirst by pressing my lips to a leaking pipe, sucking for minutes to gain enough for a single swallow. But it'll keep me alive until this squatter leaves. Or is captured by the police, or evicted by Watkins.

Or me.

At one in the morning by my wristwatch, a car pulls up outside, small sounding, bad muffler, the engine quickly off. A set of sprightly footsteps pass the boarded windows.

I hear the front door open.

"Love the place!" exclaims a decidedly down-market female voice. "Who'd have thunk such a diller cave would free up in summer?"

The door closes. Two pairs of footsteps cross my ceiling.

Is she privy to my entrapment? I am at the cellar door in seconds, pounding on its iron skin.

"Miss!" I shout. "Lady! I'm imprisoned in the cellar! Can you convince your boyfriend to open the door? Please!"

Hushed voices.

"I won't press charges. I just want out! I...I'm starving!"

More whispered conversation. "Sublet?" she finally says, her words barely audible, talking to him, not to me. Laughter follows.

"Sorry, buddy!" she exclaims with a trailing giggle. "We're on our own tonight. Private party."

"Look, you can't let him do this. It's inhumane."

The bedroom door slams. More laughter. The clink of glasses. The clanks and clunks of bottles and shoes dropped to the floor directly above me. Soon come the squeaks of bedsprings under torrid lovemaking. She moans, his wet breathing crescendos...

Someone vomits. The treated floorboards absorb nothing, the puke seeping through the ceiling to drip into the cellar at my feet...

For the love of God...

I won't be a prisoner in my own house any longer. Retribution's coming, bub.

Kneeling at the cellar door, I adjust the wire concoction in my hands: the four coat hangers I've straightened and linked into an awkward sort of probing rod.

I press this rod under the door, steering its curved form up the alcove wall. If he's left the keys in their original position, they'll be hanging just out of view from my low position.

I fish blindly. Like some carnival game back in Omaha. Or African chimps using sticks to draw out termites from their mound. Inserting and withdrawing the rod into the alcove. Bending it, rebending it, adjusting my angle, letting it snake unseen up the wall and hoping to hear the jangle of keys as my prod finds its mark.

Twenty minutes with no success, until I hear that glorious metallic tinkling as the tip strikes something high on the wall. I carefully rotate the wire. More jingling. Beautiful. Like chimes in the wind.

The keys are there.

I release a calming breath. *Steady, Jeff.*

Now to dislodge them.

I make the minutest adjustments, my fingers delicate as a safecracker's feeling out the tumblers. The wire's end catches something. Sticks a little.

Maybe, the key ring itself.

I risk a sudden jerk of the wire, an upward motion intended to push the ring up off that hook.

A hard metallic clank as the key chain hits the alcove floor. Within sight.

My pulse is racing now, hands trembling as I run the prod over the key ring. My wire won't catch it, can't quite hook the loop to pull it close.

I withdraw the wire. Bend its end into a more pronounced hook.

Footsteps cross the room above.

Has he heard? The clank? He can't have.

I shoot the wire back under the door, try to pull in those keys.

Footfalls are hurtling down the stairs now like a runaway freight train. The swish of the curtain.

He's in the alcove.

The wire hook slips underneath the key loop. Catches. I yank it toward me.

Come to papa...

A spectator shoe heel crunches down on the keys. Halting my progress.

I pull fiercely but there is little hope. One white-gloved hand plucks up the keys, the other tugs the wire away from me. His strength is Herculean. I watch helplessly as the last linked coat hanger wire slips through my fingers in an instant.

Without comment, he carries keys and wire away. A closing of the velour curtain ending the show.

For now, bub. It's only Act One.

* * *

I stand precariously atop the upright suitcase, pounding at the boarded window with a broken piece of shelf, the impact of each blow threatening to disrupt my delicate balance and topple me to the cellar floor. The glass is long cleared, but the thick MacDougal planks will not give.

Break, dammit! Did he nail these in with railroad spikes?

There is music to accompany my efforts. Off in the main room, the squatter listens to Benny Goodman on the radio, the volume high enough to drown out my work. And if not, who cares? *Come in and stop me, Jack. Open that door.*

A crunching blow. The wood splits at last.

Brick behind.

When did he have time to brick it up? Shock steals concentration and I fall, my shoulder crashing hard against the concrete floor. Something snaps. I scream. Mice scatter to the corners.

I bite my lip, stifle sobs as best I can. Won't allow any hint of injury, of weakness to drift up to that stranger's ears.

But *he* is not listening. He is changing radio stations. The Goodman Orchestra fades, and as I lay there in agony, the music is replaced by a commercial for ionized yeast, then the tones of an ominous sounding clock. Host Arch Oboler is telling us that it's later than we think, time for *Lights Out*.

Yes, lights out. I glance at the fuse box in the corner. No power for either of us, you bastard.

My shoulder throbbing, I drag myself over, open the box cover as Oboler declares:

"Tonight's program is a meditation on the horrors of the vampire, that terrible night fiend who can only enter your home when invited inside. Be wary, friends. Don't open your door to strangers."

I pull the fuse, sentencing the house to darkness and silence.

No reminders needed, Arch.

* * *

Enfolded inside absolute darkness, I lay on that cold floor, passing in and out of sleep. The stilling of the house's electric mechanisms allows more delicate sounds to reach my ears: the patter of mice darting across the floor, the chirping of a lonely cricket trapped somewhere nearby, and the passing of cars on the main avenue, a distance of thirty yards, but to me as remote as the moon.

In all this chorus of subtleties, *he* is quietest. Asleep? Away? I cannot say. At least until a brief scraping noise calls my attention somewhere toward the cellar door. Aroused by this disturbance, I reset the fuse. The single bulb comes to life, as does the radio upstairs, Perry Como singing "You Can't Pull the Wool Over My Eyes."

A saucer and plate have been slid under the door, the former full of water, the latter holding two slices of buttered bread.

Not on your life.

I pull the fuse, garroting Como and returning the house to silent darkness.

* * *

Time passes. Though ravaged by hunger, I am not tempted by the bread at the door, not foolish enough to trust his offerings. Still, as the hours pass, morbid curiosity and a lingering fear stave off slumber and gall me at last to investigate. Without replacing the fuse, without alerting *him*, I scoot over to examine the plate and saucer in darkness by touch. My hands find the victims, the bodies of two mice at the plate, a third near the saucer, this last one dying and lethargic enough to let me stroke him as he expires.

I feel surprising empathy. Kinship to my fellow prisoners with a monster in the house.

Yet, instead of being deterred by this attempt on my life, I am rallied. Enlivened. If he wishes to poison me, there is a reason. My captor is unwilling to wait weeks until I die of starvation to get in here. Maybe my presence unnerves him as he unnerves me. Or maybe he wants his electricity, his radio. Or thinks there's something of value down here.

Whatever, I'll play. Still in darkness, I dump the mice bodies and bread into the box of ornaments, pour the water into the turpentine can. Every drop, every crumb removed. I reset the plate and saucer into their initial positions, as if in thirst and hunger I've partaken of their contents. I slide my body to the cellar's center. Over the course of the next hours, I release ever-growing moans as if my belly aches, as if my insides burn with hellfire.

Then I grow still.

Still as a dead man. One with a shard of window glass hidden in his palm.

Hours pass. Maybe tens of hours. I need to urinate, but dare not move from my spot, dare not risk a sound while playing dead. Instead, I release my bladder there, the puddle adding to the illusion of death. If I could empty my bowels, I would.

Poisoned.

Come on, fellow. Step inside.

At last, I detect the sound of turning keys in the locks. I try not to swallow, to tame my muscle tremors as I hear that door creak open. My eyes close. I listen to those shuffling footsteps coming closer.

The splash of a shoe stepping into the piss puddle.

His breath close, hot, wet. He bends near, examining me. Some liquid, sweat or saliva, dripping onto my face—

I thrust up with the shard, even before my eyes pop open. The cellar still black, he recoils too slowly against my attack, his flashlight reflexively pulled up, half a face revealed. Surprise in a single glazed eye.

I stab before he can straighten, dig the jagged edge into soft flesh below the eye. Deep enough that my fingers brush against clammy, stubbly skin. The shard tip strikes bone.

His shriek is horrific, worthy of a banshee. He kicks out, the shoe heel hammering my chest with jackhammer power, sending me careening backwards, head ricocheting off the floor. My scream joins his.

The flashlight's glow speeds away like a will-o'-the wisp. Door hinges groan—

But I refuse to lose my best opportunity at freedom. Back on my feet, I catch the edge of the closing door with my fingers, dropping the glass weapon to strengthen my hold. We wage a desperate tug-of-war, but he is inhumanly strong.

The door pulls flush, a vice crushing my fingers until the grip is lost.

The door latches. The locks turned.

Sealed again.

My last chance gone.

* * *

Days pass. How many? I don't know. At least a week. Lost in a stupor of hunger and despair, I begin a slow demise. Consciousness is rare, though thankfully my keeper does not dare venture down again. Not after his wounding. I suspect he is often absent from the house, though truthfully I'm unsure of anything. My senses are expiring, can no longer be trusted. My Mary is often standing before me, asking why I didn't stay in Omaha, why I went east, why we never married. A cavalcade of phantom voices and sounds often join in. I believe nothing. So, when I hear the front door open, I'm unsure if it is a trick of the mind, an illusionary noise, or my captor coming or going.

But then I am startled by the voice of Peter Watkins shouting:

"Jeffrey, you home?"

It can't be truth.

The shout repeats. "Jeff?! You in?"

"Mr. Watkins?!" I croak, my throaty voice gravelly from disuse. "Is it really you?"

"Why don't you answer your phone, Jeff?"

No hallucination. Peter is upstairs.

A palsy in my limbs, I reign in my body, focus my addled brain, try to form coherent sentences. "I'm locked in the cellar! Get the police!" I crawl to the door. "Go! We may not be alone!"

"The police?" he asks as his voice nears, descending the stairs. "Why do we need the police? I warned you about that door."

The rustle as the curtain is shoved aside.

"Who the hell are you?" Watkins gasps, startled fear in his voice.

My stomach knots. *He* is in the alcove. Lingering. Spying. Listening to my movements as I listen to his. How long…?

"Jeff, who is this man? Get the—" The words turn to a gurgle.

"Run!" I shout, peering below the door. Those twin spectators dance an awkward dance with tan loafers, the latter kicking, stamping, trying to force separation.

"Leave him alone. Please. He's done nothing!"

A muffled moan. A snap.

Peter Watkins crashes to the floor. Dead eyes staring at me.

"Oh God! Oh God!"

The squatter kneels, picks up the body. The stairwell groans as he carries Peter upstairs.

The house turns silent as a grave.

***

Still leaning against that cellar door, I'm awakened by the sound of a poorly muffled car pulling up outside.

A car door opens. As does the front door above.

"Who is that?" asks a familiar woman's voice, the one from the night of sex and vomit. "Crackers, is he dead?"

Footsteps pass the bricked windows. A car trunk is opened. Something heavy placed inside.

"You didn't say anything about another corpse!" she shouts, voice in hysterics. "Take that stiff outta my trunk or I'm chauffeurin' him straight to the cops. Damn right, I mean it! Bodies all over town, what kinda life is this for a girl? Mother said you were a rattlecap. How am I supposed—"

Something hits the pavement.

The car springs whine as a second payload is placed in the trunk with the first. The hatch closes, *his* familiar gait shuffles around to the front. A car door slams.

In seconds, the automobile is speeding away from Jasper Lane, out onto the avenue to merge with the sounds of heavy traffic.

* * *

He returns much later without the car, opens the front door, and passes across the ceiling. His pace is irregular even by his standards, the gait off from the one I've come to know. He staggers more than walks. Is he drunk? Exhausted from his crimes? Some disease progressing? Who can know?

I hear the bedroom door open but he does not reach the bed. There are no squeaks of the springs, no thump on a mattress. Instead, there is a single hard crash on the bedroom floor.

Then stillness. Absolute stillness.

He lies on the floor directly above. Asleep or unconscious.

A reprieve from his spying.

What opportunities does this allow? The shock of Peter Watkins's murder has given me new energy and focus. But how long will it last?

My mind reels. I've learned much about my adversary this horrible day. The squatter kills with impunity, yet remains unwilling to open my door again, even to dispose of a victim. He'd rather risk hauling a body outside and dumping it somewhere else than give me another shot at him. I cut the bastard to the bone once. The bully, he's scared, he won't allow a second chance. That cellar door isn't opening again. Not while I'm alive.

If I don't get out on my own, I never will.

An inkling, an idea lingering in the brain since my imprisonment, reemerges. An option deemed too dangerous before, as tantamount to suicide, is now, in my hopelessness, a possibility. A Plan D on the table.

My career in insurance offers instruction. I recall the mob insurance scammers of Bay Ridge before the war.

Now, I emulate their methods. While my captor lays unconscious above, unable to halt my undertakings.

In the cellar's pitch blackness, I grope about over the door, pull down the bulb, grip the wires that feed it, extend them to maximum length out of the wall. With a shard of glass, I cut free the bulb and socket mount, shave away the wire insulation, bare copper feeds in my fingers.

Step One.

I open up June Watkins's suitcase, withdraw the scarf and the perfume bottle. A sniff. The perfume is cheap. Mostly alcohol.

Good.

I drench the scarf in perfume, rub it against the interior walls of the turpentine can for good measure.

Step Two complete.

Now, things get risky.

I replace the fuse, the radio upstairs comes to life. An alarm for him. If he only sleeps, I'll be caught.

But there is no movement above. Out cold, the drunk.

Did the murders weigh on his mind? Maybe he has a conscience after all. Not that it'll save him from the chair.

I place the reeking scarf on the plate, set one bared wire end to the fabric, the other to heat the dish. Whiffs of smoke tickle my nose. Then the scarf bursts into flame.

I drop to my knees, shove a plateful of flaming scarf beneath the door, sliding it across the alcove floor towards the curtain. Velour is highly flamsmable; I need only reach the drapes.

Luck isn't with me. The plate passes harmlessly beneath the curtain, but the motion dislodges the scarf midway, the remnants burning away uselessly on the floor before it.

Damn. Damn. Damn.

As Peggy Lee sings "Shady Lady Bird" on the radio upstairs, my mind turns to the mob's other method of setting fire to curtains. A cruel, gauche practice. But nobody accuses mobsters of taste.

I rummage through the Christmas box. All ornaments are too large to roll under the door. Then, snuggled away at the bottom, I find a cotton snowman ornament.

Hallelujah! I use my heel to crush the snowman flat.

I search the suitcase, seize the tampon pack. Just one left.

Two chances. Two shots on goal.

I pull the tampon from the applicator, dip it into the perfume, let it soak, then empty the bottle's remaining contents over the flattened snowman ornament.

I tie the tampon string to the tail of a captured mouse, the snowman's hanging thread to the tail of another. The strings should burn away before reaching the bodies. Least that's what the gangster said at the deposition.

Setting snowman and tampon to the bare wires, I light them aflame. Then release the mice beneath the door. Driven forward by the miniature bonfires they tow, the panicked rodents scamper across the alcove floor. The snowman's tether burns away too soon, the mouse springing free, leaving the flaming ornament well short of the drapery.

But the tampon pyre reaches the curtain just as the string expires. The velour catches. The whole drapery up in flames.

A beautiful sight. Mice and tampons, every arsonist's friend. Little burning chariots that leave no evidence. Singed feminine hygiene products? Scorched rodent bodies? Nothing unusual in a burned-out house. If the tethering strings burn away, as they always do, there's nothing peculiar for an insurance investigator to use as evidence.

Thank God for mobster ingenuity.

The fire climbs the curtains as I watch safely from beneath the door. Soon, the alcove's roof and upper walls are decorated in dancing flames, thickening billows flowing up the stairs into the ground-floor rooms. The neighbors will smell smoke, passersby on the nearby avenue surely see the rising billows. Help soon on its way.

My pulse pounding, breath quickening, I gaze at the inferno.

Burn. Burn. Too fierce for him to stop now, even if he wakes.

It seems I gain my wish. The alcove fully ablaze, the smoke and heat strengthen until I must pull my watering eyes from that door draft, find clearer air inside.

Yet the atmosphere here is changing too. A fierce heat above, I turn my vision upward. Flames crawl across the ceiling, invading the cellar along the creosote-infused rafters. The preserving oil easily flammable, the treated wood a natural highway inside.

An ember falls to blister my cheek. The first of many.

The inferno out of my control.

God, what have I done?

As the fires stampede across the ceiling, I resist the instinct to stand and run for the farthest, coolest corner. *Madness.* Heat and smoke rise, the most survivable atmosphere is the lowest. On hands and knees, as cinders fall around me, I crawl toward the water pipes along the far wall. When at last I reach them, I try to dislodge their position, to open the flow and douse my body. My strength stolen by starvation, the pipes defy my tugs, refuse to break. Desperation growing, I hammer with bare hands at the leaky seam which sustained me, but the flow does not increase, less than a trickle seeping out.

The whole ceiling is now ablaze, and even this is not the greatest threat. The smoke unable to escape the cellar's confinement, the black billows thicken, a funeral shroud around me. Even crouching on the floor, I spy nothing beyond my elbows, not even the pipes I struggle to crack open.

Blinded. But I can hear.

Shouts outside. The screams of sirens.

"Help! Help! In the cellar!" I shout. The call costs me dearly. My lungs emptied in the effort, the next breath brings smoke, scorching embers flowing into my lungs. I gag, spit up black sludge, mucus and blood. My hands abandon the pipes to cover my mouth, somehow clear my throat.

A thunderous rumble above. The ceiling gives way, fiery timbers, furniture crashing in. Fed oxygen by the gaping new hole, the flames flare, the smoke parts momentarily.

I see him again.

Amongst the fallen beams and broken bedroom furniture lies a flaming body, a Lucifer on his lake of fire. One spectator shoe yet untouched, just visible.

The sight births fresh hatred.

In death I am immolated while he feels nothing. Even now, he wins.

The fresh oxygen consumed, the shroud returns, eclipsing vision, bringing skin-scorching heat. My arm hairs glow like embers, my clothes aflame, new agonies obliterating final thoughts. The blaze sweeps over floors and walls, forcing me to stand, to flee the fiery tide. Choking, disoriented, I stumble about sightlessly in search of any pocket of breathable air. Limbs failing, consciousness fading, my delusions rise. I imagine voices, a stomp of boots, metallic hinges groaning nearby.

Spent, I am tumbling into the pyre when an outstretched arm seizes me about the waist, drags me to cooler reaches, a blanket thrown over my body, smothering away resistant embers.

"Easy, fellow. We've got you."

It is no fantasy. The firemen have entered the cellar.

II

BLUE AMBER

Originally published in Alfred Hitchcock's Mystery Magazine

Blue Amber

Latvia 1910

"You four—out!"

The Russian guards unlocked the pilot chain restraining the huddled riders inside the prison sleigh. With the groans of the damned, the captives pushed their aching bodies over icy boards and out the opened back. Stooped by their weight in irons, four figures lowered themselves to the grey-brown slush of the seaside road.

But a fifth remained tethered in the sleigh bed.

"And me?" said Fricis, holding up manacled wrists, raw and discolored from another day's labor. "Am I to rest this stop?"

"Your job's farther on." The lead guard pocketed the key, jumped from the sleigh and motioned for it to proceed. The driver clicked his reins, the thick Nordic draft horse pulling the sleigh away from the others, Fricis's slave crew fellows disappearing from his view into the eternal night of Baltic winter.

Fricis released a slow breath, a tangle of mist drifting away as the sleigh gained speed. Alone. It would be his night then at last. He would be dead in an hour's time, a fabricated "escape attempt" to mask his murder. The same fate as Juris and Alberts, the Tsar's assassins elevating four years to a death sentence without appeal to judge, jury or right of law.

Fricis Svaars would die as all suspected revolutionaries died in Rīga prison. Shot down "on the run."

He tested the black chains that connected his wrists and ankles to the sleigh bed, propped a boot on the ninety pound "anchor" tethered to the band about his waist. That the dogs claimed his comrades had run was the most obscene of lies.

Fricis was twenty-four, a handsome bull of a man in the prime of life; these shackles were not as heavy to him as they were to others, yet to flee wearing such bonds would be a comedy for his killers' amusement. He'd carried these chains a year now, dragged this foul anchor with him during every hour of slave labor, in each moment outside the jail yard. He knew their weight as he knew his own body. The Ochrana had hoped to break him, but they only made him stronger. Indeed, he might be the strongest man in Rīga prison…

Fricis did not fear death, it would end the pain. But he could not help his people dead. Or see Liva again.

Something colder than winter touched his soul. He thought of his wife alone in Liepaja, "Libau," as their Russian masters called it. What would happen to her after his killing? It should make no difference, his murder. He had told her he would not survive prison, to think of him as dead. To paint his grave portrait, say goodbye, and marry Stefens. But Liva was a loyal, hard-headed woman, her letters full of hope.

He smiled grimly. And Stefens was no Fricis.

Poor Liva.

Now, on a rise above the beach, the sleigh passed the stacked-log foundation of a lighthouse, its protective lamp steering some lonely steamship through the perils of the submerged Ventspils ridge.

Recognition brought nostalgia. How Liva loved lighthouses, collected porcelain replicas, paintings, photographs. Since their youth, diverted every beach stroll to find the nearest. This view would have moved her as it now moved him. A fitting valedictory—if she were here.

Fricis pulled at his bonds again, glanced over his shoulder at the driver and the sole remaining guard at the front. Yes, there were stronger chains than iron. One had but to remember why one lived: *Latvijai jabut brivai! Livai jabut miletai!*

Latvia must be freed. Liva must be loved.

The sleigh jittered as it ran across rocks, jarring Fricis from his musings. The driver pulled on the reins, the sleigh slowing to a halt on an icy sea cliff about a quarter mile from the lighthouse.

The young guard's voice boomed over Fricis's shoulder: "Here!" The keys landed between his knees. "Your ride's over, Svaars."

Yes....

* * *

With the driver remaining in the sleigh at the top, the guard marched his prisoner down the steep path cutting across the cliff face, Fricis gripping the cold dirt of the wall to keep from slipping down the torturous way. With no traction, weighted in irons, it would be impossible to climb again, should he be allowed.

At the bottom, a ridge of snow drifts swallowed the trunks of beach-edge firs, Fricis's boots falling through to the clumpy sand dunes beneath. Beyond, the shore itself lay bare, biting Baltic winds sweeping every grain of snow and sand towards the tree line, leaving only the heaviest of ocean treasures on the black rocks of the surf. Among the scattered branches and shells, bits of ochre reflected the distant lighthouse.

"Amber," said the guard, throwing Fricis the burlap sack, "your task today."

Amber, of course. The prison often made extra money by sending inmates to gather it for the elegant shops in Rīga and Jelgava. Baltic amber was the finest in the world, with Latvian artisans crafting exquisite wonders to sell in every port of the Russian Empire and beyond.

Fricis kneeled at the edge of the water, dropped his iron weight into the mud at his boots. No simple "ball and chain" with blades and teeth like a plow tool, the anchor burrowed into the earth when dragged, stood fast against the strongest limbs unless carried. A foul appendage designed by men who understood the mindset of bondage and passed their days engineering lives in chains.

Fricis shivered in the sea-winds, felt the aching in his crown where they'd opened his skull with a railroad hammer. Glancing down, he found pink, scarred cuticles on reddened fingers, the nails torn from both hands. They hadn't broken him. At least he took that to his grave.

He glanced at his guard, a young man, thin of build with reddish hair and sea-green eyes. Not such a formidable adversary without the rifle in his hands, not for Fricis at least...

He felt a strange intimacy with this man, such an important person in the course of his life. Fricis knew those who brought him into this world, he should know the one who would show him out.

"What's your name?"

The boy-guard shrugged, indifferent to the question. "Janis."

For the first time, Fricis detected a Liv accent in the guard's Russian. He was of native blood, though not a Lett like Fricis. Perhaps that could be of use...

Fricis picked up a crusted, impure splinter of amber, changed his tongue to a rarer language. "You want all the pieces or only the best, Brother?"

The guard's eyes widened slightly. "You know the Liv dialect? Aren't you a Lett?"

"Yes, but I wish to know all the languages of Latvia, of every tribe. It is important to remember before they die. Don't you agree?"

"So many...you will forget."

"No! I forget Russian!" Fricis spat into the surf, saliva lost in sea foam, "And I forget German. And Polish. And Swedish. A few words every day. As you should."

Janis laughed. "And they told me Fricis Svaars was a practical man." He leaned forward, resting his free forearm over the rifle barrel. "Russians pay well, almost as well as Germans. He who has the money chooses the language."

"And how much do they pay you for murdering me?"

The lack of surprise told Fricis everything. "They pay me a solid day's wage—to make you collect amber."

He pointed the rifle at Fricis. "So collect."

His back to Janis, Fricis reluctantly began his final task. He had no trouble finding amber in these shallows, the beach not as dark as it should be for four in the winter afternoon. As the lighthouse beam prowled the sea, some flaw in its mirror cast an irregular halo over the beach, splinter spotlights crisscrossing the sands, shadows climbing the sea-cliff walls.

In one light, a twinkle of blue. Moving closer to this reflection, something else caught Fricis's eye. Far down the shore, under one of these roaming beams, two figures marched his way. Bulky silhouettes walking shoulder to shoulder, in this weather, with such purpose, they could only be bound for him.

So that's why the guard waited. Janis was only here to keep him in place for the Tsar's men. The professionals would do the work, make sure everything passed the farcical investigation tomorrow. The secret police, the Ochrana, planned every detail of his demise as they had his comrades.

The lamplight shifted out to sea, the men lost again in darkness, but Fricis had little doubt their destination. Five minutes at most. Five minutes to decide if Liva was a widow, until a new crime was committed against Latvia.

Fricis moved up the beach. Not far from a sign warning boaters of the Ventspils shoal, he found the spot where he'd seen the blue reflection. On the shore lay several beautiful pieces of amber, a few even a deep wine red; they'd make excellent ornaments. But half buried in the mud, something shone a pale turquoise.

Fricis pulled it free. "Look at this, Janis, it's blue amber."

"Blue amber?"

Fricis brushed dirt from the shiny pear-shaped object in his palm. Naturally smooth, not a flaw to be seen, and the rarest, most valuable color. Not a fortune, of course, but certainly several good nights on the town. A find worth toasting.

"Throw it here."

This amused Fricis. Couldn't he wait another three or four minutes? Perhaps Janis didn't want to fight for it when his killers arrived. He recalled the old tale about three murderers who killed each other over gold.

Something sparked in Fricis. There was value in that thought…

"No."

Janis's eyes shown green in a wayward beam. "What do you mean 'No?'"

"I will not." Fricis shrugged, stuffed the amber into his trousers. "It may buy me a good meal in the afterlife. Certainly, better than my last on Earth."

"I'm the guard…"

"Yes—but you can't shoot me, Janis. You'll bungle their plans." Fricis nodded towards the unseen men. "You may lose your job, even be charged with a crime. What do the men from St. Petersburg care about a simple prison guard, a Liv from the governorates?" Fricis opened the heavy sack again, dragging it through the mud as he resumed his collecting. "I'm a political prisoner, Janis. When I die, there'll be a lot of attention. If you kill me over amber, it's the perfect excuse. 'Ah, dirt-poor Janis did it for greed, no more questions necessary.'" The fickle lights fled once more, a moment of blindness as their eyes adjusted anew to the dark. "You play into their hands, Brother. They might hang you just to appease the mob."

Janis squinted, shuffled his feet. "I won't warn you again…"

Fricis waved off his threat. "I can't let you shoot me, not in good conscience. I might have to die, but let's not get you in trouble." Inside the night, screened by the sack from hip to toe, Fricis slowly pulled the anchor from the ground. Ninety pounds with one hand, not a tick of emotion in his voice, not the slightest change in posture…

Steady, steady, before the lamp turns. "They'd call it an intra-clan squabble, wouldn't they, Janis? Those Russians…No, we'll just wait until the men arrive. Make them take the blame."

As the inexperienced do when challenged, Janis stepped forward. "Who's to say why I did what? Now give me—"

With a sudden motion, Fricis threw the anchor. Too short, it fell half the distance between them. But half was enough, as Fricis rushed past the weight, Janis just within reach of his bone-snapping grip.

A moment later, it was over.

Staccato pulse drumming in his ears, eyes wide as the moon, Fricis took hold of his situation. He reached over Janis's body, seized the unfired rifle—pure luck, Fricis, you've no right to be alive—and lay prone on the icy stones, searching…

There! The sweeping lights returned down the beach, catching the figures still marching side by side, unaware. The rules of the campfire, those in the firelight can see only a few yards beyond the flames, but someone in the darkness can observe them for miles.

Fricis chose the one nearer the sea, pulled the trigger, watched him fall.

As he bolted the rifle, the other figure fled for the trees near the cliffs. Fricis pressed the trigger—nothing. The chamber was empty. A simple one-shot rifle!

Janis…You said the Russians paid well!

With a vicious curse, he began to search the guard's body, but he had nothing, no ammunition, not even the keys. Where were the keys?

Fricis heard the neigh of a horse, the sleigh driver on the cliff top whipping his mount, the transport speeding from view. How long until he returned with a sleigh full of men?

Fricis drove such thoughts from his mind, continued his frantic search. Near Janis's boot, he found the key ring. But none of its members fit his manacles. Where were his? With the driver? The head guard and the other prisoners? Damn!

Anchor in his arms, he ran through the tree line to the cliffs. But as he feared, Fricis found no traction on the ice of the steep path. Every step slid back to where he'd stood, he finally lost his balance, slipping down onto his belly until his boots pressed against the first tree trunk.

A beam of light through the branches, distant voices. Pulling himself up, Fricis saw the opened lighthouse door, two animated shadows shouting on its steps.

He had no time.

A moment later, he was dragging the guard's body from the beach. Inside the shadows, he propped Janis's corpse against a fir, snapped a low branch, hooked the guard's belt over the stub so he stood on his own.

Balancing the rifle between a thin branch and the dead man's hands, Fricis returned to the shore.

A functional illusion, near enough to be seen, deep enough to fool. It may buy him a few moments, or a warning shot at least...

More shouts. A figure led several others from the lighthouse, lanterns in their hands. The last Ochrana had conscripted the crew.

The cliffs were impenetrable, the beach a trap. If he could get past them somehow undetected, let his enemies prowl the wrong way while he headed the other. But they would watch the tree line...

Desperate to madness, anchor in hands, Fricis waded into the surf. Felt the stabbing knives of arctic waters, muscles knotting as he pushed himself deeper. Daring the sea in irons, he must be insane.

Steaming breath in his eyes, he dipped down, shoulders beneath the surface, the black waves lashing his neck. His body began to shudder uncontrollably.

He must be invisible, camouflaged against the surf at night, but it would take only one wayward beam from lantern or lighthouse. He had to go farther. Moving along the beach, he saw the Ventspils sign, felt the rocky rise of the shoal beneath his boots, extending out to sea.

Old memories returned. Fricis had stood on this subsurface ridge once before. On a warm August afternoon ten years ago, with Liva afraid of stinging jellyfish and more interested in climbing the lighthouse stairs, he'd journeyed out into the Baltic on his own. If the tides were right, with a bit of swimming here and there, a man could walk near five miles out to sea with little difficulty, never getting his beard wet, often with his knees above the lapping waves. With the high summer sun over his shoulder and the endless turquoise ocean stretching to the horizon, it had been a stroll unlike any other in the world. To walk on water until the land disappeared behind, and the Estonian islands Saaremaa and Ruhnu appeared in the mist ahead. Paradise.

But the tides were deeper tonight, manacles on his limbs in coldest February, and somewhere ahead were those gaps where he must swim.

Three hundred yards out a buoy. Shelter behind.

He could make it.

Fricis turned his back on the beach, eyes concentrating on the pale shape of the marker, a small flag atop it bobbing in the night waves.

In line with the buoy, no matter how numb his feet, if he just went towards the flag he could not err.

He struggled to remember. Remember how cold was natural to his people, the stories of how the Gulf of Rīga would freeze over, of how his forefathers would journey out for the winter to fish. Shelters, taverns, whole communities on rails and blades.

Fricis felt his body convulse, his tongue quivering in his mouth. No, the Olden Days were long ago, he was not as his ancestors. These were warmer times; the Gulf hadn't frozen in centuries. An iceless port, that's why Peter of Russia had wanted it, why for near two hundred years his people suffered. Why Liva would become a widow.

The buoy was close. Maybe…maybe not a widow. Maybe a mother, holding his child in the summer fields of Kurzeme, violet flowers in their hair. Yes…

The sound of gunfire. A strange calm, he felt almost sleepy. Were they shooting at him? He was so numb, perhaps he wouldn't feel the bullet, know he was shot. Or maybe they fired at Janis under the cliffside? Yes, Janis…

Hold them off a little longer, Janis. Earn your pay.

With little feeling in his legs, he missed the drop in the shoal, head and shoulders plunging below the surface in an instant. Blind, with his free hand he pawed for some outcrop as he sunk, the irons dragging Fricis down to his doom.

But his mind was with him, Fricis's instincts sharp as his fingers dull, he cast the anchor out, freeing both hands to grasp something, anything to slow his descent. But he touched nothing, no rock, no protrusion, the surface long out of reach. Sinking forever into the abyss, heart drumming in his ears, Fricis said goodbye to Liva and Latvia as the air slipped from his lungs.

Then he stopped.

Somehow, he found himself suspended, swinging slowly like a clock pendulum in the depths. An unseen force held him in place, even as the shackle weight bent his limbs towards the bottom. In the silent blackness, he lay in the palm of an invisible giant who would allow him to sink no further. For a moment Fricis almost believed there was a god.

Then he remembered. Forcing an arm upwards, he tapped dull fingers on the chain extending from his waist, like some iron umbilical cord in the dark womb. Up again, a full arm's length, he followed until the links pressed against a rock face. He willed his fingers to move, to somehow contract and pull himself higher. The chain ran up an angled cliff face ending in the anchor, its blades wedged into an underwater fissure.

It was then he began to panic, the possibility of life returning, he felt the stickiness inside as his airless lungs pressed together. He tugged at the line, it slid a bit, then held firm. Fricis dragged himself higher, face across the embedded anchor. He kicked out, hoping his blind toes would find a hold. Something caught, his body elevated, an opened palm above the surface. He found a knee to support his weight, then pushed, starlight above the waves. A moment of burning air as his lips broke the surface, but the motion dislodged the anchor, it tumbled down the cliff, dragging his head under again. Twisting his body, Fricis threw both shoulders forward, hands locked about the chain, the iron erupted from the waters landing ahead of Fricis on the shallower ridge top. Forcing himself to his feet, he pierced the waves again, took a long breath, felt the warm needles of air on his skin. The other side, the first gap crossed.

That was one.

With leaden limbs, uncaring of the men on the beach, he stumbled along the ridge, waist-high in the water. Toppling forward, he collapsed against the buoy, momentarily dipping its flag into the seas. Vision blurring, Fricis wrapped his arms about it like a lost lover, hoping to never let go…

For a moment he hung there in darkness, felt the gentle swell as the tides passed under the marker. Rhythmically rising and falling, his weak breaths caressing the moon, it seemed he could touch the lunar surface. He pressed his cheek against the weathered buoy, skin to wood yet no texture, no temperature. Fricis hooked a chain across the float, to ease the weight of the anchor, and inch by inch, hand over hand, moved himself to the rear until he was hidden from the beach.

He gazed over the float, at the empty shore beyond. The lantern lights seemed far away, but he could not be certain. Distance was not…not as obvious as it had been … difficult to read, to think….

His eyes fogged. Then slowly, so slowly, he began to burn.

It started in his chest, wildfire spreading through his limbs, a molten heat erupting up his throat, incinerating all thoughts in his mind. Fricis howled aloud, not in the worst childhood fevers had he burned this way. Everything he touched seared his flesh, the icy fabric of his clothes blistering his skin, the irons seemed to melt from his wrists. The sea must boil.

Panicked, he let the chain moor him to the buoy, trying to rip off his clothes with both hands before they burst to flame, incinerating him between cresting waves of the ocean.

But the shackles would not budge, not allow him to pull free his jacket. Fricis gulped salt water to douse his innards, tongue withering inside his mouth, pulling air from his lungs.

His breathing slowed against his will, his motions dying. He must think, reason a way to shed these scalding clothes.

As he searched his fevered brain, Fricis found old memories. Of Liva, her family, her father…he had been a fisherman, capsized at sea. Told Fricis of days in arctic water, of hypothermia, when the brain releases all energy before it succumbs. One last burst of heat to save the body. Cruel stories of freezing men casting away oars, life preservers before they "caught fire" on their skin, stripping themselves naked only to drown.

Out. He must get out of the water.

He had no strength to pull himself up. Leaning back, he saw the buoy tipped by his body, the anchor weight, the flag dipping lower. A slight kick pushed him farther away, the hooked chain sliding to the center. Succumbing to sea, to the random fates, he let the tides pull him where they will, the chain slipping farther, over the pole of the flag. The buoy pulled onto its side.

There was still a chance.

Anchor weighing down the buoy he rode the next crest, rolled himself over the tilted marker. His weight fully upon the wood, the float sank into the sea, too heavy, he would drown. Yet it did not sink further, reaching a sort of unsteady equilibrium six inches below the surface. Fricis forced his legs beneath him, knees against his chest, another few inches of elevation for his torso, his lungs, heart, all organs above the waves, let the limbs die first. And kneeling on an invisible buoy, he floated there, a man in shackles upon the sea.

* * *

"He took the whole catch," cursed Vilis, spreading out the shredded net on the icy deck before him. "Just bit through the threads to take every fish. Ole white tip don't care how much money he costs us or how many hours I gotta spend fixing his thievin' work."

Vilis glanced to the bow, where the hefty, red-faced Ludis stood with his lantern outstretched, eyes peering over the sea.

"You listening to me, Captain?"

"Where is the marker?" whispered Ludis more to himself than to his only crew member.

"What?" Young Vilis abandoned the net, bowing beneath the boom to join his captain at the front. "Is there a problem?"

"I can't find the buoy."

Their eyes searched every pocket between the waves as they neared Kolka, the cape separating the Baltic from the Gulf of Rīga. Its lighthouse resting on the shore, they knew the shoal markers must appear soon.

Ludis waved the lantern over the edge, a kaleidoscope of yellows painting the waters below the boat. "There's something peculiar with that lighthouse, Vilis. The lamp's lit, but nothing moves." The captain flashed the lantern again, its signal unanswered.

Vilis scratched coarse chin whiskers. This was damn unusual. "Maybe they ain't seen us?"

"Yeah…Go sound the horn."

As he again ducked underneath the boom, Vilis took a long look at the shoreline. "Don't the lighthouse appear big to you?"

The thunder of impact, Vilis's ribs slammed against the sea rail as the ship lurched high to one side, foam showering over the bow. Nearly falling into the spitting seas, he saw Ludis thrown like a rag-doll to the deck as the sail collapsed around them. A hiss in the black air, Vilis caught a last glimpse of the boom swinging towards him and all went dark.

* * *

Vilis awoke on the deck, cheek pressed against a frozen pool of his own blood. Softly moaning, he brushed the pink ice from his lip and nose where the timber had struck him, tasted the liquid thawing in his mouth.

Slowly, he became aware of his surroundings. The sail was crumpled at his side, some sort of movement beyond. He tried to lift his head, but shards of pain stabbed his spine and jaw, light spots bursting over his vision.

Somewhere, something splashed.

He rolled onto his stomach, tried to clear his sight. Beyond the sail lay the captain's lantern, glowing fitfully on its side, the oil leaking over the deck.

It came back to him then. The impact…they'd hit something, a sand bar, ice, maybe the Ventspils shoal…

He looked back to the lantern. That would never do, oil on the deck a hazard…

Ignoring the pains, he forced his body to a knee, grabbed the rail, hoisted himself up. They were at fifteen, twenty degrees tipped to starboard side, tiny streams of melting ice flowing over the deck towards him. For the first time he wondered if they were taking water. And where was Ludis?

"Captain?"

A few awkward, tentative steps over the soaked sail, and he reached the lantern. Lifting it, Vilis took his first clear look at his new world.

In the sea, just within the lantern's range, was their rowboat moving away. Ludis abandoning ship without him?

"Captain!" he yelled, a mist of pink breath floating on air. Yet, it didn't look like Ludis at the oars, a bigger man, something reflective at his wrists as he rowed.

"Captain?"

A sound behind. Vilis turned, held the light up to illuminate the deck. Near the cabin, he found Ludis, his captain squirming, tangled in the net, bound at feet and hands by its thread. Between them, something brilliant shown in the lantern light...

Blue amber.

III

THE ANTIQUARY'S WIFE

Originally published in Alfred Hitchcock's Mystery Magazine

The Antiquary's Wife

Odessa, 1899

She had daring red hair, worn mostly back, with a few curls down the forehead, and my emotion at seeing her was simply envy. At fourteen, and a twin, I wished to be as distinctive, would have loved the colors of coral and autumn running in my hair. But the fire above did not enliven this stranger on our doorstep. In fact, the vibrancy contrasted with her grim countenance and gaunt body and the rest of her seemed a skeletal tree lost beneath a sunset.

This visitor made no effort to speak Greek, or even Russian, but went straight to English and said:

"I would like to inquire if a room is available."

I was saddened to disappoint her as I had so many others, but Mother's wishes were well-known to me. "I'm afraid the house is in mourning."

"Oh."

"We can recommend a lodging down the street. Mrs. Derevyanko is—"

This woman stepped closer. "I heard you...your home, I mean, was trustworthy."

"Trustworthy?" For a moment, I thought I had misunderstood her. My English was strong, but still, mistakes could be made. Our lodging home was many things: cozy, humble, inexpensive. I shrugged. "Well, I suppose we are. I never really thought—"

"Mrs. Jones says you are most trustworthy. I'm a friend of hers. Yes, I can say that. Mrs. Natalia Jones from—"

"From Hughesovka."

"Yes. And she says I should stay here."

There was something in the desperate manner of this foreign woman that made me a bit fearful. And for the first time, I noticed a large coach parked on the street nearby, the driver and another man carefully watching our conversation. This too made me wary. Still, if she was a friend of Natalia's…

"And your name is?"

"Mrs. Scarborough. Or Lilly. Lilly Scarborough would be best."

"I'm Anastasia. 'Tasia,' if you prefer." I tried to smile. "One moment, Mrs. Scarborough."

I retreated into our home and relayed Mrs. Scarborough's request to my mother.

Her eyes widened behind that black veil. "And you have left a friend of Natalia's on the doorstep?"

"You said no visitors, Mother."

"Such a manner-less girl. Let her in, Tasia."

I returned to the door, passing my sister sitting on the stairwell, Eleni smugly shaking her head at me in disapproval, echoing "manner-less girl" behind my back.

Oh, to be married and free of this place. "Come in Mrs. Scarborough, I 'm sorry for the delay."

"I would only stay a night or two," she said, stepping inside. "Is this too much trouble?

"That's up to Mother."

Eleni and Mother rose to greet her, while Mrs. Scarborough looked about our darkened interior. "My condolences for your loss," she said.

Mother nodded. "Thank you."

"Papa lingered for a long time," said Eleni.

"Oh, I'm sorry."

"He was just wasting away in that bedroom upstairs," my sister continued.

"Terrible."

"I can still see him, his eyes gray and watery."

"Eleni," I said. "Mrs. Scarborough doesn't want every detail."

"And how do you know Natalia Jones, Mrs. Scarborough?" asked Mother.

"I stayed with her once, and my husband did so twice. She treated us very well, as family."

"Where is your husband now?"

Mrs. Scarborough's frown deepened, and she looked down at her shoes. "He's waiting for me at our home in Massachusetts, I'm afraid."

"Quite a husband who lets his wife travel Europe on her own."

"Progressive," I said.

"Daring," said Eleni.

"Yes, a good man."

"So, you're an American?" asked my sister. "You're our first. We have Welsh all the time, traveling out to the coal camps along the Kalmius, and sometimes Scots and Irishmen, but never Americans."

"Never," I said.

"Can you tell us about Boston?"

"And New York?"

"And Des Moines?"

"I think," Mrs. Scarborough said, "if it is permissible, I will take a room and have my things brought in? I am very tired from my trip."

"Of course," Mother said with something approaching embarrassment. "Excuse my daughters' enthusiasm. We haven't had a lodger since my husband's passing." She directed our guest to the room beneath the stairs, the largest bedroom in the house and the one with a private bath and a good view of the courtyard beyond.

Mrs. Scarborough approved, paid Mother some small amount and then returned to the coach outside. We offered to assist with her luggage, but she declined. Instead, the coachman and the other man appeared in the doorway each loaded down with bags. I shook my head. How could one woman need so many things?

"Do you think she's really married?" I whispered to Eleni.

"She has a wedding ring."

"Natalia will know."

The men deposited Mrs. Scarborough's bags in her room and then exited our house. When they returned, they carried between them a large trunk of red wood surpassing five feet in length and at least three in width and depth. Both men were stout, strong-looking fellows but it was clearly taxing them greatly to move it, and when they set the box down in Mrs. Scarborough's room, a heavy thud reverberated throughout the house, a bit of dust cast into the air.

My sister and I exchanged glances as Mrs. Scarborough went to pay her men. Then Eleni, with a smile, whispered a theory in my ear. I scoffed at her in that moment, as anyone would, but she would be proven exactly right.

Or, at least, half right.

* * *

That night, I snuck down the stairs from the attic room I shared with my sister for a cup of bedtime tea. As I passed through our parlor, I noticed lamplight beneath Mrs. Scarborough's door and heard the thin, tinny notes of a music box or cylinder from within. Balakirev, I thought. Yes, certainly. Balakirev's *Islamey*. I had played this at my last lesson. Or attempted to play it, at least. Do they listen to him in America? Apparently so. I smiled. All the world loves Balakirev.

After I made my tea, I sat in Mother's worn parlor chair, my legs tucked beneath me, and simply listened. Always it was the same. The notes would slow, trailing off, but never quite finished, then came a fierce ratcheting sound as Mrs. Scarborough—Lilly, why not call her Lilly?—rewound the spring. We were not ten feet apart, divided by a door an inch thick, yet in separate worlds; she in her cozy, lighted, musical room, and I in this darkened, shrouded parlor. I wondered about her husband in far-off Massachusetts. Did our music somehow remind her of him? It must be hard to travel so far alone.

At some point, I passed into sleep, because the next I knew, it was past three, and the teacup was on the floor. A light remained under Lilly's door, the music now absent, but sounds were still drifting in. Was she speaking? Yes, perhaps she was. I inched forward in the chair, but it was not enough to hear, and when I rose, I caught only "forgive me, Anderson," before the squeak of a floorboard betrayed me, and everything turned silent inside.

A few seconds later, the light went out beneath the door. Nothing stirred 'til morning.

* * *

Whatever her thoughts on my presence outside her door, Lilly showed no alarm or concern the next day. Instead, she asked me to come along as translator when she purchased her ticket back to America, and we walked through the wide city streets, down towards the harbor together. It was a brilliant spring day, the warmth and salty air enlivening me in ways that nothing had since Father's death. The pain in our house submerged, if not forgotten, for a few hours, I twirled Lilly's sun parasol as we walked, happy to be learning the ways of the world from this older, well-traveled woman. Soon, we broached the subject of her marriage.

"My husband," said Lilly, "is the most dedicated, if not best, antiquary in Worcester."

"An antiquary is a historian, yes?"

"Not quite. A historian is concerned with the sweep of history. The antiquary is all about the details, the objects themselves from the past."

"So, he collects antiques? In an academic way?"

"Archaeological evidence and items of significance, in theory. In practice, junk," she said, though as soon as the remark passed her lips, something caught in her throat. Her face softened, and Lilly seemed to suppress some emotion with a hand to her mouth.

"Mrs. Scarborough?"

Lilly took a few moments to compose herself. "I'm sorry. I felt faint." She motioned ahead. "I'm a bit afraid of heights and those steps, before us, well…"

Her voice trailed off, but I knew what she meant. We had reached the grand staircase descending from the hillside of the city center to the harbor. The Communists in their day would rename it the Potemkin Steps, but in 1899, it was still known as the Boulevard Staircase, the more appropriate name as it is as wide as any street and very much a thoroughfare. Everyone who enters or exits the great port city by sea traverses this mammoth staircase.

"Let me help you, Mrs. Scarborough." I slipped an arm around Lilly's and steadied her as we descended. It is a strange experience, I must admit, walking down these steps on a sunny day. They are so high above the sea, the ships and people at the bottom so small that the only thing directly in your sight is the endless watery horizon itself. With little in the way of point of reference, you step down, and nothing changes. You step again and all is the same. Soon, you feel the steps are rolling up beneath you, and like the rungs in some mouse wheel, they will keep coming forever. But they don't. There are only two hundred of them, and finally, you are at the bottom, exhausted and exhilarated. Lilly's face was completely flushed, perspiration darkening her red hair, and I returned her parasol so she might have some shade. To my surprise, I received no thanks for this assistance, Lilly growing gloomy as we approached the buildings along the pier.

In the shipping office, things only got worse.

I turned from the clerk back to Lilly, resumed my English: "He wants to know what's in the trunk?"

"Only my personal things. Odessa's a free port, so what does it matter?"

I relayed this to the clerk, who shook his head. In Russian he said: "Odessa hasn't been a free port in forty years. Whoever told her that is living in the past. There are taxes, tariffs that must be paid." He looked down at the information we'd provided. "Given the dimensions of the trunk, it must be considered freight. She needs to declare its contents."

I looked at Lilly: "It's not a free port. You're trunk is so big, they need to know."

"Only clothes, shoes, that sort of thing."

"Then write it down on this." I handed her a form from the partition. Lilly released a long, theatrical sigh as she took it.

The clerk was clearly interested in her flustered manner. "She should know," he said, "that our company has the right to open any cargo it ships."

I told Lilly. She didn't like it.

"That must be illegal."

I shrugged. "I think a captain might simply wish to know what he is carrying on his ship."

"You're siding with them?"

"I'm not siding with anyone. I'm simply explaining…"

"Ignorant girl," she said, her whole manner changing before my eyes. "I should have brought the other child, Elena."

"Eleni."

"It's immaterial." Lilly shuffled through her bag, withdrawing several ruble bills. "All the other customers have their shipping stamps. Ask him how much for my little stamp."

"You want me to solicit a bribe?"

"Call it business. Just ask him."

"I won't."

"You will," she said fiercely. "Natalia Jones says you are trustworthy."

"Exactly. I won't do it."

Lilly growled something, then tried to circumvent me, holding the bills out toward the clerk. He shrunk away, looking over his shoulder at the others in the office. "Nyet," he whispered.

"He says 'no.'"

"Fine. If he won't, then he won't." Lilly stuffed the money violently back in the bag, then seized her papers. "I'll find a shipper who respects privacy, not this fat little dwarf," she huffed, marching towards the exit. "And if I can't leave tomorrow, don't expect me to remain in that mausoleum you call a lodging house. There are kennels that treat their occupants better."

She thundered through the door, slamming it so hard behind that the windows shook. A few of the men in the back laughed. One or two even clapped.

"French?" asked the clerk, when all had settled down.

"American," I said.

Outside, Lilly was already far away, past the sailors' chapel and marching up the Boulevard Staircase. Making good time with no assistance from anyone.

* * *

I sat in my attic bed, sketching lines into a book, just following my muse.

A curve, a curve again, a few more dashes, and there was Lilly's frowning face. Like a gaunt gargoyle, I thought.

Then I dropped the lines down, forming her long, thin body, circles around the base. I filled in the sketch lines. Soon I had Lilly towering among a group of children-clerks, holding out a ruble above them. I (or my muse) adding the caption: "A shiny coin for one little stamp, dears."

A catharsis, of sorts. Revenge for my scolding earlier.

I penciled in an impossibly large pestle under her legs and added an old-style kerchief hat. Lilly as Baba Yaga, the witch. Perhaps, I'd slide it under her door.

Never.

Oh, shut up, muse. And draw me something more.

I flipped over the page. Let my imagination take me where it will.

The pencil lines were longer here, smoother, more subtle. No cartoon this…Detail, detail, a body stretched out horizontal…yes, detail…a woman with watery, gray eyes…

I frowned as the idea formed clearer in my head, onto my page. Lilly, lying broken and bruised on the ground at the harbor, something shattered near her.

Where had that come from?

I heard a faint rap. *She* was at the opened door to my room, Lilly standing in the little attic landing, a music box in her hands, a contrite look on her face.

"May I come in, Anastasia?"

I said no, but she did anyway, sitting down next to me on the bed. I flipped my sketchbook shut.

Lilly settled that music box onto her lap. "It is ornate, isn't it? My Anderson gave it to me. I worry it will get damaged on the journey back to Worcester. Perhaps, it might be better if I left it with you? What do you think?"

It certainly was a beautiful music box. The body was a polished forest green, a curio drawer with bronze handle in the center, and on top a quintet of tiny porcelain horses. The Orlov Trotters, it seemed, led by the legendary silver-gray stallion Smetanka. How he gleamed.

"Do you like horses, Tasia? We have a pony in Dighton."

I liked horses.

Lilly wound the key, let the box play that familiar Balakirev tune, the porcelain horses moving in figures of eight about the top, mighty Smetanka chasing and being chased by the others.

Beautiful.

We silently listened to the whole piece, Lilly and I, watching those horses go round and round. I was moved by such a potential gift, especially knowing it came from her husband. Still, there was uneasiness. This woman had called me ignorant, insulted my home only hours ago. A mausoleum? A kennel? Did she think I didn't remember her words? What was this gift really but another bribe? Like with the clerk. Buying off amends, Lilly? Every time you make a mistake, do you simply bribe…

"Again?" asked Lilly as the notes faded away. "Another play?"

I shook my head "no."

"You haven't said two words since I've been in here. Anastasia…Tasia…I leave tomorrow. Let's part as friends. I was foolish at the harbor office. I'm sorry. You have no idea what I've been through recently." Her eyes turned watery. "Sometimes I think I won't see the next sunrise. You're only fourteen; you've no understanding of darkness, of men."

I knew darkness. I had lost a father and a brother before reaching my fifteenth birthday.

I said nothing.

When the pause had gone on too long, she finally said. "Alright, I tried." Lilly rose from the bed and placed the music box on the dresser near the door. "I'll just leave it here, so you can listen to it when you wish."

"I tried?" How humble?

"Mrs. Scarborough, if you leave it, I'll only throw it out."

Something in her seemed to shrink away. She nodded, picked up the music box, and let herself out. Husband or not in Massachusetts, Lilly was alone in this part of the world, a great pain running underneath. Part of me had sympathy for her then, but I held grudges when I was fourteen. I still hold them today.

***

I lay on the floorboards in the darkness trying to keep warm. I'd come down from the bed to the floor to ease the tense muscles in my back, to let them stretch out on the hard wooden surface. As I did every night I worried, every night I stayed awake anxious and waiting. Every night since Father died.

But tonight, the boards were as ice, some unnatural cold seeping up from below. I had no idea the source. Storms at sea can play havoc with the weather, dropping coastal temperatures to un-seasonal lows in minutes.

I watched my breath rise to the attic ceiling. *But it's May. This is impossible.*

My sister sat up in the bed. "Tasia, do you feel this draft?"

"It's simply freezing."

"I—"

Two heavy thuds rose from far below, then a great rending of wood and a scream. A scream as horrible as any I have ever heard.

In an instant, we were both out the door and down the landing. Mother was already there, and the three of us hurried to the ground floor.

The front door stood open, warm white rain blowing in over the threshold. But it was the other door, the door to Lilly's bedroom that kept our attention. It had been torn off its hinges, now lying cracked at an angle against the wall, splinters all over the floor.

I seized a lamp, lit it, forced back the shadows in her room.

Lilly was gone.

* * *

A half-hour later, I sat alone in Lilly's shattered bedroom, pulling her things from floor. We had checked every room, every wardrobe, every corner and alcove in the house. She had vanished. Mother and Eleni had gone to the streets to find her and, if possible in the Greek Quarter at this hour, a policeman. Someone had to stay. I guess I was the most timid.

That strange cold was retreating, but a scent like cured meat lingered in the air. The courtyard neighbors drying lamb near opened windows. Somehow, it made me hungry.

Nothing made sense. It seemed impossible that someone, some group of men, had broken in here in an instant and kidnapped Lilly. Eleni's theory that something had broken out was not to be considered. I glanced at that shattered door. It would take several minutes with hammers and axes… Could Lilly have done it herself? Madmen are capable of great strength. Why not madwomen?

I set the lamp down on that great trunk, the only thing in the room left undisturbed. Invincible, immovable old crate. There seemed to be no latch, no lock. Just a box really. Like those old Chinese puzzle chests, impossible to rob. Odd again.

I continued to collect Lilly's things. The music box was missing, but a diary found a photograph and gazetteer folded inside. I sat down on the trunk, pulled the light closer. The photo showed two people, Lilly in a fashionable dress, locked arm-in-arm with an attractive bespectacled man about a decade older than she. Behind them towered an Egyptian needle, the trees and flowers of some great park on the margins.

The man must be Mr. Scarborough. If so, he was more handsome than I'd imagined. Cruel that I thought an antiquary wouldn't be.

I set the photograph aside, turned to the gazetteer:

The Spade and Pen.

The Journal of the Antiquarian Society of Worcester, Mass.

I thumbed through it. On the third page was the annual membership photograph. There he was, second from the left... Yes, "Anderson Scarborough, PhD. Pre-Slavic Studies. Treasurer." The same man.

The rest of journal was only a series of boring articles, one the "Cuman and Kipchak Relics of New Russia" heavily marked up by pen.

I investigated the diary. I found Lilly's handwriting legible, easily understood, though I soon became skeptical of her truthfulness. Evidently, when she had begun her trip to Europe, Lilly's husband was *not* left at home in Massachusetts, but traveled with her to Liverpool and then down onto the Continent. They'd sailed along the Danube to the Black Sea and then overland to Odessa. It seemed a romantic trip, few troubles on the road or between the couple. I kept waiting for Dr. Scarborough to leave, but he did not.

From Odessa they went east five hundred miles to the steel town Hughesovka and the warmth of Natalia's hotel, arriving, if my calendar conversion was correct, only nine days before Lilly would appear on our doorstep.

The key events, I reproduce here, word for word:

The Diary of Lilly Scarborough—May 15th

New discoveries with more than one peculiar turn—this is what I take from such a long day in *Novoya Rossiya*. I am rather surprised to find where I am sleeping tonight. Well, we must give the details, mustn't we? I will try to recall everything I can and get it down on paper before the miller's candle fails me.

On our fourth day in Hughesovka, Anderson had pledged to go for a ride into the Ukrainian countryside. As usual, he was exactingly true to his word. By prior agreement, he arranged to borrow Mrs. Jones's horse and buggy, and we set off from our hotel, The Cardiff, midmorning and in good spirits.

It was already warm, the sun reflecting off the green roofs of the English Town, ducks and geese lounging on the slow Kalimus River, and we crossed the bridge to the Slavic side. In a short while, we'd left Hughesovka's immense factories behind and were lone travelers in a land of fields swaying in worship to the blueness of the sky, here and there slow-turning windmills like guardians of the horizon. It reminded me so of my trip to Holland as a girl, and though a quarter-century had passed and we were on the opposite side of Europe, if I closed my eyes I was in Volendam riding on the back of that Dutch farm cart, hand-in-hand with my *oma*.

I told Anderson my thoughts.

"Sentimental girl," he said.

Too sentimental for an antiquary? Oh, pish tosh.

When we had seen no one for a long while, not a lonely peasant cart or any wagon bound for the coal camps, Anderson steered the horse off the road into the fields, the heather thumping against the side of the buggy as we lurched ahead.

"Darling, the wheels are not deep enough. We'll get stuck."

"Pish tosh," he replied, stealing the fashion from me.

Soon, Anderson found a spot to his liking, and we pressed down the grasses for a lunch. A good man knows his place on a picnic and does all the work. Anderson left me happily stranded on the isle of our blanket while he assembled the meal from a compartment in the rear of the buggy. He set out the cups and bowls and bottle of wine before at last arriving with a sort of miner's kettle that had kept the lunch warm all the way from town.

"Borsch *and* cawl?!" I said.

"Natalia's kitchen, Lilly. You should have known."

It was a scrumptious bite. A bit salty, but it's the sentiment (there's that word again) that counts.

After the meal, Anderson and I lay on the blanket talking, as we rarely did, of future matters. Of his tenure, our wait for children and the state of his mother's health in Springfield. His glasses folded in his pocket he looked young as the day we married, every bit the daring, globetrotter I loved and less the obsessive, academic bumblebee one couldn't help but love (usually).

My hand across his chest, I wished for romance, but received only one close-lipped kiss before Anderson sat up and said:

"I have a surprise."

He rose and returned to the buggy. A moment later, I heard a noise like the winding of a clock, then the notes of an instrument playing vaguely Eastern music. Anderson returned with a music box in his hands, toy horses turning round on its top.

"It's Balakirev, I believe."

"Oh," I said, though I didn't know who that was.

He kneeled on the blanket and handed the box to me. "I do have a confession," he said, clasping his hands together like a choir boy before the altar. "It can't be more than ten years old,"

"Anderson, in some households new things are admired."

"Yes, but fortunately ours has taste. Promise me you'll keep the age a secret."

"A woman never tells an age, darling. I love it." Though this was not quite the truth.

"I found it at this little shop on the Slav side. They have every sort of bizarre thing in the curiosity cabinet. Human heads preserved in jars, among them. I bought this as well." He reached into the pocket of his jacket. "Though, of course, we must give it to the Worcester Collection."

"A spoon?"

"A seventeenth-century spoon, Lilly," he said, with fire in his eyes.

Oh, if that fire were for me.

We finished the picnic by late afternoon and packed our things. I yearned for English Town and a warm bath, but Anderson steered us west.

"Garrett has been insisting I see a spot a little farther on. I missed it my last time. You don't mind, do you, Lilly?"

Anderson's excursions are like his gifts—for him.

"Of course not. Adventure."

"Good girl."

We rode on for another tranquil hour, passing through villages that seemed too small for names. In the field lake beyond one, much of the community was swimming, the men and children clad in nothing, the women and older girls only in sheer garments that floated up around their shoulders as they dove and splashed about scandalously.

"Well, you don't see those in Boston Harbor," I said as we passed.

"Lilly, in Boston Harbor, we'd see nothing at all."

Soon, evening's touch was turning golden fields to gray. The landscape, too, was changing, flat lands undulating into gentle hills, and the roads falling away, swallowed inside darkening grasses.

Anderson hung out the lantern, muttering something about Garrett's vague directions. We're going to be lost out here, I thought, though I knew better than to try and dissuade Anderson when he was bent on some challenge. A good wife stands by her husband, as *Oma* always said. In the Old World, take the Old World view.

The hills rolled on. I was watching strange insects accumulate on our lantern glass when I perceived a figure standing among the gray grasses at some distance ahead. He was still and black with arms outstretched, like a wizard casting spells over the land. The view was lost to me as we descended the trough between two hills, but when we climbed the next, *he* was there.

"Here is what I wanted," said Anderson, pulling up on the reins.

The figure was a granite statue, weathered and ancient. A warrior by the look of him, a sword at his hip, though the hands, as I'd thought, were open and free.

"Kipchak," Anderson said, jumping from the buggy. "Ninth century. Steppe nomads eventually destroyed by the Mongols." He looked back at me. "This is what Garrett was talking about."

"And to think, other girls go to the beach on their holidays."

"There are a dozen of theses statues between here and Katerynoslav. But they're largest in the east." Anderson moved closer to the statue which reached perhaps to his chin. The mouth was opened, the warrior-wizard locked forever in a scream.

"He looks hungry."

"For a thousand years he's stood here, guarding this spot, Lilly. While the Golden Horde, the Tartars, and Cossacks all swept by. Think what he's witnessed."

"He's witnessed nothing, dear. He's a piece of stone."

"True, true. But a useful piece of stone. The locals regard them as landmarks, give them names."

"Well, we'll call this one 'Robert.' Say goodnight to Robert, darling."

"Lilly, get my kit from the back of the buggy, will you please? While there's still a trace of light in the sky."

"Darling, it will be midnight before we're in English Town."

"Work, dear."

This was no picnic. I fetched the kit. "What are you going to do?"

He withdrew his sampling knife and kneeled at the base of the statue. "I'm going to prove Garrett wrong. That Harvard twit thinks these statues came from a quarry up near Kharkiv, while I am certain the source is much closer to the Sea of Azov." He began to lightly scrape off small bits into his opened handkerchief. "We'll see who the real antiquary is."

"You mean you can tell where that thing came from just by a few grains of rock?"

"I can't, but our man Bonner can. You remember Bonner, Lilly? You met him at the Society dinner. He was the one you found drab and boring."

"You'll have to be more specific, darling."

"He was the fellow in the yellowish tweed jacket and the toupee. His wife left him for the lamplighter."

"Oh, the scandal."

He scraped away. "Lamplighters need love, too, I suppose."

"Don't antiquaries?"

"Not the best. They're committed only to—" The knife's edge hooked some hidden crevice, and a shard broke off into Anderson's hand.

"Well, that's a little more than I wanted."

"The thing's stood here for eight hundred years, and now you've defaced it."

"More like de-footed it, I think."

"True."

"And it's a thousand years."

"What's a century or two between friends?"

"Are we friends? He looks like quite an angry fellow." Anderson gently folded the stone splinter into his handkerchief, then pressed the bundle into his jacket's inside pocket. "He's positively livid, I think."

"And getting more ferocious all the time. Imagine someone cut off your foot."

"What would I put in my mouth?"

"Crow would do. Now can we be going?"

"Well, I'd like to take measurements, Lilly. Perhaps a detailed sketch for the *Spade*. But this old lantern will never do for such exacting work." He looked at me, a child preparing for the scolding. "Let's get to it in the morning."

"And stay where?"

"There was a windmill a few miles back. The people out here are often friendly."

"'Often' means 'not always.'"

"Well, it's either that or spend the night in the buggy with Robert here to watch over us."

Anderson can be quite convincing at times, and we soon found ourselves standing at the door of cottage adjacent to a windmill. The miller was a hard and square man, his wife, soft and round, and both equally welcoming. Their five pepper-pot children stared on curiously as Anderson negotiated the rent in his slow, confusing Russian. After a brief exchange, my husband turned to me:

"We can stay for free if you'll pluck a chicken."

"Just pay the man, Anderson."

With little fuss, we were given the Miller's and his wife's bed. (Where they or their children sleep tonight is not clear to me. I suspect some are stranded in the stable loft, others perhaps lie under the stars.) Anderson, of course, evaluated our room looking for anything of antiquarian value. He discovered a large chest of a type common, he says, in the steppes of Central Asia. It had no visible lock, and like a child with some new toy, Anderson insisted on showing me how it opened. (Pins hidden beneath the brass pieces at the corners). It goes without saying that he found this far more fascinating than I did.

The weather warm, our hosts cooked the meal over a pit grill in the yard. Lamb strips, potatoes, *salo*, and meat-filled pancakes, tough but delectable. They gave us rather strong homemade vodka that tasted closer to a whiskey. Ukrainian moonshine, I suppose. Afterwards, our heads all a bit lightened, the youngest boy told some sort of legend in front of the fire pit. By his mannerisms, it seemed quite a horrific tale. Certainly, the shadows he cast up onto the windmill behind were misshapen and terrifying. The imagination of children is universally grotesque, isn't it?

And the day is drawn to a close with little more to write. I am sunk deep into our feather bed, the candlelight so low I can barely see the page. Despite eight souls somewhere about, I may be the last awake for the house is still as can be. There were curious sounds earlier. At first, I thought them outside, but now I am certain they come from within. It is the miller and his wife making love and trying to stifle their breaths. They know I can hear them. Whenever I clear my throat, or move even a little in the bed, they go quiet for minutes.

I think of those bathers at lake. So fearless compared to New England society. Anderson would never touch me if anyone else were in the house.

Yes, there we are, another low moan. Their bed is closer than I thought. Well, let them have their fun. Time to put out the light, close this journal, and escape to the world of dreams.

Tomorrow will be a most fascinating day.

May 16th

A bizarre and threatening day, one that I fear may result in a most terrible ending by tomorrow. Anderson has once again proven he thinks of little but his own desires. Not me, not our welfare, only his wants and those of that petty and self-important society of his. He has been gone for hours, taken away by his own obsessions, and I fear the next knock at my door may bring the news no wife can bear. Perhaps, recording the day's events will bring some sense to them, some enlightenment I can't see in the moment. If it gives any comfort in these lonely hours, then it's worth the effort, I suppose.

For a day that has ended in such distress, it began in a calm and lovely manner. We were awakened early this morning by the stirrings of a rural household and, in short order, given a lavish country breakfast of homemade sausages, wheat sauce, cucumbers, and tomatoes by the miller's family. The food was rich and enjoyable, fresh from the farm, as they say, but Anderson was in a poor mood that seemed to worsen as the meal went on. He spoke little to me, less to them, and by the time we had hitched the horse to Mrs. Jones's buggy, he was almost hostile.

As we rode away, leaving the windmill behind, I bent towards my husband and asked the reason for his sullen manner.

"I expected better treatment, Lilly," he said. "I should think that the property of paying guests would be respected even out here."

"Whatever do you mean? They were wonderful."

He pulled the antique spoon from his coat pocket and handed it to me. "Some prank of the miller's children, no doubt."

The spoon's handle was horribly twisted, and the face had been punctured repeatedly by some sort of weighty, pointed instrument, the tip of my pinkie easily able to slip through the holes.

It was most certainly odd. But... "What's done is done, dear. They're just children, and it's only a spoon."

"A seventeenth-century spoon."

"That it is." Or was. But why reason with him? Anderson's sulks are best ignored. Only he can bring himself out of them. I never have.

We soon came upon a familiar figure in the hillscape. I thought it another, as we'd only set out minutes before, yet there was the mark Anderson had made at the base. In these uniform lands, distance can be so difficult to judge.

"I see 'Robert' is up early this morning. Hello, Robert."

Anderson said nothing, still sulking about his spoon. Soon he was off the buggy, measuring tape out, taking down the dimensions of the statue from every angle. I laughed to myself. He seemed an industrious tailor, getting a client ready for the ball.

"What's the inseam?" I shouted.

Anderson's glare was priceless.

In the morning light, I found details in Robert I had not noticed the evening before. The mouth was of great dimension, and despite a thousand years exposure to the elements, the teeth looked un-weathered, long and sharp. The fingers too were stiletto tips and held out in claw-like hands before the chest. All and all, the warrior looked like he had little need of a sword.

Bored, I soon left the buggy behind and wandered over the next hill. In the low valley beyond was a small pond, two lean goats sipping at the water's edge, eyeing me curiously. I kneeled at the bank, snapped a few fronds, and pensively tossed them into the pond. "Meditation and water are forever wedded," Melville had said. True enough.

Again, I thought of the bathers. What if I stripped everything off and waded into this pond? What would my husband say? Out here in the open land under the eyes of God? If I faked a cramp, and called for help would he leave his work and come running? Would Anderson jump into the pond clothes and all to save me?

Suddenly, I heard a scream!

I turned and climbed the hill as fast as I could, lifting the hem of my skirt to run faster. At the top, I gained a clear view of the shallow below. Anderson was at the buggy, wrapping his hand in some old cloth. When he saw me, he laughed.

"He bit me, Lilly," Anderson said with a child-like grin.

"What?"

"Oh, those teeth are sharp. Ran my hand underneath them when taking a measurement." He shook his head as he tied the cloth tight. "Surprisingly deep. May need a stitch or two back in Hughesovka."

I descended the slope. "You are a klutz."

"Blame him, Lilly. I think he lunged for me."

"I blame only you, dear. I guess I can't let you of sight until this work is finished."

"You promise?"

"Of course."

I regretted that commitment. Anderson continued for hours. When the measurements were through, he sketched the statue from every angle in nauseating detail, reciting from memory the history of the Kipchak peoples as he worked. It was past noon when we finally left Robert behind, setting our route at last towards Hughesovka.

The trip to Hughesovka was uneventful, though it turned frighteningly cold for spring in the later hours. Anderson dutifully draped his jacket over my shoulders, and while this was some relief from the temperature, something in the pocket kept scratching me as we rode. "Digging," I think I described it as at the time. I assumed it was that shard taken from the statue, but as there was nowhere else really to put it, I endured, hoping only to be back in English Town shortly.

At last, we reached The Cardiff, and I returned to the room while Anderson settled our overtime use of the horse and buggy with Mrs. Jones. I found that the shard had not only cut through the interior lining of the jacket, but torn apart its handkerchief and done a good bit of damage to the bodice region of my dress. All from one sharp edge and the vibrations of a buggy. Well, I knew Anderson would never throw it out, but I was not going to let it rip up the interior of our luggage on the return journey to America. I wrapped the splinter in a thick hand towel, and with a bit of inspiration, slid it into the curio drawer of the music box. The bundle just fit, though once wedged inside, I could never get the drawer open again. I can't say it bothered me.

At the back of The Cardiff, there is a restaurant that is popular citywide and filled with the mix of cultures and occupations that make up this industrial boomtown. We dined, as always, with Natalia Jones at the head table, sitting on an elevated section of the floor, underneath a sparkling chandelier, and directly in front of the oil painting of her husband with city founder John Hughes.

We were joined tonight by a retired Russian military officer whose name somehow I never quite caught. I wish that I had. He was a well-dressed man in his fifties, who seemed quite aristocratic, prosperous, and was certainly highly opinionated. Opinionated people seldom get along with Anderson because he is, well, opinionated himself.

Things started to go wrong when Anderson asked Mrs. Jones why the neighborhood was called "English Town" when nearly everyone here was Welsh.

"If you speak English, you are English," said this officer, answering for Natalia.

Anderson, of course, could not let this go. "We speak English, but we're American."

"There's no difference."

"Of course, there is." My husband then spent ten minutes listing off cultural, political, and economic differences. By the end of his speech, I felt the countries as far apart as the Martians and humans in Mr. Wells's *War of the Worlds*.

The officer sat there smoldering, clearly half listening to Anderson's points. When, at last, my husband finished, this man's only retort was, "They are the same." Then he smiled, the evil smile of one who is the turning the screw. "There is *one* difference, I grant you. The English are thieves. But Americans are twice thieves."

"What does that mean?"

"They stole their land from the Indians. Then they stole it again from the English."

"I don't think a Russian should be lecturing anyone about stealing land."

"I say it to you plainly. You are a thief, Dr. Scarborough. From a nation of thieves."

Here, Mrs. Jones tried to interrupt, but Anderson and this uncouth officer were advancing towards a most heated exchange. To make some point, my husband turned the language to Russian. The officer stood up and shouted a reply that drained the color from the faces of both Anderson and Mrs. Jones. Whatever was said, my husband thoroughly and openly refused it. Natalia then insisted the officer leave. With a glare at me that turned my blood cold, he did so.

It wasn't until we'd quit the dining hall and were on our way up the stairs to our room that Anderson informed me he'd actually been challenged to a duel!

Inside our room, my husband was in a terrible state, pacing back and forth until the residents below were banging on their ceiling in protest.

"A thief. A thief, Lilly. Did you hear what he called me? By a stranger, a man who barely knows me."

"That's the point, dear. He doesn't know you. But this challenge, are you sure we're safe? Maybe Natalia should contact the authorities?"

It's like he never heard me. "Well, if I 'm going to be labeled a thief, then I should enjoy the benefits of the title, shouldn't I?" He walked in circles at the foot of the bed. "Oh, Garrett would be so impressed. Bonner, too." He looked at me, a disturbing fire in his eyes. "Odessa's a free port, Lilly. They don't care what goes in or out."

"Anderson, what are you on about?"

"I'll get a few of those Welsh hulks Natalia always has loitering in the lobby. They'd go for a few beers, I'd reckon." He went to the wardrobe and seized his jacket. "And night is the best time to do these things, Lilly."

My stomach was twisting in knots. "Don't go, Anderson. A man out there challenged you to a duel. It's murder."

"Oh, it's all for show. They fire into the ground and depart as friends."

"Tell that to Alexander Hamilton."

"I think Alexander Pushkin would be a better example *here*, Lilly. But that only proves your point." He kissed me on the cheek. "I think we can be back by midnight. Journeys are always quicker the second time, when you know the way."

And with that, he left.

When I reached midnight alone, I awakened Mrs. Jones and asked her to summon the police. She suggested we wait. So now I am waiting, as I am bid to do, but my mind can find no rest.

Please come back, darling.

May 17th

It is past four in the morning, and Anderson has not returned. But I am not alone. I know that now. From time to time, that music box plays. I need not wind it. It plays on its own. Some fault in the spring, I thought, and locked the key. But when I became weak, crying for my husband's absence, it began to play again. I tore out the spring. It played. I gutted the mechanics, throwing them across the room. It played!

It plays now. I am convinced it will play on the road to Hell itself.

***

And those were the last words. There were no later entries for that day, and the next four pages had been torn out. The final entry was on the twentieth, the day Lilly arrived at our home. It consisted only of a brief will. Everything bequeathed to a sister in Martha's Vineyard. No mention of a husband.

At this point I put down the diary and tried to make sense of what I'd read. Perhaps, my English wasn't as strong as I'd thought. Perhaps I misunderstood so many meanings from American culture. But I could only conclude Lilly was a madwoman. The diary, the door, the disappearance all confirmed this.

Still, I wanted to know what was in that trunk.

I stood before it, the top past my waist, and ran my hands along the smooth, crimson wood, used my fingers to turn up the brass pieces at the corners. Beneath each was a wire loop, set deep in a recess. I tugged one, a click. Then I pulled the others. Three more clicks and the top rose slightly. A spring released. I lifted the lid.

Inside was a black rubber sack running the length of the box and rising nearly to the brim. A seam ran along this industrial bag, the envelope sealed by a series of iron staples, each the size of a finger.

That scent, again, far stronger. It was not the neighbors' food.

I hesitated. There was no way to open the sack without Lilly knowing. She would not be coming back. I knew it then.

I gripped the overlapping edges, strained to part the rubber skin. My heart pounding, some unnatural strength came to me, as it had come to Lilly with that door, as it came to someone, something that last night in the fields.

The envelope began to part, those staples leaving deep grooves in the bag's skin. Then it tore away in a rush, and I saw the contents below me, the flesh, the stone, the two *entwined*. I looked though for the rest of my life I wished I hadn't.

I quit the room in horror and, in my panic, ran right into my mother's breast. She and Eleni had returned with news from the harbor. Lilly had thrown herself from the Boulevard Staircase, the music box in her hands playing all the way down.

IV

KILLING SAM CLEMENS

Originally published in Sherlock Holmes Mystery Magazine

Killing Sam Clemens

August, 1867, Odessa

"My theory of fiction," said Sam, sitting at the café table across from me, "is that there are no new stories. The same tales repeat, generation to generation, civilization to civilization. Only the details change." He paused to taste his whiskey. "The modern author earns his keep only in the manner of his telling, Joe."

I smiled, sipped my cognac as Sam drank his Scotch. My name wasn't "Joe," but I wished him to think it was. "And our personal stories, Sam? The true ones, I mean. Are they as repetitive as fiction?"

"I think so. But who knows the roles we're assigned? That's where Providence will have her say...A smoke?"

"No, I'm trying to quit."

"I imagine you'll succeed. I quit every week." Sam struck a match, concentrated on lighting his cigar. As he did, I sized up this stranger across my table. Sam looked about my age, early thirties, dressed tolerably enough, nothing distinctive in his appearance really except a briar of unruly red hair and a bushy moustache. He talked more like a literary theorist than a routine travel writer with a few fiction publications to his credit.

In fact, it was his talking—and his use of English, rare as it is in Odessa—which had caught my attention at the harbor. Two Americans so far from home, we'd naturally struck up a conversation, then spent the afternoon in the café talking over spirits. I sensed Sam was growing a bit tipsy. It would make him easier to rob.

"So, this 'frog tale' was quite a success?" I asked.

Sam blew smoke rings into the humid air. "It was."

"Published in New York?"

"Nationally."

An exaggeration? That's the trouble with artists, you seldom know. My last two swindles weren't worth the effort, and I had no hankering to repeat my mistakes. An American abroad should carry silver dollars or at least rubles here in the Russian Empire, but as a writer, he might be flat broke. I certainly had never heard of Samuel Clemens.

I rubbed my bad knee beneath the table. It'd been a month since the Spaniard's wallet brought any livable monies. And I had to kill him to get it.

Sam checked his pocket watch—silver plated, a good sign—then frowned. "I've two hours 'till my ship leaves. I'm sorry to say, we should adjourn this gathering, Joe."

Well, here's the moment then. The watch was proof enough, I guess

A pity, Sam had wit.

"There's a church near here," I said as deftly as I could. "It might make an interesting account for your readers back in San Francisco."

"I've seen a half-dozen…"

"Yes, but this one has the most astonishing display of artifacts. The works are exquisite, beyond anything I've seen." I pushed my cognac away; it would be best to be sober. "They say these relics are from the days of Olga and Prince Vladimir themselves. It's your duty as a travel writer to relay such wonders to your readers, isn't it?"

He frowned. "If we hurry, the harbor's a ways off…"

"Twenty minutes, Sam. It's all the time we need."

* * *

We soon arrived at Pokrovskaya Cathedral, a square-ish white-marble structure dominating a small park off the city center. At the sight of the cathedral's golden dome, Sam shuffled through his shoulder bag, withdrawing a leather-bound notebook into which he scribbled:

Spire-topped roof resembles a great bronze turnip turned upside down.

I felt my brow furl. "Do editors pay for such observations?" I asked.

"Six cents a page." He said smugly and shoved the notebook back into the bag.

Of course. *Six cents for nothing.*

I aptly praised Sam's hard-earned skills and harkened him through the opened door of the cathedral. The interior was even grander than the exterior, snow-white marble inlaid with gold and bronze, the icons of a dozen Orthodox saints peering down from above. A small crowd was gathered near the altar, several black-clad priests among them, but these holy men were not the center of attention. All eyes were upon a small choir just beginning their hymns.

Caps in hands, Sam and I stood there quietly as they sang. Their hymns began as a barely audible hum, expanding to an ethereal chant that rose over several minutes to superhuman strength. An army of invisible angels joined in, the chorus's power turning tenfold. It was a marvelous performance, perhaps the best I had known, marred only towards the end by an elderly man in the congregation, a decrepit and destitute-looking fellow whose fits of coughing nearly brought the piece to an early close.

Still, Sam was moved. "I am not a great admirer of organized religions," said he. "But that was truly inspiring. As fine a choir as I've ever heard."

"They sing everyday at this hour. There will be an encore, several in fact." I lit two votive candles, handed one to Sam. "But your ship will not wait and there is much to see."

"Where are these artifacts?"

"In a vault below. Come."

We hurried out the rear of the cathedral to a shaded yard loosely separated from the surrounding park by a crumbling white-stone wall. There was an antiquity in this secluded garden, the shadows of the Ottomans hanging in the air. Among the scattered stones we found a series of weathered steps leading down into the earth, the opening of a tunnel just visible.

"There, Sam," I said. "Our passage to the vaults is within."

At this entrance, I slowed to read a notice affixed to the keystone. Two children—a boy and a girl—had been lost in these tunnels weeks ago. By order of Odessa's governor, all known entrances to the catacombs were to be sealed in a month's time to prevent further tragedy.

I paused, trying to calculate the days since posting.

"It is out of date," said a priest who had trailed us into the yard. He reached up, tore the paper from the stone. "I should have done this much earlier."

"What do you mean, Father?"

"The children are safe. They found their way out a day after this sign was hung." He smiled. "To emerge unharmed, when the search parties had given up, a miracle."

"Yes, a miracle."

"What is happening?" asked Sam, rather flustered and reminding me he knew no Russian.

"Two children were lost briefly, but now are home. We can go."

The priest started to protest our path, but I turned away, ushered Sam down the steps. We felt the drop in temperature as we reached the bottom, the air so much cooler than the burning summer surface. As always, I regretted the absence of a coat.

I glanced at my companion. Sam seemed unflustered, stoically squinting behind that candle, the flame light sparkling in his narrowed eyes, his attention focused on the high-but-narrow white-stone corridor stretching ahead.

"This tunnel is just one of many, Sam. These are the largest catacombs in the world, greater than those of Paris and Rome combined. Men who journey inside are often lost forever. It's a wonder those children found their way out."

"Where is the vault?"

"A little ways on. Not far." I motioned ahead with my free hand. "The path is straight, we'll have no trouble."

Sam held his watch up to the candle flame. "My ship leaves in a little over an hour."

"We'll have you on the surface in ten minutes. You can get a carriage-for-hire. I know a driver who is usually at the corner this hour."

"You visit this cathedral often?"

"Four times before. You will be the fifth."

He grew quiet. We probed the darkness in silence. With every step our light forced back the gloom, the spectral-white tunnels extending forever, our two candles birthing four shadows to keep us company.

"These passages are surprisingly sterile," I said when we were some fifty yards inside. "I've never seen a rat, seldom glimpsed a bat. Even insects are rare. Lifeless, it's like tunnels inside the moon."

"And as cold."

"Well, this may warm your soul, Sam." I knocked on the dusty wall. "We are directly beneath the cathedral, and the choir above will sing momentarily. It is even more magnificent down here. I am no architect—I know nothing of acoustics—but their voices are magnified inside this tunnel. It is as if the hymns are piped from Heaven itself, Sam. Overpowering, amazing, awe-inspiring, I have seen stalwart atheists brought to tears."

"I would welcome such rapture, if it occurs."

"Worthy of your travel reports, yes? You will send me a clipping from your newspaper in San Francisco?"

"If it is as thrilling as you say."

"It will be."

I motioned ahead. In a matter of a few steps, we reached the spot where the Spaniard had died. *"No mas. No mas,"* he'd screamed, his cries drowned out by the chorus above. I had walked back innocently through the cathedral afterwards, no suspicious glances from priest or congregation, even pausing to put three useless Spanish half céntimos in the tithe box.

But only three. *No mas.*

I slowed my steps, let Sam grow closer. When the choir sings...

A strange notion entered my head then. Perhaps it was the familiarity of the scene, but I thought of Sam's theory that all stories repeat. How many murders—real or imagined—had occurred in the murk of dungeons such as this? I recalled a favorite.

"Have you read 'The Cask of Amontillado,' Sam?"

"I'm no friend of the Dark Romantics."

"But have you read it?"

"Yes. And I can't abide the ending. The murderer gets off Scot free."

"Indeed. It is one of my pet tales. The two men winding through the gloom of the catacombs, much like us."

"The end of similarities, I'd hope."

"Yes."

We laughed, though I longer than he. We were as friends. I knew the roles now, no Providence needed. I was the trusted Montresor leading Sam's Fortunato down to his doom as in Poe's tale. This cheered me greatly. It was all black theater, wasn't it? As he said, only the details change.

"Is this vault near?" he asked.

"It's just beyond the archway, Sam. Can you see it?"

"No."

"There." I pointed to a small opening at the end of the corridor. "It's the width of a man and half the height. We can just squeeze through."

He muttered something, gritting his teeth, Sam a skeptic by nature. Beyond the archway, I would do it. Choir or not, we would be too far in, I hoped, to be heard.

"Here we are," I said as I ducked under the low arch. "You will marvel at the beauty on this side, Sam."

"I should hope it's worth the effort."

"My hope as well." I shoved my candle into a nearby crevice, blew it out. "Ah, I've lost the flame," I shouted from the other side. "Will you help me relight it?"

Crouching in the darkness, I pulled the knife from my pocket and waited for Sam to emerge through the gap.

A backlit silhouette appeared in the opening—I stabbed—but struck only cloth, his bag pitched ahead of him as he tried to force his body under the archway. The power lost, the blade ripped up to Sam's shoulder, grazing him and severing his carrying strap. The bag fell between us. Sam shoved me away and overextended I tumbled to the floor, my breath rushing out as I hit the earth. I whipped the knife around, but he was gone in that instant, back through the archway.

The tunnel turned black.

I reached a knee, listened to Sam's screams for help, his fleeting footsteps echoing down the corridor as he sprinted away. Pursuit? No, he had too much of a lead. Cursing, I scooped up his bag, retreated deeper into the catacombs.

Pulse pounding, panting breaths echoing all around me, I struggled to think, to grasp this turn of events. What would Sam do when he reached the surface? He would seek help from the priests, from the police. Yes, but it would be difficult to make himself understood, to find someone who knew English.

I had time. I'd flee into the lower tunnels; find an exit far from the cathedral.

But I made a foolish error. In my haste and panic, I'd forgotten to retrieve my candle. I knew it impossible to go back. If Sam's calls had already been heard...

Instead, I sped into the inky depths of the Earth, cradling the bag in one arm, my free hand extended out to deflect any unseen wall or overhang. In this absolute darkness, I missed the turns I knew, blindly ricocheted from wall to wall, and lost all perception of direction. When calmness at last reached me, I spent hours in systematic attempts to map my progress through the maze, but I only became more and more hopelessly lost.

Hours passed, perhaps days. It was impossible to know. I grew tired and hungry. The air was desert-dry, and a horrible thirst overtook me. By chance, my opened palm came across a damp spot in the wall. I hoped it touched some underground stream. Picking at the rock with my knife,

I carved out a finger-length trough to collect moisture, even pressed my mouth to the stone and tried to suck water from the earth. I split my teeth on that rock and earned not even a drop. Useless. I moved on, thirst unabated.

Three times I slept in these passages, haunting the bowels of the Earth like the damned in Hades. "This will be your tomb," a voice said. But I drove it away.

At last, there was a hope. My groping fingers came across two familiar indentions on the wall, my initials! The long, straight first letter, the second curved, I had found the spot where I'd carved them after my first robbery, my self-made marker for the exit, a safeguard for lightless passage. Circles! I had walked in circles all this time, never journeying far from the entrance. The cathedral yard was near.

Relief washed over me, the voices slowed. I would soon be free. A close call, but I had kept my reason in the maze and survived. If Sam had missed his ship, I might have revenge. Yes, revenge…

Yet, all was not as it had been in this familiar passage, the very corridor where I'd dumped the bodies of previous crimes. My searching hands found no remains, no skeletons, no tattered clothes left in the abyss. Gone. Unless the dead walk, someone had cleared them away.

The children's search party? Sam's police? Who else could it be?

I crept cautiously towards my escape.

At last, I reached the low archway where I'd assaulted Sam. I gripped the welcome stone edge, but my fingers pressed on a texture of wood beyond. The exit was sealed, a thick door fastened snugly across it.

No…

I pounded on this obstruction, kicked it, threw the bag harmlessly against its pane. How? How could it be sealed? There wasn't time…

I pressed rough fingers to my temple, tried to recall the date of the notice, the one the priest had torn away. What had it said? What were the priest's words? Or was it Sam? Sam and his avenging police, accelerating the sealing? Yes…Enough of the catacombs for the governor. He would solve the problem forever. Seal it tight as a drum.

I pummeled the door, battered it until my fists were bloodied and raw, then collapsed to the floor and lay there for uncounted time. On the ground were bits of wax, the fashioners of this barrier having burnt candles during its construction. Starving, I devoured the remnants of the wax, even ate pebbles to fool my stomach. With my knife, I scraped at the base of the door, cut away until the blade snapped in my hand. Yet, the door remained steadfast, scarred but little diminished by my efforts.

At last, there were voices. *New voices.* A rescue party? I would face the gallows for a scrap of food, a single drop of water. No…their words were too pretty, too harmonious. My heart sank. It was only that damnable distant choir, their hymns so faint and far away, I knew my calls would never be answered. I sobbed in despair, my cries unheard by man or God.

Two days at the door, I lay. I learned to judge time by their performances. I had never experienced such hunger, yet it was the thirst that would finish me. My tongue sat fat and immobile in my mouth, my lips swollen, saliva as thick as pudding, I could scarcely swallow.

Sitting in endless solitude, I tried to distract myself from my coming doom. I dug deep into Sam's bag, discarding clothes, letters, a matchbox. At the bottom, I gripped something hard and rectangular bound in leather. I imagined it his billfold, and though it wouldn't bring salvation, there was a bittersweet satisfaction in having taken it from him. Perhaps he would be stranded in Russia, moneyless as I had been. But it was only Sam's notebook. I cast it aside, felt my strength ebbing, collapsed forward onto my belly, hoarse breaths rising from my throat. This was the end. I was fading into a sleep from which I would never wake.

But I wouldn't die face down like a beggar. I rallied, rolled myself over, shoved the bag under my head, tried to reach comfort in my last moments.

I found only injustice.

Wasn't I Montresor, oh, Providence? I raged. *Wasn't I meant to leave the tunnels unharmed and triumphant?* Sam had switched it. Instead of his perishing here, it would be I who would rot into…

A palsy took my hands. I pressed them to stillness against the floor, my fingers touching on a lost strip of wax melted into a crevice. A portion of wick remained.

It seemed an answer.

With one of Sam's last matches, I lit the wick, pulled his notebook near. With shaking fingers I turned the pages, vowing to know the mind of my murderer.

The book was filled with the routine observations of a travel journalist, simple sketches of foreign cultures, a few caricatures of politicians and pilgrims; tucked inside was a photograph of a pretty young woman, and towards the back, the outline for a novel: a nostalgic book about a boy in Missouri, his friend, his sweetheart, and a murderer entombed forever in the caverns named Injun Joe.

V

POMPO'S DISGUISE

Originally published in Ellery Queen's Mystery Magazine

Pompo's Disguise

Rome, AD 55

I recognize him, of course, despite the wig of black Parthian hair combed consciously down over his forehead. No one long keeps their identity hidden from me, a tavern thief of thirty years. Even on a bustling holiday like tonight, every face in the Hospitium Hermetis has my attention, and wig or no wig, I well remember the pale blue eyes, the slight chin, and the scruffy neck-beard of the seventeen-year-old mama's boy at the corner table. He's not one you forget, not when seen in the flesh.

On the Neptunalia holiday not eight days ago, he had slipped into this very tavern sporting a faded sun hat and wearing the reeking rags of a Tiber fisherman, then gotten drunk upstairs, vomiting down the stairwell until his friends took him home. Now, with the Ludi Victoriae Caesarae chariot races in their third day and the house packed with thirsty spectators, this thick-necked fool has returned in a new guise, dressed as an urban fop in an over-embroidered black tunic and strumming an ivory-framed lyre. Every sighting brings a new role, it seems, another persona, a fashionable identity.

A strange hobby, but I try to understand his reasons. If I were he, I might do the same.

The house girls, Nona and Virginia, their professions advertised by their own bright blond wigs, press their ample bodies against this boy, begging him to play "Cleopatrae amator" on his lyre. Instead, Pompo, as he calls himself on these ventures, recites self-penned love poetry while the whores feign interest on the bench beside him. The rhymes are crude, the imagery cruder. Ovid, he isn't.

Save for these girls, the tavern takes little notice of Pompo. As I should ignore him. As every pickpocket in here should.

But there is temptation. And real danger.

See, despite the youthful face, the dressing up, and something of a wastrel's reputation, Pompo is from *the* family and easily the wealthiest man in the tavern. And in Rome, more than any other city in this world, wealth has become power.

Pompo remains untouchable. Best to let it rest there.

So, time for another mark.

My eyes search the room. Now take this man—Decimus. He's more the type. Old soldier, done from the wars at fifty. Still muscular, still fierce, he'd snap a little man like me in two if he could catch me. But catching me isn't as easy as it sounds, friends. I've worked this tavern and hundreds like it throughout all Italia since I was thirteen. No one has ever gotten their money back.

Well, except my sweet Antonina and a few of my other lady friends over the years. You see, I've a weakness with the fairer sex. I can never quite con them. I lose *denarii* every time I try. Some inherent and unfortunate nobility left in my character that keeps me from being a master thief. A pity.

Luckily, there is absolutely nothing feminine about the hairy, bulky, and dirty Decimus.

This should be easy.

I wipe the summer sweat from my brow and, using the crowd as camouflage, I approach the public bench where my target is sitting. Decimus's great calloused fingers strum his leather coin pouch on the table, while he complains to a drunken friend about his harrowing life: about the disgraced Thracian legion, about losing his pension and land grant, how he has to gamble for a living now...

Pig. Yes, Decimus, your life is so difficult as a gambler: When you win, you collect. When the other man wins, he ends up facedown in the Tiber. Well, I'll collect for those you've strangled. For Marcus, for Lucius, for little Publius who trusted you.

I thumb the tortoiseshell amulet hanging down into the folds of my tunic. Mercury, guide the dead to the fairest spots of Hades, and grant me victory, Lord of Thieves, over this Umbrian thug. I check my fingertips and thumb. No impressions from the tortoiseshell.

A good sign.

With the god's blessing, I slowly sit down on the bench next to Decimus. His back remains to me as he confides with his friend, but the companion arches his neck a little at my arrival, giving me a long, fog-eyed stare. Nothing in my manner apparently arouses his suspicion and he eventually returns to their conversation about the empire, complaining to Decimus that life was better under Claudius, that the new reign cares nothing for old soldiers like them.

They live in the past, these two. But I live in the present...

And *at present*, I bide my time, try to make small talk with others at the table: a pair of Greek merchants, apparently too busy in negotiations to chat with me, and a young scholar using the free candlelight to write some important work on Euclidian geometry. All of little use.

But then the trusty fool Pompo assists me. At the next table he begins playing his lyre and laughter soon arises at the poor pitch of his instrument. All heads turn in his direction. While Decimus watches, I slip my hand out, over the table, just adjacent to the money pouch. It won't be hard. I simply have to wait until he moves his hand away to take his cup of wine....

There!

Not so difficult after all. Mercury has shown me the path to victory. I slide the pouch off the table, pinch it tight between my fingers as it falls, then let my arm go limp at my side, the bag hanging in my hand, just off the floor. Yes, there we go. If Decimus reacts, if he moves, or if some do-gooder shouts in alarm, I'll drop it, pretend the pouch fell there by accident, and as an honorable Roman, I'm trying to pick it up.

Honest Quintus, they'll call me.

But no one says a word. Decimus remains oblivious and drunk, watching the fool with the lyre. Now comes the difficult part. Anyone can knock a bag from the table, but who will walk away with it? Only a thief. There's the intent. The guilt. The robbery.

I rise from the table, slowly, but not unnaturally so. Just a tired man, bent from years of labor. Taking the pouch, I press it close to my belly—no slipping it inside the tunic, no advertising that I've something I wish to hide. In fact, I toss it up a few times in the air as I walk away. Relaxed. Casual. What sort of thief would do that?

Decimus's table long behind me, I press my way towards the door, jostled continuously by the flow of incoming customers. The races are over and there's barely room to breathe in this tavern tonight. Near the exit, I pass the owner, Gnaeus Festus Gallus, who is trying to explain to an angry German tribesman that they serve no beer on the Italian peninsula, only spiced wine or water on the holiday. I fear their shouting match draws attention in this direction, but at last I am out the door, stepping free into the humidity of the summer night.

I smile. Well done. No wonder they call me "Quintus ingeniosum."

Quintus the Clever.

But then the smile fades from my lips.

The street is full of soldiers.

They stand dressed in their brown off-duty tunics, without helmets or armor, theoretically unarmed, though I can see the hard impressions of their *pugio* daggers hidden at their breasts. So many—six—eight—ten—by Mercury, more?!—is it twelve?—or twenty-five!? With others at the corner? With eyes watching from the shadows beneath the aqueduct bisecting the street?

I retreat back into the tavern. Let out a slow breath, slip the pouch into my tunic, and watch Festus argue with the German over beer. I doubt the soldiers would be wary of a middle-aged man, unarmed and casually carrying a common coin bag in his hand. But their sheer number gives me pause, and squeezing past an armed guard is far from my first choice.

The odds are better with Decimus.

Of course, the moment this thought enters my mind, the gods must have their jest. In that instant, Decimus appears from the crowd and, seizing me by the tunic, heaves me across a serving table. Bowls, plates, and regrets scatter everywhere, as I tumble off the other side headfirst, falling facedown to the floor under a rain of cheeses, pears, and blackberries. Something snaps at my ribs.

Half stunned, I lay there wondering who it was that actually called me "Quintus the Clever."

Oh, yes, my Antonina. Such a sarcastic woman when she wishes to be.

Painfully, forcing myself over—is that rib moving?—I find Decimus standing above me.

"Where is it, Quintus?" he shouts.

I wipe the blood from my chin. "You've got it wrong, my friend. I would never—"

"Only you, Quintus!" He cocks his great battering ram of a fist. "Only you. I'll crush your skull to powder in one shot."

"Let's not be rash, Decimus—"

Fortunately for me, ole Festus throws himself between us, shouting out that there is no fighting in his tavern. It takes Decimus by surprise, and they stumble back into the crowd. While the owner struggles with my opponent, I crawl away towards the other end of the chamber, not quite able to get to my feet with the sharp pains emanating from my rib cage. The crowd parts ahead of me. So great is their fear of Decimus, of his murderous wrath, that not one person offers a hand to help me up.

Thirty years coming here and not one hand.

Life of a thief, I guess.

And maybe death.

At the next bench, *the last bench,* sits Pompo. His back to the altercation, playing his lyre, he seems ignorant of the fighting, probably willfully so. With nothing to lose, I crawl up onto the bench next to him. His blue eyes turn to me, frown. To my surprise he stops playing.

"Yes, child?" he says.

"Continue your melody, please," I plead, trying to overcome the pain to speak. "It was as moving as your performance at the Theatrum Marcelli."

"You saw me at the theater, you say?"

"I did. The day your mother received full honors."

His frown deepens. "Who are you, child?" Then he adds with aristocratic distaste: "And what has happened to your chin?"

Being called "child" would be amusing under other circumstances as I am more than twice Pompo's age. But at the moment there is no humor. Decimus has fought his way past Festus and is storming across the room.

"I am only a loyal *civis imperil*," I answer hurriedly. "As for my chin, well, that man you see…"

My words are cut off as Decimus arrives and seizes me by the throat with one hand, forcing me down on the bench, knee on my damaged rib cage. His fingers cut deep into my flesh, choking the life out of me as he did three of my friends at the river.

"Where is it?" he growls, patting me down with his other hand.

"There is nothing.…" I hear a cracking sound at my trachea, the pressure cutting off my speech.

Pompo, still sitting on the bench, disapproves. "Child, I was speaking to this man first. Leave him be."

Decimus isn't one to be told what to do, especially by a foppish lyre player in a tavern. With his free hand, he shoves Pompo back harshly, tipping the young man off the bench. Legs in the air, he falls hard to the floor, his woolly wig rolling off to reveal a low forehead and short-cropped blond hair.

The room changes instantly. Those near the scene rush back, fearing Decimus's expanding violence, while others farther away laugh at the boorish spectacle, but a few, those who have spent time on Palatine Hill, or stood at the front of the grand parade, or ever considered the statue of honored Agrippina and her son closely, they do not respond. In fact, they stand dumbfounded. I hear Festus gasp.

As does Decimus, his hand slipping from my throat.

"By Jove," he whispers.

Still on the floor, Pompo pulls the wooden whistle from beneath his tunic, blows it loudly. The volume is not needed. His men are already on their way, bursting through the tavern door. Dressed, as I have said, in the tunics of common off-duty soldiers, their movements now are too precise, too rehearsed and trained to be anything other than that of an elite bodyguard emerging from hiding.

For, you see, their master likes to join the common people on his holidays, to go out in disguise along the *Via Lata*, to the baths, or the taverns just as any other Roman might; those who know him say he longs to discuss the arts, or sports, or even politics with the plebs of the city; to feel as if he is one with Rome itself.

Up to a point.

But correct him, confront him, or dare I say shove him, as my unfortunate adversary has done, and you'll find there is nothing common in Pompo's response. The rumors are true. I see the evidence now with my own eyes as the Praetorian Guard drags poor Decimus away.

Though my damaged voice croaks more than speaks, I offer to help Pompo to his feet, but the illusion is now pierced, and the guards won't let me lay a hand near him. He will rise on his own, not as a boy-man but as a man-god, and all in the tavern instinctively step back. More than a few shout prayers aloud. Festus drops to his knees, crying out to Minerva for mercy.

Through the doorway, I see Decimus thrown into the street. There are screams, sobs, a flash of knives, and then harrowing silence. Great Mercury will soon take another soul down to Hades.

I collapse onto the bench, exhausted. It might have been me the wing-footed one carried off tonight. Blessed as Mercury has been to me, I have no need to meet my god just yet.

Feeling my pains, and wondering if it was worth the trouble, I pull out the money pouch from under my tunic and withdraw a few silver *sestertii*. They are new and shiny coins engraved with the image of our young Emperor Nero.

A last glance at Pompo as he exits.
There is a resemblance.

VI

ON RECORD

Originally published in The Saturday Evening Post

On Record

Bruno Williams pressed the button on the recordable turntable and spoke into the microphone:

"This is a confession. A reluctant one, but my crime has been witnessed, and there is no way out. I killed Sonny Bumbass, my neighbor of fifteen years in this Brooklyn tenement, today, July 12, 1959, at roughly 9 p.m. and in cold blood.

"You would have, too, if you had endured the years of sleepless nights and constant noise, if each of your legal avenues to get him to shut off the incessant music had failed. You would murder, I contend, as I have murdered.

"Sonny began bootlegging records three years ago. Two hundred a week, all hours, playing them on one turntable and recording them on the microphone of another table to make the duplicate. A low-end affair, he maxed the volume to get the sound. Others complained, but it's my bedroom that shares a wall with his bathroom, where he records— 'for the acoustics.' I appealed directly to Sonny, but as the landlord's nephew, he laughed me off.

"Twice I called the police. Someone is on the take, and they never came. This apartment was grandfathered to me. I can't afford another, not since I lost the job at the plant. For falling asleep on duty.

"Bumbass...even though he's dead, I still hate that name...

"For thirty months, we argued to the edge of violence. But in these last weeks I changed my tactics. I charmed. I don't know if I planned to kill him, but I wanted Sonny to like me, to take me into his apartment, to let his guard down. He began to invite me over to listen to his favorites. Always the capitalist, he played the redneck music and boogie-woogie that is so popular with the kiddies these days. Nothing with taste.

"Tonight, I arrived with something better: 'Ellington at Newport.' Duke sells, so Sonny was willing to play it. When we reached Gonsalves' famous sax solo, Sonny closed his eyes to take it in. I beat him to death—in four time—with a plaster bust of Beethoven.

"At that moment, I considered I might get away with it. Sonny was a black-marketer, connected to riff-raff far more suspicious than a veteran like me. But then I saw a horrified face looking in through the window—Frank Malone. Out to sleep in the cool air of the fire escape, Malone dropped his mattress and fled down the ladder. By the time I reached the window, he was two levels below me. He descended to the street, turned a corner, and was out of sight.

"Malone will bring the police, of course. So, I have taken Sonny's recordable to my own apartment, where I leave this message as my final—"

Three hard knocks at the door.

"They've come. Well, I'll say again that you'd have killed Sonny too. All that noise, all those years. They might convict me, but they'll never blame me."

Bruno clicked off the machine and opened the door to his fate. In rushed Fidel Canada, a first-floor tenant, nearly out of breath.

"You got a phone, Bruno?" he said between gasps.

"I had it pulled years ago. No one could ever hear me over all that noise from—"

"Frank Malone's dead."

"What?"

"Yeah, I saw the whole thing. Frank climbed off the fire escape, and went tearing into the street still in his pajamas, all panicked, shouting something we could never make out, then got bulldozed over by the Chauncey Street bus."

"My God."

"There's an ambulance down there, around the corner, though it won't do him no good now. The police got the whole street blocked off. I gotta call my cousin in Queens. He was real close with Frank."

"Yes … Yes, you do that, Fidel. Try Mrs. Polk on the 14th floor. I think she has one."

"I'll go on up, Bruno. This'll break her heart, too."

"Yes, break…" Bruno glanced at the disc on the recordable turntable. When Fidel was gone, he picked up the record, opened the window, and tossed it away.

Freedom!

Emancipation!

Quiet!

His confession eviscerated into a thousand pieces on the cement eleven stories below.

Or so he thought. Instead, the disc spun away like a rebellious Frisbee, slamming unbroken into the seam in Sonny Bumbass' window. It wobbled as it hit, as if something out of a Chuck Jones cartoon, then hung still, wedged solidly in the gap. A circular black flag on the building's exterior.

Bruno stared in disbelief, cursing the gods of music and aerodynamics, then reluctantly eased himself out onto the rickety fire escape. Bumbass' window was more than an arm's length beyond the banister, but if he could just lean out a bit…his fingertips could almost touch…yes, he could feel success within his grasp…a tad more…

Through the dusty pane, he could see Bumbass' body lying still…he laughed, though the banister pressed hard against his ribs...*you deserved it, Sonny, you son of a bitch...play Chopin once and a while, and I might have forgave yah...*

Just one more inch...

* * *

"Never seen a banister give way like that before," said Officer Moody, kneeling over the broken body of Bruno Williams. "Nasty fall."

"It happens on these old tenement fire escapes, Sid," answered Officer Ureno, standing nearby. "You should never lean on them, especially a big man with all that weight." He shook his head. "First Malone, now this guy. Tough night for the building, losing two people."

Moody fingered one of the countless black shards covering the pavement. "What was this record in his hand anyway?"

"Unlabeled."

"Give you ten-to-one it was recordable, and he was a bootlegger. Moving his wares out the back fire escape late at night." Moody grimaced. "A conman stealing from Bing and Dean and everyone else with talent. Kinda got what he deserved."

"That's heartless, Sid. And even if you're right, I'd go on record saying the punishment didn't fit the crime."

VII

DEADLY SIGNALS

Originally published in The Saturday Evening Post

Deadly Signals

As we sped through the heartland night, the car's crackling radio kept all our minds on the war in Manhattan:

"Enemy now in sight above the Palisades," said the radio newsman, the fear penetrating his professional veneer. "Five ... Five great machines. First one is crossing the river. I can see it from here, wading the Hudson like a man wading through a brook ... A bulletin's handed to me ... Cylinders are falling all over the country. One outside Buffalo, one in Chicago, St. Louis..."

"Doozer of a news flash," sighed Judith, shivering in the passenger seat. "Who could be behind it, Henry?"

"Bet them cylinders are German. Hitler's got the scientists to pull this off."

"Germany's too far," said Bill, leaning in from the backseat. "Gotta be closer, Canada or Mexico."

"Yeah, it could be the Canucks, couldn't it? Bastards."

"Poisonous smoke drifting over the city," continued the reporter, a cough in his throat. "People in the streets see it now. They're running towards the East River, thousands of them dropping in like rats..." His words suddenly cut away.

I fiddled with the volume knob, growing more annoyed. Annoyed because we'd missed the beginning of the broadcast, because we didn't know who was attacking our sovereign nation, because the radio was cutting out in these backwoods, and most personally annoyed because the whole thing distracted us from our plans. Murder isn't an undertaking you try half-focused. I know. I'd done it before.

I looked over at Judith, my only fem three years now. So innocent-looking with her farm-girl hair and doe-eyed baby blues. I'd told Bill she was cheating, though, dynamiting Rob Fingers when I was away. I'd said I couldn't be no cuckold, and *we* had to do something about it. Now! Bill, unthinking ape that he is, went along.

Hope it worked.

Electric lights came through the trees. I pulled into one of the last roadside stores that sold booze before we crossed into the dry counties of Missouri. The place was a worn-out dump, single gas pump in the mud, undersized jack-o'-lanterns by the door.

I said I'd be a minute, then exited the Roadmaster and went inside. At the counter, the clerk and another fellow listened attentively to their radio, another news flash coming in:

"...Washington for a special broadcast on the national emergency..."

I shuffled to the back, ignoring the cardboard ghosts and adverts for candy, and found what I wanted: adhesive tape and beers. Returning to the counter, the clerk rang me up without a glance.

"Sounds pretty bad," I said.

He shrugged, "Not so bad."

From the radio came a stately, familiar voice begging the people to remain steadfast, to have faith in the military, to pray to God for America.

Roosevelt? Futz, it had to be him. Who else spoke like that?

"Yeah, not so bad," I said sarcastically and left.

I put my goods in the trunk, next to my shotgun and spade, then went around and got inside. Judith and Bill had the radio off.

Good. No distractions.

Work time.

* * *

We arrived in the bleak, post-harvest cornfield. I turned off the engine, shut down the lights.

"What are we doing here?" asked Judith innocently.

"It's a party. Everyone out."

A minute later, I was at the opened trunk while the others stood on the bare ground nearby. I'd just loaded the gun when Bill grabbed Judith's arm.

"Got any last messages for Rob Fingers, Judy baby?" he shouted.

I raised the gun. "Step away from her, Bill."

His face drained of color, but Bill did as he was told.

"What's this about, Henry?"

"I told you she mighta been cheatin'. Not that I believed." With my free hand, I tossed a roll of tape to Judith. "You been set up, Billy-Boy."

She bound his hands from behind, then fastened tape across his mouth. All the time, I kept my sights squarely on him. We led Bill to the hole Judith and I had dug yesterday, told him to sit. She tied his ankles, then kicked him into the ditch with a giggle.

"You see, Bill, Prohibition's long over, but we ain't pardoned for those crimes. You been chirping to the coppers." I stood at the edge, barrel aimed at his forehead. "Nobody cuts a deal at my expense."

Judith laughed. Then a masculine voice shouted: "What are you doing here, son?"

I glanced over my shoulder. Back by the car stood a man in overalls, a farmer by the look of him, pointing a rifle right at me. Behind him were another three men similarly dressed and armed.

I dropped my shotgun. "Just a party, fellah. Why you here?"

"Hunting little green men," he said, glancing down in the ditch. His eyes turned colder. "But you don't look like Martians."

"We're from Cleveland."

"Just as bad."

* * *

They used my own tape to bind me, threw me in the backseat of their car while two more followed with Judith and Bill in mine. It was a long, uncomfortable trip into town. Despite having interrupted a murder, all their thoughts were on the radio. The Martians had taken America's cities and were expanding into the countryside, our armies destroyed in a matter of minutes.

It seemed impossible, yet perversely gave me hope. The government would need men to fight the invaders. My record showed I was good with a gun, a natural leader, a big macher—they'd want me in the resistance. I might get out of this a hero...

But then Mr. Orson Welles came on, told us the broadcast was over. That it had all been a Halloween production. The newsmen, Roosevelt, were actors. No Martians, no invasion of any sort. All faked. The farmers laughed with embarrassment and relief. It became a joke even as they felt ridiculous for hunting radio extraterrestrials.

Not me. I sat silently the chump, and remained so as we pulled up to the Hannibal police station.

All excerpts from the radio play of The War of the Worlds *by Howard Koch have been used with the permission of Peter Koch.*

VIII

HAGIOPHOBIA

Originally published in Alfred Hitchcock's Mystery Magazine

Hagiophobia

Hagiophobia: A dread of holy places and things.

Kurzeme, Latvia

Horseplay raged for hours between Boriss and his friend Jorens. Inside the abandoned cathedral, far from any town, no one stopped them. They boxed and wrestled, shoved, and chased each other through archways and down tunnels into something that might once have been a crypt, though neither boy paused to notice.

Here, Jorens, sixteen and wiry, wrapped his opponent in a fearsome headlock. But Boriss, three years older and oxen built, simply hoisted Jorens off his feet, up past his own shoulders, and threw him to the floor. To both boys' surprise, Jorens fell through into darkness.

Boriss heard the scream.

Then the thud.

And he thought of recent tragedies.

Boriss dropped to a knee above the hole where his friend had vanished, pressing a muscular arm into the unseen below. He touched nothing, sensing great depth.

"Jorens!" He shouted. Only an echo answered.

He kneeled there for several moments, listening to his own breathing. As the shock ebbed, Boriss drove away self-pitying emotions and began to grope about in the darkness for something, anything, to help his friend, some stray cord left by the renovation teams, or a fallen timber that could be lowered down into the depths. But the chamber was murky this low in the earth, and what little light emanated from the upper levels of the cathedral failed to reach the dark corners of the under-earth. Nearly blind, his outstretched hands touched only dust, fallen stones, and the brittle bodies of dead insects. As his fingertips slid across coarse and ancient surfaces, Boriss began to appreciate the oddity of his surroundings, noticing how the crypt bottom was wooden rather than stone and that the Gothic pillars rose up through the floor instead of resting upon it. Even ignorant of architecture and engineering, Boriss could well see this was a false bottom, a flimsy and decaying platform resting above the real floor. He recalled his papa talking of Soviet times, when the Communists used churches and cathedrals to store vegetables and grains, sometimes even hiding machine parts in underground vaults and tunnels, and that they'd often partition lower chambers into shallow compartments for these purposes.

Boriss trusted this word "shallow." It gave him hope that Jorens had not fallen so far, a confidence he welcomed as he lowered himself into the hole where his friend had disappeared. About a meter down, the toe of one sneaker pressed onto solid stone, flat and smooth, extending away underneath the platform. The other foot, however, remained hanging perilously in space, and with an athlete's agility, Boriss swung himself beneath the false bottom, crouching in the recess below. He found himself on the edge of an octagonal pit set in the original stone flooring, Jorens unlucky enough to have broken through above its edge and presumably fallen deeper. Extending out from this chasm's mouth was a gloomy meter-high world of pillar bases and smashed statues from the days of the cathedral's glory, the tiled floor littered with whitened watermelon seeds and infested by daddy longlegs, the tiny spiderlike creatures bobbing and weaving on their extended legs in fear of his presence. The air here agitated Boris's lungs, his coughs hurricanes among the longlegs, sweeping them away into the shadows.

Leaning over the pit's edge, Boriss peered down into darkness, wondering how deep it went.

"Jorens," he said sadly.

A voice answered. "Boriss?"

"Jorens! Are you all right?" He felt a moment's relief, then blank stupidity for asking such a question. "I can't see you."

"Boriss...it's my legs...I can't stand."

"How far did you fall?"

"The bone's broken through my jeans, Boriss."

"Yes, but how far are you *down* there?"

A pause. "I can't tell. I can't see anything." A soft sob echoed up from below. "It's cold in here, Boriss. Like winter almost."

"Try your phone."

"I am. Nothing's happening."

"All right." Boriss's eyes flipped up to his level, searching for an anchor or foothold down into the pit. On the opposite edge stood the sole unbroken statue beneath the platform, a bishop by his dress, his raised cross pressing up against their wooden ceiling. If Boriss could find a rope, he might be able to tie it to the base of the statue and rappel down. But cracks crisscrossed the pit wall below the bishop, and Boriss suspected the whole thing might give way under human weight. It would never support two climbing out.

"I'll get help, Jorens. Stay here."

Another pause. "Where would I go?"

But Boriss didn't hear his friend's reply. He was already up onto the platform, scampering for the stairs to the surface, all the while wondering what the authorities would say after yet another incident and how he would ever keep Jorens quiet.

* * *

Two minutes later, Boriss slipped through the half-rusted renovation scaffolding to escape the cathedral. The flat plains and high trees of the Kurzeme countryside stretched out before him. On the road, a Chevrolet truck approached, trailing dust into the afternoon air.

His first thought was to hail the cab for Jorens's rescue, but the old fears told him to flee, to remain anonymous. For now at least.

The truck honked an acknowledgement.

Indecision brought confusion. Boriss stood in place.

The vehicle, a large black four-seater cab with an extended bed, pulled off the road, flattening the grass near a fallen cathedral spire. Out of the expensive truck came a skeletal old man dressed in casual summer wealth. Through sparse dyed hair, the Baltic sun shone white off his scalp, contrasting with a triangular birthmark stretching from his temple past the crown of his head.

Everts Gūtmanis. Everyone out here knew that birthmark.

Gūtmanis closed the truck door and walked up the path toward the cathedral steps. "Hello. You with that lady reporter?"

Boriss did not reply.

Gūtmanis squinted, an air of recognition on his face. He ran a hand through his thin hair over that birthmark. "No, you're Valts's son. Boriss, right?" The rich man placed his hands on his hips, frowned. "What are you doing here again? You keep away from this place."

Boriss said nothing, walking around Gūtmanis out along the side of the truck toward the fields. He knew this man directed the renovation. If Jorens was alive, he'd find him. If Jorens had died, well, he'd find him then, too. Boriss could do nothing more.

A wolflike dog popped its red-gray head out of the truck bed, the animal playfully barking at Boriss, licking his arm with its heavy, wet tongue as he passed.

Boriss shrugged it away.

But Gūtmanis was more persistent than his pet. "Hey, I'm talking to you, Boriss." The old man followed him. "How long you been out here today? Your little sidekick in there, too?"

"No."

"Bet he is. You're what, nineteen, Boriss? Twenty? Why don't you get some work instead of hanging around in the boondocks?"

Work? Like he'd given his papa *work*? "I tried working for you. I didn't last a day."

Gūtmanis laughed. "I own lumber companies, Boriss. You think I'm gonna trust a fallen hockey star with a chainsaw? With all those PEDs scrambling your brain? After you busted up your teammate's spine on the ice for no good reason? You ain't got no restraint, just like your old man, Valts."

Boriss slowed, turned. The rich man grew closer. "Of course, at least your daddy's a drunk, Boriss. A man, if not much of one. You? With those hormones you got in you, you're half horse or bull, can't even think human."

Gūtmanis neighed liked a horse, then poked Boriss in the chest with a bony finger. "Everyone thought you'd be the next Kārlis Skrastiņš, a true great of the game. Instead, you're off the national team, out of university, and wasting your days with kids four or five years younger 'cause you can bully 'em." His eyes narrowed, the amusement fading from his voice. "And I know it was you over at Tukums. If I ever prove it, Boriss, I'll put you away. Like I did your papa."

Boriss grabbed Gūtmanis under each arm, slammed him up against the truck, and bent the old man backward so his head and shoulders were pressed into the bed. Gūtmanis's eyes went wide with surprise, his feet kicking at Boriss's thighs. The dog growled but backed away.

"Nothing happened at Tukums." Boriss seethed, shoving him down.

The old man stared on.

"And my papa ain't a drunk, you see?"

He dropped Gūtmanis. The old man collapsed forward out of the bed, crumpling to the ground at the base of the rear wheel. For a moment, Boriss felt relief and elation at having finally stood up to the richest man in Kurzeme. Then Boriss noticed the crimson dripping from the tree spike in the rack of the truck bed. He glanced down.

The hole in Gūtmanis's head was bull's-eye center in that birthmark.

Boriss stood in the warm Kurzeme breeze for a moment, then pressed a massive hand to his face.

God, this had been the worst day.

DEEDS OF DARKNESS

* * *

Yes, Mom. I'm on my way. I'll call you after the interview.

Santa pressed send on her mobile phone and returned her eyes to her driving. Twenty-five and still a child, she thought. Her little Toyota jittered on these Kurzeme back roads, an hour out of Liepāja, and twenty minutes from the closest village. Where was this place? It's not even on the GPS. Nothing but lowlands, wheat fields, and forests. Though, less forest than there used to be....

Of course, that was the point, the real point, of coming here. In theory, Santa would be interviewing Everts Gūtmanis, the "Baltic Timber Baron," about his charity renovation of some old cathedral in the middle of nowhere, a location so remote neither Rome nor UNESCO could be bothered to assist. She'd take a few quotes and photos, do a fluff piece for *Baltic Beacon* about what a charitable man he was. That's what she'd told Everts's assistant on the phone three weeks ago and his press secretary at the cafe in Rīga on Monday morning, too. In reality, Santa had another agenda.

Santa smiled. She rather liked ambush journalism. In fact, she specialized in it.

One hand on the wheel, Santa thumbed up Everts's name on her mobile, pressed call. After the usual clicks and pauses, it rang, rang, then went to voicemail. "This is Everts Gūtmanis. Leave a message," it said, first in English, then Russian, then Latvian.

Latvia last? Where's your nationalism, Everts? Or did you sell that, too? You octogenarian prick...

"Hello, Everts," said Santa, ignoring his surname to show they were equals. "This is Santa Ezeriņa. I'm a little ahead of schedule for our three o'clock meeting..." This was a lie. Or might have been a lie. It was only two-thirty, but she had no idea how near or far she was from the destination. Santa was fairly sure she was still in Europe.... "So, I decided I'd take a drive around the area. Everts, please call me when you're approaching the cathedral. I'm in a red Toyota Aygo in case we pass each other. *Ciao*."

A bit informal, but that was the game. Let them relax, take you lightly, then ask the unforeseen questions. Questions like, "Why have twenty percent of Latvia's woodlands disappeared since entering the European Union?" Or, "Why is no one replanting the Old Growth forests of Kurzeme?" Or, "Why are you destroying a poor country's—your country's—greatest resource for the easy profits of Swedish and British furniture companies?"

Santa slammed the brakes as a sounder of wild boars darted into the road, four or five sows and their piglets snorting and glaring at her before disappearing into the weeds on the other side. She released a heavy sigh, let her pulse drop, and waited a few minutes for them to get far, far, *far* from the Toyota. All she'd need is to hit a pig half the size of her car.

She drummed her fingers on the steering wheel, checked the clock in the dashboard. Well, if we're stopped, we might as well look around. Santa turned off the ignition and climbed out. A warm spring breeze was blowing the grasses on either side of the car, herons flying high in the blue sky. Far from her—perhaps a kilometer—a tractor was making its way through a sea of sunflowers, but there was no obvious path through the fields to reach the driver and ask directions.

Well, no choice now...

Santa took off her shoes and climbed onto the slanted hood of the Toyota, standing unsteadily at her full height to survey the land.

Nothing.

She mounted the roof, hoping she wouldn't dent Mother's car....

There it was. Santa could just see the spire of the cathedral behind the distant treetops. Probably another five minutes on these muddy roads.

She hopped down, tossed her shoes in the passenger seat, and climbed inside. All right, she thought as she started the ignition, all problems solved.

Everts would get the interview of his life after all.

* * *

Boriss rolled Gūtmanis's body down the embankment into the underbrush, then stood at the roadside nervously appraising his situation.

They'd find it soon, of course, but this would buy him time to run. With luck nobody would go down there until the police came out with dogs. By then Boriss would be home, some alibi concocted to protect him.

But there was Jorens...

Boriss looked down at the iPhone in his hands, the one he'd taken from Gūtmanis's pocket. It had rung twice, then gone silent. Someone wanted the old man.

Some instinct told Boriss to key in Jorens's number, to connect his friend to Gūtmanis. If the police thought it was one of them, a fifty-fifty chance, then the phone records would be evidence in Boriss's favor. Something to balance out Jorens's being in that pit.

He'd tell the jury Jorens killed Gūtmanis, tried to hide in the cathedral, fell...

It would never work. Half in frustration, Boriss pressed call. To his surprise, someone answered: "Hello?"

"Jorens?"

"Boriss?" The voice grew stronger. "You got a phone? Is someone with you?"

"Your mobile survived the fall?" He whispered more to himself than his friend. "You... you make any calls on it?"

"Boriss, I can't send out. Call 'Emergency.'"

He walked in circles to buy time, shooing away Gūtmanis's dog. "I'm going to do that, Jorens. I am. But..." He scratched his sweaty face. Maybe another angle.

"Look, Jorens, you gotta promise me you'll say you were alone out here. No matter what happens."

"Alone?"

"And you don't know who made the emergency call. We been friends a long time, Jorens. Your papa and mine, too. You need to prom—"

"I wasn't alone," Jorens shouted. "You threw me in this hole. Call Emergency, Boriss!"

"Jorens, listen. Promise me."

"No! I got two busted legs thanks to you. Why won't…"

Boriss clicked it off.

He stood there silent many moments, glanced at the dog away beneath the tree.

No options. Just like at Tukums.

Boriss walked to the truck and began rummaging through the cluttered bed.

* * *

A few minutes later, Boriss kneeled above the pit's edge, beaming a flashlight down on Jorens. The drop to his friend was five meters at least, the bottom covered with fossilized seeds and communities of bobbing longlegs. Rust stains and drill holes in the pit's wall showed where a metal ladder may once have rested, but it was long since removed.

"Did you reach Emergency?" Jorens said weakly, appearing pale and forlorn in the light's yellow oval. He'd torn off the bottom of his shirt, using the cloth as a tourniquet for the leg where the bone had punctured the skin. The other leg, bent back at a sickening angle, looked nearly as bad.

"I called them, Jorens. They said forty minutes."

"Forty minutes?"

"We're a long way from town. And if we leave you down there in that tourniquet, you'll lose the leg." Boriss tossed him one end of the rope he'd found in Gūtmanis's truck. "Here, tie this around your waist. I'll pull you up."

For once, Jorens did as he was told. "Where'd you find this stuff?"

"The renovation crew left an equipment box tucked away behind the old water basin. We walked right by it."

Jorens pulled the knot tight at his belt. "Okay."

"Keep your hands on the rope, now." Boriss squatted on the floor a meter back from the mouth of the pit, right behind the bishop statue. He set the flashlight at his feet, the beam stretching across the hole so he could watch the rope coming up cleanly over the edge.

"Ready?"

"Do it slowly, Boriss, so I don't bump these legs."

"All right."

Boriss began to pull. The rope came up easily; Jorens couldn't weigh more than seventy kilos. Not even a workout at the gym.

As he reeled in the rope, Boriss calmed Jorens with reminisces of their friendship. Reminding him of childhood summers on the Majori beaches, collecting shells in the midnight sun, and their hikes into the high hills of Sigulda. Of all the secrets Jorens had told him—of laced cigarettes, a pregnant girlfriend at fourteen, and even shoplifting for the thrill of it—secrets Boriss had kept buried to this day. As a good friend should.

At last, he saw the top of Jorens's head rising over the edge, his once-spiky hair matted to his skull by sweat and dust. With one last tug, his face became visible. Their eyes met.

"You should have promised, Jorens."

"What?"

"I can't have another incident."

Boriss released the rope. For the second time today, he heard Jorens scream.

This time, he welcomed the thud.

Boriss retrieved the flashlight, then bent to one knee over the opening. Jorens lay unmoving directly below, head against the pit's wall. No draft from his nostrils disturbed the dust that coated everything, no breath dislodged the crawling longlegs from the wall.

Satisfied, Boriss pulled Gūtmanis's wallet from his pocket, then threw it next to Jorens's body. He'd keep the iPhone awhile, make a few more calls to establish that Gūtmanis was alive another hour or two, long enough to coincide with Boriss's alibi, whatever it might be. Then he'd toss the phone in the Daugava River near home.

Just one more thing.

He pressed his shoulder against the statue, pushing with all his strength.

But the bishop stood firm, even as Boriss strained and grunted in the darkness for minutes. He felt the heavy burn in his thighs as he had all those hours in the training hall, as he had every day on the weighted sled for Coach Ozols. It reminded Boriss of better days, when people asked nothing of him other than to put a puck in a goal. When he was a hero, not a screwup.

A cracking echoed throughout the chamber, fresh dust rising to tickle Boriss's sinuses. With one last ferocious shove, the ancient bricks beneath the statue came loose, and the whole edge gave way. Boriss stepped back as the statue toppled forward, taking much of the pit's upper wall and masonry with it.

Burying Jorens beneath cathedral stones.

* * *

The Toyota's engine revved, wheels spinning, as the little car fought its way through the muddy road. Santa willed it forward. Come on, she thought, this is not the time to get stuck. A girl's got an interview.

She shifted again, heard the gears grind, smelled transmission smoke.

If I have to call Aunt Ieva for a tow...

The tread found traction, and Santa fell back into the seat as the car sprang forward down the road, passing a blur of trees on either side and into the sudden light of the Kurzeme afternoon sky. The ancient cathedral came into view through her windshield.

Santa whistled, slowed the car to take in the scene. Not quite what she expected. Oh, the cathedral's form was familiar enough from the Wikipedia photographs: one tower upright, one half collapsed, both set against a modest stone building. Nothing special, really, other than its age and rarity in Latvia.

But Santa had never seen it under renovation, the impression more unsettling than she'd anticipated. Instead of the crisp edges of a finished building set against the clear sky, the scaffolding built all around it with its translucent tarps and skeletal additions blurred the boundaries in the air, making the cathedral seem hazy at a distance, a mirage, something resting partly in this world and partly in the next. Rusted poles protruded from every meter of the cathedral's skin, somehow bringing to mind that ghoul from *Hellraiser*, while here and there tarps had torn free of their moorings and hung like surgeon's gauze on Gothic saints or over high, pointed arches in the towers. Dissection rather than refurbishment came to mind, as if something old and holy were being torn apart before her eyes.

She wondered if Everts Gūtmanis was happy with the progress.

A last turn in the road took her around to the rear of the property. She parked under a clump of Scandinavian pines, two weathered bicycles chained to the nearest trunk. Somebody does live out here, she thought. Unless, old Everts peddled all the way from Rīga with one of his mistresses.

Santa opened the Toyota's door, breathing in the relaxing scents of pine and honeysuckle as she checked through her purse before exiting. Mobile phone? Yep. Camera with battery and flash? Yes. Pepper spray handgun, full magazine? Unfortunately, yes.

Santa sighed. A pity to carry the pepper gun, but one could never be too careful these days. Only last week in the village of Tukums, someone had dragged a girl into one of Gūtmanis's lumberyards at night, assaulted her, then tried to cover up the crime by dousing the victim in petrol and lighting her aflame. A heinous, sickening act that had all of Latvia, indeed all the E.U., outraged and hunting for the culprit. Well, the victim would certainly be Santa's next interview. If the poor girl lingered that long.

Santa grimly shouldered her purse, closed the car door, and walked up the path toward the front of the cathedral. Despite her negative impressions, clearly a great amount of money was going into the refurbishment. Tiles and bricks stood stacked everywhere, construction equipment littering the yard, all supposedly paid out of Everts's own pocketbook. A noble cause, in theory, yet she wondered why he would bother. Kurzeme, like most regions of Latvia, was predominantly Lutheran, the Catholic population too scattered to come out to a cathedral in the middle of nowhere. Foreign tourism didn't really extend much beyond Rīga and its nearby beaches. Who did he expect to see this?

And if it wasn't to be seen, then what was his motivation? The few who dared to criticize Gūtmanis hinted at laundering money for Polish organized crime or paying old political debts from his boyhood spent in Latgale, the one Catholic region of Latvia. But Santa had dug deeper than her competition. She'd spent much of last week in Russia, sifting through the Soviet archives at Moscow State University. She knew the truth.

God doesn't take bribes, Everts. Not when you're destroying her land.

Santa rounded the corner to the front of the cathedral and was little surprised to see another road heading into the yard from the fields. That useless GPS, she thought. Might as well have thrown darts at a map.

Parked in the rough near this road was a large, new-looking long-bed truck; Gūtmanis's prize-winning Saarloos wolfdog was tugging on something in the underbrush just beyond. She whistled for the animal but it didn't flinch, unwilling to abandon its catch for a stranger.

With no one in sight, Santa called Gūtmanis's phone.

The ringing in her receiver was echoed by another outside and close by. Both quickly went dead. Santa thought she detected a movement behind the scaffolding near the cathedral entrance.

"Hello?" she called out.

She received no answer.

Santa called the phone again.

The ringing *did* come from the scaffolding, and it went dead a second time. From the webwork shadows beneath the scaffolding emerged a burly young man of about twenty, dressed in dusty jeans, tennis shoes, and a muscle T-shirt with karāts rīga, Latvia's preeminent amateur hockey team, on the front. His arms filthy, his hands scraped and scarred, she assumed him a construction laborer.

"Good afternoon." She withdrew a business card from her breast pocket. "I'm Santa Ezeriņa. I've an interview scheduled with Everts Gūtmanis about the renovation."

The stranger seemed hesitant to respond, and when he did speak it was with a voice high-pitched for a man so large. "Yes, the journalist. I've been waiting for you." As he moved close enough to take her card, Santa observed sweat stains up and down his T-shirt and spots of acne on an otherwise handsome face.

A hard worker, this one.

"I'm one of Gūtmanis's men in the lumber division," he said, then motioned toward the truck. "Pretty much his official driver too."

She nodded, waited for him to say more. He didn't.

"Do you have a name?"

"Davids."

"I assume Mr. Gūtmanis is about, Davids?"

"Not yet. I dropped him a couple of kilometers back. Somebody got out of line at a log clearing. Wouldn't want to be him with the boss, you know?"

"Why do you have his phone?"

"Boss left it on the dashboard. I figured you might call, so I kept it on me."

Another nod. "All right."

His face flushed a bit. "Don't mean to off-put you, lady. This is how we do things out here." He stuffed the phone down into his jeans pocket. "Mr. Gūtmanis tells me he'll be here in twenty minutes with three of the renovation engineers in tow."

"Good."

"I can take care of you until then if you'd like."

"Don't let me trouble you, Davids. I'll do exteriors until Mr. Gūtmanis arrives." Santa pulled her camera from her purse, attached a wide-angle lens.

Took a picture in his direction.

He frowned. "Was that of me?"

"No." she half lied. "I wanted the truck next to that fallen spire over there for scale. Though you might have drifted into the frame."

"I'll be famous."

"Famous might be an exaggeration. Keep it a secret, Davids, but our circulation is less than five thousand."

"Mom will still be proud." He smiled broadly, revealing fine white teeth. "Would you like to shoot the inside of the cathedral, Miss Ezeriņa? While we wait for Mr. Gūtmanis?"

The truck, the phone, the dog… he had to work for Gūtmanis, didn't he? Yet, something in her hesitated.

She shooed it away. "Yeah, all right."

* * *

The interior of the cathedral left a far different impression on Santa than the exterior. Inside, the scaffolding was untarnished by the elements and rose in neat columns above a wide, pewless floor to a domed ceiling, painted with angelic figures that would have made Michelangelo proud if they weren't quite so vibrant, so screen-saver rich, their majesty reduced by the obvious newness. The reliefs, too, along every side chapel had been scrubbed clean of the grime of centuries, their saints and biblical figures recast in fresh white plaster leaving them ghostly spectators watching from the margins. An afternoon sun, peeking in through placeholder glass in high windows, cast the whole scene in a pleasurable yellow-orange tint. It did little to cheer her.

As she had for the past five minutes, Santa walked through the forest of columns, snapping pictures while Davids tarried near the door, repeatedly, it seemed, checking his battered wristwatch. He spoke only when she asked a question, seemed to know the layout well, but little else. Not unexpected, Santa supposed, for a young working man from the countryside. Yet, his silence made her feel rather alone.

Santa paused from her photo-taking to thumb through the pictures in her camera's display. Each image popped off the screen, so false and cheery, like Las Vegas replicas of the old and European. More like a shoot for a commercial travel guide, than an exposé.

Terrible.

"Is there any part of the cathedral that hasn't been renovated?" Santa said, the frustration evident in her voice as she walked down the nave toward Davids. "A room with the original decor? And less scaffolding?"

"You want before-and-after photos?"

"Something like that. For contrast."

"The crypt is relatively untouched."

"The crypt? How marvelously pleasant," she said, brightening. "Who's buried there, Davids? An ancient cleric? A Livonian knight entombed on his shield?"

"I really can't say, Miss Ezeriṇa."

"Well, let's find out, shall we?"

With a last glance at his watch, he led her toward the apse. There, tucked away inside a narrow archway lay a staircase, descending into darkness.

"Ladies first," Davids said.

Santa withdrew a penlight lamp from her purse, followed the steps down into a gloomy, vaulted chamber. She instantly knew from the softness of their footsteps something was unusual. One shine of the flashlight revealed a scarred wooden floor, a stray daddy longlegs crawling across her beam.

"This is a false bottom," she said, jumping up and down slightly, feeling the give in the boards. "The Soviets used to build compartments to store cabbages, potatoes, grains."

"Watermelons, too, I think."

"Yeah, maybe." Santa made one bounce too many, and the heel of her shoe punctured the thin flooring. She lurched forward, pressing a hand on a cold granite column to keep her balance.

"Careful," Davids said, a hand on her arm. "There are holes everywhere."

"Yes," she flashed the little penlight about, "there's quite a large one up ahead. A girl could fall through there."

"Or a man," said Davids. "But don't worry, Miss Ezeriṇa. I've got you."

"Thanks," she said dryly. They continued deeper into the chamber. "You know these grain stores were valuable after the Second World War, Davids." She wondered how well he knew his boss. "What if I told you that in nineteen fifty-three Everts Gūtmanis, as a seventeen-year-old Soviet soldier, shot an anticommunist partisan he discovered stealing grain in this very vault?"

"Mr. Gūtmanis killed someone?"

"Shot him against that pillar over there, by all accounts." She turned the light to a large column in the center of the room. "Under orders, of course." She looked into Davids's eyes. "Communist ideology of the times aside, if you had murdered someone in a holy place, wouldn't you try to appease God? Clean up the crime scene and erase the murder? Even if it took sixty-five years?"

"I wouldn't care if God knew what I'd done. Only men."

"I see." She turned the light ahead, down into that wide hole before her. "A practical philosophy, Davids, if shortsighted, but…but…. There's someone in there!"

"What?"

Inside the hole was another hole, at the bottom a teenage boy, half buried in rubble.

"There's been an accident."

"Kids are always playing in here," shouted Davids, pressing against her to peer into the opening. "He must have tied the rope to the statue, and the whole thing collapsed over—"

The boy's hand moved slightly, a low cry emanating from his lips.

"He's alive." Santa pulled her mobile phone from her bag, started pressing keys. "I'll get someone. We won't let him die."

"Yes, he just won't die." Davids slapped the phone from her hand—it went scattering across the platform—then he shoved her, and Santa's body fell into the darkness. She just caught the edge of the stone pit below, her purse tumbling from her shoulder to the bottom, the penlight smashing against the stones. Everything went dark.

Santa pulled herself into the recess beneath the platform as Davids pawed at her from above. One heavy blow stung her shoulders, yet she maintained her grip, and crawled farther back into under space.

Still half in shock, Santa eased her breathing. She could hear his footsteps centimeters above her head. He attempted to swing down to her level, but she smashed his foot with a stray stone, and he retreated above.

Why? A robbery? It must be, she thought. Some rural hick after Everts's truck, his payroll...that's why he had the phone....

As if on cue, the dull bluish light of a mobile phone seeped through the seams in the boards above her. Then a sneakered foot thundered through, splinters spewing everywhere as Davids kicked his way down.

He's inhumanly strong, she thought, rolling back on her haunches, as boards exploded against her with each concussive kick. The acne, the high voice...all steroids.

Well, they can strengthen muscles, but not tendons. Santa grabbed the foot, and just as she'd been taught in class, twisted with all her strength, till she heard the terrifying *pop* at the knee. Davids screamed, his leg thrashing in her hands, his heavy arms tearing away her wooden ceiling. In this maelstrom, the other leg came crashing through, bruising her thigh, his knee barely missing her chin. Santa seized him at the ankle and twisted again.

The last boards fell away as his bull-body writhed, and he stood above her on two tottering legs, with his torso exposed. One hard kick sent him tumbling back over the pit's edge and out of sight.

* * *

Something snapped as Boriss hit the pit floor. Then, a startling nothingness. He never lost consciousness, though light spots exploded across his vision, and time seemed to skip. Where the seconds went, he did not know, but when awareness returned, no sensations ran across his muscular back, and no feelings remained in his stout limbs. His body refused his order to sit up, to rise, to scream at the woman high above who had cast him here. All that emerged from closed lips was a child's groan, weak and feeble.

Yet, she answered. Santa was speaking to him. Yes? No...no, she had retrieved her phone, calling the police. It seemed far away and unreal. A dream.

Somehow it was too much for his mind. He wished to curl up like a baby, to cease to exist, but instead he only lay there on the flooring, immobile as the fallen statue nearby.

Then, they began to crawl over him.

He could not feel the dozens of legs, of course, but he saw the ochre bodies on stick limbs climbing over his skin, up his jeans. Some movement was herding the daddy longlegs in his direction. Something they feared, and proved, by instinct, the little creatures no longer feared him.

From out of the murk crawled a bloodied and battered Jorens, his belly on the floor, his legs lifelessly dragged behind. Hatred burned in his gaze, the sharpest stone Boriss had ever seen clutched in his hand.

And Boriss was grateful he could feel nothing at all.

IX

VOICES IN THE CISTERN

Originally published in Ellery Queen's Mystery Magazine

Voices in the Cistern

AD 50

Cicero, the great Roman orator and master of Latin prose, famously wrote that even hardened thieves have traces of honor buried deep in their natures. That every rogue lives by a system of ethics, though it may be scant and unfathomable to civilized men. That no soul is wholly black.

But Cicero never met Vibius Vitellius Pansa. A twilight hour with him and the ole patrician statesman would have been running for his life, his philosophy changed forever. Certainly, I should be running now. People don't live long around Vibius. Two of my company have already met their ends by his sword, leaving me the only expatriate thief left in this frontier town. By Mercury, god of thieves and travelers, I *will* live to return to Rome.

But I won't be leaving today. This town is surrounded. And so am I. Vibius has me penned near the back of the tavern, his heavy, muscular body eclipsing the light from the opened doorway behind him, the table we sit at turned to box me into the corner. No escape.

He says, "Listen," so I listen. What choice do I have?

"Do you remember," he whispers in that lispy voice of his, "what you told me on the Vinalia holiday, Quintus? The night we got drunk in this very tavern?"

There is menace in his tone, the usual evil in his dark eyes, and my mind reflexively tries to recall what foolish thing I might have said during that celebratory night. Did I admit to sleeping with his Sophia? Or slipping *denarii* out of Vibius's coin purse while he lay passed out on the floor? Or was it something about his "dealings"? Did I grumble aloud that I felt it treason for Vibius to smuggle Roman steel to the Scythians with the war going on, that it would end in crucifixion for all of us? Who knows? I'm a fool when drinking wine. It's cost me wives, friends, even a prize horse or two. Yet I couldn't have voiced such suicidal ideas. Not to Vibius and still be breathing....

"Quintus," he says, clearly tired of my delay. "You told me you were an excellent swimmer."

"A swimmer?" I repeat, relieved and a little confused.

"A diver for pearls in your youth."

"Yes. At Myus Hormus for a few years." Actually, only one stormy season, and I'd spent more time stealing from others than diving. But why tell Vibius that? Let's see where this is going.

"They used to call me the 'King Crab,' Vibius, 'cause I could split open oyster shells so naturally." I click my teeth, trying to imitate the sound of a cracking shell. It's a pathetic charade. "Why do you care about my diving?"

"I want you to salvage something from a lake, 'Crab.'"

Well, this is interesting. Our city, Chersonesus, has been under siege for sixteen days from the long-haired Scythians, the whole town isolated on a tiny peninsula jutting out into the Black Sea. There isn't a body of fresh water in held territory. So, Vibius's "lake" is either really the sea, or he means we must go over the wall into Scythian lands. An act of suicide. Even blessed Mercury wouldn't help us there.

But I'll play along. "Which lake?"

"Never mind," he barks. "When you agree, we'll talk location."

"What are we looking to recover?"

His voice lowers, though there's no one to hear him. The tavern is deserted, merrymaking long ago a casualty of siege rationing. "Quintus... you remember Appius Domitius Nepos?"

"Soldier from Herculaneum?"

"He's dead. I killed him."

Surprise, surprise. As a professional, I should let this go. Unfortunately, divine Fabulinus taught me too well to speak.

"Why?" I ask.

"Many reasons. Nepos was stealing from my money pouch."

"Oh?"

"And he may have bedded Sophia."

"The cad."

"But the chief reason was profit, Quintus." His voice lowers further. "Nepos possessed an amulet fashioned in sapphires and gold, one he'd found during the looting after the Mauretanian Revolt. Kept it hidden from his betters for ten years, he did. Nepos showed it to me once as collateral in a deal he and I were concocting. Said it could fetch ten thousand *aurei* in Rome or Alexandria."

"Ten thousand!"

"Ten thousand, Quintus. He was a fool to reveal such a treasure to a man like me." Vibius smiles, a pride in his greed. "So, I lured him to this lake…"

"I still don't understand why a lake?"

"Let it be. We'll simply say I convinced Nepos to paddle his *ratiara* out into friendly waters. A place he couldn't run from me," he whispers, drawing his sword from his sheath and raising it high above the table.

I lean back on my bench. By Orcus, he is Mors unleashed.

"When the time came, Quintus, I stabbed Nepos in the throat with my *gladius*, a powerful thrust that made him spit blood, then a second blow up against his skull right here." Vibius digs the sword point into his own scalp, pushing so hard even he winces as a trickle of blood runs down his forehead. "Nepos was dead the instant I cut him. His knees buckled at the force of the blows, his eyes clouded. I saw the amulet around his neck then, Quintus. I nearly grasped it—ten thousand *aurei* almost in my hands—but he fell too quickly away, out of the boat into the water."

A tremor runs through his body at these words, regret birthing a sickly swoon in my compatriot. It takes a long moment for Vibius to regain his senses. At last, he says: "Nepos must have been wary of me, Quintus. He wore a *lorica* underneath his robes. The body sunk, carried straight down by the steel armor to the bottom. Out of reach."

"Why didn't you go after it?"

"I can't swim. But you can, Quintus. A quarter-share if you bring up that Mauretanian amulet."

Well, well... "I want half."

Something out of Hades flickers in those eyes, but his answer is immediate. "If you need it, then all right. There'll be enough to go around."

Victory scares me. Vibius doesn't give up money easily.

"Meet me at the Temple of Apollo Medicus tonight, 'King Crab.' We'll be rich men by morning."

* * *

Rich by morning? A jest worthy of Bacchus himself. It's long past the third watch, and we're not one *quadran* richer. Instead, I wait for Vibius, pacing over the loose stones on the edge of the Apollonian Plaza. It is a hot, sticky night, and despite the war's curfew, I am far from alone. Dying bodies cover these hallowed grounds. Injured townsfolk lay strewn across the temple's steps, a dozen others resting against the heavy Doric columns above, even more huddle around the dry fountain at the center. They are gamblers, betting their final hours that Apollo will appear in his *Medicus* form, as the great physician and bringer of medicine. A sad fantasy. Though the priests deny this, it is well known the Scythians are a more pious people than we Romans. If the gods intercede at all, it will be on the enemy's side.

We are on our own.

I spit out a few of the salted sesame seeds I've been chewing and continue my walk around the plaza, my circuitous path allowing me to observe the crowd from every angle. The horrors within are plentiful. Among the dying are children injured at the last assault, when the Scythians stormed the walls and roamed free inside the city for half a day. With so few soldiers remaining since the *legatus* sailed for Rome with his legions, the people of Chersonesus stood alone to beat back their enemy. Women, slaves, the youth of the city all fell in the defense. Me? I lay drunk during the heroism, blacked out under a table, cradling a wench whose name I can't even recall.

I've no regrets. I'm a bandit with allegiance to no one. But to see the results here, the raw, open wounds in mere babes... Well... I'm no Celsus, no student of legendary Hippocrates. I know nothing of the medical arts. What can be done?

A sigh, something cold slithering down deep in my soul. My guardian *genius* haunts me, taunts me. I ignore him. After all, a conscience is a terrible liability in a thief. Great Mercury seize it, strangle it, take my morals from me. I beseech you, wing-footed one, listen to my prayers at last....

Dark glances in my direction interrupt these tired old pleas. Walking among the temple-goers, three guards keep order, one of them eyeing me suspiciously as I tarry too long on the plaza's edge. In a community this small, I've earned a reputation. It would be wise to slip out of the light into night's darkness, let them forget about foul Quintus, hooligan from Rome...

Oh, but where is Vibius?

"Quintus," whispers a lispy voice.

I turn my attention to the narrowest, darkest side street off the plaza. In the shadows, far from the entrance, stands the hulking form of Vibius. He motions for me to join him, and I follow my compatriot deeper into the alley. Soon, we are far from the temple district, slinking wordlessly along the twisted streets set down by our Greek predecessors, keeping off the newer, wider Roman avenues. At last, we arrive in Chersonesus's oldest neighborhood, so close to the eastern edge of the city I can see the torch flames of the sentries stationed on the outer wall. Perhaps Vibius *does* intend to take us into Scythian lands? I slow my steps, drop away from him...

One word about going over the wall, friend, and I run. We can't spend ten thousand *aurei* on the deathly shores of Elysium.

But my fears prove unfounded. Vibius stops at a two-story *insula* apartment and, producing a bronze key from the folds of his tunic, ushers me inside. Another key and another door, and we are standing in the darkened apartment of a lower-class Roman family. A horrid and familiar stench fills the room.

Even in the darkness, I know. "How long have they been dead?"

"Less than three days," smirks Vibius in a singsong voice. "Casualties of the Scythian attack. Still, what the Fates take from others is a boon to us, you know?"

He lights a candle. I see the family. I wish I hadn't.

The wounds are too clear.

"Since when do the Scythians use short swords, Vibius?"

"Since I sold them short swords," he grunts, eyes narrowing behind that candle. "Questions are unhealthy in our profession, Quintus."

"It seems so."

"Nepos asked questions, too."

"And where is Nepos exactly?"

"There." He points to a large black object in the rear of the room. In the gloom of a single candlelit chamber, with my attention on the deceased tenants, I had failed to notice it before now. A small, two-man boat rests on its side against the far wall.

"You expect to take that over the wall? Unseen by friend or enemy?"

He mutters something about me being slow-witted, then pries the boat from the wall to reveal a large hole chiseled away in the mud brick behind. The candle flame flutters in an incoming breeze, hinting at a deep passage beyond.

Well, what is this? A passage to Tartarus? My *genius* rises again.

Ten thousand *aurei*, Quintus. Ten thousand.

At Vibius's order, we rotate the boat and press it bow-first through the hole. It just fits, clearing the craggy break-in by the narrowest of margins. Then I follow Vibius inside, crawling through dust and over broken bricks, wondering at the bargain I've made with this traitorous son of Ephesus.

We squeeze into a thin passage, our bodies pressed to the walls by the bulk of the boat. The candlelight dancing in the draft, the flame remains just strong enough to illuminate. And it is truly revealing. The masonry in this tunnel is superior to the crude apartment we have left, much of it fashioned in solid Roman concrete, and the walls are decorated with familiar Neptunian frescoes. I finally grasp our situation. In the twisty backstreets of the old Greek neighborhoods, Vibius had led us to an apartment adjoining the great Cistern of Chersonesus. We have tunneled into the city's water supply.

So, this is Vibius's "lake."

He gives me no time to consider these circumstances, barking out orders to lift the boat and carry it onwards. It is a snug fit, the hull scraping paint from the frescoed walls as we progress and every few steps we must shift our positions, rotating the boat to find some new impossible angle to wedge it through. At last, we descend a series of wide steps, the passage opening into a chamber beyond our candle's ability to illuminate. There is great depth to the darkness, a feeling that the unseen somehow extends forever.

We set the boat down on wide tiles inscribed with Greek characters. From a pile of bricks nearby, Vibius produces a large tar-headed torch, lighting it with the candle flame.

Even jaded as I am, it is a magnificent scene that materializes before us, a vision out of the days of Homer and Hesiod, when men like Diomedes were strong enough to fight the gods. We are standing on a stone platform jutting out into the city's great cistern, greenish waters extending as far as the torchlight can reach. The air is as fresh as the open sea, with a slightly copper smell to it, and from the surface of this man-made lake rises a forest of green-gray Ionic columns, easily thirty feet in height above the waters, reaching up to the great vaults that form the Atlantean ceiling, a golden rooftop suspending the weight of the city above us.

"Enough fresh water to support the population ten months in times of drought," says Vibius as he slides the boat into the silent waters. "Or under siege."

"Why did you bring Nepos down here?"

"To kill him, of course," he says bluntly. "And get the amulet."

"I mean, how did you convince him to come?"

He shrugs. "This is the most private place in Chersonesus at night, Quintus. We often do deals down here. I told Nepos we had an offer for his amulet, said the buyer was waiting on another landing, all we had to do was ferry across…"

"Rather like Charon."

"The dead's ferryman earns a single coin for his services, Quintus. I'm after ten thousand *aurei*." He picks up a wide plank from the refuse on the landing, tosses it into the boat. "Let's go."

Vibius hands me the torch and we descend into the boat. He casts us off with a grunt, then uses the plank to paddle our boat away from the platform, through the gloom, into the heart of the cistern.

We cross in silence, me kneeling in the bow with the torch, Vibius behind, steering us through. The columns are endless, like massive trees in the Pontine swamps southeast of Rome. As we pass close to one pillar, its girth half the width of our boat, I reach out and touch its coarse skin, disturbing the white mineral lines marking high water of years past.

I marvel at the columns' age. By their inscriptions, these predate the Roman settlement, the sections stolen from Greek temples on the surface and reassembled down here with little care for harmony or aesthetic. Fluting is mismatched, capital pieces rest stacked on their sides or even upside down. All is functional in design, not meant for human eyes.

And yet, as we pass, I see new landings in the distance, each with its own staircase entrance. There must be a half-dozen official openings descending from the surface. And how many clandestine ones made by men like Vibius? I remind myself, despite the magnificence of the scene, that we sail on Nepos's grave.

"There she is," shouts Vibius, with clear satisfaction. He slows his paddling, nods ahead. "The column with the Gorgon head, Quintus.

Nepos, the old scoundrel, went in there, fell against the pillar as he sank."

We drift up to a particularly damaged-looking column with deep cracks in its higher sections, and a mosaic of crusted gold-green minerals over the lower. High up in the gloom, an enormous Medusa-head capital stares down upon us disapprovingly.

"If she turns you to stone, you'll reach the bottom quicker, Quintus," chuckles Vibius with what, from him, passes for humor. "Might have a hard time getting you back up, though."

I stand up in the boat, touch the ancient pillar. "You're certain this is the right one?"

"One hundred sixteen columns in here, Quintus. With twenty or so Gorgon capitals, all upside down. Except that one." He laughs. "Someone erred in the construction, it seems, since the city planners forbid Medusa to be set right-side-up. Thought it bad luck. Certainly was for Nepos."

The mirth drains from his voice. "And unlucky for me, too, as I didn't get the amulet. Let's get to work, 'Crab.' No currents in the cistern, and with that heavy *lorica*, the body's got to be near the base somewhere."

I hand Vibius the torch, remove my sandals, belt, and tunic, and, fully nude, move to the edge of the boat.

Diving for the dead. The gods must not approve.

A last glance at Vibius—expectant, impatient, smoldering greed in his black eyes. Great Mercury, vengeful Dirae, if I perish down here, drown this Ephesian rat in waters a thousand times deeper than this cistern. Leave his ghost to wander the floor of Oceanus cold and alone for all eternity.

With such a prayer to the gods—*any gods* who'll listen—I jump into the cool waters, surfacing again to fill my lungs once more, then diving down as I did all those years ago at Myus Hormus on the Red Sea. I descend headfirst, kicking quickly to build inertia, then slowing the pace to conserve air. Vibius's torchlight does not reach far below the surface, all is quickly black, and I keep a guiding hand on the mineral-laden pillar as I swim down, feeling the column's girth expand as I move towards the base. The depth of the waters is surprising, my body soon straining under the effects of pressure, a tightening pain building in my ears and temples. I grip my nose, blow into my sinuses to balance the air. The headache subsides.

Yet it takes too long to descend, and I have little air as I reach the bottom. Like some half-blind hermit crab, I grope over the silky floor tiles, extending my hands in arching motions out from the column base. Nothing.

By Mercury, if this is the wrong column....

I blow out a few bubbles, feeding the body's need to exhale. A cold, coppery taste comes with it. My lungs aren't what they once were, my heartbeat rising steadily. I resolve to swim around the pillar base once before surfacing. With one hand on the column and the other dragging along the bottom, I kick through inky blackness. Three-quarters around, I touch something coarse and leathery, the shape familiar. A boot! My pulse races at the discovery, eating up the last of my air. The boot adjoins a leg, up then to a host of floating robes rising off a body.

Nepos lies facedown, forty feet below the surface.

I move my hands up to the torso, feel the steel bands of the *lorica* beneath his tunic. If I can just find the shoulders, the neck opening...

A sticky contracting pain through my lungs, my pulse thundering in my ears... no... not this time. Rise now, or I'll never reach the surface.

I push off the floor, a flurry of kicks propelling me upwards. Halfway up my aged lungs fail as my body forces an exhale, bubbles erupting from my mouth, choking waters rushing in. But I keep my will, remembering my diving days.

Rise, rise, no matter what...

I gasp as I break the surface, a painful, roaring breath worthy of Ulysses ascending from the sea at Scheria. Black spots bursting over my vision, I reach out, cling to the column, keep my limp body from slipping back into the abyss.

As my sight dissolves into blackness, I catch one image. A glimpse of truth sent by Minerva herself. Vibius leans over the opposite side of the boat, his back to me. His muscles coiled, he holds the searching torch out over the waters with one hand, his sword in the other, high and ready.

Then the blindness overcomes me. It takes several long breaths, gripping that column, refilling my lungs, for my sight to clear. When vision returns, Vibius is facing me in the boat, his weapon sheathed as if never drawn.

"Well, Quintus? Did you find him? Did you get it?"

"No," I say, still panting, "it's too deep. Perhaps when the waters lower..."

His face contorts at this news. "Lower?"

"With the siege, Chersonesus has no other source of water. The levels will drop quickly. In a few days, with Mercury's blessing, we can try again."

He trembles with such rage that the boat rocks beneath him. "And does Mercury think me a fool as you do? You'll be down here to fetch the amulet for yourself the moment I turn my back." He draws his *gladius*, slicing the air between us. "If you wish to see the sun again, Quintus, you'll get that treasure now."

I slide around the column, away from the boat. "Kill me and who'll dive for you, Vibius?"

"Better to find another swimmer than to trust Quintus the Liar with such a valuable secret. Go on. Dive! Your life depends on it."

Tip the boat over, drown him... Do it, Quintus... please.

Later.

"All right, all right, friend. By Jupiter, I'll give it one more attempt."

With Vibius watching me, I take another lungful of coppery air and descend again. My limbs are weaker this time, a powerful ache running throughout my body. But I know the course now. Nepos will welcome a final visitor.

Then we let him sleep forever. It is only fair.

Soon I am at the bottom once more, floating in the darkness above the corpse as my hands slide over Nepos's shoulders to the opened collar. My fingers numb at this depth, it takes too many heartbeats to find the cold chain cutting through the death-bloated neck flesh. When at last I touch these twisted links, they run down to the chest, the amulet itself pinned below the body.

By Mercury, why is nothing easy? The corpse won't budge. Nepos is a huge man, half-titan he seems, and weighted down by the steel *lorica* under his robes, he's too much to pry off the bottom. The air already dwindling in my lungs, I lower my feet to the cistern's floor, trying to find the leverage. *Think of the riches, Quintus! Lift! Pull!* My back arches, my posture leaning farther and farther away until I'm looking directly upwards as I strain. The yellow orb of Vibius's torchlight shines far above, like a full moon high in a cloudy night sky, his boat a swaying silhouette at the luminosity's edge.

But why is it swaying?

The answer is immediate. The tides of another craft rock the little boat, the swaying growing stronger as a great black square with six oars in the water glides into view. A moment later this craft—it seems a large raft—gently bumps against our boat in an almost peaceful motion. Then Vibius's corpse plunges into the cistern above me, crimson clouds billowing out from his opened neck, wings of white foam forming in his death twitches!

I instinctively gasp, a flood of bubbles rising from my mouth to mix with the dead man's blood. Panicked, I release Nepos's body, clumsily, desperately swimming away over the cistern floor.

For mindless moments, I kick through the depths, heart pounding, unable to judge distance or depth. It is all I can do to make the next column. Half blacking out, I rise behind the pillar and try to muffle my gasps as I break the surface.

Scythian voices answer back. Can they hear me? How far am I from them? It is several long moments, willing my painful breaths to slow, waiting for the depth blindness to pass, before I dare to peer around that column.

I am farther than anticipated, not one or two, but three pillars away. Burning torches held in the hands of the enemy illuminate the scene. Against our little boat floats a fir-tree raft, at least a dozen helmed Scythians standing upon it. Several hold torches, others languish at the oars. One, he appears the captain, stands in our boat, his short sword drawn, poking at Vibius's unmoving corpse in the water. With guttural call, he seems satisfied that Vibius is dead and returns to his raft. The oarsmen resume rowing. At the back several muscular men use cattle scapulae to scoop a yellowish powder from high clay jars, dumping the mixture into the trailing waters. Even at this distance, I can see an occasional uncrushed leaf among the grains. Deadly hellebore.

Poison. They are fouling the city's water.

More torchlights. In the distance, beyond this raft, move two others. And a new set of lights on my side of the column, sailing towards me...

I sink down below the surface, deep enough, I hope, to be invisible.

But I can't remain here long. Fortuna, goddess of luck, protect me, for there is a single choice. The closest exit, the one I know must be open, is reached only one way. I push off the column praying to remain unseen as I glide beneath the approaching raft. Ten, maybe fifteen feet below the surface I silently swim.

Please, fickle Fortuna, don't let them be looking down....

With a few slow, silent kicks, my body passes within their torchlight, yellowish beams painting my naked skin shades of orange. Then, the dread clouds of hellebore descend as I reach the rear of their raft. I close my eyes, lock tight my lips. Not one sip, not a drop must reach my tongue. I feel the tickling texture of the deadly powder all around me, the grains collecting on my face and shoulders as I swim through the hellebore clouds. Finally, their powdery touch fades. I refuse to slow, won't rise until my lungs are spent. When I do break the surface at last, I open my eyes, risk a glance backwards. The Scythian raft has long passed me, gliding over to join the others near the Medusa column. The enemy voices remain low and calm.

Fortuna, sweetest of goddesses, I'll sacrifice a goat to you every morning. Just let me survive.

The time for stealth over, I plunge ahead, swimming as fast as I can over the surface, churning the water towards the nearest landing, the one from which Vibius and I cast off so recently. The instant I touch those old Greek stones, I pull myself from the cistern waters, sprinting through the darkness to the stairs. Scythian shouts rise far behind me. I imagine their bowmen taking aim at my nude body, their unerring arrows piercing my neck and back. I drive this image from my mind, hurling myself up the steps in a blind ascension, scraping my bared skin against the walls, finally tripping and falling like the old Fool in a Plautine comedy. But I won't be caught. I continue my feverish climb and soon that familiar stench of death is near. My groping hands find the chiseled hole into the apartment. I scamper through, hesitating just long enough to seize a tunic. I don it with a prayer to the deceased, and rush out into the dark streets.

Safe on the surface, I slow outside the *insula,* catch my breath. Take a moment to realize I live, that I've escaped Pluto's realm once more. How many gods will I thank in their temples tomorrow? A fortune in sacrifices to make…

Yes, a fortune… but divine offerings are premature. Riches remain at stake. What shall be your next move, Quintus?… Think… think.… Where is my *genius* now? Where is the inspiration?

I glance at the sealed door of the apartment, imagine the path down to the waters. The Scythians will be gone by dawn, when the cistern is opened to the public. If I wait for tomorrow night I can dive again, undetected by my fellows, and retrieve the amulet for myself. Ten thousand *aurei,* a princeship in my hands.

Your son won't be a pauper much longer, honored Annia. I'll give you a luxurious villa on the shore of Lake Trasimene surrounded by servants…an honest life…like you dreamed for me, dear Mother.…

Yet, even this triumph is spoiled. My *genius* awakens, interjecting unwelcome truths into my mind. A dive tomorrow evening will leave a full day for the townspeople to draw from the fouled water. Imbibing on tasteless hellebore, they may think their illness is disease from other sources. Rotting siege food. A plague. Or an act of the cruel gods. So many will drink on these hot days. Hundreds, thousands will die.…children first.…

I double over, fight off this cursed *genius.* If I listen, if I alert the city, they'll drain the cistern, allow the springs to fill it again unpolluted. But before it fills, they'll find Nepos, the amulet....

Mother... what did Cicero say about honor among thieves? No, this is not a fair test, great Mercury... not a fair test at all...

I scream aloud, and feeling dizzy, stumble over to an outcropping of stone beneath the city wall. For a brief moment, I understand Vibius, why he swooned so when Nepos went in....

I crouch forward on the stone, pondering, cursing for ages it seems. In my convulsions, a weight rubs against my thigh. An irritant felt even among these agonies. I investigate its source. In the pocket of the dead man's tunic is a coin, an old bronze *as*.

A sign.

Can it be? An answer given by Fortuna? Or Mercury? Or a deception? A trickery from the owner's unburied shade? I examine this weathered coin, seeking my way. It is nearly a century old, shaved on the edges and slightly bent, a relic from Republican times still in circulation out here. On one side is a galley filled with supplies bound for a city far from Rome. I trace the engraving with my thumb, feeling its smoothness, a skin worn away by the thousand fingers that have touched it over its life. Merchants, soldiers, gamblers, and thieves. From citizens and priests to slaves and slave children. Generations leading to me. I feel them all.

It is an honest coin.

I turn over the *as*. On the reverse is the two-faced deity Janus. God of beginnings, endings, and change.

Change. For me. To shed a conscience at last.

"Heads or ships?" The child's game. Ten thousand *aurei* against a thousand Chersonesian souls.

Yet I'm afraid... more afraid than I ever was of those Scythian brigands.... Invisible Fortuna determining the course of a life... of lives...

I throw the coin a hundred times in my mind before I let it go. It takes all my courage to watch it fly, see it land. The result clear.

A sigh. I throw it again. And again. Janus changes nothing.

And Cicero was an old fool.

Ignosce mihi, mater.

"Guards, guards!" I shout at last, rising from my seat and running toward the sentries at the walls. "There are voices in the cistern...."

X

THE LAST WALK OF FILIPS FINKS

Originally published in Alfred Hitchcock's Mystery Magazine

The Last Walk of Filips Finks

Found Amongst the Private Memoirs of Doctor Alvis Mārtiņš, Late of Rīga.

Filips Finks was still alive when I reached the windswept courtyard on that dark April morning in '32, though I could see from his injuries that his time in our world would be short. To lift his battered body from the damp cobblestones, I quickly deduced, would only hasten his demise. Instead, we found a good Samaritan amongst the gathered crowd to fetch a cup of soup and a blanket from his quarters, and I fed the dying Filips, comforting this stranger during his agonizing final minutes in a role closer to a minister or priest than a night-watch surgeon.

Before the light faded from his eyes, Filips's utterances formed a narrative of sorts, a bizarre and superstitious tale I was made to repeat at the trial of his murderer weeks later. How the courtroom laughed as I spoke that day, and I was forced, for reputation's sake, to denounce Filips's words as folly, the delirious product of an injured mind slipping toward the abyss. Now safe in old age, I can admit I perjured myself then, for I believed much of what was said, and have come to believe more.

As I finished my testimony and descended from the stand, I made a last glance at the accused. A dark and maddening intelligence passed silently between us, and a subtle nod of her chin told me we were in secret agreement. This confidence with a suspected murderess chilled me to the bone, and though I was not again admitted to the courtroom, I followed the case feverishly through the newspapers to the wanton determent of family, practice, even health.

After the unsatisfactory sentencing, through my own determined investigations, I came to piece together the events that consisted of the last walk of Filips Finks. I set them down here for your consideration. Think me a mad old fool if you will, what I write is truth.

Procul his. Condemnant quod non intellegunt.

* * *

The beginning is easiest, when no one disputes the order of events. A little after seven o'clock on that final night, Filips Finks, chemist, scholar, and junior member of the House of Blackheads, stood before his looking glass preparing for his evening stroll.

"You shouldn't go out," said his wife, Ilze, standing behind him. "There's work to be done at home. The baby's window needs brickin' up with the white nights coming soon."

Filips nodded. It was true what she said. Their child had been born with illness and could tolerate no daylight. Window shutters often gave way in the gusting Baltic winds and the high-nosed neighbors wouldn't let them board it up. The only way for the boy to be safe was to seal off the window forever.

He glanced at the pile of white bricks balanced precariously on the wooden platform adjoining their opened balcony and just beneath the child's window. They had been sitting there a week, the trowel and pan perched on top showing a touch of rust from the spring rains. He should finish his work, it was already half done.

Still, he had stronger desires this evening. Why couldn't it wait? The white nights were months away.

"Let a mason do the job tomorrow, Ilze," said Filips, fastening his cuff links. "I need the exercise of a stroll through my city. You know what the doctor said about my lungs..."

"Brickin' is exercise."

"Enough, Ilze."

"You'll be going to the bordello then?"

He feigned surprise, though this accusation was far from rare in his home. "Ilze, not since our marriage vows."

"I smelled perfume on your collar last evening."

"The barmaid at Fisher's wears too much of the French stuff." He slipped into his horsehair jacket, buttoned it tight. "The jasmine smothers all customers."

"A lie."

He watched her through the mirror, arms crossed, face beet red. She was not the woman he had married. The wretched pregnancy had ravaged her body more than most, and if he was honest with himself, he wished to leave her, child or not.

But, then, he'd never make full member. The Blackheads tolerated many scandals, but divorce wasn't one of them.

"You should learn to trust me, Ilze. You'll be the first woman in our young republic to die of a stroke at thirty-three."

"Heed the words, Filips: 'The price of a prostitute is only a loaf of bread, but a married woman hunts down a precious life.'"

He tried not laugh. *The price of a prostitute is certainly more than a loaf of bread, my dear.* "Who said that? Rainis or Shakespeare?"

"Proverbs 6:26, my husband. If you'd attend sermon, you'd know."

This irked him. "I'll not ask permission to leave my own house, woman. Good night to you and our child." He donned his homburg hat and left.

* * *

Through the cigar haze, a well-tailored man asked: "Why not go with us to the brothel after drinks, Filips? It has been a long time."

Filips sighed and watched his breath push back the smoke above his glass. "I promised Ilze I would be a good lad tonight."

They laughed at this, all Filips's friends crowding the bar in Fisher's smoky pub, one of the many English-style cigar taverns that had cropped up on Kungu Iela since Latvia's independence from Russia. A favorite haunt of the westward-looking Blackheads, the senior board were all here tonight, roaring drunk and ready to roast Filips for his new prudish lifestyle.

"Since when do your promises to your wife have value?" asked the heavy, clever-eyed Otomars, pushing another shot glass of black balsam toward Filips. "I can think of a thousand lies you've told her."

"A thousand, but not a thousand and one, my friend. And it won't reach that count this evening."

This answer engendered drunken boos among the members even as ancient Ludvigs Baumeisters gripped a bony hand over his shoulder, squeezing tight through the jacket until Filips winced. "Finks, you've refused to partake, since…since…" Baumeisters frowned at the memory loss, then scowled over at the American negro jazz band disturbing his concentration with their foreign music. "…since…oh, what was her name again?"

"Let's not discuss it," Filips replied with a bravery he immediately regretted. To be flippant toward one like Baumeisters… He could feel their curiosity ebbing toward annoyance.

As always, Otomars arrived with the solution. "We'll flip a coin, Filips. You win, and we pay your bar tab. You lose, and you tell." He pulled out a shiny five-*lati* coin from his breast pocket. "Shall I?"

Filips looked down. How could a junior member resist the senior board? "Aye."

The coin was flipped, the result clear.

"Talk, Filips."

He downed his licorice-tasting liqueur and shrugged off the alcohol in it. "What is to be said, friends? I sponsored a girl across the river for almost a year. Not so different than many of you. Who doesn't have a mistress over in Pārdaugava?"

"The girl's name!?" demanded Otomars. "And the story."

"Lelde. Beautiful, sweet Lelde from a Zemgale hamlet, though raised in one of the finest bordellos in Rīga before I set her in her own apartment."

"Things were better for you then."

"Things are still good for me, Rubess," Filips answered, irritation in his voice. He traced circles in the moisture of the bar top with his finger. "Anyway, it went well enough for some months. I saw Lelde daily. There are moments, images, erotic sensations that enliven my dreams to this day." His fingertips felt the coarseness in the wood grain. "But the girl began to expect something more of the visits. Promises were made. In the jest of romance, a man can be quite foolish, can't he? For this, I am guilty. But it was all part of the theater she unfortunately took as truth."

"A girl like that should know," said Baumeisters.

"Lelde began to press me for meetings outside her room, for walks, the museums, plays, dinners, excursions… until it became uncomfortable. She once came to my home unbeckoned, though fortunately, Ilze was away. Can you imagine my nerves? Finally, I told Lelde the sponsorship must end, that there would never be anything like the courtship she coveted, that we must never see each other again. It was then she…"

"She what?"

Filips's eyes grew distant, haunted: "Lelde found a pistol and shot herself through the heart. An hour or so after I left her apartment."

Murmurs of surprise arose among those who had never heard the story, while a few stodgy fellows asserted that they had read something of the matter in the *Jaunakas Zinas* newspaper a year or so before. One junior member, too intoxicated to be taken seriously, attested that there was more to it, rambling incongruently about arson and murder and the like before he was hushed by his betters. At the height of this drunken din, Otomars asked softly:

"You are certain you had left, Filips?"

"Of course."

"It's not your fault, Filips," shouted Baumeisters with an air of indignity. "A backstreet strumpet with greedy ambitions toward a man of station."

"And toward your future," added Otomars.

"Exactly," continued Baumeisters. "It would have ended in blackmail anyway. It always does if you give out real names." The old man's eyes widened. "You didn't tell her your *real* name, Filips?"

"No," he said, the tone unconvincing.

"And that is why you so seldom join us in our outings to the brothel these days? Misplaced guilt?"

"It's not so plain, Otomars. You know a life with Lelde was not the farthest thing from my mind. With this girl, if she had only been my equal... Lelde once talked of children."

"Oh, Filips, you don't mean...?"

"Well," he laughed. "It would take little to place her ahead of Ilze at least."

"Understandable."

A few chuckles arose at this, then someone on the margins gave an impromptu toast to fraternity. In the pause afterward somehow the discussion of Lelde crumbled away. The others turned to private conversations on trade and profits, citing bloated numbers beyond the capacity of junior members to appreciate. Alone, in the eye of the conversational storm, Filips lit a cigar, and took a long puff, deep in dark thoughts.

All witnesses agree Otomars approached him then, and more than one patron saw the heavyset man slip the note into Filips's jacket pocket. Of this, and Otomars's dangerously persuasive abilities, there is no doubt.

***

Alone and quite drunk, Filips climbed the steps up from Fisher's hours later. The street chilled him after the warmth of the basement bar. The night, too, was darkening, storm clouds following the great river inland. By the winds, they would break on the city soon.

Well, he'd have shelter for an hour or two soon.

Filips continued through the lighted city center, strolling along German-style streets, between blocks of stone buildings covered in folklore facades from the *Jugendstil* boom of three decades before. He soon passed beneath the mammoth square tower of the Dome Cathedral, whose heavy bells toll by legend when an adulterous woman walks by.

"Fortunately," Filips said to himself, "the belfry is silent on the sins of men."

He now crossed the gray-flowing Daugava by bridge, to where the city turns low and wooden, the architecture a composite of Scandinavian, Slavic, and Baltic native. At this hour in the "wooden district," there were no streetlights, but somehow Filips found the address Otomars had given him on a sloping street down by the river shore, stopping before a warped, peeling building with pincushion hearts hanging in the window. He tarried outside, strangely nervous, laughing at himself for acting like a boy calling on a sweetheart for the first time. Finally, growing cold in the river winds, Filips went inside, climbed the stairs, introduced himself. Bought a room.

She smelled of honey and apricots.

There were no nerves or regrets when the man left two hours later. Filips kissed the girl at the steps, handed her a calling card, made promises he'd never keep.

As he headed down the street, he checked his pocket watch—past two o'clock—then considered the weather. The storm clouds hung above the city now, crowding the top of distant St. Peter's tower and darkening every route home, the air still and pregnant with moisture.

But what was a little rain? He felt a new man and decided to take a circuitous path through the wooden district, planning to cross the river again by another bridge closer to home. It would take him through the poorest and darkest alleys of Rīga, but who would harm a member of the Blackheads? Soon, he thought, *senior* member, if Otomars's promise held.

Though the lampless streets Filips went at a leisurely pace. No companions walked with him at this morning hour, and only the growls of a dog chained in a shallow yard and the repetitive squish of his boots in the road mud disturbed the brooding storm silence. Here and there between the buildings were open lots used in summer for gardens and animal pens, though they sat empty and dead this early in the year. Through these spaces, Filips could see out across the expansive river. On the opposite shore, the lamps burned even at this hour in the windows of a well-known bachelor, famous for his late-night gatherings. The distance to this sole sign of life, however, made him feel terribly alone, and with each step the angles changed, the buildings cutting off the river and choking away the last rays from the distant window. The black night, somehow, grew blacker still.

Filips began to whistle a seafaring tune Ilze had taught him during their brief, unhappy courtship, and he hurried his steps a bit for he was no longer enjoying his walk. He soon turned onto a narrow paved way penned in by the tall black shapes of linden trees on either side, their branches brushing across the low rooftops in the slowly rising storm winds. He had not gone far when Filips realized he had frequented this street before. He was approaching, though by opposite way, the very corner where poor Lelde had lived and died. The spot was now an open lot, for in the panic when her body was found, a lantern had been kicked over, and the building consumed with all its residents.

Though a year had passed, nothing had been built in the opening other than a small mourners' bench set before a few crooked wooden crosses left in remembrance. His vision clipped by the night, it was not until he had nearly passed the entire lot that Filips realized a woman sat silently on the end of that isolated bench.

Despite the gloom, certain features could be made. She wore a faded maroon dress, bonnet, and mourner's veil. He thought it very odd to be grieving here so late, and alone. She must live close by. A friend of one of the deceased, perhaps the woman had even known Lelde herself.

She then raised the hem of her dress slightly, revealing the white of her petticoats.

Ah, a street girl, he thought. All is explained.

"No, thank you, my dear. I can't stop tonight." And he tipped his hat respectfully.

She pulled the hem up to mid-shin. He did admit to himself an ache of arousal, for even sitting in the dark, he could see the woman had a most pleasing shape. But he was satiated, and even if not, preferred the privacy of the brothel to a pickup in the street.

"You are very pretty, madam," he said with another bow, "but it is too late to tarry. And I am wanted at home."

She patted the space on the bench beside her.

"I'm sorry. Another time." He continued on his way, but had gone perhaps a hundred yards before a queer feeling rose up his spine. He turned over his shoulder to see that this woman was but a few steps behind.

She must be desperate for money, he thought and regretted the compliment he had given her. "I've spent my salary elsewhere, girl. There's no reason to be following me."

The woman nodded under that veil and held out a hand toward him. Though he had nothing to fear—she was only a helpless female, after all—there was something dreadful in the silence of this vagrant, and he hastened his steps to expand the distance between them. In the twisting, turning alleyways of Pārdaugava, she was soon out of sight.

The encounter troubled Filips, perhaps more than it should, and he was only just regaining his composure when he reached the iron pontoon bridge that connects Pārdaugava to Rīga's lighted center and home. Filips hurried across, relieved to be walking again beneath the brilliant streetlamps and over firm, tightly bricked roads. The presence of other people, even if at considerable distance, cheered him greatly.

He was only a few blocks from home when a woman's shadow stretched up the wall and he heard the click-clack of boot heels on the road stones behind. He glanced back. She stood not ten feet away.

"Confound you, stranger. I told you I had no money. What do you want of me?"

She did not answer, but took a few steps closer, and with halting, bird-like movements, opened her palms wide to him, beckoning for an embrace. In the brighter light of the center, Filips discerned details hidden before. Her dress was coated in a clinging gray dust across the chest and shoulders; the skirt, too, was marred with deep creases as if it had been long folded in a box or closet, and her veil, while obscuring the particulars of her features, was just thin enough to reveal wide, black eyes and an unhappy mouth. Though no individual point was truly terrible, the composite birthed in him the strongest revulsion. Filips felt his pulse rising and his breath quickening as he said:

"Go back to your own side of the river, girl! People will see us together. They'll make assumptions."

She didn't stir during his outburst, though a sadness radiated from her very form. The woman's only reply, when it came, was to unfasten the top buttons of her dress and bare a breast before him. As his eyes widened in surprise, she motioned for Filips to come closer.

How gauche, he thought. "Have you no shame?" He turned and marched away, determined to be rid of her, and aware how dangerously close to home he was. If some friend of Ilze's burning the midnight oil should see him with this backstreet tart….

She tried to take his arm, and desperate, Filips jogged away, then burst into a full sprint, dashing through Cathedral Square as the bells tolled three o'clock. He eased his pace in the narrow streets beyond, snuck through a side passage to the very edge of his apartment courtyard. Here he paused at last, adjusting his hat and wiping the perspiration from his brow. The stranger was nowhere to be seen.

Irritated, sweaty, pulse still pounding in his ears, Filips walked briskly along the iron fence that separates his building from the road, the small square on the other side darkened save a few lights shining bright in balcony windows above. Reaching the entrance, Filips unlocked the gate, passed inside, and had just relocked it when a feminine hand reached between the bars to caress his wrist. He looked up to see two dark, pained eyes staring at him. This close the translucent veil hid nothing, and to his great horror, Filips knew the face beneath. A beautiful, pale, half-burned face that yearned for him, desired him fully. His alarm increased as Filips realized that the dust which covered her dress could only be ash, and that she, or it, now had a firm hold on his wrist. But the greatest terror, that which drove him mad in his final moments, was what he saw at the base of her bared breast. Directly above her heart lay an open bullet wound, the black liquid pumping out in rhythm with her pulse, a heartbeat that quickened as she looked at him longingly. And smiled.

Filips hurled himself from the gate into the narrow courtyard. But she clung to his arm, somehow through the fence, embracing his body, whispering "my love" in his ear as he collapsed with her atop of him. Filips's scream split the night before she silenced it with a kiss and he succumbed to her amours as the world came crashing down.

***

By the time the night watchman reached my surgeon's station, it was too late for Filips Finks. All in the crowd around his broken body knew his injuries were fatal, and as I sat with him and he relayed his tale to me, many raised white candles high to light the path to Heaven for his departing soul. There was a moment of somber tranquility while all silently considered the fragility of life on this planet. But this passed, as did Filips, and then the incessant and fiercely logical investigation into what had happened to the man began. It was a matter of a few minutes before the first, and only, suspect was arrested.

At her trial, Ilze Finks maintained that she didn't mean to kill her husband then. That after a long night continuing her watch for him on their balcony, she only meant to startle Filips and the woman he was embracing in the courtyard below, that her aim was to simply separate the lovers when she swung the trowel with manlike strength, severing the support braces on the platform beneath her son's window and sent its deadly payload of bricks raining down upon her husband five stories below.

It was a terrible thing to hear in court. Her frank admittance to killing her husband, if not murdering him, was a subtle difference lost on the newspapers that vilified Ilze as a monster and threw the investigation into chaos, adding to the innumerable problems for the police.

Chief among these, of course, was the matter of the mysterious stranger.

It remains the rarest case in Latvia's brief history, where only murderer and victim agreed, for no one but Ilze and Filips saw a woman in the courtyard that night. No tenants called to their windows by screams or the great crash of bricks that followed spied anyone in that plaza save the broken and bleeding Mr. Finks. The judge, in his own primitive investigation, also concluded it extremely unlikely that any human could have slipped out through the courtyard's only exit, a locked gate no less, and remain undetected by the eyes of alarmed citizens. Ilze, herself, never satisfactorily explained how the bricks could crush her husband but leave the lover he held unscathed and capable of flight. In the end, the judge told the jury to ignore references to this stranger, "for what was unseen is unlikely to have existed." A most dubious maxim, surely.

Before the return of Stalin, though, Latvia was a kinder place. Ilze's life was spared, and she was committed to the upper ward at Sarkankalns Hospital. If she wasn't mad before she entered that cold asylum, she soon became so. Ilze was known to remain at her window deep into the night, the white light of the electric torch she held in her hands becoming something of a beacon or landmark for that region of the city. In my nightly rounds as a surgeon, I more than once passed within sight of Ilze's shining window and would raise my lantern in solidarity to our shared secret. For I knew she didn't stand waiting for the spirit of her husband, as some speculated, nor for the return of her child given to relatives in far-off Canada. No, from that high window, she probed the maze of streets stretched out before her with unblinking, forever eyes, much as I watched the road over my shoulder on cold and dark mornings on my way back from some fatal accident in the "wooden district." Together we searched though we never found what, or more accurately, "who," prowls Rīga's backstreets in the early hours of the morning. I don't have to tell you her name: a young woman raised in a brothel who lost her grip on Filips's love not once but twice. In life and in death, cruel Fate cheated poor Lelde every time.

Imprimatur.

XI

MATRICIDE AND ICE CREAM

Originally published in The CWA Anthology of Short Stories: Mystery Tour

Matricide and Ice Cream

It was a burning 35°C in the Kiev train station when I bought the first two tubs of ice cream. A kiosk on the second level, sandwiched between overstacked magazine stands and flowery souvenir shops, sold a range of Ukrainian frozen delights. With President Poroshenko's trade restrictions choking off Russian imports, European products filled the gap, flooding Ukrainian shelves with goods in trendy Western packaging. A little digging in the freezer, however, and I found the tubs made of the old-fashioned materials I needed: insulated cardboard packages little changed since Soviet days. I purchased *Витчизна* brand—"Homeland" ice cream—in chocolate and banana-strawberry flavors and hurried back to the train and the compartment I shared with Mother.

Soon we were on our way, the unending passenger train chugging west over the Dnieper Upland on a fourteen-hour trip towards the border town of Uzhhorod, where my fiancé and her expensive tastes lay waiting. The summer was the hottest in Ukrainian history. Passengers lay drenched in sweat, infants crying, the elderly cooling themselves with cheap hand fans bought at the station. No one drank the national alcohols; only water would do at such nightmarish temperatures. Few moved, fewer still could think. It was Hell. It was opportunity.

At the Lviv station, along the route, I found two more *Витчизна* ice cream packets.

At Skole, in the first foothills of the Carpathians, I bought the final pair. Six in total. I hoped it would be enough.

Returning from this last ice-cream purchase, I slid open the door to our compartment, the cabin little more than an emaciated broom closet: two small bunks climbing one wall with Mother resting in the lower, a solitary window, and a recess over the door where we'd shoved our luggage, the whole bag collection looking like it might crash perilously down on us at the slightest bump or change in acceleration.

"Well, Milo," wheezed Mother in her gravelly voice, "what did you buy this time?"

"Some treats for us. And a present for Vika when we get to Uzhhorod. Another four hours or so…"

"The money of mine you spend on that girl."

"Mother, I'm a man. I'm thirty-eight. I don't—"

"You're thirty-eight, Milo. But you're far from being a man. At this rate, you'll never get there."

"Thanks, Mom."

"It's the truth."

"Just because it's true, doesn't mean you need say it."

Mother propped herself on one elbow, watching me as I set the ice-cream tubs in the bag with the others. I could feel her disgust from here.

"Does Vika realize that I'm cutting you off? I won't support two, Milo. Or three if you plan a family."

"Mother, all Vika knows is that you are coming to the wedding, and you're very excited about meeting your new daughter-in-law. These should be happy days for us all. Let's not argue."

She held up a cigarette-yellowed index finger. "Not a cent after the honeymoon, Milo. Not one—"

Her words were cut off as her wheezing breaths turned into a succession of coughs, her fleshy face contorting in pain…

"Mother?"

The coughing grew more aggressive, her skin turning purplish as she tried to get air.

The sight didn't completely displease me. Still, I pulled a bottle of Bon Aqua from among our things and poured the water into a plastic cup.

"Here, drink slowly, Mother…"

After several choking minutes sipping the water, the cough faded, her color returned.

"Did you take your medicine?"

"Yes," she said as if it were somehow my fault that she'd smoked three packs a day for fifty years. But then most things were "my fault."

"You know the physician at the hotel said you shouldn't travel today, Mother. It's too hot with your emphysema. And Doc Folger back in Rochester didn't even want you to go abroad this summer."

"Well, what was I supposed to do? Miss your wedding? You'd never let me live that down."

"I'm just telling you, Mom—"

"You're in no position to tell anyone anything, Milo."

"Fair enough." I sighed and gently took the cup from her. "Have a rest, Mother."

She lay back on the bunk and closed her eyes. I sat on the floor, as always, the dutiful son at her side, listening to the train pull away from the station.

My thoughts growing ever darker.

* * *

Once twenty minutes had passed and I was sure Mother was asleep, I took her large foot-wash tub, which she'd carted with her all the way from New York, and quietly exited the compartment.

The corridor outside was nearly empty, only a few children at the other end of the car looking out the window at the rising terrain of the Carpathian foothills. I went in the opposite direction, to the public toilet, stepped inside, and filled the washtub to the brim with water. I felt its weightiness, the water shifting from side to side with the train's every shudder. A glance in the mirror and I discerned weight of a different character, one of consequence, of pending fate. *Mother or Vika?* Who gave me more pleasure? I couldn't live with both. And Mother might linger another twenty years...

A man has his rights.

With a remorseful sigh, I returned to my cabin. Mother slept on.

I set the washtub at the foot of her bunk. Next, I withdrew a pair of scissors from our luggage and an ice-cream packet from its plastic bag. I carefully cut out the large, semicircular dry-ice coolant bar from the packet's bottom, and set it on the cabin table.

Mother stirred, coughed a bit. I waited her out.

When she was again restful, I removed five more dry-ice bars from their packaging and placed them with the first. Then I closed the window and, taking an old Cornell University t-shirt from my things, I rolled it up and set it along the bottom of the cabin door.

With the window shut and the door draught blocked, the room's already sweltering temperature quickly rose. Perspiration rolled over my brow and dripped off my nose as I worked, my shirt growing damp and stained.

With something between a prayer and a wish, I dropped the first dry-ice semicircle in the washtub, then the second, and watched the white clouds rise to fill the lower half of the cabin. By the third dry-ice bar, the tub's water had nearly evaporated, and I had to use every last liter bottle of *Bon Aqua* as I fed it bars four, five, and six.

The mists thickened. I could barely see Mother on the bunk, but I could hear her coughs as her frail lungs tried to pull usable oxygen through the clouds. I climbed up to my own bunk, up with the free air that had been pushed higher by the heavy dry-ice clouds. There I waited and listened.

Her coughing grew hoarser, more violent. I thought of my boyhood. I thought of Vika, of sex and money.

I awaited freedom.

My gold-plated birthday watch, the one with the digital display, said the temperature in the sealed cabin was 111° Fahrenheit and rising. At 115°, Mother's gasps and explosive coughs reached their apex. I thought I heard her call my name. Or maybe it was only my conscience speaking...

By 122° Fahrenheit, both Mother and conscience were silent.

I waited another ten minutes, then climbed down and checked the body. No pulse. Eyes dilatated. A perfect smothering.

Emancipation.

I'm not certain I truly thought in the next few minutes. I only reacted, mindlessly following the plan I'd imagined a thousand times before. I opened the window to air out the cabin, and when the clouds were dispersed, I lifted the t-shirt from the bottom of the door and stuffed it into the luggage.

Taking the washtub and shutting the compartment door securely behind me, I followed the corridor again to the toilet, passing a young woman in a flower-print dress carrying a little dog. She smiled but said nothing. Inside the restroom, I emptied the remaining water into the toilet bowl and washed the tub clean of any film with paper towels. Then I flushed the towels and water down the vacuum of the train's drain and returned to my cabin.

That first foray into my new murderous reality exhausted me. Several contemplative minutes passed before I found any strength for further action. When I did, I dumped the ice-cream packets out the window, casually, one by one over a half-hour. Let them be lost forever in the Ukrainian wilderness.

I scoured the cabin for anything I'd missed.

Empty water bottles? Not suspicious in this heat.

A pair of scissors? Nothing unusual. Still, I slipped them into a pocket of the luggage. Why answer questions about what I was cutting?

I looked through the plastic bag, discovered a receipt for ice cream, and had just thrown both bag and receipt out the window when a knock came at the cabin door.

I shut the window, gave a last glance around the room, calmed my nerves then answered the door.

It was the young woman I'd passed in the corridor earlier, her dog down on a leash, a chocolate bar in her hand.

"Would you like a sweet?" she asked in accented English, a smile on her pleasant twenty-something face.

"A sweet?"

"I saw that your ice cream had spoiled. So, I thought you'd enjoy a chocolate bar."

"My ice cream spoiled?" She'd seen me eject the last packet…seen it from her cabin window…or the dining car…

OK, OK, I was a litterbug. What of it?

I willed my pulse to slow, answered her in a whisper. "Please excuse us. My mother is sleeping. Would you mind coming back later?"

"Oh. I'm sorry. Forgive—"

"No trouble. And take your pet…" I pointed down. Her dog—a toy beagle—had curled up on the floor at our feet.

The woman laughed loosely, her hand on my shoulder. "He likes it here. Pocket beagles can sense kind-hearted people, you know." She bent down and picked up the dog. "Maybe he'll drag me back to you one day."

"Another time," I said firmly.

"Enjoy the chocolate."

"Thank you. Good day."

I slid the door shut. Locked it.

I released a long breath. Well done, Milo. The first conversation was over, though it had shredded my nerves. Again, I searched the room, checking for any final detail that had escaped me. All looked clear. I scooted the washtub below Mother's bunk, then, with a bit of inspiration, pulled off her colorful stockings, shoved them into a bag overhead, and sprinkled droplets of water over her feet from the remnants in my last Bon Aqua bottle.

Done.

With my preparations complete, I relaxed, ate the chocolate bar the stranger had left, and dumped its wrapper out the window.

One had to be consistent.

At last, I pooled my courage for the penultimate moment. I reclosed the window, let the temperature rise again, then threw open the cabin door and shouted: "Help! Help! Someone, please…my mother…she's not breathing!"

A buzz of Ukrainian voices filled the corridor, faces popping out of every cabin door.

I screamed again. "Please! Somebody help us!"

Porter Panchenko came running up the corridor.

"It's my mother," I cried, my voice cracking. "She won't wake up."

The hefty porter shoved his girth into the compartment and bent over my mother on the bunk. For several minutes, Panchenko examined her, muttering sad-sounding words in Ukrainian. At last, he said in thick English, "The heat has claimed another one."

I thrust my face into my hands. "It's my fault, my fault. She has allergies and emphysema. And I had the window shut..."

"Mr. Capela, don't blame yourself. This happens all the time with older passengers. There are warnings in the stations for those over sixty not to travel on days over thirty centigrade."

"I can confirm the heat was stifling, porter," said a feminine voice. That stranger with the beagle appeared in the doorway. "My dog collapsed when I visited this cabin not half an hour ago. I had to lift the poor little thing out, didn't I, Mr....?"

"Capela. Milo Capela," I said between sobs.

"Beagles are well-suited to high temperatures, Porter Panchenko. They're among the most heat-tolerant of all canines. To affect my dog in mere seconds, I'd guess the room was what, Milo? Forty degrees centigrade? The dog lapped up a quarter-liter of water as soon as I got back to my own cabin."

My opinion of the woman changed drastically. Perhaps, she was helpful after all.

The porter sighed. "It's a tragedy all too common this time of year. I'm sorry for your loss, Mr. Capela. There's nothing we can do until we reach the Mukacheve station, I'm afraid." He offered me his hand then, unsure of American customs during a tragedy, sheepishly retracted it. "Unfortunately, every cabin in the train is occupied. If you don't wish to travel with the deceased, I can offer you only the porter's booth."

"No one should be alone when losing a parent," said the woman. "He can stay in my cabin, if he wishes, Porter Panchenko. You'll remember my colleague missed the train and left an open spot."

"Thank you, miss," I said. "I may take you up on that offer. But, for the moment, I wish to be by myself. This is so…so…shocking."

"Of course. If you need me, I'm in berth sixty-four, two doors down in this car."

"Thank you."

The woman placed a gentle hand on my forearm. "She wouldn't want you to grieve, Mr. Capela. Life is for the living. Your mother is waiting for you in a better place."

"If I need you, I'll come."

She disappeared from the doorway. Porter Panchenko reiterated his condolences, then told me he'd return shortly with some paperwork.

Soon, I was alone.

So far, so good…

I shut the cabin door. Took a Valium. Changed my shirt. I considered texting Vika, but it occurred to me the beagle lady was quite attractive.

How sympathetic might she be to a man who'd suddenly lost his mother? European sexual morals, after all… I put on some cologne.

Leaving Mother to her fate, I set out for berth sixty-four. I found the door open. The woman sat inside, reading a Rankin novel, her dog curled up on the floor at her feet. She'd changed out of her dress into casual jeans and a form-fitting black t-shirt with "Miss Quote" across the breast.

"Hello," I said, rapping on the door frame. "Is that invitation still open?"

She looked up from her reading and smiled. "It is."

Her cabin was larger than ours, with a full-sized twin bed on each wall. I sat across from her, the pocket beagle jumping up onto my lap.

"He likes you."

"Yes," I said, scratching the dog's head. "Very friendly. How old is he?"

"I'm not exactly sure. Young, I think…"

"And his name?"

"You wouldn't be able to pronounce it."

I smiled. "How long have you had him?"

"A week. I solved a murder on a tour bus in Kiev. This little fellow was a gift from the victim's family. I'm headed to Bratislava now. I don't know what I'm going to do with him at the EU border. I hope they'll let me take him through."

"Solved a murder, you say?"

"Yes. And not my first, frankly. I'm a journalist. Trouble follows me everywhere."

"A nice girl like you?"

"Not so nice. You don't know me."

I felt my pulse rise in an unexpected way. "Are you famous? Should I ask your name? Or is it something else I couldn't pronounce?"

"Santa Ezeriņa."

"'Santa Ezeriņa.' Did I get the Ukrainian right?"

"It's not Ukrainian. I'm Latvian. Don't get your Eastern Europeans mixed up. Balts are not Slavs. You'll offend us if you do. Have you never been to Rīga?"

"No. Should I?"

"Everyone should go to Rīga at least once. You may never go home."

"What brings you to Ukraine—besides murder?"

"Journalism in theory. My colleague came on assignment and I tagged along. Of course, she met a boy, decided to take another train, and left me all alone. Typical of Līva." Santa crossed her legs and rubbed a knee as if it troubled her. "It's my first time in western Ukraine. That's why I was looking out the window at the beautiful Carpathian uplands when I saw you throw out all those ice cream packets. I counted six…"

"Six, yes. But how did you know it was me?"

"The gold watch on the wrist of the discarding hand. I observed you wearing it in the car's corridor when you were carrying that tub to the dining car."

"To the toilet, actually. I'd just washed my mother's feet and wanted to pour the dirty water into the sink."

"What was wrong with the ice cream?"

"Spoiled. I was saving the rest for later, but the first was so disgusting that I didn't even risk the other packets. Ejected them all, as you observed."

"Ukrainian ice cream always spoils. But in Rīga… Oh, I'm sounding like a tour guide…"

Her voice trailed off and we sat for several moments listening to the chug of the train in the growing altitude. Finally, she said: "I'm sorry to bring up the tragedy of the evening, Milo, but given the rancid quality of the ice cream, have you considered that perhaps it was food poisoning that took your mother's life?"

"Mother didn't have any."

"Maybe she had a taste whilst you were taking the foot tub to the toilet? Or simply had your back turned?"

"A taste wouldn't be enough to make her ill, much less kill her."

"Forgive me. I was only looking out for you. As a journalist, the stories I've heard about what is found in food in this part of the world…well, it would make your skin crawl. I did a story in Tallinn about what a woman discovered *still living* in her pecan yogurt. Ninety thousand euros she got in the settlement.…"

"We have enough money, thank you, Miss Ezeriņa."

"You and your mother?"

"Me and my fiancé in Uzhhorod, now."

"I see."

My attraction to this "murder-solving" journalist had waned. I set the beagle on the cushion next to me and got to my feet. "I should be going. There'll be much to do about Mother. I just wanted to thank you for the support with the porter. And the chocolate bar, of course."

"You're welcome, Milo. You seem to be holding up well. I only wish I could do more."

"Have a pleasant journey."

I left berth sixty-four and headed back to my cabin. I discovered the door open and Porter Panchenko waiting inside, holding a folder full of papers.

"Mr. Capela," he said as I entered, "we'll be arriving at Mukacheve in thirty-five minutes. I should tell you what will happen. At that station, the police will come on board, as will a medical official, a doctor named Zima. He'll do an examination of the body, and you'll formally identify the deceased. A death certificate will be issued, and the police will submit—"

"No autopsy?"

"Not unless you request one. Or the doctor or police feel there are unusual circumstances. In this heat, sad as I am to say it, we lose an elderly traveler twice a month. I'd be surprised if the examination and paperwork took fifteen minutes. I did the same for a Moldovan gentleman on Sunday. The procedure went so quickly, we left the station on time. Not a second's delay. No less tragic, of course."

"Of course. Tragic."

He withdrew a document from his folder and held out a pen. "If you'll sign here, sir, we'll provide for transportation of the remains to any Ukrainian city with an international airport. You can then fly home to America with the body, if that is your intent."

"What am I signing exactly?"

"That you won't sue our company, sir. That all involved accept that this death was a result of natural causes with no party at fault."

"Can we say 'natural causes' before the doctor's evaluation, Porter Panchenko?"

"As I said, sir, two deaths a month…"

I took the pen, signed.

He seemed relieved. "I'll have an English copy printed out for you at the station, Mr. Capela. The death certificate, too. With the bilingual papers, you should have no difficultly leaving Ukraine or retrieving the remains in America. These are international documents accepted by all countries."

"Thank you, Porter Panchenko." I handed the pen and document back to him.

"It's heartbreaking that these things happen, sir. I wish the procedure weren't quite so routine." He bowed and went out the door.

I laughed internally. A doctor's certificate in English saying "death by natural causes" and clearance back to America. With no siblings, aunts, or uncles to question anything.

The perfect murder.

I shut the cabin door. Texted Vika the single letter: "V."

V for Vika. V for Victory. V for Vindication.

I'd never been so happy.

***

I was dreaming a strange dream—about Freud talking backwards—when a knocking on the cabin door awakened me. I slid off the top bunk, careful not to disturb Mother on the lower one, and stumbled groggily to the door.

The knocking repeated.

I slid open the panel. "Yes, Porter Panchenko…"

It was Santa Ezeriņa. "I'm sorry to bother you, Milo," she said. "But we might consider more seriously the food poisoning possibility. I no longer believe your mother's death was temperature-related. It simply wasn't as hot in this cabin as we thought."

I patted my bed-head hair into place. "Miss Ezeriņa, you're quite a fussbudget…"

"Hear my reasoning, Milo. You washed your mother's feet to cool them, yes? And afterwards, she put her stockings back on. If it were sweltering, I don't think she would do that. She'd want her feet to remain open to the air."

"You are mistaken. Mother didn't put them back on. Look, they're off now."

Her eyes didn't stray from mine. "They were on when I visited your cabin while she slept, Milo. That was after you'd emptied the washtub. She wore rainbow stockings, unusual for an older woman. I remember them clearly. And I can see by your face that you do too."

"No…no…they were lying on the bed by her, not worn. And it was boiling hot, Miss Ezeriņa. After all, your dog swooned."

"There are many reasons a toy beagle might swoon."

"Such as?"

"Gas."

"Gas?"

"These old, Soviet-era trains reek of diesel fumes. This could affect a little dog."

"Please, enough." My voice turned harsher. "You've many wild theories, Miss Ezeriņa. Diesel fumes. Food poisoning. What imagination! You'll blame extraterrestrials next. Now, have some respect for a son in mourning, and kindly leave me in peace."

"Insist on an autopsy when the authorities come aboard, Milo. Have them check the stomach and lungs, blood, and body tissues. I can help you communicate if you want. I speak fluent Russian and some Ukrainian."

"I think I've 'communicated' with you all I want, Miss Ezeriņa." I began to shut the door.

She caught its edge. "Milo, if there's any reason you'd fill a washtub other than to wash feet, you need to tell me now. It'll be better for all of us."

I forced the door closed. Locked the bolt.

I paced in the cabin, feeling the vibrations of the car beneath my feet. For the first time, I avoided looking at Mother.

What did Santa Ezeriņa know? Nothing? Just a sleazy reporter, grasping at straws for a story.

Still…

I called Vika. It went to voicemail. I redialed. Voicemail again. I left a message. Tried to relax, rest.

When at last my beloved called back, Vika's first words were: "Did she suffer?"

"No."

A pause. "She should have suffered after all she's done to you."

"Listen, sweetie. There's a change of plans. Is your Schengen visa still valid?… Good. Find us a flight tonight to the EU. Doesn't matter where. Budapest, Warsaw, Rome. We're eloping, getting out of Ukraine.…no, the body, too. You'll need to arrange it with the airline…use Mother's credit card number. Price isn't a factor anymore."

A fresh knocking at the cabin door.

"Santa Ezeriņa!" I shouted, "If that's you, go away…no, no, sweetie, I'm alone. Just a nosey girl…I assure you she's not even attractive…please, sweetie, just get the tickets. I gotta go…yeah, everything's all right. Love you too." I ended the call.

The knocking repeated. Harder.

"Miss Ezeriņa," I said through the door, "if you're here to harass me further, I'll be alerting the porter."

"This *is* the porter," replied a masculine voice.

"Oh." I unbolted the door and slid it open.

Outside stood Porter Panchenko, a fresh document in his hands, a slightly sour expression on his face.

"What is this?" I asked.

"Your 'request for postmortem' form, sir. I can help you fill it out if—"

"A postmortem? An autopsy? You said no autopsy!"

"The young woman in berth sixty-four asked for it on your behalf. She said you were confused by our procedures."

"No! No! No!" I plucked the form from his hand, tore it up, and threw it back at him, the pieces raining down and sticking to the sweat stains on his plump body. "There's no confusion. And no autopsy. Do you understand my English?"

"Only trying to assist, sir," he said, brushing the paper from his uniform, then stooping to pick up the litter.

"You can assist by letting me grieve in solitude. And fulfilling our agreements."

"Yes, sir." He turned abruptly and headed up the corridor, growling something in his mysterious language.

I stood in the doorway, tempering my anger. When rage passed, and reason resumed, I stepped into the corridor and slid the panel shut behind me. I had to nip this inquisitive reporter's interference in the bud before we arrived at the station and the doctor came aboard. Frankly, I didn't think I'd be able to stay reserved if she asked pestering questions in front of authorities.

I found her door open, Santa Ezeriņa sitting on her bunk, stroking her little pet. Ernest Blofeld came to mind.

"Come in, Milo."

Her dog jumped down to greet me. I ignored it, remaining in the doorway. "I wanted to let you know, Miss Ezeriņa—Santa—that I've taken your advice on the autopsy issue. No need for your kind assistance. I called America. The best pathologist in Manhattan will examine Mother on Tuesday afternoon when I arrive with the body."

"You'll miss that appointment by twenty years or more, I'd say."

"What? What do you mean?"

"You'll be in a Ukrainian prison unless the U.S. government seeks your extradition, which is unlikely once the facts are known."

"Are you accusing me of some crime, Miss Ezeriņa?"

"Only matricide. The autopsy, performed in this country, will show excessive carbon dioxide in your mother's lungs and blood. Not poisonous, but in enough volume to indicate inert gas asphyxiation in a confined space. Am I wrong?"

Sharp pains shot through my stomach, and I leaned hard against the door frame to keep from trembling. "As I said, Santa, you've got quite a perverse imagination. Previously, you thought it was food poisoning."

"Food poisoning was a ruse to test your resistance to an autopsy. No imagination was needed, however, when I kneeled to pick up my dog on my first visit to your cabin and smelled the sour scent of dry-ice gas, i.e., carbon dioxide. I knew then. Sublimated carbon-dioxide gas is heavier than air, Milo, opening the window dispersed it in the cabin above, but let invisible traces linger at floor level. That is why the beagle grew lethargic." She shrugged. "It was a simple matter to deduce where it came from on a train: the mixing of the coolant from the discarded ice cream and water in a washtub that was never used on feet. In that tiny compartment, six bars were enough to smother your sick mother as surely as if you'd thrown a pillow across her face. You gambled on murder, and for now, you've won."

"Well, this is a perfectly disgusting theory. You reporters will make up anything for a story. But you've no evidence to detain me or the body. Those ice cream packets are lost in the wilderness. By the time you find them—if you find them—I'll be in another country, Mother long cremated."

Santa lifted her iPhone from the cabin table. On the phone's screen was a waifish woman, casually dressed, with long, Michelle Phillips hair to her waist. She stood in hilly grasslands alongside a set of railroad tracks, a Витчизна strawberry-banana ice-cream tub in her hands. Santa swiped to the next image, a close-up of the packet, the opened and empty cavity meant for a dry-ice bar clearly visible.

I felt suddenly dizzy.

"Your mistake was throwing the packets out the window sequentially. By the fourth packet, I found it curious enough to use the GPS of my phone to record the locations. My colleague's train is an hour behind ours. When your mother was discovered dead, I sent the last three packets' coordinates to Līva, had her get off at the nearest spot. She's already found two. Your fingerprints will be on these, and the coolant has clearly been removed," said Santa. "For what purpose, Milo?"

A kind of palsy seized me, my hands shaking with rage as I pointed at her screen. "You and your friend are doctoring those yourselves…for your newspaper. It's your word versus mine…The police will never believe you…"

Santa sighed and flipped to the next image: a man stood in the same hillscape, the same ice cream tub in his hands. "This is Līva's beau, First Lieutenant Andrey Karpanko of the Dnieper Homicide Department. They met in Kiev when I solved the bus murder. They're inseparable now; they're even travelling this way in a private train compartment—'The Honeymoon Cabin.'" She smiled sardonically. "Līva always did have a thing for men in uniform. I think they'll have more influence with the police than you. And in Ukraine influence matters as much as evidence. Perhaps more."

I stepped quickly into the cabin, the dog yipping at my shins.

Santa slipped the phone safely into her pocket. "No, Milo. Līva and Andrey know everything, and it's all in the cloud anyway."

"What do you want? Money?"

"Justice," she said bluntly. "To murder the one who gave you life, Milo? I know seven languages yet have no words for what you've become. Maybe there is a tongue somewhere with something worse than 'satanic.' Or perhaps we'll coin a term just for you."

I reached into my pocket, nearly stumbling as the train decelerated as it approached the station. "I've fifty dollars here. And another two thousand in my mother's bag. You, Līva, Lieutenant Karpanko, can split it. It's yours. With more, much more, when I get the inheritance."

"Do you have enough for them too?" She nodded towards the window.

The train pulled up to the Mukacheve platform. I dropped my money in horror. A dozen uniformed policemen stood waiting, some with dogs, others in body armor sporting automatic weapons. The flashing blue lights of police cars parked nearby gave the scene a deeply surreal glow.

"With the militant problems in Ukraine these days, they take no chances with reports of killings on public transport," said Santa. "We called ahead."

She picked up the beagle, set it in her lap. "I'd be careful in the way you move. The Ukrainian phrase '*Stiy, ya budu strilyatu*' means 'Halt, I will shoot!', Milo. Just so you know…"

XII

THE HOUSE IN GLAMAIG'S SHADOW

Originally published in Nancy Pickard Presents Malice Domestic 13: Mystery Most Geographical

The House in Glamaig's Shadow

1989

The red conical summit of Glamaig lay ahead of Nigel Boorman, a path as treacherous as the man upon it. An abundance of slippery scree covered these slopes, the great Corbett a stimulating climb requiring balance, endurance and patience to conquer. One careless step and an unlucky hiker might betray his footing and find himself sliding down the coarse gradient with ever-growing speed, a terrible inertia carrying him along four hundred meters of rock-filled slope, depositing him very much worse for wear into a lonely Highland glen.

But the forty-six-year-old Englishman was determined to reach the apex, where he might gaze out over the other Red Hills south of Glamaig or at the Black Cuillin Mountains that form the backbone of this Isle of Skye. When visiting Sgurr Mhairi, as the Highlanders called Glamaig's summit, Nigel would look across the glittering sound to the rugged Isle of Raasay or seek a glimpse of the Scottish mainland beyond. Stirring vistas materialized with every dawn on Skye, inspiring imagery useful to a professional writer like Nigel.

Most of all, he desired to see the spot where his benefactor, Lyle MacPhate, had died, to touch the jagged rocks at the summit where the greatest Highland writer of his generation collapsed after ascending Glamaig eighteen years earlier.

A tragedy for Scotland.

A loss for world literature.

A boon for Nigel Boorman. It made him rich. Or, more accurately, made him once rich, those monies long spent.

Surmounting the summit, Nigel followed a worn, winding path to the place of MacPhate's demise. Flowers, books, and notes left by the literary devout lay pinned beneath stones here, these remembrances weighted down securely to resist heavy Hebrides winds.

Nigel found this makeshift shrine amusing for reasons all his own, a mirth tempered when, after a few minutes rummaging through the mementos to MacPhate, his eyes fell on a black stone dedicated to someone else. On its surface, in wind-smeared chalk, was written: "Nigel Boorman."

His pulse, just recovering from the climb, began to rise again.

He lifted the stone.

Beneath was a small, clear plastic bag. He picked up the package, wiped off the grime, and weighed it in his hand. The packet was little more than a sandwich baggie, the contents nothing but the jumbled pieces of a child's puzzle.

Odd.

Nigel felt a knotting dread. He disliked being associated with MacPhate, especially at some ramshackle remembrance on the late author's home island. People were ruthlessly protective of their heroes out here.

Nigel suspected conspiracy. What kind of prankster would climb treacherous Glamaig to play a game with him? And who even knew he'd planned to hike the Red Hills today?

The owners of his writers' retreat in the valley were the obvious answer. The pub-goers in Sconser another. He'd drunk too much the night before. Talked too much. Anyone on Skye could have dropped in at the public house, overhead his ambitious plans to reach Sgurr Mhairi.

He felt his face flush in anger. Well, he sure as hell wasn't going to assemble a puzzle on any windswept hilltop. Nigel slipped the baggie into his jacket pocket, zipped it tight. He was the sole occupant of Gill Hall for the next two months. Plenty of time to figure this out.

He walked away over loose, shifting scree to the edge of the downward slope. Nigel's gaze found his lodgings far below at the foot of the Corbett. Despite being known as a hall, the Gill Writers' Retreat was little more than a stone cottage. A river skirted the building on two sides, a grove of oaks cutting off the view of a small dirt road that connected Gill Hall to the world outside. Roe deer grazed on the golden autumn grasses that grew beside the hall's gate. A perfect scene. A perfect place to write.

In theory.

At this height, nothing looked real to Nigel. The hall, the road, river, trees, and deer were props on a museum panorama, accessories to a child's train set. The view from Glamaig made man's incursions on Skye feel inconsequential.

Nigel took a robust breath, made sure the baggie was secure in his pocket, and began his journey down the slopes of Glamaig.

* * *

Sitting near the Gill Hall study window, with the river waters rushing below, Nigel typed:

At work
I watch the clocks
At home
Alone
I listen to them

His fingers drummed on the desktop. You're a piss poor poet, Nigel Boorman, you know that? He tore the paper from the typewriter, slipped it into the bin, then caressed his tired brow. Three weeks. Three weeks and less than forty pages, half of those unusable...

He calculated the cost per day, the cost per page for staying here. He must be as mad as they said. Nigel glanced at the clock on the desk. Three a.m.

No more.

Nigel set the cover over the typewriter and sat in the study, listening to the river outside. Beyond, if he concentrated, if he held his breath, he could hear the distant roar of the sea. Impossibly large, this Highland country.

Nigel breathed slowly. He should be inspired here. This landscape was magnificent, this house's study a miracle, a perfect muse to any writer who ever set foot in Gill Hall. The "Cascading Study" he sat in exceeded in fame the retreat itself. Mirrors positioned on walls and ceiling magnified the small waterfall outside, pulling river vistas in through wide curtainless windows. With the laws of physics reversed by clever reflection, waterfalls cascaded up walls, and the river flowed backwards across the ceiling. Except for the desk, chair, and a single black door, the whole room appeared crafted out of surging, white water. London Times best sellers were written within this beautiful maelstrom, masterpieces drafted by authors who felt serenity with Nature or the touch of God himself.

Yet Nigel's talents remained inadequate to the wonders around him. All poetry and prose tonight binned.

He sighed. Whisky. He needed whisky.

Nigel exited through the black door, left his comfortable, modern upstairs, and descended a narrow stairway to the ground floor which the absent owners had decorated with stiff period furniture. The whole house in darkness, the only light came from the embers of the dying hearth fire, and above those, from the suspicious, yellow eyes of the Gill Hall cat, its black form lounging on the fireplace mantle.

He flipped on the electric light in the kitchen, found the Talisker Skye whisky, and poured himself a glass. As he took a sip, Nigel's eyes strayed across the counter to the puzzle bag he'd left there. He took another drink. He told himself he wouldn't touch that riddle until five pages— publishable pages—were written. But even that magnificent study above couldn't keep him focused on writing or dampen his curiosity about what lay inside that packet affixed with his name.

An itch needed scratching...

To Hell with the five pages.

Nigel pulled up a stool, untied the baggie, and depositing the pieces onto the countertop, fended off the cat to assemble the puzzle. It quickly became evident this was a promotional puzzle for Blackadder the Third, Rowan Atkinson, and Hugh Laurie dressed in flowery period costumes. Odder still was the handwriting made in marker over the puzzle's face. When assembled the writing said: *Picture the End of Gill Hall* followed by a sequence of numerals and letters:

U35 T41 O23 E12 M53 O39 O21 L21 N23 A24 G33 A21 Z05
R04 E14 O12 F53 S34 N27 N05 E38 A17 O18 O22 C11 D05
A13 T42 Q23 O48 A33 N23 A24 G33 A21 Z05 R04 E14 O12
F53 S34 N27 A05 E12 E28 L56 O23 Z06 X01 D02 A03 C04
U07 I08 Y09 E28 A13 M33 Q05 R04 R31 T43 S34 O33 V23
A15 A12 A21 K27 O42 G23 Z07 E12 A14 O33 A23 A05 P53
P21 D23 T11 O31 E23

A cipher! His favorite hobby at Oxford. Obviously, some old compatriot had come to Skye, discovered he was in residence at Gill Hall and decided to play a trick. After all, Nigel loved Blackadder. He'd even worked on a treatment of his second novel with Ben Elton before it all went sour.

"Picture the End of Gill Hall," he mumbled.

Picture...?

Could that be a reference to something other than a mental image? A literal picture? A physical photograph or painting? There was only one picture hung in all of Gill Hall, an observation he'd made while pacing the floors during nights of writer's block.

Nigel retreated to an alcove under the stairs where the picture hung crooked and dusty, half-eclipsed by a potted fern. He pulled the picture from the wall. It was a framed print comprised of ten portrait photographs arranged in two rows of five. He knew them well. They were the first ten authors to reside at the retreat.

Dougal Andrewson, October-December 1968
Fiona Quillan, February-April 1969
Crag MacDonald, September-November 1969

Elspeth Selkirk, LLD, January-March 1970
D. P. MacManus, February 1971
Lyle T. MacPhate, March-May 1971
John F. Reid, October-December 1971
Raymond Philpott, MBE, December 1972-January 1973
Alexina O'Cain, March 1973
William Boyd, April-May 1973

Gifted authors all, conservatively dressed in their portraits as befitting the Tartan Tory affiliations of the Hall's owners. Only grizzly, unshaven MacPhate wore casual clothes, a jumper with the words Townsend Brewery broadly across the breast, a jumper he'd famously been buried in after his heart attack atop Glamaig. Nigel was always surprised they'd included such an informal photograph among the studio portraits.

But who could omit MacPhate? The population would riot.

He took another swig of Talisker and set his mind to the cipher's challenge. "Townsend" was obviously connected to the "end" referenced in this puzzler's note. If one assumed Townsend as the starting point, he thought, then the digits may be offsets from MacPhate's position among the portraits.

This proved correct.

After a few minutes in the kitchen, Nigel moved to the desk in the mirrored study, pipe firmly in mouth, note and picture before him, working out the game. In the end, it was a rather simple cipher for a pro like him, taking too brief a time to be entertaining.

The first numeral indicated the offset from MacPhate; the letters determined the direction of counting. Consonants were counted backward, vowels forward. The last numeral showed the letter to be used within the selected author's name. So that U35 revealed an 'I' from Alexina O'Cain while T41 was an 'F' plucked from Fiona Quillan.

He continued transposing the code. The message when revealed sent a shot of cold adrenaline through Nigel's body:

IF YOU'RE SMART ENOUGH TO READ THIS, BE SMART

ENOUGH TO PAY. LYLE MACPHATE COMES FOR HIS MONEY TUESDAY

Nigel leaned back in his chair, those spinning mirrored waters suddenly dizzying. A message from the past, one that stabbed at his heart, turned his skin cold and clammy. MacPhate's death brought fortune to Nigel. Now, years later, someone wanted payment for that long-ago-spent wealth.

He thought back to uneasy days. Gulped his whisky.

Nigel had arrived at Gill Hall for the first time in 1975, four years after MacPhate's death. Nigel's own writing proceeded slowly during that first residency until he discovered a complete manuscript stuffed inside a wall crack behind a study mirror. Why the notoriously secretive MacPhate had hidden it remained a mystery, but after sending out feelers to the publishing world, Nigel concluded the work and its subject were completely unknown outside these walls.

MacPhate's loss became his gain.

Nigel published the manuscript under his own name eleven months later. An international best seller, *Remembered Tomorrows*, made his career, brought him fame, women, riches. A series starring Brian Blessed premiered on *BBC One*. A movie adaption in America sold for sixty thousand dollars.

However, Nigel was never able to match this success. Sales of follow-ups, crafted by his own pen, were lukewarm at best, the reviews torturous. He became a "one-hit-wonder." A joke. A hack who somehow produced one masterpiece, then fell out of public favor.

The affairs dwindled. Nigel married for money, a tolerable enough arrangement until Daphne grew tired of supporting him. Now, her alimony to him paid his Gill Hall fees.

Nigel clung to *Remembered Tomorrows*. It was all that sustained him.

And now someone knew his one success in life was a lie.

* * *

"Mornin', sir," said Gillies, the courier for Hebrides Custom Delivery. "Did you enjoy your hike?"

"I did." Nigel sat on an oaken stump outside the Hall's gate, smoking his pipe. The old deliveryman approached by bicycle, his basket loaded with Monday parcels. The courier resembled an aging hippy forced to conform, with a salty grey ponytail flapping from behind his delivery cap and astrological tattoos peeking out of the cuffs and collar of his drab uniform.

"I even made Sgurr Mhairi. See me up there, Gillies?"

"No, sir."

"Then how do you know I was hiking?"

Gillies slowed to a stop in front of him, dismounted. "Why, I delivered those mountain boots to you weeks ago. Figured you'd put some wear on them, with the great scenery we have around here."

"Fair enough."

Gillies plucked a large parcel from his basket, offered him a pen.

"Another package for you, sir. Sign here, here, and here. Lots of papers for this one."

"Should be. It's a family heirloom." Nigel stood, took the package, and scribbled his name across the documents. "Old dueling pistol from my grandfather. World War One variety. Grandpapa shot some Austrian over Grandma's hand in marriage. Good thing for me he did."

"Dueling pistol? No wonder the special forms. What are your plans for it, sir?"

He looked at the courier blankly.

"Defend the family honor."

"Sir?"

"Kill things, Gillies. Kill whoever creeps over the Gill Hall gate after dark."

* * *

Three hours later, Nigel fired the family heirloom at stones along the gate wall, pretending they were the faces of Lyle MacPhate's collectors, peeking over at night.

He was a damn good shot, had been since his army days. His string of bulls-eyes remained unbroken until somebody shouted:

"Stop!"

Nigel turned to face the road. A burly constable emerged from a police cruiser two sizes too small for him.

"Good afternoon, Officer."

"Constable MacAskill," he said gruffly, a stern expression above his red whiskers. "You have a license for that handgun, Mr. Boorman?"

"I have a collector's permit to own rare firearms."

"But not a license to fire them?"

"No. Not in Scotland. Not since they changed the bloody law last year."

This answer troubled MacAskill. "Look, Mr. Boorman, I don't want to bring you in. I agree. Why should lawyers in London tell us what to do with our guns up here?" A slight smile appeared within the beard. "My family adores *Remembered Tomorrows*, you know. You've a Scottish perspective rare for a John Bull. Impressive."

"I'm obliged."

That smile expanded. "We've a small jail cell. You wouldn't like it. No writing desks. We even had Lyle MacPhate in for brawling back in his days. He had to dictate his work to an assistant through the bars. No room for two." He clasped Nigel on the shoulder. "So, stop shooting. All right? Mind that gun only as a collector."

"Certainly."

"Good. We'll chat soon. Sheep are blocking the A87 presently. Can't find anyone else to drive 'em. away." The officer retreated to his car.

A curious thought came to Nigel.

"Constable MacAskill," he shouted, "how did you know I was firing a pistol?"

"Heard the shots from the road."

When the squad car was lost behind the oaks, Nigel took one last shot at a stone on the wall, listened to the thin pop of his antique gun.

And wondered how anyone could hear it from the road.

* * *

Tuesday passed. Then five weeks without incident.

Nigel began to tentatively hope nothing would come of the message, prayed he'd made erroneous assumptions about the meaning of the ciphered note. Yet he remained uneasy at Gill Hall and spent his days in the village, writing until closing time at the local pub. Fear became his muse. A plot mimicking life came rushing up from his subconscious. At last, the words began to flow.

Nigel intended to finish the first draft late one Friday night, had the portable typewriter out of his backpack, but was pulled into a conversation with the local pub-goers. He bought them drinks, told the young Scots he was an author researching a detective novel set in Skye. The girl with the perfect bum wanted her copy as soon as it was published. He kept enough sobriety not to take her home.

Sometime past midnight, Nigel bicycled back towards Gill Hall. It was a cool night even for November, mist in the air, red Glamaig rising above all save the moon in the heavens. As he followed the edge of the Corbett around, the hills cut off the glow of the village behind. Ahead remained only the homestead lights of his nearest neighbor, Angus MacDonald—weren't they all MacDonalds out here?—and when that house was passed he found himself briefly peddling into darkness, navigating as much by the feel of the bicycle as by sight. He enjoyed sensing the changes of gravel, grass, and mud beneath his wheels, and it pleasantly startled him as it always did when he passed over the hard-stone bridge across the River Sligachan. Now and again he heard the bleating of sheep, and his eyes caught the shaggy shapes of Highland cattle grazing at the roadside.

At last the hills parted, and he saw the outline of distant Gill Hall, the porch lights turned on by his landlord's electric timer. Nigel expected this to be the only manmade illumination, but some hundred meters from the house, at the base of mighty Glamaig, the pinpoint light of a lantern shown. It rested in unsteady hands, or perhaps was buffeted by unfelt winds, for the light with its peculiarly red cast shook visibly.

As Nigel grew nearer the lantern went out.

He waited for it to relight as he rode up to the Gill Hall gate, but the lantern light did not return. Perhaps the owners were climbers attempting a nighttime ascent of Glamaig by moonlight alone. That seemed an ill-advised plan. He thought briefly of poor Alexina O'Cain, lying comatose for years in that hospital on the mainland. He briefly wondered what became of her manuscript here.

Nigel set the bike against the old stone wall, opened the gate, and was soon at rest in the mirrored study, the moonlight waters of the river swirling around him. A soothing scene that put him at ease as he composed at the typewriter...

Until a coffin rose up the wall.

For a fleeting moment, Nigel believed he'd nodded off, dreaming of impossible things. Or that somebody at the pub slipped a slow-acting narcotic into his beer. But the phantom coffin did not dissipate. It remained inside the room, as visible as his own hand before him. After climbing the waterfall, the casket floated across his ceiling and down the other wall.

At last Nigel comprehended. The bizarre sight was a reflection up from the river below, twisted by the funhouse mirrors about him. Gazing through the window, he saw the same coffin bobbing among the waters, carried by the current toward a rocky bend at the mouth of the oaken grove.

Up on Glamaig, that unsteady lantern light was shining again.

By the time Nigel exited the house and reached the river, the current had driven the coffin into the edge-water stones, the worm-eaten wood shattered like egg shells.

A skeleton thrown over the rocks.

DEEDS OF DARKNESS

Nigel's electric torch hid nothing. He saw the empty eye sockets, the long switchblade fingernails, and the rotten fabric of a jumper on the body, "Townsend Brewery" clear as day on the front.

Lyle MacPhate had come for his money.

* * *

"Vandals, Mr. Boorman," said Constable MacAskill, sitting in a Gill Hall chair, gently stroking the retreat's cat. "Someone's idea of a ghoulish joke. Diggin' up poor Lyle and dumping him in the river. We get sick ones out here sometimes. The vastness of the wilderness can affect the mind…"

"I think I was meant to see that corpse, Constable," said Nigel tersely, standing behind MacAskill's chair. "I'm certain of it."

"Why do you think so, Mr. Boorman?"

Nigel balanced answers and omissions. "MacPhate was an alumnus of Gill Hall. I'm in residency now…it seems a local has an axe to grind with this retreat. Wishes to drive me away. Probably some sad Skye writer rejected for a place."

"That's a flimsy reason to dig up a coffin, Mr. Boorman. And to deface MacPhate's grave especially. We love Lyle MacPhate out here. He's family to us. If someone means to discredit him, they're from the mainland. Probably not even Scottish."

"Who would trek all the way out here for a prank?"

"With motivation, men will travel anywhere, Mr. Boorman. But I doubt the defiling has anything to do with you personally." He shrugged. "If it did concern you, as you claim, would this tickle your blood?"

MacAskill withdrew a paper from his jacket pocket, a familiar pattern of letters and numbers written across the page:

A48 A21 O42 T44 S54 E15 E42 M41 N05 A23 S05 R27 O37
M53 F23 I22 U35 I27 C24 A12 Q53 U26 U27 S23 U05 I12 C54
S01 I21 O24 G55 U35 P54 E38 R28 B28 B47 A24 U24 H42 J42
O05 J12 I31 I32 I37 A33 C06 B05 K04 A14 O22 C05 U14 E41

B34 M27 H05 E16 P28 U46 F26 T47 A21 Z11 E31 J02

"I found it scrawled in chalk on MacPhate's gravestone near Achachork, Mr. Boorman. Can't make heads or tails of it. Any ideas?"

"Never seen anything like it."

"I read in your book bio, you were a cipher expert at university. Thought you might want first crack at it."

"It's gibberish from some juvenile hooligan."

"Looks like a code to me." The constable returned the page to his pocket, set the cat aside, and stood to leave. "I'll send it to Edinburgh next week. We'll keep you informed of any developments."

"Thanks."

"You leave that pistol in its case. Understand?"

"Of course."

"Where'd you get the gun, anyways?"

"I had it sent from home, had Gillies from the courier company bring it here."

"Gillies is a good man. But he reads his clients' mail. Lost his job at the Royal Mail for it. Spent a year in prison. Been working at different private delivery services since. If you need confidentiality, Mr. Boorman, don't have Gillies deliver anything."

"I'll remember."

"Good."

When Constable MacAskill was out the door, crossing the mossy stepping stones toward his police car, Nigel shouted:

"Will that cipher be published in the papers?"

"No time soon, Mr. Boorman. We don't want copycat crimes."

"Then do me a favor. Leave a duplicate of the script."

The constable smiled, returned to the cottage, and handed Nigel the note. "You can keep this copy if you agree not to publish it."

Nigel didn't publish it. But as soon as MacAskill was gone, he translated the script:

BRING FIFTY THOUSAND POUNDS TO GLAMAIG'S SUMMIT. ALONE. TEN AT NIGHT. SATURDAY.

* * *

Nigel Boorman's climb to Glamaig's summit was slow going that Saturday. Finding secure footing at night, with a creeping sea fog reducing visibility further, made the ascent tortuously slow. He arrived at Sgurr Mhairi late and found no one waiting. He loitered on the hilltop, more from fear of descent in such weather than any threat brought by his blackmailer.

Cold and tired, with despondent thoughts in his brain, Nigel sat on the rock pile that marked Lyle MacPhate's demise. A chance turn of his electric torch revealed a large stone chalked up with the Boorman name.

Girding his strength for whatever might come, he rose, approached the stone, and moved it aside. Beneath was a ram's horn, rimmed to serve as an alarm or musical instrument. Tape

affixed to the horn said, "Blow."

At least it wasn't another bloody cipher.

Seeing no alternative, he blew the horn. It echoed throughout the endless Highland night.

Nothing. He blew again. In some distant vale, dogs barked in response.

The second set of echoes had barely died away when a red glow appeared over the summit's edge, the source somewhere on the south face of Glamaig.

Nigel discarded the horn and withdrew the dueling pistol from his jacket pocket. Summoning his courage, he walked to the south edge of Sgurr Mhairi.

He was surprised as he looked down. The fog had thickened since his ascent, covering the lower section of the Corbett so that the hilltop Nigel stood upon seemed a perfect cone of red rock floating on an endless, grey-white ocean. The ridge that connected Glamaig with the other, lower Red Hills to the south was submerged below the fog level. Yet the figure of a man could be seen on that ridgetop, standing unmoving within the mists. He might have been invisible save for the red lantern shining brightly in his hands.

"You're late, Boorman!" came a voice from below. "Did you bring the money?"

"I did."

"Throw it down."

Adrenaline in his veins and hyperaware, Nigel noticed the lantern light was not directly upon him. Instead, the blackmailer's steady beam remained focused on the Corbett slope five meters below. Atop this summit, he must be little more than a shadow in his opponent's eyes.

Now was his chance.

Nigel raised the pistol. Fired three shots.

The man's body shuddered. The lantern fell and went out. The silhouette sunk into the fog below.

All went silent.

Pulse drumming in his ears, fingers trembling, Nigel reloaded his gun. Then he stood on the summit, his electric torch beam searching the mists. Nothing.

What now?

He could not assume his nemesis dead. Despite all instincts, Nigel trudged down to the ridge, enveloped within the surrounding fog. The dread of blundering blind off some precipice quickly eclipsed the fear of any wounded man. The ridgetop was saddle shaped, deep slants on either side dropping away to sheer cliffs. Beneath his mountain boots the scree shifted and slid, like walking on marbles, threatening to topple his balance with every step.

Nigel crept unsteadily along the ridge's center to the spot where the man had stood, his perception confirmed by the broken lantern just within his torch's range.

Yet there was no body. Pivoting on the unsteady surface, he rotated the beam outward—

There!

Down the western slope of the ridge, a man lay unmoving on the ground, the dark, bulky form resting where the incline fell away to a cliff.

Family honor, he thought. Nigel took a few cautious steps down the slope to make certain his blackmailer was dead.

He heard another's boots scraping over loose stones nearby. Heavy breath shifted the fog.

He started to turn, but a brutal shove sent Nigel toppling forward, chest and stomach hard against the ground, pistol jarred from his hand, the torch lens shattered into darkness.

Shock and pain were quickly replaced with horror. He was accelerating forward, sliding faster and faster down the blind slope. Nigel grasped at stones too small to slow his descent. He dug his fingers into the earth, the effort scraping away skin, tearing off nails, but it was too late, the momentum had grown beyond his power to stop. He plummeted through fog and night, sliding toward his death.

Seconds before Nigel Boorman went over the fatal edge, he glimpsed the body, passing near enough in his slide that even darkness and mist could not obscure the figure—the decoy—he'd shot from Sgurr Mhairi's heights.

The man was a straw scarecrow stuffed into an old delivery courier uniform.

* * *

"If there is anything more we can bring you, Miss Brown," said Gillies, handing the parcel to the latest writer-in-residence at Gill Hall, "please don't hesitate to call. I work all hours."

"It's kind of you," replied the East Anglia poetess, a censure in her gratitude. "But it's Ms. Brown. And I can visit the post office myself."

The courier chuckled. "As you will. But take the roads. Stay off the Red Hills, especially after dark. The scree is deadly slippery when it rains."

She thought of poor Nigel Boorman, two years earlier. "I'm no hiker."

"Wise. If you need letters or manuscripts routed, just give us a ring. We've delivered for all the Gill House greats—MacPhate, O'Cain, Boorman—"

"Goodnight, Mr. Gillies."

"Inspiration, Ms. Brown. I look forward to reading your work."

When Gillies had bicycled out of sight, and Sandra was certain the courier would not return, she left Mother's parcel in the kitchen and climbed the stairs to the "Cascading Study." Silently, tense for no real reason, she moved back the ancient-looking glass and withdrew the rolled papers wedged into a crack in the wall. The Gill Hall cat, its black form reflected in every mirror, watched Sandra unfurl the manuscript.

LESSONS OF SGURR MHAIRI

by

Nigel Boorman

It was a nearly complete manuscript. Easily the best thing Boorman had done in two decades. The publishing world, the revivalists needed to know...

Or should know. Sandra wondered if anyone else was aware of this novel-in-progress.

Dark possibilities hung on the edge of her consciousness. She could break into the prose fiction market at long last.... No more academia.... Who would know?

Sandra flipped toward the end to finish the epilogue interrupted by Gillies's arrival. Clipped to the last page was a scrap of paper, on it a bizarre series of characters:

U28 L53 A48 E44 O42 S23 I29 G45 G44 J51 R24 A33 I21 O42 M28 T27

The soon-to-be-infamous Sandra Brown did not solve the message's puzzle. Somehow, she never considered it a warning.

XIII

CLEOPATRAN COCKTAILS

Originally published in Ellery Queen's Mystery Magazine

Cleopatran Cocktails

I stare at my reflection in the jewelry case's glass. I'm not a young woman anymore. Lines in the forehead and under the eyes. A bit jowly at the cheeks. A middle-aged face if I'm honest. Well past time to do something with life.

> *Bob Beamon's leap lasted twenty-three years before being broken.*
> *Roger Maris's sixty-one home runs made it thirty-seven years.*
> *Dan Marino's passing yardage a mere twenty-seven.*

I could never break an athletic record. I'm terrible at sports as much as I love them.

Beneath the case's glass, on a lavender silk pillow, lies the Tabatskaya Necklace: a string of pearls conservatively valued at thirty million dollars. The third most expensive in the world.

So, here we go.

I glance over at this room's lone guard. Ronnie's away from his station, at the museum window as he always is on schooldays at this hour, waving down to his wife and son in the convertible. Her name is Joyce, the boy Jonathan. Ronnie introduced me last week.

A before-school tradition. Very sweet.

And it gives me an extra thirty feet.

I pull the hammer from my purse, smash the glass, seize the necklace. Alarms go off. People scatter. They don't know I'm unarmed.

Ronnie sees me. Shock in his face. The exhibition security is designed to keep thieves contained, each exit accounted for. Automatic iron doors descend over the windows and stairwell.

But I don't wish to leave.

I run towards a washroom. Not the ladies', but the handicap and baby-changing facilities. A sole occupancy bathroom. No stall. No surprises.

Ronnie is closing fast.

The race is on.

> *The Statue of Liberty, at 225 tons, is literally the biggest gift in history.*
> *A record that's lasted 131 years.*
> *No dice.*
> *I can't lift fifty pounds, can't afford even an Amazon gift card.*

> *The Thuggee strangler Behram killed 931, the last in 1840.*
> *A murder mark still standing 177 years later.*
> *I could never harm someone*

> *That Russian woman, Mrs. Vassilyeva, who bore 69 kids.*
> *Twins. Triplets. Quintuplets at every birth.*
> *The final set born in 1765. 252 years.*
> *That much time in labor?*
> *Forget it. I would rather harm someone.*

> *World records all.*
> *None even a millennium old.*

Ronnie won't pull the gun, it's there for defense, intimidation. He'll try and tackle me. But I've made the washroom. One small toilet. No interior walls, no stalls. One bolt to keep out the rest of the world.

I latch it. Hear Ronnie pound on the door.

He doesn't carry any keys. He'll call the office on the ground floor. Probably, five minutes to find the janitor. Three more to bring them up in the security elevator.

CLEOPATRAN COCKTAILS

I lower the diaper-changing platform, withdraw the Styrofoam cups, rubber mortar and plastic safety scissors from my purse. I remove the two heavy packets of vinegar from my ill-fitting C-cup bra. Clip the packet ends with scissors. Pour the liquid into the Styrofoam cups.

Cutting the necklace string, I slip the pearls onto the changing platform. Crush them to dust with the mortar.

The Gewandhaus Orchestra of Leipzig, Germany formed in 1743.
The longest running musical group in history at 274 years.
And you thought the Stones were old.

Swedish newspaper Post- och lnrikes Tidningar established 1645
Still published.
I can't write a word in another language.

The Nishiyama Onsen Keiunkan company of Japan, founded in 705.
1312 years.
A family-owned hotel for fifty-two generations.
Thirteen centuries of operation is impressive...
Millions upon millions of manhours.

I'll eclipse them all today.

As Ronnie beats on the door, and alarms blare outside, I brush the pearl dust into the cups, let it dissolve inside the vinegar. My stomach knots, and I feel a little dizzy as the priceless powder disappears within the murky liquid. Somehow, I forgot a spoon. I stir with my finger.

Then I drink the first cup.

And the second.

And third.

Most would gag at this much vinegar, but I've practiced months for this...The vinegar is acidic, the pearl remnants a natural balancing antacid.

No mistakes. I've waited millennia.

The door latch turns. Ronnie has obtained a key. Only one cup to drink.

> One morning in 41 BC, to impress her lover Marc Antony with her wealth, Cleopatra VII of Egypt dissolved a single great pearl earring in vinegar. By historian Pliny's account the pearl was worth ten million sesterces. Estimated value today? Fifteen million five hundred thousand dollars. Antony and Cleopatra shared the drink. An aphrodisiac. The most expensive breakfast in history. A record that lasted 2,057 years. Until now.

Ronnie throws open the door. Gun in his hand. A custodian and another guard at his side. They see the cups, the empty packets, the bare necklace string. Their eyes fix on the mortar. Confusion covers their faces.

I down the last cup.

Thirty million dollars for breakfast. None will ever think of little Janet Millsap as a listless unemployed divorcee from Panama City, Florida again. One whose life will pass unnoticed by history.

Now, friends, look upon the woman who surpassed Cleopatra, Queen of the Nile. As none has in two thousand years.

Today, forever, a record-breaker!

I lick the last of the pearl solution from my lips. Cleo was right. It is an aphrodisiac. Where is my Antony?

Somehow, I doubt poor Ronnie here is in the mood...

XIV

KUTSENKO'S CAGE

Originally published in Curiosities 3.

Kutsenko's Cage

1905, Odessa

There were two remarkable things about Doctor Kutsenko:
He was the most handsome man Tasia ever knew.
And he owned a cage.

He and *it* arrived one sunny spring morning while Tasia was down at the market shopping, her usual habit as Mother was away working in Yalta. When Tasia returned to their family's lodging house past noon, she found her sister in a grand mood.

"We've a lodger," said Eleni before Tasia stepped two feet into the house. "Arrived an hour after you left."

"A lodger?" asked Tasia as she set her basket on the parlor table. "No more lodgers while Mother's away. Remember what happened with the last one?"

"He's a doctor. And very charming. I've given him the second-floor room."

"Eleni, we can't live un-chaparoned with a man. The neighbors will think us a bordello."

"The neighbors *are* a bordello, Tasia."

"Yes, but…"

"And I'll wager even they don't pay four rubles a week."

"Four rubles a week?"

"In advance." Eleni withdrew the coins from her skirt pocket and presented them to Tasia.

"Four a week, my word…"

"Let me introduce you." Eleni gripped Tasia's hand and pulled her up the narrow stairwell to the second-floor landing. There the door to the spare room stood open. Inside was a man of no more than thirty-five, well-dressed in a felt suit and sparkling black shoes. He stood at the bedroom dresser, atop of which he had laid the tools of a doctor's trade on handkerchiefs. His head bent down as he organized the instruments, Tasia could see a sun-bronzed face furled in concentration, a strip of white skin at the hairline telling her he wore a hat outdoors. And when he turned those auburn eyes on her, Tasia wondered how she'd ever objected to such a striking man's presence in their home.

"Doctor Kutsenko," said Eleni. "Please meet my sister Anastasia."

"Call me, 'Tasia,' Doctor."

"Very glad to make your acquaintance." He bowed slightly. "Two such hospitable young ladies as landlords? How could I help but be pleased?"

"Doctor Kutsenko has just returned from quite a journey, Tasia," said Eleni.

"Oh?"

"Yes, six months on the Subcontinent." He said zestfully. "I was telling a few yarns in your parlor earlier, wasn't I, Eleni? Well, none I can't repeat to you Tasia, should we find the time."

Tasia found that she liked this educated, active and extremely good-looking man. She stepped from the shadows of the landing into the full light of the bedroom.

And Doctor Kutsenko frowned. "Are you twins? Eleni, you never mentioned…"

"Yes," said Tasia, feeling sheepish. "We are."

"But not identical. Eleni is a little taller, and your faces aren't quite the same—though both pretty, I should say."

"Whose is prettiest?" asked Eleni with an over-broad smile.

"Impossible to judge. It's like choosing between *Venus with a Mirror* and Melzi's *Flora* in the Hermitage. As soon as you pick one, the other calls your heart."

"Doctor, do you always flirt so with twenty-year-old landladies?"

"You misunderstand me, Anastasia. My interest is purely academic." He shook his finger as if to pretend to scold her. "Twins, you see, fascinate me scientifically. Identicals are best, of course, for long-term biological study, but fraternals have their value too." He pressed his fingertips together below his chin. "My eyes show me that you are similar. Now, if you will humor me, let your voices say how you are different."

The sisters stood in thoughtful silence for several moments to this strange questioning before Eleni, with a shrug, said, "Tasia can't cook."

"And Eleni *won't* cook," laughed Tasia. "She's lazy."

"I'll cook for polite people. I'll cook for *him!*"

"Ladies," Doctor Kutsenko said with a chuckle. "You show me your differences are far more than cooking."

Eleni laughed, and Tasia was about to join in when the edge of her eye caught motion somewhere in or around a trunk near the window.

Tasia blinked, unsure what she had seen. Nothing moved again, if it ever had. It was quite an odd trunk, really, large and perfectly cubical. A sail-like cloth was pulled tightly over its form. And was that the impression of bars beneath?

"Doctor Kutsenko, please pardon me for asking, but what is that…that structure underneath the tarp? A cage?"

"Yes. My specimen cage." He said without emotion. "Besides being a medical doctor and surgeon, I take interest in biological diversity in all its myriad forms. I regularly contribute to zoos and university collections throughout Europe." He sat back against the dresser, his hip disrupting the neatly aligned scalpels. "On this journey, though, I failed to gather anything of interest. The cage lies empty." He seemed to steel himself against the disappointment. "Much to the dismay of my backers, I should say. Still—Tut! Tut!—there are other ways to make money, aren't there?"

"I thought I saw movement inside."

"The bedroom window is open, and the breeze simply ruffles the cover."

"Oh."

"I helped him carry it in here," whispered Eleni. "It's too light, I think, to be anything but empty."

Tasia nodded.

After a pause, Doctor Kutsenko said, "Well, I really should return to my unpacking. As you raised the subject of cooking, Eleni, I'll remind you to please serve my dinners before four o'clock. Any later, and I have the ghastliest nightmares. A temperamental condition I've been cursed with since a child."

"Anything you wish, Doctor."

"And I'll mention to you, Tasia, in case your sister hasn't, that I intend to resume my medical practice now that I've returned to Odessa. As a surgeon, I may have callers at ungodly hours. I hope the sum I'm paying for this room offsets the inconvenience of a few bleary eyes. Can I depend on you and your sister to lend some small assistance when needed?"

"Of course, Doctor Kutsenko," said Tasia. "We would find it most interesting."

"Wonderful. We're all going to be great friends."

As they left the bedroom for the landing, he muttered: "Twins—such possibilities."

A step down the stairs, Eleni whispered: "Did you hear him, Tasia? He said we had possibilities."

"Possibilities for biological study."

"Marriage is a form of biological study, isn't it?"

"You've been reading those ladies' journals at the English Club, Eleni." Though Tasia couldn't help but wonder who the doctor might prefer…"He does seem very nice. But what do you think about that cage? Are you sure it's empty?"

"Not absolutely certain, of course. That cloth covers all of it, and it's fastened tight as a drum at the base. But, even so large, it was a feather when we carried it. It had to be empty."

"My mistake, I suppose."

They descended the last steps into the parlor. Tasia went to her market basket on the table and withdrew the newspaper she'd bought.

The war with Japan dominated the front page, but when she turned to the second, Tasia saw the inside headline:

ROSE THIEF STRIKES AGAIN

"Another robbery," she muttered.

"Where was this one?" asked Eleni, coming up behind to read over her shoulder.

Tasia read aloud:

" 'A trio of Repin masterwork paintings were stolen Saturday night from the Vorontsov Palace, three playing cards left in their places. Police believe the thief may be a foreigner, as the cards, which substitute the suit of diamonds with roses, are of Ottoman origin.'"

"Foreigner?" scoffed Tasia. "Anyone can buy those cards at the Privoz bazaar for a kopeck a pack. And they're Persian, not Ottoman."

"That article's slander. It doesn't mention anything about the charitable things the Rose has done. Leaving bundles of money—and those cards, again, old news here—at orphanages, churches, hospitals…"

"A pittance compared to what he's stolen, Eleni."

"He gives to those who need it. Like that famous English thief. 'Something…Hood,' wasn't it?"

Tasia tried to recall what she'd read in the London papers from the English Club. "'Hook,' I think it was."

"That's it!" Eleni snapped her fingers. "Hook! *Captain* Hook."

"Yes," said Tasia, flipping the newspaper page. "Well, let's hope your Captain Hook leaves a little money around here. We could use some good luck…"

* * *

Sometime past four in the morning an exhausted Tasia opened their front door. A man outside in a hooded cape stepped forward, the cowl pulled so low she could only see his thin lips and stubbly chin. With a metallic scent in his breath, he said:

"Is Doctor Dikopavlenko here?"

"Dikopavlenko?" repeated Eleni, standing behind Tasia, a kitchen knife hidden in her robes. "Who's he?"

"We've a Doctor Kutsenko," said Tasia firmly. "Is that who you want?"

"That'll do." The man lurched hard against the door, knocking Tasia from the threshold and forcing himself into the house. Both women shouted, and Eleni readied the knife, yet the effort of barging inside sapped this stranger of his strength. He toppled forward, Tasia barely able to catch him before he hit the floor.

"Eleni," she said, straining to keep the big man up. "Help me."

Eleni pocketed her knife and slipped an arm under his shoulder. They both shouted for the doctor.

He was already on the stairwell. "Take him up to my room."

"He's bleeding," said Eleni.

She was right. Red droplets were falling from inside the hood, some landing on Tasia's bare feet as they hauled him across the parlor. Doctor Kutsenko joined them at the stairs, hoisting the man up, half across his shoulders as they climbed the steps. Eleni had an arm and Tasia a leg, but it was like carrying nothing. The Doctor ably shouldered the load alone.

When they reached Kutsenko's room, they set the wounded man down on the bed, propped his head upon a stack of pillows. The doctor pushed back the hood.

Eleni, not at all squeamish, let out a breath.

The remnant of a wine bottle protruded from his opened skull, the cylindrical shard lodged just above the cheekbone and encompassing all the right eye socket. Dried blood covered his face and neck, new crimson seeping over the pillows.

"Doctor…"said the man, his one visible eye cloudy and distant. "I…"

"Artur Kutsenko," replied their tenant.

"I can't pull it out. Something's hooked in there, Doc."

The doctor patted the man on the shoulder, then moved to the dresser to select his instruments. He silently shuffled through them for a moment, lifting a wiry hook and something resembling rose prunes, before he glanced at the girls:

"Eleni, Tasia, please close the door on your way out. This is no scene for young ladies."

* * *

"You saved his life."

"I can't say that for certain, Tasia. Only that procedure went better than expected."

"How could a man in such dire condition walk out of here so alert and seemingly in good spirits a day or so later?" Standing in Doctor Kutsenko's airy, morning bedroom, Tasia folded up the stained sheets on which the patient had lain for two days before leaving. "Doctor, you are a miracle worker."

"Hardly. What I did most competent surgeons could have done if they applied themselves." His voice turned gruff. "It's only that they *won't*."

She looked at him curiously, folded the last sheet.

"You see, Tasia, this twentieth century we've entered has no limitations, scientific or otherwise. Daring medical practitioners—those outside the conservative schools of the establishment—can mend tissues, cure ills our forbearers never dreamed possible. We are not far, I think, from keeping the Reaper at bay forever. A worthy man, if properly maintained by his lessers, may live indefinitely. Are you open-minded, Tasia?"

"I think so."

"Let us see." He began to unbutton his shirt.

"Doctor Kutsenko!"

He laughed. "Nothing of that sort, Tasia. Observe..." Turning away from her, he pulled out the tails of his shirt, then hoisted it up to his shoulders. In the center of his back, on either side of his spine, were two thick oval scars. "I live on the kidneys of another man. Two, in fact."

She'd never heard of such things..."Is that possible?"

"If it weren't, I wouldn't be standing before you now." He let the shirt down, turned back to her. "A surgeon living along a remote tributary of the Ganges performed the first operation, the second was in Peking by a soon-to-be-murdered physician loyal to Prince Qing. Great men, great methods chased into the shadows even in their own nations by centuries of imperialism. I learned the methods from my benefactors. Now, I return the favor to those in need."

It seemed something out of Verne or Wells…"Are there any drawbacks?"

"Only moral. But if it saves lives…"

"Then it's worth it."

"Yes. We are similar, aren't we, Tasia? You can inform Eleni, if you wish, but please keep this conversation within the household. The closed-minded, you see…I won't let men die, Tasia, waiting for some committee of medical bureaucrats to say what I do is permissible. I'd rather take the risk, than lose the great man."

So brave…"You're not a criminal, Doctor Kutsenko. You're an angel."

"Well, some might say. But angels have wings on their backs, not scars." He tucked in his shirttails. "Anyway, it's well past time you called me 'Artur.'"

"Artur."

"And it's you, Tasia, who may yet see the angels. Angels in the architecture along Yekaterininskaya Street, that is. I invite you for a city-center stroll and fine dining tomorrow night. Unencumbered by your sister, of course."

This surprised Tasia, nervous butterflies fluttering about her stomach. "I think such…such…meetings with our male lodgers are against the rules, Artur."

"Oh. You are certain, then?" His disappointment was palpable, more than a hint of offense in his tone.

Tasia felt a silly girl. She was twenty, after all, without any serious suitors. What had he said? *I'd rather take the risk than lose the great man…*

Stop being such a prude, Tasia.

"Of course, as you say, Artur, rules are made to be broken. Mother might never know."

KUTSENKO'S CAGE

* * *

Tasia flipped another page in *Tess of the d'Urbervilles*.

"Where have you been all night?"

Eleni tossed her umbrella in the door basket, stripped off her raincoat. "The Medical College Library."

"To nearly ten o'clock?"

"I've been checking surgeons' registries." She hung the coat on the wall peg. "There's no listing for a Doctor Kutsenko in Odessa or the whole oblast."

"He never claimed to be a *registered* surgeon."

Eleni pushed over a footstool, then sat down on the divan next to Tasia. "But there *was* a listing for a Doctor Isa Alexandervich Dikopavlenko, Practicing Surgeon, in three consecutive volumes. Until he was expelled by the Medical Council in December 1900."

"Why?"

"The registry didn't say."

Tasia shut her book. "Artur's a good tenant, Eleni. Why are you suddenly so skeptical of him? You saw him save that man with a bottle through his eye."

"I did. A man who called him 'Dikopavlenko.'"

"A man with a head injury. He might have called Artur anything in such a state."

"Including his actual name. I don't trust a doctor living under an alias. How many tragedies have we suffered because of lodgers with false identities?"

"Are you sure, Eleni, this change of heart regarding Artur isn't merely jealousy? A bit of envy because a handsome surgeon asked me to dinner tomorrow night instead of you?"

"You know that's not true."

"I wonder. One of our tenants has shown interest in me, for once, and now you—"

It was more a bleating than a scream, like the cries of some dying animal echoing up from the Feliski slaughter yards. In an instant, both sisters were sprinting up the stairs to the second floor. The cries came from their tenant's room.

"Doctor Kutsenko," shouted Eleni, pounding on the door. "What is happening in there?"

There was a rustle inside, then something like the clinking of metal on glass. The metallic sound repeated, and the screams—whatever they were—subsided. Heavy footsteps followed, then Doctor Kutsenko tore open the door. He stood in his robe, hair disheveled, face night swollen.

"Artur," said Tasia. "Is everything all right?"

"Nightmares!" He half-screamed. "Eleni, why did you tempt me with the chocolate mousse past six? You know I can't have food at night."

"You ate it well enough."

"Well, I'm sorry for the screams. It was a manifold vision even Goya could not slumber through. I should think that I shall not disturb you anymore tonight, though. I've taken a sedative." He began to shut the door.

"Isa Alexandervich!" shouted Eleni.

He paused. "Why do you call me 'Isa'?"

"To see what you would do."

There came a knocking from downstairs.

"The front door," said Tasia. "At nearly ten..."

"Another emergency, perhaps," said the doctor wearily. He locked his own door, and the three of them descended the stairs together. When Tasia opened the front door, the same man in the hooded cape was on their step, his eyes clear and stern. Tasia noticed for the first time he had *heterochromia*, one iris blue, the other, the one in the socket where the bottle had been and now encircled by a ring of Doctor Kutsenko's stitches, was dark brown.

"Doctor," he said. "Your assistance is required."

The doctor nodded—and it seemed to Tasia that some unspoken communication passed between the two men. Their tenant returned to his room. In moments, he was back down the stairs, dressed in a tan waistcoat, medical kit in hand. "I've disturbed you enough tonight. Please don't wait up, ladies."

"As if we would, Isa," said Eleni.

Tasia watched from the door as the pair climbed into a horse-drawn buggy and sped away into Odessa's night.

* * *

"It's nearly eight o'clock, Artur," said Tasia, looking through the menu at elegant Fanconi's Café in the city center. "You'll eat too late…"

He laughed at this, glancing up from his own menu with those mesmerizing eyes. "I'll risk a few nightmares for a scrumptious meal at last, Tasia. Not that your sister's cooking isn't enjoyable, but…"

"No apologies. No one eats Eleni's dishes. I've lost so much weight since Mother's been gone… This dress hardly fits me…"

"Well, I think you look elegant." He said and his gaze lingered on her figure.

"Thank you." Tasia felt herself blushing at the compliment and wondered if he could tell. To be out, free and un-chaperoned with a man like Artur at Falconi's, the legendary "hanging gardens" restaurant where the tycoons and nobility of the Russian Empire dined…. Simple ethnic Greek girls of Tasia's class never ate here. She probably couldn't even merit work at Falconi's as a dishwasher…and these prices…

"Artur…our meal will cost three weeks rent. With the war, food is so expensive, it is not fair to you—"

"I have the means, Tasia. Enjoy yourself."

She nodded. Yet, his answer begged another question. One that perhaps should not be asked, but the wine in the park before dinner had made Tasia brave and improper: "If you've monies available, Artur, then why do you stay at so simple a place as ours? Why not a fancy hotel? Or purchase a home?"

He frowned, a firmness in his response that made Tasia regret her question. "Isn't it evident? My work demands a residency off the 'society' path. At least until the medical boards de-criminalize my methods." He took a long drink of his merlot and it seemed to Tasia his hand gripped the wine glass very tightly. "Every year I make overtures, always I am rejected. Idiots! How many Russian elite will die in this conflict with Japan whom I might have saved? If my techniques were applied these brave officers would still breathe."

"Only officers? Surely all soldiers could benefit?"

"Of course, of course," he drank more wine, "the heroic deserve to keep what is born theirs. But the supply must come from somewhere, Tasia. The common soldier will lay down his life on the battlefield for his commander. Is it much different to make that same sacrifice in a hospital bed? We'd win this war if men like Admiral Vitgeft had been given another spleen."

Tasia wondered if she was misunderstanding these rather curious words...."These skills of yours, Artur, do many others have them?"

"No white man does. I can say that for certain. The Swiss and French, leaders here, can only stew in their juices with envy. Racists! Jingoists! They fail to look East. The Chinese surgeon Bian Que was performing organ replacement centuries before Christ's birth, as was the great Indian physician Suśruta. The chaos of imperialism has pushed the knowledge to the corners of their societies, to hidden schools in lost grottos and Himalayan valleys seldom trod by Europeans. But they can be found by an intrepid scholar-adventurer who dares- and I am the one who has done so. When they told me my kidneys were failing, I sought legendary places. If I live by a transplant, others here can too."

"And Odessa is very glad you're alive. As am I."

He did not smile. "Well, Odessa will be. Soon. That I guarantee you. If we...."

His words were interrupted by a looming presence within the restaurant. The head waiter led a tall, serious-looking police constable past them to a fine-tailored elderly gentleman alone at the next table.

"You are Baron Kurakin? Owner of the Osmanov Warehouses?" asked the waiter.

"What is it?" replied the old man sternly, as if the waiter should know to whom he spoke. "Why do you interrupt my soup?"

"I'm sorry, sir," said the constable stepping forward, a tremor in his voice despite his towering size. "But there is a problem at your warehouse property. Our men have cornered the Rose Thief and his gang. We are breaking down the doors."

"At last," said the baron. "We'll kill that rogue, yet."

* * *

Arm-in-arm Tasia and Artur walked above the seaside along Nikolaevsky Boulevard, a perfectly paved street skirting the edge of the Odessan Plateau; the gilded roofs and wrought-iron gates of palaces and mansions to their left, a viewing wall overlooking the harbor on the right. And, far above the branches of the white acacias lining the roadside, floated oriental lanterns launched from one of Odessa's many great plazas ahead. They lit up the April night sky, a manmade constellation of glowing orange orbs flying over the city, slowly being carried away by the winds to cast their lights on the dark waters of the Black Sea.

Tasia had never seen a more beautiful night.

Yet her escort possessed a different view. "All these Oriental lamps," said Artur looking high into the heavens, "it is an ill omen for this struggle with Japan. We will lose this war…"

Tasia patted his arm. "They are Chinese lanterns, not Japanese. Take them as signs your work will be accepted…"

"What a pleasant interpretation. You are a remarkable woman, Anastasia Karadopoulina."

"Hardly."

He kissed her—a moment before she knew he would.

"Artur…we are un-chaperoned."

"This is what un-chaparoned people do, Tasia. Have you never been alone with a man?"

She pushed him away gently, unsure if she wished to…"People will see us."

"Maybe another kiss when we are home?'

"Eleni will be there."

"You can't hide behind a sister forever. Is she as chaste with her sweethearts as you?"

"You and I mustn't be in the same house, Artur. If you wish to court me, you might find other lodgings."

"I'll do so, Monday morning."

"It's best."

They walked, silently holding hands for a few minutes. Tasia unsure of her own intentions... He was handsome, and a healer, but some of his recent words unsettled her. She'd ask Eleni. Jealousy aside her sister was always truthful. Blunt and tactless but truthful.

After several minutes, the Chinese lanterns fading to mere pinpoints over the sea, they passed into a plaza with the great neo-classical statue of Duke de Richelieu, and Odessa's famous Boulevard Staircase descending forever down to the harbor. At the top of these mighty steps, a portly police constable stood watch.

"Is it over?" Asked Artur as they passed through the plaza. "Did they catch the Rose at last?"

The constable shook his head. "Word is, he slipped away once again, sir, curse 'em. Twenty men with that devil at bay, and still he escaped. We took a few of his men, though."

"You'll never finish him. Not with our best off at war. And oafs like you left to mind the house."

"Well, never mind the war, sir. We aren't so incompetent as you say. There *was* blood on the road stones afterwards, some of our bullets found their marks. It didn't drop the devil, but it may take the bloom off the ole Rose, yet."

"I'll keep my wager on the great man."

"As you wish, sir."

After they'd exited the plaza, leaving the offended constable far behind, Tasia asked: "You admire the Rose Thief, don't you, Artur?"

"I admire his willingness to go outside the law for what is right, what is needed." His voice dropped to a whisper then, his words so low Tasia wondered if she was supposed to hear what was said next.

"And I understand his obsessions. God help me."

* * *

When they returned home, they found the front door ajar and the lodging house empty.

"Eleni!" shouted Tasia.

But there was no answer.

"It's unlike her to leave the premises unlocked," continued Tasia, checking the back courtyard for her sister.

"My door is open as well," said Artur, peering up the stairs to the landing above. "Someone's been in my room."

"Eleni would never invade a tenant's privacy."

"The evidence would suggest otherwise, Tasia," he said tersely and began to ascend the stairs, when something stopped him…

A man had appeared in the front door.

"Doctor Dikopavlenko!" shouted this visitor. Tasia half-expected it would be the familiar hooded patient. Instead, this new caller was stockier, slightly older, dressed in a long black coat and red bowler hat. "We need your help!"

Artur stepped back, down to the parlor. "What help?"

The man stared at Tasia, "Is the lady…?"

"She's with me," said the doctor. "Speak freely."

"They shot the boss through the liver, Doc. He don't have long, lest you can do something. Can you come with me?"

"I'll get my surgeon's tools. I'll need your help to take everything. It's none too heavy. I've only one left."

The man in the bowler grunted an affirmative, and the two climbed the stairs to Artur's room, Tasia trailing behind. There followed a whirlwind of activity as the doctor collected his blades, saws, and medicine bottles from the drawers and dresser tops, only pausing when he remarked about missing a scalpel.

"Doc, we got no time," said the other man. "The boss is half in his grave as is."

With his satchel pinned beneath one arm, Artur and this visitor lifted the cage from the floor, hefting it past Tasia as they went from the bedroom to the landing.

It seemed to her something moved within. An inkling, an irrational suspicion, came to her then that somehow equated the motion inside with her missing sister. It made no sense, yet Tasia still found herself reaching out a hand to lift the tarp's edge…

Artur slapped it away.

"We've no time for that, Tasia! A man is dying."

"What's in there, Artur?"

"Later!"

This resistance only increased her fears. They were halfway down the stairs, Artur first, bearing most of the weight of the cage when Tasia gritted her teeth and grabbed at the covering again.

The man in the bowler struck her hard in the jaw with his elbow. Tasia, lost her balance, slid down the few remaining steps to the parlor's floor, more stunned than injured. The men sped by her, carrying the cage through the room and out the front door.

"I'm sorry, Tasia. That was uncalled for," said Artur as they stepped into the street. "He'll live to regret that. I assure you as a gentleman."

Through the opened doorway, she could see them slide the cage into the back of a black horse-drawn van. The two men shut the rear door, then went around to climb into the seats at front.

Her wits returning, Tasia rushed to her feet, reached the doorway. The van was just pulling out into the night.

"I'll explain everything, Tasia, soon," shouted Artur from the passenger seat. "You'll forgive me, I know. If you're a woman worthy of love, then you'll forgive. But, now, a brave man is at risk…"

As the van distanced itself, that cage moved again, independent of the shuddering of the carriage over the street stones. She knew then. Knew whom that cage contained.

"Eleni!" Tasia sprung from the front step and sprinted after the van. "Eleni!

"I'm here!" came a shout behind. Tasia turned around to see her sister and three police constables running up the street towards her.

The sisters embraced, Tasia whispering, "Thank God, thank God."

"Where's Doctor Kutsenko? Where is that cage, Tasia?"

She pointed up the road.

"Is the cage empty?"

"No."

A moment later the constables were lost in the gloom of night, last seen in a vain pursuit of the van. The sisters returned to their home.

Under the lamplight of the parlor, Tasia could see Eleni looked impossibly tired, lines in her forehead, shadows beneath her eyes. She appeared ten years older than she had this afternoon. Though her own jaw stung, and was quickly swelling, Tasia felt the need to comfort her sister. But Eleni wanted nothing—no tea, no food, no blanket. Only to sit on that parlor chair, head in hands, and recover her strength.

"Tell me what happened," Tasia finally said softly.

"Don't you know?"

"How could I?"

Eleni lifted her face, eyes red and puffy. "Then you didn't see? You haven't seen?"

"I've seen nothing."

Tapping some new well of strength, Eleni moved her chair closer, leaning a shoulder against Tasia, as if she needed physical support to tell of her tale. Finally, she told her story in the hoarse, cracking voice of a much older woman.

* * *

Eleni's Encounter

"I had been alone some hours this evening when I heard those familiar cries coming from our tenant's room. The long, shrill, bleating sounds he says he makes in his sleep when the nightmares come. But Doctor Kutsenko was away—out courting you, Tasia. Who or what then was up there? I listened to those shrill screeches for only a few seconds before I seized the spare key from the cabinet, and with lighted candlestick in hand, climbed the steps to the landing before the doctor's room. Only then did I pause, Tasia. The noise was horrifying, like a despondent creature awaiting the fall of a butcher's axe. It took all my will to slip the key into the lock and turn the bolt. As I opened the door, the cries went silent. Whatever made those noises was aware of me, knew I was inside the room with it. After those incessant shrieks, the quiet itself somehow became frightening.

At first glance, the bedroom appeared undisturbed, exactly as it had been when Doctor Kutsenko was present. I used the candlestick to light the chamber lamps. The doctor's wardrobe was open, few clothes hung inside, and I could see that nothing of any size dwelt there. Of course, my attention went to that covered cage by the window. As I grew closer, and the boards creaked beneath my feet, an impression appeared underneath the tarp, as if a hand, or perhaps a face, were pressed against the fabric, trying to peer through. It quickly faded. I stared for several moments, but the face—if had been a face—did not return. Still, I pulled one of Doctor Kutsenko's scalpels from the top of his dresser and kept it ready as I approached the cage. Gripping the pen's corner at a full arm's length, I shook it slightly, then harder. Nothing moved underneath, though it seemed weighted down, heavier than when I'd helped the doctor carry it in a week ago."

Tasia brushed her sister's hair with her fingers, feeling the perspiration, the warmth of great emotion on her skin. "I observed him carrying the cage tonight, Eleni. Artur has a way of bearing all the weight. It might seem light to you no matter the contents."

"Could be. Could be, Tasia. All I knew at that moment alone up there was that the cage was too heavy *now* to be empty. Keeping the scalpel ready, I hiked up the end of the tarp nearest me. What I saw inside drove waves of revulsion through me, sick, primal emotions that sent me scampering back a few steps. They didn't last, Tasia. Thank God. As I recovered, a terrible pity took my soul. It was a boy inside, maybe fifteen or sixteen, emaciated, wearing only a loin cloth. I couldn't tell his race or ethnicity, I could see little of his features for he was huddled at the other end of the pen back to me. His face in profile, peering over his own shoulder, I could see but one terribly-pained intelligent dark eye staring back at me. Oh, the poor creature. On the boy's back ran a thin, oval scar outlining where his left kidney must be. Or must have been. His bare skin too was pockmarked by countless needle scars, he must have spent this last week, or much longer, drugged into delirium. The boy was the saddest sight I've ever seen. And there were signs, Tasia, hints that the cage's population wasn't always so sparse. That perhaps two or even three souls might have occupied it recently. I didn't attempt to communicate with the prisoner. I wasn't thinking then. I knew only that I wished to free him. I quickly found a set of keys in the drawer of the wardrobe, trying the members until I discovered one that fit. I opened the padlock, pushed the tarp higher, and pulled open that door. The captive stirred at the motion, turning towards me, tentatively at first, but faster as he gained resolve. As he did so, more of his form became visible. His chest and stomach were covered in those damnable uniform, deliberate scars. Scars made not by some terrible accident, but by the precision of a surgeon's knife. He had prominent mark at his throat, but the most gruesome lay at the face. His other eye, the one initially hidden by his posture, was missing. Instead, the eyelid over the socket was pulled tight and flat, a fresh suture along the upper cheek holding it in place forever. No bulge of any eyeball remained beneath. It had been removed, Tasia. All these horrors I grasped for but a moment. The boy crawled forward to the opening, face nearly in mine, and tried to speak. But only the hideous bleat erupted from his lips. It was no foreign language, something had been taken. His speech stolen from him.

"I lost my composure then, Tasia. I dropped the scalpel, it fell beside the cage, but, I failed to retrieve it. Instead, I tugged down the tarp, blocked the sight of him, fled out the room and down the stairs as those blaring bleating cries erupted from behind. It was a cowardly act, I admit. By the time, I reached the parlor I'd regained *some* of my senses. That creature, that poor boy out of a Mary Shelley nightmare, was not the monster. He was a victim. Doctor Kutsenko was the true monster. And then I thought of you. That devil Kutsenko was somewhere in this city with my sister. I panicked then. I didn't know what he might do to you out there, Tasia. He might have a dozen flats, a dozen cages… I fled the house searching for a policeman. When I returned, you were here, and I'm grateful to Mary, Jesus and Saint Symeon that you are. But that tragic child…. Why would he cut him up like that?"

"He's a harvestman, Eleni. But if I told you what that fiend was harvesting, you'd never believe me. The possibilities—and the horrors—of the twentieth century are endless."

She looked at me. And she knew.

* * *

The police found the van less than an hour later. It was off on a side street near Frantsusky Boulevard, the horses standing calm, the carriage quiet, the rear door ajar. The driver, his red bowler floating in a pool of crimson on the floor, had fallen onto the leads when he died, pulling the reigns tight and slowing the obedient stallions to a standstill. His throat, like Doctor Kutsenko's next to him, had been slit from behind by "a precise instrument well-suited for the task." The police suspected the weapon was one of the surgeon's own scalpels. In the van, a cage was found empty with the door open, the remnants of a shredded tarp nearby inside.

The murderer of Doctor Kutsenko and his associate has never been found.

XV

MURDER WITH A FLICK OF THE WRIST

Originally published in Ellery Queen's Mystery Magazine

Murder with a Flick of the Wrist

I

Latvia

The most dangerous day of Santa Ezeriņa's life began with the exclamation: "Wait until I get my bra on!"

"The camera won't be pointed at you, my little sunshine," said her lover Geofreys, turning the DSLR on its tripod and focusing it towards the one windowless wall of the cottage bedroom. "It'll only be me."

"In your briefs?"

"I'm only filming waist up." Geofreys pinned his largest quilt to the wall, the one in EU colors with "Euro Critic" embroidered upon it in gigantic lettering. "Do you think that's straight?"

"Straight enough," Santa answered, tiptoeing around the empty champagne bottles and opened food containers to find her blouse and jeans. Her head still spun from last night. This wasn't how she'd envisioned a romantic weekend in the Sigulda countryside. Happy birthday, indeed.

"Do you really have to do this now, Geofreys? I haven't even showered."

"Sunshine, the movie opened *yesterday* in America. If I don't get this review up, other Internet critics will steal my viewers." He watched her as he buttoned a plaid shirt over his bare chest. "Two million subscribers, Santa. Two million, and we're set."

"You're set," she said softly, pulling on her clothes.

"Santa… It's my work." He paused, gathering his courage. "And I need you to go outside. I can't shoot my video with you watching me."

"Thousands of people will be watching you on the Internet, Geofreys."

"Not while I'm making it, sunshine. I'm shy."

Santa pulled on her boots, stuffed her hair into a knit cap, and fetched her jacket. *If he calls me "sunshine" once more...*

Geofreys settled himself onto a chair in front of the Euro Critic quilt, finger-combed his sandy blond hair into place, and blew Santa a kiss. "Press 'record' on your way out, my sunshine."

She did not press record on her way out. Instead, Santa stepped out onto the front step, shutting the door behind with enough force that snow from the overhanging roof tumbled down over her cap and shoulders, the ice slithering into her jacket collar to freeze her neck and back.

Nice work, sunshine, she thought.

Santa sighed, felt the bite of winter air, and stared out over the sloping landscape. Their cottage rested midway up a steep, snow-covered hillside, the surrounding peaks and high ridges of the Sigulda wilderness breathtaking under a morning sun. The "Switzerland of Latvia," they called the Sigulda region, though these "mountains" were mere high hills really, closer in scale to the highlands of Scotland than the incomparable Alps. Still, in winter, it was a romantic enough place, perfect for lovers of the outdoors, or lovers who stayed *indoors* and wanted true seclusion for their amours. Another world only forty-five minutes from the tensions of political, conflicted Rīga.

Santa dug through her jacket and found a crushed packet of cigarettes. She'd thought she'd quit, but why not make this weekend a complete return to hedonism? She pulled a stick match from the pocket and lit up.

That's better.

More relaxed, she took a few steps away from the cottage into the knee-deep snow. After the shuttered darkness of the house, the sunlight and unending whiteness burned Santa's eyes, and she squinted hard to focus her surroundings. A virgin snowfall last night had covered everything. Mother's Toyota, borrowed for the weekend, was little more than a boxish outline down by the road, and the hill's only other structure, an old manor house from the days of the Baltic-German lords, looked like something out of a fairy tale themed snow globe: pointed towers, dark stone walls, all under a glaze of New Year's ice. Walt Disney would have approved.

Santa released a slow breath and watched the tobacco smoke rise in the air. She wondered if their little leased cottage had once been a guesthouse or servant's quarters for the larger estate. It was obvious there was no renting the bigger house now. "Private Property" and "No Trespassing" signs surrounded the great manor, written in four languages and posted prominently.

Santa didn't need her reporter's instincts to conclude that the manor's owners preferred solitude, so she was genuinely surprised when a little man waved from one of the doorways in the great house and then hurried across the lawn to the main gate.

"Good morning!" he said enthusiastically, entering and exiting the gatehouse and trudging through the snow towards Santa. "Fine day for January, isn't it?"

"Global warming, I think," she said with a smile. "I blame the Americans."

"And I'll thank them if it gives us more days like this!"

He was an older man, the sort of regal fellow who looks better at sixty than he must have at thirty. His thick grey-black hair was gelled back, and a thin beard surrounded a large mouth from which hung the curved shape of a lighted briarwood pipe. His attire was the selection of beiges and tweeds Santa expected in a wealthy country gentleman, though the knee-high rubber boots he wore as he fought through the snow stole a little of the dignity in his demeanor.

Santa instantly liked him. A cache of goodwill well needed when the stranger reached her and said:

"And how was the lovemaking last night? Did you both climax?"

"Did…I…we…?"

"These mountain winds carry every sound. No secrets up here, my dear!" he said with a laugh that made it almost all right. He cupped his ear. "And now your lover is telling another guest—in English—that he was disappointed with the latest Daisy Ridley film. Am I right, my young friend?"

Santa smiled despite herself. "He's doing a videocast for the Internet—alone."

"Ah, buggers!" The old fellow snapped his fingers. "I should've known, should've known. Yes, you'd never have a guest in such a small cottage during a night of passion, and there are no tracks in the new powder for a visitor to arrive this morning. He had to be alone!"

"Elementary, my dear Watson," said Santa, throwing away the cigaret.

"Not Watson, but I am a doctor. Dr. Peters Balodis, inventor." He extended his hand. Santa shook it. "And now that you've punctured my detective persona, a confession! It's not the winds that carry information. We've audio amplification and detection equipment all over the estate. You never know who might slink by in the night."

Santa frowned. "Whom are you expecting?"

"Whom did Faust expect in his last days, my dear?"

"Hello!" shouted a voice behind them.

Santa turned to see Geofreys on the cottage step. He'd donned his trousers but was still barefooted. Without a care for the elements, he bounded over to them, a wide smile on his face.

"Your feet will freeze," Santa said.

"It's good for the circulation, sunshine," he replied with a wink. He shook Dr. Balodis's hand. "Geofreys Aboltins, film critic. The Internet's twenty-second most-viewed and rising."

Dr. Balodis laughed. "Well, that's practically royalty, my friend." He looked from Geofreys to Santa. "Then come into my abode. The staff is still on the New Year's holiday, but I can fix a…"

A clear plastic beach ball skittered across the snow to land near them.

"What's this?" exclaimed Geofreys, and he took a step closer to the ball. Santa immediately saw it wasn't right. The sphere's skin looked sturdier than a typical beach ball, and in the center rested two black cylinders, a digital readout between them.

Dr. Balodis grabbed Geofreys' shoulder, shoved him to the ground, then turned to Santa. "Get aw—"

Sound ceased. Santa saw the blue of the Sigulda sky, red streaks over the snow, and then her body hit that cottage wall harder than she'd ever hit anything before.

II

Somewhere, someone said: "She's awake."

In a rush, sound and movement existed again, consciousness preceding awareness by mere heartbeats. Santa found herself staring up at the ceiling lights from a hospital bed, a Styrofoam cup filled with water in her hand, a yellow straw sticking out. Her lips were wet, cool droplets on her chin, yet she had no memory of the drink she must have taken only moments before. Santa set the cup on the tray at her bedside, the motion of lifting her arm an agony, everything twisted inside her body. As she released the cup, Santa noticed her normally cheery fingernails had been shattered.

She wondered how this happened.

A plump, fifty-ish woman in a nurse's uniform appeared above her, leaning slightly over the bed to take Santa's hand. Her thick palms smothered Santa's fingers, eclipsing her broken nails.

"How do you feel today?" asked the nurse.

"Everything hurts," Santa said, surprised at the clarity in her own voice.

"Any nausea? Dizziness?"

"No... I don't think so."

The nurse patted her hand. "You'll be fine, dear. The doctor will be in shortly."

"Can she hold a conversation, Nurse?" asked a masculine voice just out of view. Santa tried to turn her neck to see the speaker, but shards of pain rose up her spine. Indeed, *now* there was nausea.... Santa closed her eyes, tried to right the spinning world. In her self-imposed darkness, she heard the nurse reply: "The doctor should evaluate her. Head trauma like this..."

"Run and fetch the doctor, then," answered the gruff voice.

"One moment, Inspector."

The nurse's footsteps trailed away.

Santa lay there a moment gathering her strength. When she at last opened her eyes, a square-jawed, diminutive man of about thirty was staring down at her. He looked familiar, rather like a young Peter Falk from television.

"You're a lucky woman, Miss Ezeriņa," said the man. "Certainly, much luckier than the others. You took the least of that bomb."

That word "bomb" brought back sudden, terrible memories. Memories of why she was in the hospital, of that hillside explosion, of…

"Geofreys!?" She sat up in the bed. "Is Geofreys here? Where is he?"

The inspector held out a palm as if to steady her. "Geofreys Aboltins is in serious but stable condition in Ward Five. A lot of pain. He never lost consciousness until the ambulance arrived, poor fellow." He lowered his hand. "Dr. Balodis's condition could be called stable as well. He'll be buried Wednesday. Closed casket. Though frankly, they could fit what's left of him in a wastepaper basket."

She winced. No. Nothing like Peter Falk. The great Columbo would never talk so flippantly about the dead.

And she had a vague sense she'd spoken to this policeman before.

"Who did this?"

"That's the real question, isn't it?" He pulled a chair close to the bed and sat down. "And I assure you, Miss Ezeriņa, my men will find out."

Something in the way he said "assure" was accusatory. Now closer, down in that chair, Santa could see he was older than she initially thought, forty or forty-five with crow's feet at the eyes and a diagonal scar across the lip. No, this face wasn't of the American reruns from which she'd learned her English. "You're Inspector Kalvans from Rīga, aren't you? I recognize you from the newspapers."

"Indeed. Senior Inspector Roberts Kalvans, Miss Ezeriņa." He leaned forward and seemed to be looking through her eyes into her mind. "Your head seems clear enough. Can we make our talk official at last?"

She *had* spoken to him before. He had hounded her bedside all week.

It was coming back to her now. "Fascist" Kalvans—the sensationalist investigator who always got his man, usually by maiming a few innocents along the way.

Well, she'd been maimed enough. "With no doctor present, and no lawyer, there's no conversation to be had, Inspector Kalvans."

He frowned, compressing those crow's feet. "That's unsporting of you. Imagine if the interviewees for that newspaper of yours, *The Baltic Beacon*, demanded a lawyer at each conversation. You'd never print a single scandalous word." He leaned back in his chair. "Be that as it may, you're improving, and I should inform you of recent developments. Your lover—and that is Mr. Aboltins's relation to you, isn't it?—is under hospital arrest as a prime suspect in the murder of Dr. Balodis."

If she were healthier, or the questioner less perceptive, Santa might have hidden her emotions. Instead, Kalvans smiled slightly and said: "This surprises you?"

"Go on."

"Your boyfriend has accrued more than seventy thousand euros in debt—credit cards, bank loans. I can see by your face this also surprises you. You are not such a close couple, yes?" He scratched his chin. "Well, Aboltins admitted to his debts from his hospital bed not ten minutes ago. He said his mother even took out a lien on the apartment she inherited from Soviet times to stave off the financial wolves at the door."

Kalvans raised a bushy eyebrow. "The relevancy of this? Well, the victim, Dr. Balodis, had been reporting to us for months that someone was attempting to extort money from him via anonymous death threats. Now, Balodis is dead, and your boyfriend, a man in financial distress, is one of two people close enough to deliver the bomb that killed him. You being the other."

"We were victims of the explosion too."

"Thirty percent of bombers are injured or killed by their own devices. Explosives are a delicate business. Criminals, I find, are indelicate people. If you help us, Miss Ezeriņa, I assure you little prison time."

"Prison time?"

"Any prosecutor would conclude that a lover at the killing scene was an accomplice. Aboltins would likely have transported the bomb in the car you borrowed from your mother and hid or assembled the device in the one-room bungalow you shared with him on the mountain. You can't credibly 'not know.' Assist us, and we'll say you were forced into the crime by a desperate but dominant male. The penalty would be minimal."

"No one forces me into anything—criminal or not, Inspector."

Something approaching a sneer spread across his dark lips. "You might want to rethink your words, Miss Ezeriņa, lest the burden fall fully on you as well. I've no desire to send a woman away for life."

The nurse returned with the doctor. Santa remembered his name... Rikters, she thought.

"Dr. Rikters, can we vacate the room of visitors? I am feeling nauseous again."

Kalvans pushed back the chair, stood up. "Turn over everything to the police, Miss Ezeriņa. Give us Geofreys Aboltins. It's your only hope."

* * *

Santa lay beside Geofreys in his hospital bed, her arm draped across his chest, her eyes looking up at his bandaged, burned face. She was grateful, for both their sakes, that the worst of his injuries were concealed. Occasionally, when he spoke, the medical tape would come loose at his neck, and she'd see the thick tubes digging down into his throat. Or she'd glimpse under the gauze and padding to see the ragged edge of a skin graft. The thought, more than the sight, made her uncomfortable. And she felt guilty and disloyal for the emotion.

"The debts," he said in a voice too old for such a young man, "emerged from business start-ups, technology classes, the best DSLR and servers I could buy, those kind of things. They just sort of snowballed."

The night policeman yawned outside the door. Santa wondered if he spied for others.

"Inspector Kalvans showed me receipts from your credit cards, Geofreys. Thousand-euro bills at gentlemen's clubs, escort agencies…"

"Did he?" She felt his pectoral muscles tighten beneath her hand. A tension in his body usually reserved for the apex of their lovemaking, now so different in cause and meaning. It made her impossibly sad.

"They're fake receipts, Santa. Kalvans is trying to separate us. He's as bad as his reputation."

She said nothing.

"You do believe me, don't you, sunshine?"

"He gave me another receipt, Geofreys, one from a travel agency. You were preparing to leave Latvia?"

"With you. A surprise spring trip to Abu Dhabi. So you could swim in the sea."

She could swim at Večaki beach, just thirty kilometers away. Freer and more nude than she ever could in the Arab world.

They sat silent for minutes. She listened to the policeman's shift end outside. His replacement, a woman officer this time, peeked in a moment, then softly closed the door.

"I'm having doubts again, Geofreys," Santa said when the door was shut.

"Because I have debts?"

"Because you have secrets." She gently turned his bandaged face to hers. "I'm a news rag reporter. I don't believe in secrets."

He looked at her, pain in his one unbandaged eye. She stroked a rare patch of undamaged skin near his chin, felt the stubble, the perspiration. The emotions welled.

"Don't worry," she said with a weak finality.

They tried to sleep.

III

Gazing up from the frozen roadside, Santa had a clear view over the ascending hillside to the gates of Dr. Balodis's house, police tape crisscrossing the entrances to the main building and to the nearby cottage she and Geofreys had once rented. A weather-warped sign affixed to a post midway up the hill read "Police Crime Scene. No Admittance" in large printed letters, with a handwritten annotation in heavy marker below. "Info? Call," it said, followed by a number she recognized as belonging to Inspector Kalvans's mobile.

The weather was colder than it had been the day of the murder, and all surrounding hillsides remained white with powder. But Inspector Kalvans had cleared this hill of every snowflake. All that remained was a mountain of black frozen mud with patches of shriveled winter grass and the footprints of countless policemen. Santa could only imagine the manpower needed to search a hill this large. Well, Kalvans always got his man, guilty or not.

She just hoped that man wasn't poor Geofreys.

As Santa examined the scene, she went over the evidence in her mind, or at least what she'd gleaned from a hospital bed and conversations with the police. The only tracks on the hillside or road, prior to the ambulance team, had been those of the victim, Geoffreys, and herself. Dr. Balodis had been alone in the house, and even if someone was hidden on the premises, the assailant could never have escaped without leaving tracks. The manor's powerful security equipment showed and heard nothing. No aircraft had been in the air to drop anything. The bomb, roughly the weight and dimensions of an inflated basketball, was not self-propelled.

Everything pointed to it being thrown, probably at short distance.

Santa scooped up a gloveful of slush from the road, patting it down into a ball, adding more until the sphere was the size of a grapefruit. With a grunt, she heaved the ice ball up towards the hilltop. It landed not a quarter the distance to the house, well short even of the police sign.

Difficult to believe anyone threw something as weighty as that bomb from down here and reached its target. She pulled the portable laser range finder from her coat pocket, scanned the adjacent hilltops. All were the same—beautiful, uninhabited, and too far away to be meaningful.

With one exception.

Across the valley, on a towering ridge, was an old blocky Soviet structure complete with monolithic gray walls surrounding a drab, featureless building. It was difficult to tell at this distance, but this enormous blot on the landscape looked like a warehouse or factory, though Santa could only guess what they used to store or manufacture up there. Sigulda had generally been spared the ugly construction booms of Latvia's two Soviet occupations. Whatever that thing was, it stood out, the sorest thumb in a region of castles, wooden villas, and German-style mountain cottages.

Santa took note of this, then recorded the distance to that ridge and several others, before pocketing the range finder and pensively walking up the sludgy road toward Mother's Toyota. She climbed inside the car, avoided glancing up at her bruised face in the rearview mirror, and started the ignition.

Soon she was driving along the winding valley road. Up ahead on her right, she spied chimney smoke, then a small, darkly wooded winter lodge, the muddy car park in front empty except for the hoofprints of deer and one lonely, beat-up white van.

Santa parked next to the van and went inside. The interior atmosphere was warm, even hot, under the sway of an enormous stone hearth and the furious fire it contained. Large wooden tables dominated the room's center, an ill-fitting brass bar extending along the rear wall.

A fortyish woman, trim and attractive, with long red hair to her waist, greeted Santa somewhat reluctantly. She seemed surprised to see a customer.

Santa sat at the bar, better to converse with the locals, and ordered *zāļu* tea. While the woman prepared it, Santa observed the photographs on the walls. Most were of the beautiful Sigulda region in the early nineteen hundreds. She noted that Dr. Balodis's manor house was prominent in a picture dated 1895, while that Soviet monstrosity was absent from area photos as late as 1964.

The woman turned on Latvian traditional music in the overhead speakers. Santa wondered if she thought her a tourist. She feared the post-trauma swelling in her throat had temporarily affected her accent. When the steaming tea arrived, Santa thanked the hostess in the clearest

Latvian she could muster and then said almost offhandedly, "A shame about the Dr. Balodis tragedy. A bombing out here in this clean country."

The woman ignored her. Turned up the music.

Santa persisted. "Did Dr. Balodis ever come in here? This must be the closest lodge?"

The woman nodded, but avoided eye contact.

"Did he have friends? Enemies?"

The hostess disappeared into the back room without comment. Santa sipped her tea, frustrated.

The woman returned, a wet scrub towel in her hand, and began to clean the bar top. After several hard, revolving wipes, she said reproachfully: "I don't think it's wise to speak ill of the neighbors, do you, girl?"

"Well, I'm a journalist…"

"I know who you are. Your face was all over television. You were involved in the murder of the timber lord Everts Gūtmanis last May."

"If by that you mean I brought his killer to justice…"

"I mean *involved*." And she moved from the bar to aggressively scrubbing the tabletops.

Santa watched her work, cleaning things that were already spotless, trying to look busy. Santa just had to come up with the right offer.

She's too old to be a waitress out here, Santa thought. *I'll bet she's an owner….*

"A shame," said Santa, "that a cozy place like this is so empty on a Sunday. Maybe I can help business. A glowing review in *The Baltic Beacon*? English and German editions, too. The tourists see those."

She shrugged. "I don't know what you'll say."

"My byline is yours. Everything wonderful about your lodge makes it into print. Guaranteed." She flipped a business card onto the tabletop in front of the woman. "And everything rotten about these neighbors stays between us. Deal?"

The woman crumpled up her rag, threw it into the bar sink, and with a reluctant sigh took a stool next to Santa. *"Labi,* but you heard none of this from us."

Santa nodded.

The woman thought deeply for several moments before speaking, the hearth's firelight reflecting in her green eyes. At last, she said: "Peters Balodis used to have a friend, another doctor, Ivors Turks. About the same age, I guess, though more weathered somehow. They'd have long discussions in front of our hearth. I'd serve them *kakao* on winter days. Often, they were the only ones in here."

The woman added a hint of thrill to her tone. "Those talks could turn fiery. Shouting matches were common. One time—the last time—they came to blows. Dr. Turks put Balodis in a headlock, and I swear he meant to press his face into the fire. By the time my husband separated them, Balodis had burning embers in that fine beard of his."

Santa sipped her tea. "What was the altercation about?"

"Don't know. But after that, they were never together. Dr. Balodis began to come in with outsiders. Frenchmen in Italian suits. Italians wearing French cologne. Russians sporting both. They spent a lot of money. If Turks was here when they arrived, his face would turn a heated red, and he'd storm out the door. More than once, I had to chase Turks into the car park to get him to pay his bill."

The woman grimaced, and Santa thought the retelling was somehow painful for her. "I think Peters—Dr. Balodis—liked driving Turks off. There was something cruel in it. He could have had these men to his villa, a far more elegant place than our lodge, if I'm honest. He wanted Ivors Turks to see them together for some reason. In the last few months, Turks stopped coming at all. Now, without Peters, no one comes. You're our first customer since the tragedy. Other than the police."

Santa nodded sympathetically. "Where can I find this Dr. Turks?"

"It's easy enough. His home is across the valley, atop one of the highest hills. The ugliest building in all Sigulda…"

* * *

Santa drove the Toyota along the high ridge overlooking the valley, a twisting, turning path that would lead to the home of Dr. Ivors Turks.

As she went, Santa noticed what a clear view she had of Dr. Balodis's manor on the opposite side of the gorge. Though it was a considerable distance, this ridge's climbing elevation seemed to enliven the possibility that something somehow could be thrown or glided across. Certainly, it seemed within reason to launch a bomb from these heights with the right device.

She'd talk with Dr. Turks about those options very soon.

The Toyota took a last turn around a collection of icy boulders, passed through a thick screen of firs, and Santa's destination came into view. The structure was exactly as it had looked from the valley floor. Monotonous, heavy, and gray, decorated with the meaningless lines and geometric patterns of an architectural style that had disdain for history, religion, wealth, and nation. Santa glimpsed just enough to decide that Dr. Turks's home was, or had once been, a factory, though much of it looked close to ruin. Then motion around the building's exterior drew her eye. Dozens of men with snow blowers, shovels, and icepick axes swarmed over the landscape, surging this way and that into the open courtyard and digging up the mountainside to the very edge of the cliffs. Among these huffing, grunting laborers were more serene, trained professionals. Police forensic specialists collected data, bagged items, and grouped around their van, holding coffee cups while deep in discussion.

A heavily muscled, uniformed policeman motioned for her to stop and roll down her driver's-side window. When Santa did, he said:

"You shouldn't be here, Miss Ezeriṇa."

"How do you know who I am?"

The big officer smiled. "We always know our top suspects, ma'am. They usually return to the scene of the crime."

Santa was going to argue this wasn't technically the scene of the crime, but the number of police beginning to encircle her car gave her pause. And real concern. "Probable cause" for Kalvans's men was notoriously minimal. She threw the Toyota into reverse, swung it around, and sped down the road before someone shouted, "Halt!"

When Santa's car had disappeared among the firs and boulders of the ridgetop, the muscular officer pressed his mobile's speed dial for Senior Inspector Roberts Kalvans.

"Boss," he said flatly. "The fly is out of the web."

IV

"They chased me off the mountain, Alberts. I'm lucky to be free."

"It's karma, Santa," replied *The Baltic Beacon*'s second-best reporter on the other end of the phone. "After what you did to Geofreys, breaking up with him while he's in the hospital…"

Santa tried to juggle her mobile while relayering the blankets over herself on the couch at her Rīga flat. Why, oh, why had she forgotten to pay the heating bill?

"I didn't break up with him, Alberts. I simply said I had doubts."

"Word on the street is, you're single." She heard Alberts lick his lips. "How about dinner Thursday night?"

"I may have to eat it in jail, my love. Now, what have you got for me?"

"Well…" She heard the quick clicks of a keyboard. "I had to dig deep into ancient history, you know."

"The Livonian League?"

"The nineteen eighties. Remember *perestroika?*"

"Before my time. But yeah, I know it, obviously." She shivered. More blankets needed.

"Well, when privatization began, rather than having stock or percentages of companies, some misguided individuals instead took their shares by owning physical assets outright. If you had a restaurant, someone owned the chairs, another partner the tables, another the food. Some sap got stuck with the menus."

"That'd be rough."

"Owning physical objects was considered wise when currencies were in constant flux. Now, here's the ironic thing, Santa. When they left the communist world behind and first went private, Doctors Peters Balodis and Ivors Turks drew straws for first choice of assets. Turks won and took the laboratory, the building that is now his home. It made sense. It was a functional lab, employing dozens. Intellectual property was a fuzzy concept in the socialist world. So, when Balodis took all the patents as his share, it seemed like he'd gotten the worse of the deal. Literally the short straw. When those patents were later declared international, no one thought much of it."

"Go on."

"Yet, like so many ex-Soviets, Turks and Balodis weren't ready for the competition of the capitalist world. Their lab went bust within six months of Latvia's independence. They spent the next twenty-seven years commiserating over drinks at that lodge in the valley, two old scientists telling half-humorous war stories about their brief venture into world business. But markets change, and suddenly those old patents applied to new technology. I'm not technical, but their designs for Soviet Arctic communications were now relevant to dead of winter Wi-Fi. A bidding war ensued, and they sold collectively for nineteen million euros to a Parisian company in March of last year. As the sole owner of the patents, it all went to Balodis."

Santa whistled. "So Balodis and his family are set for generations, and Turks is left with an old, outdated lab off in the mountains that Dr. Frankenstein wouldn't set foot in. Sad."

"Still not as sad as Geofreys."

"I thought you wanted to replace him?"

"I'm a bastard but a sympathetic one."

The phone beeped.

"Hold on, I'm getting another call." She switched lines.

The new voice was heavier and less friendly than her colleague's. "Miss Ezeriņa? It's Senior Inspector Roberts Kalvans. I trust your head has recovered and is finally thinking properly?"

"A few cobwebs left, Inspector. But they're clearing. Do you know about Dr. Turks's relationship to the deceased?"

"About their soured businesses? Yes. That Turks felt he'd been swindled out of millions? Certainly. I also know that Dr. Balodis believed the death threats he received were from his old business partner, who, by the way, once tried to very publicly push Balodis into a blazing tavern hearth. Have I missed anything, my dear?"

"Well, then, why is Dr. Turks free?"

"He isn't. We arrested him yesterday morning. But we can't hold him long. Turks had no method to deliver that bomb."

"There is a clear view of Dr. Balodis's house across the valley from Turks's front gate. With the height of that ridge and the right winds, it's possible he may have been able to throw it across."

He laughed. "I presume the valley tavern owner told you Dr. Turks hadn't come in for months. Did she tell you why?"

"I don't think she knew."

"Turks had a stroke in October. He is confined to a wheelchair and can't even lift his arms above his chest. Still want to tell me he threw that bomb clear over the valley, Miss Ezeriņa?"

"A stroke?"

"I had department doctors evaluate him this afternoon. He is, to use an old-fashioned term, thoroughly 'crippled.'"

Santa paused to take this in, drummed her fingers on the couch armrest, then said: "Well, he's got to have caregivers, right? He could have persuaded one of them to do it."

"All live in Rīga. All accounted for. None was able to drive in that day because of the snow. The same snow that delayed your own ambulance three hours. Turks was alone."

"Are Dr. Turks's mental faculties still strong, Inspector?"

"He's as sharp as he's ever been."

"And his hands still function?"

"Passably so."

"Then maybe he built a device and launched the bomb across?"

"Where? Up the chimney? My men have been over every centimeter of Dr. Turks's complex—the lab, the house, the whole mountain. The collective man-hours are in the thousands. Where is this cannon? This catapult? There is nothing there."

Santa found her voice rising. "Listen to me, Senior Inspector. He might have disassembled the launcher until the parts were unrecognizable. It could be sitting in plain sight, looking like...I don't know, a toaster, a ski boot.... Have you looked closely at his Xbox?"

He snorted. "I'll suggest a more likely scenario, Miss Ezeriņa. That Dr. Turks, being an invalid, had someone commit the murder for him. Someone in debt. Someone in proximity to the victim and able to deliver the bomb. Someone we caught trying to return to *her* master only yesterday."

Santa's stomach dropped. "That an accusation, Inspector?"

"Consider yourself under house arrest. I've men coming to collect your passport and driver's license. Be there to receive them."

"I can't work exclusively at home. I'm a journalist."

His voice turned colder somehow. "You are the only suspect extended this courtesy, Miss Ezeriņa. Don't thank me. I've a sentimentality for the weaker sex."

She hung up, switched lines. "Alberts?"

"Still here. Was that Geofreys crying for..."

"Tell Daks I won't be coming in to the paper for a few days."

"Yeah, okay. What's going on?"

"And ask Alla Bikova at the university physics department to call me. Give her my cell. My *alternate* number."

"Sure, but..."

"I've gotta go borrow Mother's car before the police take my license. Then find a bomb launcher."

"A bomb launcher? Please tell me that's a cocktail."

"Thanks for everything, Alberts. Ciao."

She hung up the phone. Santa threw off her blankets, threw on her shoes and coat, then exited the apartment. She took the stairs to the roof, where she moved rooftop to rooftop along the contiguous block of Lāčplēša iela until see reached the Jaunais Rīgas theater with its rare-for-Rīga fire escape. Descending again to the street level, Santa glanced back along the avenue.

The police car was just pulling up to her apartment entrance.

Santa tugged her coat closer and disappeared into the snowy Latvian night.

V

Santa Ezeriņa hammered the latest climbing spike into a crack in the old Soviet stone, placed her booted heel on its flattened head, and pushed herself higher until her fingertips just caught the lip of the great wall around Dr. Turks's home. With a grunting effort, she pulled herself up, resting on the wall top to take in her surroundings. The great factory lab loomed before her, dark and brooding. Past two A.M. and the police had long gone home, their signs and half-translucent yellow-green tape serving as warnings to all visitors. With Dr. Turks in custody in Rīga, there should be no one to disturb her.

Santa threw a rope down on the other side and descended the five meters to the alley between the outer wall and factory building. Now safe from the eyes of late-night wanderers outside, she unhooked the sport flashlight from her belt and turned on the beam. The alley around her was a mire of crisscrossing snowdrifts, teetering piles of icy scrap metal, old timbers, and bricks. At waist height, and repeating a story above, stretched lines of windows, grimy, glazed, each about a meter square. Santa set down the light and withdrew a utility hammer from her belt pack. She'd spent a fortune this evening at the sporting-goods and hardware stores of the Domina Mall in Rīga, buying all she could before Kalvans had remotely shut down her bank and credit cards.

Well, she'd make do.

Hammer in hand, Santa smashed the nearest window, cleared the glass, and crawled inside. She lowered herself onto a cavernous factory floor, dark and echoing, little warmer than the outside, and now in a state of slow disintegration. Judging by the frequent drill holes in the concrete, huge equipment blocks the size of motorcars had once populated the chamber, all surely filled with the Soviet grandeur for the enormous but now long since removed. Strings of plastic, rubber, and aluminum tubing hung limply from the shadows above, one tube dripping liquid to the floor, rats collecting around the puddle. By the number of eyes shining bright from the gloom, they had many fellows.

Santa did not pause. Her footsteps echoing and the rats scurrying, she hurried over the factory floor to a steel door at the far end. Santa rotated the heavy lever that served as its latch, and passed through into a smaller, marginally warmer room. This appeared to be some sort of planning center with ancient purplish chalkboards on two walls and drafting desks with built-in chairs in the middle. The two doors that exited the room were adorned with remnants of torn police tape, tattered strips resting on the floor nearby.

Wishing a better look at this hub, Santa found a heavy industrial light switch, flipped it on. With a mechanical buzz and a whiff of ozone, electrical lights came to life above.

A thin bald man in a wheelchair said: "Who are you?"//
Santa stepped back in shock. "Dr. Turks? I thought you were in jail?"//
"I've a good lawyer."//
He raised the pistol in his hand. Fired.//
Santa felt it hit her neck. She staggered away, black spots in her vision, trying to reach the door, to turn that heavy lever…//
He fired again. The second dart pierced her shoulder.//
She collapsed at the foot of the steel door, silent and unmoving.

VI

Santa awoke on a cot in some sort of storeroom. A little electric lamp perched on a shelf gave just enough light to see and a reddishly glowing space heater on the floor kept her from freezing to death.

Her back hurt, her neck hurt, and it occurred to Santa briefly that she was making a habit of passing out in the Sigulda mountains. A poisoned-dart gun? Really? From a man in a wheelchair? What was this, *My Man Flint? Austin Powers?*

She patted her clothes down. Everything appeared in place, even her underwear. Dr. Turks might be a decrepit murderer, but he didn't seem a pervert.

Of course, who can really know? Her phone, hammer, and flashlight were gone. No surprises there. At least he'd left Santa her watch. 9:19 A.M.

Santa pulled herself off the cot using the frame of the supply racks to stand. What could she fashion to exit this dungeon? She glanced at the empty shelves. Very little to work with. Why couldn't they have rerun *MacGyver* more often in Latvia? Only *Gilligan's Island*, again and again in her youth. And those castaways never escaped anywhere.

She unplugged the lamp, broke it open, and using the minimalist glow of the space heater, tried to twist the light's thicker wires into a lock pick. When she had an assemblage that *might* do something, she went to the storeroom door, kneeling at the lock and working furiously. She prodded and poked, twisted and retwisted for minutes, but nothing turned the bolt.

This only works in detective stories, she thought.

At last, the majority of her wire pick broke off in the lock. Cursing in each of the seven languages she knew, Santa was viciously trying to pry it free when a key entered on the opposite side and firmly pushed the whole concoction out into her hands.

The door opened.

Inspector Kalvans stood above her. "Good morning, Miss Ezeriņa. I hope you slept well?"

Dr. Turks wheeled up behind him. "You'll pay for that lamp, girl."

"He drugged me, Inspector."

"She's a prowler," spat the doctor. "Cost me a window and a lamp."

"Children, children," said Kalvans faux-warmly. "Where would you all be without my steady justice?"

The inspector ordered her out and Santa found herself in a small entry room off the building's front courtyard. Officer Zaķis, the hulking policeman she'd met from her car window two days ago, clasped handcuffs on Santa's wrists. They escorted her through the courtyard towards the cars.

"Inspector, I would like to speak with you privately," said Santa.

"There'll be plenty of private conversations at the station, Miss Ezeriņa. Some more pleasant than others." Kalvans glanced back towards Dr. Turks in the doorway. "We'll return soon for you, Doctor. Your lawyers won't keep me at bay forever."

He laughed. "You've nothing on me, Senior Inspector. Except a coming lawsuit for harassment."

"Can I say something?" asked Santa.

"No."

"You'll want to hear it."

Kalvans sighed. "Well, what, girl?"

"I've found the bomb launcher."

"Miss Ezeriņa, you're a trespasser, a suspect, and a fugitive. Anything you've discovered is both inadmissible and likely planted."

She held up her opened hands. "Do you think I planted these?"

"What do you mean?"

"The trunk of my car is unlocked, Inspector. Open it. All will be explained."

Dr. Turks wheeled from the gate towards them. "If she's stolen something from the laboratory, I'll hold you responsible, Kalvans! I'll have your job!"

"Relax, Doctor," growled the great detective. He nodded towards the big police officer. "Zaķis, do the honors."

With Kalvans and Turks following, Officer Zaķis walked Santa to the little Toyota parked at the cliff's edge. He popped the trunk, searched it.

"Two basketballs," said Zaķis. "And a can of phosphorescent spray paint."

"There used to be five basketballs, Inspector, but I did some experiments before visiting the doctor here last night," said Santa. "I needed the paint to see the balls in the dark. You did say the bomb was the weight and shape of an inflated basketball, correct?"

"Miss Ezeriņa, we've already experimented...."

"Who did?" She nodded towards Zaķis. "Him? Only him? Are you sure he's up to the task?"

"I threw in Beijing," said Zaķis.

"That's impressive, Tiger. But can you hit the murder site with a basketball?"

"No. Even Kristaps Porziņģis couldn't. The great Stephen Curry couldn't. It's impossible. That's the point."

"But they're athletes. You need to think like a physicist, as Dr. Turks would...."

"Miss Ezeriņa," said Kalvans, "it is cold. We have things to do."

"Let me have one shot. One shot, and I'll tell you everything I know about Geofreys Aboltins, Dr. Turks, and the whole sordid affair. Willingly and without protest."

He sighed. "If it means a quieter ride to Rīga... But only one. Let's be fair, Zaķis. Take the cuffs off for her throw."

"No need, Inspector," said Santa. She stretched out her hands as wide as the handcuffs would allow and plucked a basketball from the car's trunk. Holding it in front of her, Santa walked to the ridge's edge.

"Now, Dr. Turks can't lift his hands above his breast, so neither will I."

She squatted on her haunches, took a moment to line up the directions, and then simply dropped the basketball off the cliff, giving it a hard backwards flick of the wrist as she did.

The ball dropped like a stone.

The policemen laughed.

Dr. Turks sat silent.

As it picked up speed in descent, the basketball began to peel away from the cliff face, like an airplane coming out of a nosedive, the angle stiffening until it looked from their vantage point to be flying nearly horizontal to the valley floor, the basketball gliding through the air of the gorge, farther and farther, and *still* farther away, until it bounced harmlessly off a chimney on the roof of the Balodis Manor.

"Overshot the mark a bit," said Santa, looking back at the astonished men. "It's known as the Magnus effect, Inspector. Again, think like a physicist. As Chairwoman Bikova from the university has done for me. As even your 'lab boys' might if you didn't leave the on-site experimenting to ex-jocks."

She glanced at Zaķis. "No offense."

He said nothing.

"Of course, I shouldn't besmirch all athletes. Are any of you golfers? Practice jai alai? Lacrosse?"

No replies.

"A pity. Well, on a cliffside, we already have elevation. Give the ball a good backspin and you'll get both lift and forward thrust, a lift and thrust which increase as the ball gets closer to terminal velocity. Our host here didn't need strength in his limbs or great range of motion. With a mere flick of the wrist, the Magnus effect shoots a ball—or spherical bomb—far more distant than a physically challenged Dr. Turks could otherwise throw from a precipice. Almost unimaginably so."

Santa shrugged. "No heroic heaves needed." She pointed at Dr. Turks. "This man had motive, method of delivery, and, unlike Geofreys Aboltins, the skills to build the bomb in the first place."

Turks's face had turned ashen gray.

"I am sympathetic," said Santa. "Dr. Turks views himself, perhaps correctly, as having been cheated out of millions by his old partner. When Dr. Balodis flaunted that 'unjust' wealth by bringing business associates to the lodge they both frequented and then purchased a beautiful seventeenth-century manor right across the vale from Dr. Turks's useless and crumbling laboratory, it was too much. Then his body failed him and he entered a very dark place. Turks demanded payment, made threats, and when ignored, turned his scientific mind to homicide. Once the bomb was constructed, he only had to wheel out his door for revenge."

"This is madness," shouted Turks. "Even if the Magnus effect can carry a bomb across the valley, you could no more steer it than a feather in a wind tunnel. How could you ever hit a living target?"

"Well put, Doctor," said Kalvans, "We must test it. Zaķis! Vacate the chair!"

The bulky officer pulled the screaming, protesting doctor out of the wheelchair, heaving him onto his shoulder. The inspector replaced Turks in the seat, then wheeled to the cliff's edge.

Kalvans looked to Santa. "Well, Miss Ezeriņa? What are you waiting for? Pass me the ball."

Santa took the last basketball from the trunk, threw it to Kalvans in the chair.

"This was the spot the wheelchair tracks revealed Turks went to the morning of the murder. And we are close to the hour of the killing, too," said the inspector. "But could he hit it? Living up here for decades, he'd know Balodis's habits and the valley winds as no other. As Zaķis and our lab men could never know." Still in the chair, Kalvans lowered the basketball to the front of his knees, then released it lightly with backspin as Santa had. The ball sailed across the vale to the very spot where Dr. Balodis had died.

"A shot worthy of Michael Jordan," said Kalvans, satisfied. He smiled at Santa. "Officer Zaķis, place Dr. Turks in the backseat of my police car. If he complains, make it the trunk. And handcuff him. The old fellow can kill with a flick of the wrist."

"Boss," whispered Zaķis meekly. "We've only the *one* pair of handcuffs."

The famed inspector laughed. "Take them off Miss Ezeriņa, you fool." He stood up from the wheelchair, took a great winter breath, then bowed towards Santa and the others.

"Once again, your Inspector Kalvans gets his man. No need to thank me."

XVI

MURDER IN THE SECOND ACT (OR THE RELUCTANT CLAQUEUR)

Originally published in Alfred Hitchcock's Mystery Magazine

Murder in the Second Act (or The Reluctant Claqueur)

I. Doorway Visitors

Odessa, 1904

"Let us go to the theater, Tasia," exclaimed my sister suddenly from across our bedroom. "And be *paid* for the trouble."

"A grand idea," I said and laughed at Eleni and her schemes. We were fraternal twins, yet as different as sisters could be. "And who exactly is going to pay for us to attend the theater?"

"The lodger who arrived last night. He's a thespian, Tasia. An understudy in Chekov's *Uncle Vanya*..."

"On Deribasovskaya Street?"

"Far from it. Some little production in the French Quarter. You don't think a player in the Grand Theater would be staying with us, do you?"

"We're not so shoddy."

"We'll agree to disagree. Anyway, our lodger, Oleg, he's got the lead tonight, and he wants enthusiastic supporters to be in the crowd to sway the audience in his favor."

"And so he pays us to clap?"

"And cheer. And start ovations. And say to our audience neighbors, "Isn't Oleg Olehno fabulous? Isn't he amazing? He should be the lead full-time. No one else can play Dr. Astrov as Oleg Olehno does. Throw the other guy out!"

I smiled at her enthusiasm. "Well, I didn't speak with him as long as you did, Eleni, but he certainly *is* fabulous-looking. But to be paid to deceive the crowd... is that ethical?"

She shrugged. "Ask him yourself, Tasia. He's standing behind you."

For an instant, I clung to the hope her words were said in jest. Eleni has a most peculiar sense of humor, after all, but that smug, too-familiar smile on my sister's face left little doubt. I felt a flush of embarrassment and swiveled about on my sewing stool to see that, yes, Oleg Olehno was indeed leaning into the opened frame of our doorway.

"I didn't mean to startle you, Anastasia," said our tenant in the long "o" accent of Muscovite Russian. "My sincere apologies if I did. I simply wanted to know if your sister had convinced you to accept my offer regarding theater work?"

Despite the pleasant appearance of this man—trim, thirtyish, with center-parted hair and a thin mustache decorating a handsome face, a face whose strong jaw and cleft chin jutted aggressively out over the collar of a fashionable frock coat—despite *this* attraction, which any poor Russian-Greek girl from our neighborhood would have to such a man, he was an unwelcome sight in the moment. I felt betrayed by Eleni, and, more seriously, wondered what sort of tenant climbed the stairs to peer into the bedroom of two unwed twenty-year-old sisters without announcing himself. If Mother were here, instead of working the winter as a maid in Yalta, she'd have thrown him out, sole lodger or not. To her, any man who reached our top step without a wedding ring was fit for the gallows.

I prided myself on being more liberal than my parent. Still, decorum must be maintained even if those around me failed.

I rose, curtsied, and then sat down again before answering. "No, no, Mr. Olehno, you didn't startle me. I simply didn't hear you come in, shout as Eleni does when she speaks." I donned my most professional smile. "Is your room satisfactory? Would you like me to prepare your lunch now?"

"Later. And the room is fine, though I believe there are bedbugs in the mattress. But what about the theater work?" he asked earnestly. "The

MURDER IN THE SECOND ACT (OR THE RELUCTANT CLAQUEUR)

curtain rises in five hours. If it's not for you, I must find someone else immediately!"

"It just seems like a form of deception," I said.

"Everything in the theater is deception, my girl. But I offer you opportunity. The *claqueur*—that is the industry word for a paid leader of the audience—is one of the most important professions in all theater, a match in stature with the finest actors. Some say more important than those." He clapped his white-gloved hands. "It is coveted work, girls, difficult to acquire. Do a good job for me, and I may recommend you to the guild. A convincing *claqueur* works all over Europe. Vienna. Paris. Moscow. A lifetime of seeing the greatest dramas in the world's most exciting cities. And to be compensated for it?! What can be better than that?"

I glanced at Eleni, and though her face was bright with the possibility, I knew her thoughts. As she knew mine.

"It sounds wonderful, Mr. Olehno," I replied. "But as far as Vienna or Paris, we have to remain here to help Mother with the lodging house."

"She can't manage it on her own," added Eleni.

"Ladies, there is no future in a flea-box house like this. You'll end up destitute spinsters. See the world while you're still young. You know that I..."

Oleg's speech dropped away, his face draining of all color as his gaze fixated down through the window at something in the street below. From my sitting angle I could not see what he'd spied, but it induced a terrible trembling fear in him. His lithe form twitching and panicked, when Oleg finally pulled his eyes from the pane, he glanced about the room like a cornered animal desperate for any avenue of escape.

"He's here," Oleg mumbled as he rushed past me, deeper into the room. "He's found me at last, the Devil."

"Who's here?" asked Eleni.

"What are you talking about?" I said, alarmed by this suddenly distraught man.

Oleg ignored us, flung open the door to our wardrobe, and crawled up inside the cabinet, clothes shoved aside, dresses and overcoats falling to the floor, the whole thing rattling against the wall to contain him.

"He's mad," I said.

"Get out of there!" Eleni shouted as she tried to tug him out by the arm.

Oleg shook her off, and pulling his knees up to his chin, fumbled at closing the wardrobe door in front of him. "Tell that monster I'm not here. I'll pay you anything," he said, tears running down his cheeks. "Anything I have, just keep him away. Kill him if you must."

"Kill him?" I started.

"You're sitting," Eleni lowered her voice here, "on our undergarments. Please, Mr. Olehno, come—"

Three thunderous knocks reverberated up from the front door far below.

Oleg's watery eyes widened. "He'll knock it down," he sobbed in a pathetic whine somewhere between that of a hungry child and wounded puppy. "He's done it before. Caved whole walls in to get at me."

Why can't we ever have any normal lodgers? I thought, and I marched down the two flights of stairs to investigate. It was only as I reached the front parlor that I realized Eleni had not descended with me.

Typical.

The front door pounded in again, so hard I thought it might give way on its hinges.

"Yes, yes, we're coming," I said, pausing before opening the door. It's a mild December midday, I told myself, the street full of passersby, filled with witnesses. No one can hurt you, Tasia, just don't let him in.

I unlatched the door before I lost my nerve and pulled it open. What I saw astonished me, and it took all my composure to stifle a gasp. Giants were real, my friends, in Odessa in 1904. I swear to this day. The man outside was the largest I have ever seen before or since. No athlete, circus freak, or monstrous prehuman skeleton preserved in a museum could compare in stature. Though I was a tallish girl, his body stretched up to such towering heights above me, that even as I stood on our high front step and he on the street, my vision was scarcely in line with the bottom of the weathered vest that hugged his torso. This garment, like his jacket and trousers, was of the finest material but now greatly worn and patched, a damaged grandeur extending up to a smokestack hat jutting into the stratosphere above his head, its tubular crown bent midway and veering off at a perilous angle.

These details I noticed during the conversation that followed, and in still later, more sinister encounters with the man. At the moment, as I recovered from the shock of his enormity, it was the giant's distinctive face so high above that called my attention. He had a pointed nose and chin, odd, almost kidney-shaped ears half covered by bushy dark hair, and his eyes, small as they seemed in such a head, were piercing and blue. From his mouth protruded fine yellow teeth, the sun gleaming off them metallically, and as he spoke, I realized they were fashioned in gold.

"Greetings, my dear," said he in an accent somewhere east of the Volga. "I was wondering if you were housing a friend of mine, Nikolas Nukov? A handsome man of thirty-three years. He was seen looking for lodging on this very road last night."

I shook my head. "No, sir. No one of that name."

"Oh? Maybe under another name, then? Oleg Olehno? Yuri Yanokovich? My friend likes alliteration in his aliases." The giant laughed, flashing those brilliant teeth. "A childish game he plays. The scoundrel thinks he's so clever."

"No, sir. We've nobody like that."

He frowned, brooding a moment over my answer, then turned his eyes up toward our bedroom window. I saw Eleni's hand pull the curtain tight.

The visitor returned his gaze to me. "A shame. Let us say, young lady, that I'm rather tired from searching for the old fellow. I'll take a room to rest these weary bones. Don't worry about my height; we can press two beds together end to end."

"I'm sorry again, sir. We've no vacancies."

"Peculiarly quiet for a full house, don't you think?" He cupped an enormous hand to one of those kidney ears and listened. "You wouldn't be lying to me, would you, little miss? That would be a truly dreadful mistake."

"No, sir! Never!" I exclaimed, pooling my courage. "Our tenants are winter coal shovelers, you see, working the terrible night shifts deep in Factory Town." I closed our door behind me. "We should be careful not to wake them even now. It's awfully hard work. They need their daytime rest."

He gazed at me silently from his great height. I stared back, feeling the growing winter's chill. Somewhere, a dog barked.

Odessa's citizens passed to and fro on the road behind him. I was about to excuse myself when he said at last:

"Are there any other houses nearby where I might enquire about a bed? Or the whereabouts of Nikolas Nukov?"

With relief, I pointed up the street. "Mrs. Derevyanko has plenty of rooms, sir. Just three blocks that way, opposite side of the road. You'll see it."

"Thank you, my dear." He tipped that smokestack hat, took several enormous strides up the avenue, then paused and glanced back toward me. "If you're full, miss, you might remove the rooms for rent sign from your parlor window. It deceives."

"Of course. I'll take it out right away."

"I know you will."

With a last golden smile, the stranger strode away, dwarfing shocked onlookers, and disappearing down a side street well before the block with Mrs. Derevyanko's lodging house.

I returned inside. Oleg was sitting on the stairs, head in hands, sobbing. Eleni sat a few steps above, a forlorn look upon her face.

"Well," I said to our tenant. "What's this about?"

"Terror, persecution, and the dread that each day may be your last," said he, lifting his face from his palms. "And the right for a man to make a living at his trade."

"Who was that man?"

"Man? He's no man, Anastasia. 'Troll,' 'monster,' 'demon,' I call him. He's a debt collector for the Moscow Claque. I don't know his name."

"Out with it, Mr. Olehno," I said, hands on hips and doing my best impression of Mother. "I'm not used to sending away lodgers, especially those who pay for two beds at a time. Give us everything, or next time, the giant gets a room."

Oleg's face whitened at the possibility. He took a few moments to tame the tremors overrunning his body, then spoke with the choking voice of one who has been through a great ordeal. "I acquired debts while working the Moscow theaters. A bit of cards, lady friends, nothing unusual for a young man of fashion. To pay these, I borrowed from the claque—the league of professional *claqueurs*. All was well for some months. I worked hard to pay back the loan, but it was not enough. One night before I was to premier in *Othello*, the *chef de claque* arrived in my dressing room. 'The debt has become too large.' he said. 'Pay now or else!' he demanded. I told him I could not, and he stormed out. When I appeared on stage, instead of cheering me, the claqueurs planted in the audience booed, hissed, shouted insults, threw horse dung and rotten vegetables at the stage. Never in major theater had there been such a scene. *Othello* was shut down, and I was driven from Moscow in disgrace.

"I am a polylinguist. I applied at the Jockey Club in Paris, but was told that unless I paid my debt, I'd receive the same treatment as in Moscow. These claques all communicate. Blacklisted by one, and you're blacklisted by them all. Though I speak perfect English, the Covent Garden laughed at me, the Metropolitan rebuffed my enquiries. I was forced to turn back east, working in smaller and smaller productions until the local *chef de claque* discovered my identity and forced me away. Finally, it was amateur theater in the mining towns of the Urals and commissioned one-man acts before petty aristocrats, new moneyed idiots where a smile at the wrong debutant can cost you your salary, your supper, and possibly your life."

"I was traveling homeward through Kazan when this debt collector set upon me for the first time." Oleg threw off his coat and tugged down the collar of his shirt. The flesh and form from the base of his neck to outer shoulder was jagged and purple with the look of permanent discoloring. "The only time he got a hand on me, he broke my collarbone in five places.

It was but for a moment. What a grip that demon has! I thank God every day he never touched my neck."

He leaned back on the stairs and shook a fist up at Heaven. "The fools! How can I repay my debts if I can't earn a living? Once, I was Nikolas Nukov, the mesmerizing new king of Arbat Street. Now, I slink from theater to theater anonymously, earning what little I can under assumed names until the claque discovers me or that marauding collector chases me away. Even Lucifer did not fall so far. Even he ruled his Hell. How pathetic am I? Driven to asking lodging maids to be my claqueurs? I'm sorry, girls, for what I've brought into your home. I'll be the end of everything."

"We've had worse," I said. And sadly, this was true.

Eleni moved down a few steps to put a reassuring hand on our lodger's one good shoulder. "We can still help you earn a little money, Oleg. We'll be the most rousing claqueurs you've ever had, won't we Tasia? You needn't pay us. We do it at our pleasure."

I frowned, squinting in annoyance at my sister. Eleni had a habit of taking in strays. And now she'd collected another. I was still unsure about the ethics of this claqueur business. It seemed untrue to the spirit of the arts. But I couldn't let Eleni go alone. Not with Oleg being hunted and desperate as he was.

"All right, Mr. Olehno. We'll help. But I'm not as generous as my sister. You can add Eleni's original fee to mine."

II. Uncle Vanya Ruined

He was terrible. Absolutely terrible. The worst performance I'd seen in years. I placed my face in my palms. I couldn't do this.

"Bravo! Bravo!" shouted Eleni, standing up in the sparse crowd as the curtain came down. "Roses! Roses for Nikolas Nukov! Roses for a master thespian!"

"Eleni," I whispered from my seat, half in despair. "They don't give roses after the first act."

"Well, they should for Nikolas Nukov. What acting! What pathos! And so handsome! If I weren't engaged to a wealthy surgeon from St. Petersburg, folks…" She sat down, nudged the woman on the other side of her. "Have you ever seen such acting? I've seen a lot of actors act, but that was some brilliant acting there."

"Eleni, you're the worst."

"No, *you're* the worst, Tasia." She glared back at me, keeping her voice low. "You haven't even smiled. What's he paying you for? Do your job!"

She had a point. I was as poor a *claqueur* as Oleg was an actor. Feeling guilty, I began to clap lightly.

"Oh… what… stage lighting… my heavens, such fine… punctuality … started right on time, they did—"

The man next to me said, "Hush!"

* * *

During the intermission, Eleni and I walked through the labyrinth foyer to the lobby restaurant, observing the frayed glory of the building and, indeed, within the crowd itself. This theater at which Oleg performed was far from Odessa's finest, though there were hints of a richer past in the decorated façade, exquisite woodwork, and fine but threadbare carpet. The French Quarter had previously boasted the best of everything in the Russian Empire: museums and theaters, restaurants and gardens, academies and libraries. Once populated by aristocrats who'd fled Robespierre's Razor in Paris and been given asylum by Catherine the Great, their descendants, who milled about us in surprisingly common dress, had spent most of the money in little over a century since *La Révolution Française*. French still remained the language of the wealthy, of government and *proper* theater, but Russian was increasingly popular even in this quarter, as was Yiddish, Greek, Romanian, and, lately, the shouted Ukrainian of nationalists who marched in the streets.

Thankfully, *Uncle Vanya*, billed as a tribute to the recently deceased Anton Pavlovich Chekhov, was performed in the original Russian. A wise move, though I almost wondered if Oleg had prepared in some other tongue. His portrayal of Dr. Astrov was an unmitigated disaster so far. He fumbled lines, turned left when the other actors turned right and stumbled through scenes he was supposed to carry. I felt a bit sorry for him, though even *more* sorry for us who must cheer him, and I wondered if Oleg's concentration had been rattled this afternoon by the visit from …

"That debt collector," whispered Eleni. "He's here."

"Where?"

"In the park, across the street." She pointed through the lobby window to the sludgy fields of Richelieu Botanical Gardens."

In the glare of a Black Sea sunset I saw little. Children playing snow games in the open space before the entrance, a few bundled street vendors near the corner.

"Are you sure?"

"An eight-foot man with gold teeth and a smokestack hat? Yeah, I'm sure." She pointed again. "He went into that grove of linden trees."

I saw that dark hat gliding by behind the tree limbs. My stomach twisted.

"He should never have been billed under his real name."

"We'd better tell Oleg."

"Yes."

We hurried through the crowd to the backstage entrance. A cold-eyed, bearded man guarded the door.

"Tell Nikolas Nukov that Anastasia and Eleni Karadopoulina must speak with him," said I. "Immediately."

"Ladies, the second act is about to start."

"It's urgent."

"A matter of life and death," pleaded Eleni.

With an unsympathetic frown, the man disappeared inside the door. A moment later, he returned.

"He doesn't know any ladies with such names."

Eleni and I exchanged glances.

"He must," I said.

"Try again," said Eleni. "He lodges with us."

"Ah, the actor's life," said the man wistfully. "Living with women whose names he doesn't even know." He folded his arms across his chest. "Can't help you. Sorry."

We returned to our seats, confused.

"Why wouldn't he acknowledge us?" I asked Eleni. "Because we're *claqueurs*? Because he didn't want people to know we're his plants?"

"Maybe that fellow didn't give him the message?"

"Why?"

"Don't know."

The lights dimmed; the curtain rose.

Eleni elbowed the woman next to her. "Pay attention now."

"Showtime," said a man a few rows ahead of us.

The scene to begin Act Two was a wealthy country dining room during a storm, artificial lightning flashing through the set's windows, sheet metal thunder rattling from offstage during pauses in the dialogue. A few minutes of dramatics passed before Oleg's Dr. Astrov entered, dressed in a distinctively flowery nineteenth-century jacket but without tie or waistcoat. Soon, he and the titular Uncle Vanya had driven all the other characters to the margins. I worried Oleg's concentration had little improved since Act One. My fears were soon justified:

"A woman can only become a man's friend in three steps," announced Oleg's Dr. Astrov to the audience. "First, she's an affable acquaintance, then a lover, and only after that..." His brow furled.

"...only after that..."

The frown deepened. Light laughter arose from the audience.

"A friend!" shouted someone in the crowd.

"Yes, a friend. Thank you, *my* friend. Only after that, a friend."

"He sounds drunk," said Eleni next to me.

"The character *is* drunk. But he's overplaying the part."

"As a habit, I get drunk once a month," Oleg said in character, stumbling about the stage. "When I'm in this condition, I become extremely provoking and daring. I feel equal to any challenge. I compose my grandest plans for the future."

"He's missing lines left and right."

"I have my own… philosophy," Oleg continued, face ghastly pale in the stage light, "…according to which all of you, my good friends, each and all of you…" He winced, placing a hand on his belly, then gripped a stage chair to hold himself up. "…each of you appear… as insignificant as insects… or microbes."

Oleg collapsed face forward onto the stage.

Some in the audience laughed. Eleni began to clap, but I placed a restrictive hand on her arm. I had seen *Uncle Vanya* before. This was not in the script.

The other actors rushed to Oleg, the one playing Vanya turning him over. Oleg's face was twisted in pain, his eyes closed shut, a yellowish foam bubbling out over his lips to soak his chin and collar.

Screams arose from the crowd, people standing, shouting as it became evident this was not part of the play. Someone called for a doctor, one was quickly found amongst the audience, and my last memory of the scene was that physician kneeling over Oleg, using bare fingers to try and clear his throat enough to breathe. Then the curtain lowered, mercifully cutting off the tragic view from the crowd.

Eleni and I, like much of the audience, were stunned. We sat in our seats, unsure what to do until the stage manager, that same steely-eyed bearded man we'd seen at the door, came out and told us all the bad news.

Nikolas Nukov had died.

The play was canceled.

Everyone exit, now.

* * *

Outside the night had turned dark and cold, relieved only by the glow of streetlamps stretching up and down the avenue. As the crowd thinned away, Eleni and I waited outside the main lobby doors hoping to catch a departing theater official, to tell someone, *anyone*, what we knew about

Oleg's past predicament. As a cruel winter storm moved in over the city and small hailstones bounced off our hats and coats, we spied movement down the block. A wrought-iron gate opened, and a horse-pulled cart with a single driver emerged from an alley adjacent to the theater. In the cart's bed lay something or someone beneath a thin sheet, a sheet quickly blown away by the growing storm to reveal the gray-skinned, lifeless body of our thespian tenant, Oleg Olehno.

The sight of his corpse shook me to my soul's depths, and it was several taut seconds before my wits returned, and I recognized the cart driver as the audience physician we'd last seen trying to save Oleg's life upon the stage.

My sister, however, suffered no such delays.

"We're the deceased's landladies," said Eleni, walking briskly toward the cart. "Tell me, please, to which morgue are you taking the body, Doctor?"

"No morgue yet," he said gruffly, whipping the horse. "To the police. This man was murdered, I believe. Make way!"

"Murdered? Then it's as we feared."

"Aye, and a painful death it was," he replied with a dark glance in her direction. The cart pulled out into the street, heading quickly up the avenue.

"Then to which police station?" Eleni shouted. "Doctor!?"

He gave no answer and the cart was quickly lost inside the mist of falling sleet. The weather was worsening, a battering storm that even extinguished the light of one far off streetlamp.

No, no, the lamp wasn't extinguished, but simply blocked. Blocked by a head held high enough to eclipse the bulb.

That giant stood watching in the storm!

"Police! Police! There he is!" I shouted, running toward the feared debt collector. "Police, that man! Murderer! Murderer!"

"Tasia, wait!" screamed my sister behind me.

"Eleni! Quickly!"

As we sprinted through the interminable weather, it proved difficult to chase the fleeing giant, his shape only a gray nightmare slipping in and out of sight inside the storm. With an echoing laugh, he turned off into a side street, then another, and by the time we rounded the second corner, he was gone, vanishing into the tempest night as if some creature from the spirit world.

Eleni cursed in a very unladylike fashion, then muttered: "He ducked into ..." She threw up her rain-soaked hands. "...into somewhere."

Yes, *somewhere, my sister*. Even in the storm-clipped range of our vision, there were countless doors, alleys, and courtyard entrances visible off this dilapidated old backstreet. And this road mirrored a hundred others. No city is a maze like Odessa. Even on a fair day, you can pass through half the city without using the main roads, moving courtyard to interlocking courtyard unseen. And below everything stretches the catacombs, the largest in the world. We'd discovered this with the unfortunate Englishman, Mr. Humble, years before. With so many options, it was simply impossible to trail someone in the Southern Wonder who didn't wish to be followed.

Even an eight-foot murderer.

III. Cat on a Cold Tin Roof

The night of Oleg's death was a difficult one in our lodging house. I tried to sleep, but the tension stiffened my back and I was down on the floorboards every hour trying to stretch out the muscles. Still, compared to Eleni, I slept like a baby. She scurried about the house, investigating each room at every hour: in the parlor one moment, checking the windows or doors next; fluttering about Oleg's room at midnight, digging through my sewing cabinet at two o'clock to make some repair that couldn't wait till morning. I thought I caught her sleeping in the bed around five, but she was up by six preparing breakfast.

It was about seven in the morning when a knock came at the front door. Both of us were slumped over the tiny parlor table, sipping the strongest tea in the house, and it took a moment to realize the sounds we'd heard weren't illusions out of our sleep-deprived minds.

"Are you going to get that?" I asked Eleni.

She pressed her head to the tabletop, closed her eyes. "No, you can."

Too tired to argue, I lifted myself from the thin chair and went to the front door. On our step was a bearded policeman.

"Excuse me, miss," he said, when I opened the door. "Is this the last residence of Nikolas Nukov, the actor?"

"Yes," I said, waking in the morning breeze. "And we're very glad you're here. We were at the theater yesterday when Mr. Nukov died. We have reason to believe he might have been murdered."

"Well, some of our boys think that a possibility as well."

"My sister and I can describe a suspect for you in great detail."

He held up his hand. "Oh, that's above my level, young lady. I'm just here to collect his things."

"Yes. Certainly."

I led the young policeman up the stairs to Oleg's room while Eleni, apparently only half awake, watched us from her chair. In the deceased's bedroom I found my sister had already packed all of Oleg's clothes and toiletries into a tight bundle. The policeman collected the bundle, then glanced about the room.

"Is this everything?"

"I think so."

"You are certain?"

"Yes."

He nodded, and we descended again to the parlor.

"Will an inspector be coming here to talk about what we witnessed?" I asked.

"I can't say. They tell me very little." He stepped toward the door." Well, thank you, misses. If you're sure, this is all of it?"

"Oh, officer. There is one more item," said Eleni, perking up. "Mr. Nukov's frock coat. He left it here before the theater."

"On such a cold day?" asked the constable.

"He went in costume," said Eleni, pulling the coat from beneath her chair cushion, then rising to hand it to the policeman. "The Dr. Astrov character would never wear such a fashionable coat, you see."

"Fair enough, ladies. Thank you." He bowed and went out.

I watched him walk up the street through the parlor window. "That's no policeman."

"Of course he's not," said Eleni. "Did you see his trousers?"

"They were too long?"

"Exactly. A common beat constable could never have trousers down to the boot heels. He'd step all over them, fray them. He might even trip while pursuing some criminal. And did you notice when I handed him the coat, he took it with his left hand?"

"So?"

"The belt loop for his club was on the wrong side for a left-handed man. No, that was a costume, one poorly fitted for its actor."

"Are you saying, Eleni, that was someone from the theater group?"

"You know who also was left-handed, Tasia? That doctor who took Oleg's body away. He whipped his horse with his left. Imagine that same doctor with a glued-on beard and some makeup to appear younger. Voilà! Our policeman here! An easy enough disguise for a theater troupe."

"There are many left-handed people, Eleni."

"Well, we can observe when they return."

"Return? For what?"

"For what I found sewn in the lining of Oleg's frock coat. I have to say, it unnerves me. I may have nightmares—"

"What did you find?"

"It's in Mother's bedroom. I won't go in there alone to get it, Tasia. I think it's something of dark magic, something haunted."

"Haunted? You can't believe that. We're in the twentieth century, Eleni."

Her eyes turned cold. "Remember Lilly Scarborough, Tasia? Remember what happened to her five years ago? How can you say there isn't something very odd and demonic in airs of this city?"

"Everything has a logical explanation, my sister. We were simply too young to understand those events back then."

"Perhaps," Eleni said sullenly, and led me up the stairs to the door of our absent mother's bedroom. She withdrew the key from the folds of her dress, unlocked the door, and we stepped inside. Despite two wide windows, in the late dawn of winter the room remained completely dark. Eleni lit a candle on Mother's dresser. The gloom receded.

On the bed, near where Eleni had placed the protective icons of St. Phanourios and St. Maximos, was a silver brooch in the form of a cat with blazing green gems for eyes.

"I think its body is made of solid silver, Tasia. I felt it in the lining of Oleg's coat when I was packing his things last night. He must have been hiding the brooch from that debt collector. It certainly looks valuable."

"Certainly."

"But you haven't seen the half of it." She blew out the candle. "Wait."

"For what?"

"Patience."

We stood there like fools a few minutes, then the morning silence was disturbed by the rumbling of an approaching Pirotsky trolley car on the road outside, the car's electric lamps shining bright through the windows.

As the trolley neared, the cat's eye-gems turned from green to a piercing angry red. Redder and angrier the murderous eyes grew until the car had passed and they returned to soothing green.

Eleni shuddered. "It's like the motion of the trolley enrages it. I tell you, Tasia, there's some type of hex on that brooch. It thinks. It feels."

I, too, was astonished. But for very different reasons than my sister.

"It's Alexandrite, Eleni. No hex or magic about it." I relit the candle, moved to the bed, and picked up the little brooch, so smooth and cool in my hand. The cat's gemstone eyes glared at me. "Haven't you heard of it? Named after old Tsar Alexander Nikolaevich years ago, found only in the Urals. Alexandrite stones are the only gems in the world that change color depending on the light. Green as emeralds in firelight or sunlight, a fiery red or maroon if you shine an electric light upon them, as the trolley lamps did through the window." I looked at my sister. "This cat is priceless. You can't simply take it. People will come for this brooch. The same people who murdered Oleg."

"Yes, they'll be here tomorrow evening about nine."

I started. "What do you mean? What have you done, Eleni? Tell me!"

"I replaced the cat with a stone, wrapped it in a note, and sewed them back into the coat we gave the constable. The note said we've removed the brooch from our lodging house to a safe location, but it will be back at nine o'clock tomorrow night to be sold to the first customer, price of four hundred rubles." She winced. "Of course, last night, I thought it was only silver and probably cursed, not invaluable."

"Eleni, you've invited murderers into our home."

"They'd come anyway. Now, we set the agenda."

"You're awfully confident."

"I'm relieved, actually, Tasia. I thought I was dealing with a cursed relic. Something beyond understanding." She laughed. "Now, it's only men. Those I've had wrapped around my finger since I was thirteen."

"You underestimate the situation. They're not men, Eleni, but monsters in disguise. I pray we see them coming."

"Me too," she said softly.

***

Eleni's plan was clearly both dangerous and difficult. We knew if we went to the police, corrupt as they were, they'd simply take the brooch and leave us at the mercy of Oleg's enemies. We also knew that whoever found the note would be unlikely to wait until our proposed meeting time. So, we set our watch early and waited for them all day, each of us taking turns receiving visitors at the door while the other spied for hidden accomplices on the front street or in the rear courtyard from the upper windows. The view through these panes was limited, and with my growing paranoia that we ourselves were being watched, I found myself more and more often slipping out of Mother's bedroom window to spy on prospective visitors from our neighbors' adjoining roof.

One such visitor, a heavyset yak of a man in thick furs with a gray beard and Bulgarian accent, arrived at a little past eight that same night. It was Eleni's turn at the door, and though she insisted we had no rooms, this caller was determined to get a bed for the night. Too determined, I thought.

As he debated with my sister, the traveler ignoring her suggestions of other lodging houses, I moved from window to window on the floors above looking for any accomplices prepared to join the Bulgarian in robbing us. I noted from my own bedroom window another fellow lurking in the street nearby dressed in the blue-and-white striped shirt of a Russian seaman, but from this angle I could see little of his face or demeanor. I moved to Mother's room to spy from her window. A bit closer now, I could see the seaman was a trim fellow with muscular arms leaning against the front wall of the synagogue across the street. He was smoking a cigarette and clearly took interest in the heated discussion taking place on our doorstep.

Such apparent interest almost disqualified him for me. Surely, a real accomplice would be more subtle. Still, I wanted to get a read on his face. For the third time tonight, I opened the window from Mother's room that led to the roof of our neighbors. Their building was lower than ours, and their tin roof was steeply slanted on both sides, with numerous pipe chimneys that made perfect handholds and footholds. It was an ideal spying position. I could slip onto the back slant and peer over the roof's apex to watch the street or reverse the game and observe the rear courtyard safely from the front. This time I did the former, leaning my belly against the cold tin, and watching over the edge as my sailor puffed away on his cigarette.

Time passed. I grew cold and bored. The sailor finished cigarette after cigarette but did nothing else. At last, an electric trolley rolled down the street and in its lamplight I finally got a look at this man's face.

I thought I recognized him.

A minute later, I heard the front door shut and I observed the Bulgarian stomping away down the street bag in hand, muttering disappointments. The sailor threw down his last cigarette and ambled away in the same direction.

Eleni shouted my name from inside the house. I exited the roof, slipped through Mother's window and was descending to the parlor when I met Eleni on the staircase.

"I'm certain that Bulgarian was our policeman-doctor," said Eleni. "Different beard and clothes, but the same eyes. And he slipped up on his accent once or twice when I made him angry."

"There was a sailor out there who might have been the stage manager from the theater, Eleni. Clean-shaven now, but it could be him. I think they're trying to infiltrate us." My stomach twisted at the thought of it. "I told you this was a bad idea, Eleni. We should take that brooch and go join Mother in Yalta!"

"And endanger her too? If we don't know the faces of our enemies, we'll be looking over our shoulders the rest of our lives."

"You were right. That cat *is* cursed. Oh, why did you take it?"

"Because it should go to someone better than a murderer, Tasia. And I don't want to die a destitute spinster like Oleg said I would."

"I—"

A fresh set of knocks on the front door.

Eleni's eyes widened. "Positions!" She ran back down the stairs.

"It's my time to man the door."

But she was gone.

Grumbling, I returned to the nearest window. Down on our front step, my sailor was now demanding a room from Eleni. Wondering if the Bulgarian was about, too, I slipped out onto the roof for a better look.

In the shadows of the roof, I encountered Oleg Olehno.

Before I could scream or pull myself back through the window, he grabbed me and dragged me down the roof's front gradient to him. He clasped a hand across my face, and I felt his warm breath against my ear.

"You're not seeing ghosts, Anastasia. But scream out, and you'll join the spirit world soon enough." He scooted us down the slant to the roof's edge, wedging my body between a chimney pipe and the freezing tin. "You have something that belongs to me. A man doesn't fake his own death to live a pauper. Where is that brooch? I won't ask twice."

"It won't be back in the house until tomorrow," I said between gritted teeth.

"If that's true, you won't live to see that day."

Oleg's sailor accomplice appeared in the street below. "Nikolas, that young landlady's locked the door. We'll need a battering ram to knock it in. Can you slip through—" His eyes widened at the scene on the rooftop. "What are you doing?"

"When I snap her neck, Denis, I'll throw the body down. You go through her clothes for that brooch, hear me?"

"Nikolas, this was supposed to be a simple burglary. You didn't say anything about hurting women." The Bulgarian walked up behind the sailor, the same horrified look on his face.

"I'll do the hurting, boys," spat Oleg. "You just catch the body."

The sailor shook his head. "I want no part of this, Nikolas. I'm sorry." He darted up the street, away from the house. A moment later, the Bulgarian joined him.

"Denis! Pavlo! Get back here you cowards, you'll cost us a fortune."

Eleni appeared in Mother's window. "Your sailor's abandoned ship, Oleg. Now let go of my sister."

"Eleni," I shouted, "Go! Run..."

Oleg pressed a gloved hand across my mouth. "Give me the brooch, Eleni, and I'll spare her. I swear to Saint Avaakum, I will."

"Release Tasia, and I'll get it."

He shook his head. "No deals until you show me the brooch."

Eleni looked at him darkly for several moments, then reached into her dress pocket and withdrew the silver brooch, the cat's gemstone eyes glittering in the streetlight.

Oleg smiled. "There she is. Now, come out a little on this roof, Eleni."

"Eleni, don't," I whispered.

She seemed to consider the situation, then took a few tentative steps out onto the tin slope. When Oleg inched closer, she held the brooch out threateningly over the nearest chimney pipe.

"This is not such a nice neighborhood, Oleg. This chimney leads directly to the parlor of a brothel. Good luck figuring out which of the working girls ran off with your precious cat."

"It's mine!" he shouted and lunged at her. Oleg caught Eleni's wrist, they struggled in a tug-of-war for a moment, and then they and their brooch-cat prize fell over the roof's top edge, tumbling down the back slant out of my sight.

Horrified, I climbed to the ridge of the roof's apex, fearing what I'd see on the other side. Eleni was but a few feet below me, her arm wrapped around a gas pipe, still clutching the cat in her free hand. Oleg had fallen farther. He stood unsteadily at the very bottom edge of the roofing, his foot wedged into a deep rain gutter, this act the only thing preventing him from plunging down into the courtyard below. Despite his precarious position, his eyes remained on us and the Alexandrite brooch, his face a dreadful mixture of concentration, hatred, and greed. Wobbling over the abyss, he reached into the folds of his jacket, withdrew a heavy pistol, and pointed it at us.

"Prepare to meet thy God, ladies!"

A mammoth hand rose from the darkness of the courtyard, seized our assailant as child seizes a doll, and pulled Oleg off the roof in an instant.

It was, of course, the gigantic debt collector. As I helped Eleni into a more secure position, he shook Oleg thunderously until the pistol flew from his hands, the gun rattling across the courtyard stones. Then the giant grasped our old tenant by the head and began to twist it, slowly, hideously around.

It was a most horrific sight. Oleg screaming, his arms flailing, hands twitching, all the while the bluing head inching around on the neck, farther and farther, beyond man's natural limits to turn. Though he had tried to murder us merely moments before, I felt pity for Oleg and desperately wanted to end this sickening scene, to avert his execution before us.

My sister felt the same.

"Spare him, please," said Eleni.

The giant ignored her.

She threw down the Alexandrite cat. "Maybe this will pay off his debts."

The collector released his captive to catch it. Oleg scampered off through the courtyard's rear tunnel, his head now hanging off his shoulders at a grotesque angle.

The giant examined the brooch, nodded approvingly. "Aye, it's the finest of what that actor-gigolo stole from Mother. I thank you." He pocketed the cat, then pulled Oleg's pistol from the courtyard stones. "But it won't avenge her! There are still scores to settle."

He cocked the gun, and with long strides that propel him as fast as a smaller man runs, he too disappeared through the courtyard's exit.

Though there were reports of gunfire throughout the Greek neighborhoods that night, nothing ever came of it. We never saw Oleg Olehno or his pursuer again.

* * *

There is but one postscript to this story. More than seven years later, when the newspapers were full of the Lena Massacre, I came across an obituary of interest. Alexander Ivanovich Verkhoturov, a member of the Order of Saint Stanislaus, had been killed in a mine collapse near Orsk. His family was known for their coal and gemstone excavations throughout the Urals, and Alexander renowned for being the rare aristocrat who preferred to handle important matters personally rather than through subordinates. Also famous for being afflicted with gigantism, Alexander numbered among the tallest men the vast Russian Empire had ever produced. He'd come to head the Verkhoturov family after his own widowed mother had died in a carriage accident under suspicious circumstances, but Alexander, being of the highest character, was never suspected. In the last years of his life, he routinely told friends the matter of his mother's demise was "resolved."

After his death the Verkhoturov family donated his set of twenty-four carat gold dentures to the Hermitage Museum in St. Petersburg. Still more impressively, they also leant a silver cat-shaped brooch fitted with Alexandrite stones for eyes. The brooch was kept in a naturally lighted display room. I saw it myself in 1913, marveling at my own brief history with the priceless heirloom.

I visited again in 1930. The communists had moved the brooch to the building's interior, placing it forever under burning electric lights.

The cat's gemstone eyes glared at me then: Fiery, angry, and red.

XVII

THE THREE CAMILLAS

Originally published in Alfred Hitchcock's Mystery Magazine

The Three Camillas

Rome, AD 40

In our house dwelt three Camillas: the haunted, spinsterish oldest sister, Camilla Prima, aged twenty-seven; the beautiful, kindhearted middle sister, Camilla Secunda, just nineteen; and me, Camilla Tertia, the baby, then twelve and already considered far and wide the scoundrel and gossip of the family.

Siblings with identical names, especially amongst girls, were common in conservative and affluent Roman households. And our family was nothing if not conservative. As for affluence? Well, we hoped against hope in those mad imperial times to remain wealthy a generation longer. To that end, Camilla Secunda's recent engagement to a prosperous young praefectus, sealed with an invaluable diamond and emerald ring, seemed to strengthen our family's future considerably.

But Discordia would throw a deadly golden apple our way. And much of it was my fault.

The trouble began one late spring day, when I, tiring of my poetry, began eavesdropping on my sisters in the house's central atrium and heard Camilla Secunda say:

"I envy you, Prima. No man to rule over you…such freedom."

The hesitant voice of our oldest sister answered: "Whatever do you mean, Secunda? Father rules over us all."

Camilla Secunda laughed at this. "Father dotes, Prima. He lets us do whatever we like on the rare occasions he's even here. No, I mean you've no husband…you can spend your days as you like, no orders, no false smiles, no wifely duties…bliss."

"I'd sacrifice my dowry to Juno if she'd reward me with a single suitor, Secunda, much less a husband." Her voice broke at these words, for our dear sister had been waiting a decade for a man.

"Oh, sweet Prima. You only remain unmarried because you wish to be. Why, you're an independent lady of newest Rome. Yes, you are. But for me, in a month's time, I'll be as if enslaved. I'd endure Scaevola's fire to switch positions with you."

"You really don't wish to marry Drusus?"

"Betucia Minor and I were calling him 'frog-face' behind his back yesterday. His touches repulse me."

"Then break it off."

"Mother has put so much work into the match. But worse, Drusus is close to the imperial family. With the emperor confiscating estates to pay his debts, I'd hate to spite a praefectus and have him add our names to the list. We could lose everything."

"The emperor is mad; he can't last long."

"That's what they said about Tiberius…no, I wish I were as happy as you, dear sister. I fear after the wedding, I will never be happy again."

"I—did you hear a sound, Secunda?"

"I'd wager Tertia is listening in again."

"Camilla Tertia!" shouted my oldest sister. "Is that you behind that column? Come out here at once!"

I darted out of the atrium into my bedroom, barring the door and remaining in hushed silence until long after the servants had put out the last lamps.

Much to think about.

* * *

A few days later, Camilla Prima and I made our way from our home near the Servian Wall down the slope of Esquiline Hill, shaded by ancient Italian oaks that predated Romulus and Remus, and past gardens, fountains, and the lavish *domus* of the wealthy. Ahead and below, nestled in the valley between the west and south spurs of our great hill, lay the Grand Bazaar, already teeming with people early in the morning, its tents and stalls fed goods by canals off the little stream that ran through the marketplace. Though the Esquiline district was mainly residential, here and there temples sprouted up among the opulent homes. At every place of worship we passed, the heads of statues had been removed and, be they god or goddess, replaced by the visage of our emperor. It was madness, blasphemy, and treason all rolled into one. Yes, the emperor was always deified on the margins of the empire, as propaganda to conquered peoples, but no one took it seriously at home. No full-blooded Roman had ever considered a living emperor divine.

But Emperor "Little Boot" had declared himself a god and demanded tribute. Father thought it was a gambit to absolve him of his debts. Mother said the emperor was insane and shouted riddles at the moon from the roof of his palace, waiting all night for answers that would never come. Whatever the case, it had thrown Rome into a religious crisis, and, as always, spiritual uncertainty brought unfamiliar religions imported from the far reaches of the empire. Some were merely curious, like the followers from Greece and Judea who thought they could solve all worldly problems by bathing in the river, others blatantly bizarre. Strangest of all were the "mystery religions" from far to the east, cults whose rites were known only to their members. Their devout donned strange costumes and pranced through the city streets playing music and carrying idols, men dressed as women, women dressed as men, both genders as beasts, gods, or monsters. As Prima and I trekked down the lowest slope of Esquiline, we could see a few of these cultists dancing along the canal edge and another group at the market's entrance, singing. I wanted dearly to avoid them all.

All these thoughts and fears were fleeting, however. Rome may be searching for new gods, but I was looking for a different sort of answer.

"What should we do about Secunda's wedding, Prima?" I said as we slipped past the cultists into the marketplace. "We can't let her go through with it."

"There's nothing to be done, Tertia. As you undoubtedly know from your spying." She said with distaste. "Secunda will just have to learn to love Drusus."

"A kind soul like our sister deserves happiness."

"We all deserve happiness, Tertia."

A thought occurred to me, an old memory tugging at my consciousness. "Do you remember Aunt Camilla's tale of her first suitor? The one before she married Uncle Rufus? Do you remember why it ended?"

"She lost the engagement ring at sea. On a boat trip to Portus Luguidonis, wasn't it?"

"Yes. And the suitor's family called the wedding off the next month. They thought the loss of the ring a bad sign."

"A similar thing happened to my friend Sabina Minor. She dropped hers down a well. They fished the ring out, but it was considered an ill omen and the marriage canceled."

"Then, if Secunda's ring were to disappear, Drusus or his family might break the engagement."

She looked at me and knew what I was thinking. "If the gods choose it to be so, it will be so, Tertia. But they won't appreciate your meddling."

I shrugged. "The gods…our god these days is a lunatic named after soldiers' footwear."

"Hush, Tertia!" said Prima, looking about greatly alarmed. "If someone important should hear you…. You know he hates that name!"

"No one can hear me over the chanting of all these cultists! I tell you, Prima, this country is slipping into the hands of *Dīs Pater*."

"Tertia, you speak like an old woman. When you're young, you should be more open-minded."

"When I've figured out the world, why pretend otherwise? I'm not required to humor the ignorant."

Camilla Prima didn't dignify that with a response. Instead, she pressed deeper into the marketplace, and I, being the younger sister, had no choice

THE THREE CAMILLAS

but to follow. Soon, we passed an open spot cut off from the greater market by a bend in the little river. Here, a small crowd was watching the *vigils urbani*—the fire and police brigade that kept daily order—whip a bandit who had been caught stealing inside the bazaar. Whatever his theft, it was minor enough to avoid far worse punishments. Still, I saw five lashes and heard five terrible screams before Prima and I left the gruesome scene.

It got my mind thinking.

"Well, hello!" shouted a high-pitched, barely masculine voice. "Is that Venus *Verticordia* I see?" Out of the crowd came a plump man in his early twenties dressed in a centurion's armor. I'd seen him somewhere before…

"Marius Calvisius Zosinus! Are you back from the war?" asked my sister.

"Only yesterday, Camilla Prima. You look ravishing."

She blushed, then motioned toward me. "You remember my youngest sister, Camilla Tertia?"

He grunted, nodded, and kept his eyes on her. "And what brings you to the market, Prima?"

"I was buying radishes."

"Buying radishes. I procured radishes for a whole legion of men in Gaul. For three years, nothing but men, men, by Mars, more men, and radishes. I'm good at finding radishes, Camilla…. Really good. It's time I procured radishes for a woman, wouldn't you say?"

"Then perhaps you could help me find the most succulent radishes?"

"Oh, why, yes. We'll find our radishes together."

They stared at each other.

Somewhere, those cultists played a song. But it went on too long.

I finally said: "I'll go to the fish market and get some catfish, then, Prima, as you're busy."

"Uh-huh…"

"And I'll see if I can find some fresh olives."

"Yes."

"Then I'll light myself on fire as a sacrifice to the god of kindling."

"Okay. Bye-bye then, Tertia."

Leaving them to their radishes, I started for the fish market when an idea changed my course. Instead, I walked down to the riverbank where that thief I had seen punished was tending his wounds. He was a thin, small man of about thirty, dressed in a tattered tunic and dusty in places where the river water hadn't touched him. But there was a handsomeness to his face and a plebian nobility to his demeanor. I decided he might be worth speaking to.

"Greetings," I said from a safe distance. "Are you a good thief? By that, I mean good at stealing things?"

He looked at me suspiciously, splashing water over his burning back. "Good enough. Seventeen years thievin', and this was my first time caught."

"And your name?"

"Why should I tell you?"

I tossed him the coin pouch meant for shopping. "You can prosper by these monies. Or, if you still refuse to give the name, I can call the *vigils* and claim you stole it from me. What will they do to you then?"

"Quintus," he said begrudgingly.

"Quintus? The fifth son?"

"Yes." He shook the pouch, found it full. It satisfied him.

"I'm Camilla *Tertia*, the third daughter. How would you like to earn a fair wage, Quintus? Working for the benefit of a great family and thereby of Rome itself?"

He looked at me coldly, with deep blue, almost purplish eyes, skepticism in his whole manner.

"By doing what?"

"My sister is engaged to a man we don't wish her to marry. We think if the engagement ring disappears, he'll call it off."

"You want me to steal this ring?"

"Why else hire a thief?" I pointed over to the center of the bazaar, where a clump of stone buildings stood among the tents. "See that fountain of Eros near the alley entrance? I'll lead my sister, Camilla Secunda, there tomorrow, precisely at noon. Be waiting to rob us. Don't hurt her, of course, but be armed so she takes you seriously. You're a bit on the scrawny side."

He shook his head. "There's too many guards around the marketplace. I'll get worse than a whipping robbing ladies of your class."

Who was the employer here? "The fountain, Quintus! I'll give you another bag of coins a day or so after the ring is stolen. You can keep the ring to fence as you like, too. It's a *praefectus's* gift; should fetch more than an urchin like you can steal in a year."

Those eyes narrowed. "You're quite a convincing little girl."

"A 'girl' of good family, Quintus. Someday, I'll marry a great man of Rome. A senator or better, who'll rule this city. And I'll rule him. A simple burglar like you could use an ally like me."

"So I could."

"Be there tomorrow. At noon, Quintus."

* * *

"Camilla Tertia, for the thousandth time, I don't wish to go to the market with you today!"

"But why, Secunda?"

My sister lay on her eating bed, tasting slices of fresh goat cheese, that gaudy ring on her hand. "It's overcast, muggy, and I have a headache. And I've no desire to march all the way down there just to purchase some fruit."

I climbed the step and reclined on the mattress across from her, my torso propped up at one elbow. "Please, Sister. I don't wish to go alone."

"Take one of the slaves."

"They never pick out the best produce."

"Then go with Prima."

"She's at the Lamian Gardens with Marius Calvisius Zosinus."

"Really?" Secunda raised an eyebrow. "Now that is an interesting development, don't you think?"

"Come with me to the market... I'll pay you."

"Pay me?"

"Well, yes, if I must."

She sat up fully, tucking her feet beneath her. "What are you up to, Camilla Tertia? I can always tell when you're scheming."

"Nothing. I just wanted to spend time together as sisters. Before you leave us after the wedding…"

This clearly touched her, but suspicions remained aroused. "Well, rather than the market, we can play tabula. Far easier to chat here over the gameboard than walking through the crowded old streets."

"Okay. But let's wager. I win the game and we go to the market. Fair enough?"

"Fair enough, Tertia." She quickly pulled the blue and white board from a shelf beside the bed and set it on the mattress between us, then handed me the *pyrgus* box for throwing dice. "But remember Sister," Secunda said with a cunning laugh, "the goddess Fortuna seldom smiles on you at tabula."

"I feel my luck is changing, Secunda." I shook the pyrgus. "As Caesar said: *'Alea iacta esto!'*"

* * *

"Alea iacta est," indeed.

Three lost games of tabula later, and I walked through the drizzling rain to the market alone. Mother had sent a slave to accompany me, but I'd ditched the superstitious fellow by a jaunt through the supposedly haunted Esquiline necropolis. Nobody could see me meet with the thief. I'd probably have to pay Quintus for the postponement.

By the time I reached the Eros fountain, the rain had abated a bit, but there was no sign of the thief. I checked the nearby bazaar stalls—nothing. I investigated the alleyway between the stone buildings but found only emaciated market cats.

Where was Quintus?

Maybe with the cloudy heavens, he could not read the sundials clearly or ascertain the position of the sun in the sky? But it was noon, and my hired thug remained absent. Most likely, the bandit had simply run off with my money pouch.

I heard the pounding of a drum, the shrill ringing of tinny instruments, and songs sung in an unknown language. One of those mystery cults was dancing through the market street, a troupe of a dozen men dressed in the veils of Eastern women, finger cymbals on their hands, odd barbarian chants erupting from their lungs. In their center stood a heavyset man with a drum strapped to his chest, beating in time to their bizarre singing.

I watched them prance about in their euphoric celebration as good Romans in the market stood amused, confused, or terrified. Finally, their drummer grew tired, ceased his pounding, and sat on the edge of the fountain, wiping his brow. His silence seemed to break their spell, for immediately, all revelers stopped their dancing and singing.

One of the larger, more muscular, veiled men looked at me strangely.

"Camilla Tertia? Is that you?" he asked.

"Melanion?"

He rushed over, giving me a bear hug, lifting my feet off the ground and twirling me about. "Look how you've grown! You're a fashionable young woman now, Tertia."

It was Melanion the Rhinoceros. The greatest man-killer Rome had yet seen. A gladiator of such ability, he'd won his freedom in the arena and lived off the renown for years. Our father, a fan of the sporting life, had Melanion as a regular guest at our *domus* since the day he'd become a freeman. We showered him with gifts, he us. He was almost "Cousin Melanion."

Finally, he set me down. "And how is your family? How is Prima?"

"Prima is still unmarried, but Secunda is engaged to Drusus Placidius Vopiscus."

"Ugh! Secunda can do much better. Drusus has the face of a frog."

"So I've heard. And what of you?" I pulled at the thin fabric of his veiled gown. "Such a strange costume…"

"After so much killing, I've found peace at last in a religion of the East."

"In a mystery cult?"

"It's only a mystery to outsiders, Tertia. Maybe your father—"

A masked figure jumped out of the shadows.

"Surrender your jewels and money, ladies!" he shouted, brandishing a knife in hand. "Or face the wrath of—"

Melanion slapped away the knife, ripped off the mask, and in an instant had the scoundrel pinned to the wall by the throat.

"What did you say, thief?"

"Surrender…" Quintus winced, "your…jewels and money…uh…*ladies?*"

"And face the wrath, thief." Melanion dragged him into the alley.

I stood at the entrance. "Now, Melanion… maybe you shouldn't be so hard on him." I flinched as I heard a snap, then a scream. "These are difficult times; he probably was only doing it to feed his family." Another hideous shriek. "Remember, you've found religion, Melanion."

The drummer at the fountain began to play again.

Melanion emerged from the alley. "That bandit isn't in any position to threaten you now." He cupped his ear. "Ah, the divine music calls me." The "Rhinoceros" pulled up his veil and skipped away toward the others. "Say hello to Secunda for me, Tertia…"

"I'll do that, Melanion."

I watched his procession disappear deeper into the bazaar. Then I went into the alley.

The battered thief was lying on his back among the refuse, a stray cat on his chest licking his swelling face.

"*That* was your sister?"

"No, that was Melanion, the gladiator. Slayer of fifty-two men."

"Oh, of course it was. Now it all makes sense…"

The cat hopped off.

"You're lucky I was here. You might have been the fifty-third."

"Pardon me if I don't thank you." Quintus rolled over onto his stomach, cupping his jaw and mouth. "I've lost three teeth!"

"None in the front. No worries."

As he swooned in the dirt, muttering about his precious health, my mind moved on to the next course of action, looking for inspiration.

"What shall we do now, by Juno?" I snapped my fingers. "My father has purchased a new slave abroad, Quintus. A Thracian eunuch named Belus who's never been to the house. No one's seen him. *You* will be our Belus."

"I'm not a eunuch."

"No one will check. We'll give you a few days for those bruises to heal—and really be more careful next time, Quintus, we can't suffer any more delays—then we'll host a banquet at the *domus*. During the festivities you arrive as Belus and steal the ring."

He stared at me a long while. "You're an insidious little girl."

"Oh, I'm just an apprentice. You should see Mother."

"Well, I'm not doing it."

I walked over to him, glaring down. "What kind of bandit are you? Lose a few teeth, loosen a few ribs, and you quit? Isn't there treasure to be won? A year's monies gained for an hour's work?"

"Yes…I suppose…"

"And haven't you already been paid an advance?"

"Unfortunately."

"Well, then be an honest man, Quintus, and rob my sister!"

* * *

"Oh, it is a beautiful engagement ring, Prima."

"Thank you, Secunda. It's Gallic gold. Marius said he was thinking of me every day during his long three years on the Rhine."

"If so, he might have written you," I said.

"Quiet, Tertia," said Secunda, with a glare at me before turning her attention back to our eldest sister. "We should have our weddings on the same day, Prima. What do you think? Juno can give her blessings to both unions at once."

"And funeral rites to Father, with all those dowries to pay out," I added.

"Tertia," replied Secunda sharply, pointing to the hall. "Go help the servants prepare for the banquet."

"But—"

"Now, by Jove! Or we'll be a two-sister family."

I went, though not far, lingering in the doorway and listening.

"You must be careful with this ring, Prima," continued our middle sister. "Find a good hiding spot for it. I keep mine under the mattress of my sleeping bed when not wearing it."

"Oh, I trust all our slaves."

"It's not the servants I am worried about." Secunda began glancing about the room suspiciously. "Have you wondered why our sister has been so insistent on having a party tonight? With Father gone and our fiancés unable to attend? Tertia's scheming again, Prima, but I don't yet know her game."

This seemed like an appropriate time to exit, and as Secunda's gaze turned in my direction, I slipped out of the doorway, down the passage to our *triclinium*. In this luxurious dining room overlooking our gated garden, the guests had already begun to arrive. Aunt Camilla lay semireposed on one dining couch reading my poetry while Uncle Rufus was on another of the nine *klinai*, already imbibing in his wine "barbarian style," that is, undiluted by water.

Keeping away from my suspicious sisters, I was helping Mother and the servants set out bowls of lintels, plates of cheeses, and the literal fruits of Father's travels—Pontus cherries, Persian peaches, and Damascan plums—when the door chimes sang their song.

"I'll get it!" I shouted before any servant took one step toward the door. I hurried down the garden path to the gate. There stood Quintus in a neat blue tunic, shaven-faced and wearing enough powder to hide his bruises and appear appropriately effeminate.

"You look perfect!"

"This is not going to work, Camilla," he said with a crestfallen expression. "I want more money."

"No labor negotiations once an undertaking begins."

"I could simply go away."

"And I could scream for the *vigils*. Say you propositioned me."

THE THREE CAMILLAS

"Propositioned you? You're too young!"

"Exactly. Oh, I'd hate to be in your boots when they caught you, sicko!"

His shoulders drooped.

"Inside." I opened the gate. "Of course, this is going to work. My plans always work. I know for a fact the ring will be hidden under Secunda's sleeping mattress during the meal. Easy pickings. Have confidence."

I ushered him through the garden back to the dining room. Prima and Secunda had joined the gathering, and all faces looked inquisitively at the newcomer.

"I am Belus the Thracian," said Quintus, announcing himself with sarcasm that I prayed only I noticed. "The new slave. The master has sent me back from Puteoli to help with the banquet."

"Puteoli?" asked Mother. "I thought my husband was in Baiae?"

"He... he has moved on to Puteoli, Mistress."

"Oh, that man never tells where he is," she said with a sigh, then moved closer, circling Quintus and appraising the newest servant. "My husband's always had good taste in slaves." Mother caressed him under the chin. "You're not bad-looking. A pity you're a gelding," she whispered.

"I'm not—"

I flashed him a hard stare.

"—not opposed to helping you in any way that I can, Mistress," he murmured reluctantly.

"Good," she said with a smile. "We'll talk about your creativity later. Now, please help the cook kill the goats."

***

The party proceeded well, if uneventfully. More guests arrived. Uncle Rufus entertained all by reading from his latest work, *The History of the Britons*—a history, per Rufus, which consisted of those northern islanders painting themselves blue, killing each other over sheep, and waiting for the generous Romans to civilize them—while everyone more interested in romance or fashion admired Prima's and Secunda's respective rings.

But all jewelry was put away when the greasy, sticky main course of goat, chicken, and mackerel garnished with rue was served. I'd insisted the cooks add all sorts of messy sauces to make certain every ring was removed. My efforts were rewarded. Before the meal was over, a subtle nod from Quintus told me he had it.

Now, to get him out of here.

The conversation had turned to the emperor's announcement that he was moving the capitol to Alexandria, Egypt, where the Egyptians knew how to properly worship man-gods, when the door chimes rang once more.

The servants' arms full with dishes, Secunda excused herself to get it. As she did I noticed the familiar engagement ring had returned to her finger.

I glanced inquisitively at Quintus, but he missed my stare, his own gaze at the latest arrival.

A very thin, Mediterranean-looking man walked in from the garden.

"Hello! I am Belus. The new slave. The master has sent me back from Baiae."

"Belus the Thracian?" asked Mother.

"Yes."

"But we've already got one."

"You can never have enough Thracians," said Uncle Rufus, downing his fifth goblet of wine. "Though 'Belus' is a drab name. Not sure we need another of those."

"I'm confused," said Aunt Camilla.

A scream erupted from the backrooms, and Prima came rushing out into the *triclinium*.

"It's gone!" she shrieked. "Gone. The ring is gone!"

"Now, just stay calm, Prima," pleaded Mother. "It must be here some—"

"It's a sign! An omen!" She started spinning around madly, bumping over vases, eyes bulging, pulling her hair violently in every direction. "The gods don't wish me to be married. I knew it! I knew it! Never! Never! I'll have to move to a cave on Lesbos!"

THE THREE CAMILLAS

"You're getting hysterical, Prima," said Secunda. "Please…"

Such a terrible sight, my poor, poor sister, weeping there. It crushed the *spiritus*.

What choice did I have?

"He's got it!" I shouted, pointing at Quintus. "He's got the ring! Him! The false eunuch."

"What?" the thief said, eyes a mile wide.

"Get him!"

Quintus tried to dart for the garden exit, but the real Belus caught him in a headlock. They crashed to the floor, and the dinner party descended upon the little bandit, Camilla Prima's fists flying.

* * *

I snuck down the darkened hall toward the storeroom door. I unhooked the latch, pried open the door, and stared into the blackness of the recess.

"Quintus?"

No answer.

"Quintus," I repeated.

"Go away."

I glanced over my shoulder to make sure we were still alone. Satisfied, I lowered my voice further. "Camilla Secunda is asleep, Quintus. I've got her ring. The right one this time. We'll get you out with it through the kitchen."

"I don't trust you."

"How can you not trust me? I've gotten you this far, haven't I?"

"Camilla, since I've been in your employ, I've been assaulted by a man in drag, strangled by a eunuch, and pummeled into submission by your hefty oldest sister. You're not doing much for my masculinity…"

"Look, we've little time. Camilla Prima and Mother are out searching for guards. You're a repeat offender now: You'll be crucified along the Appian Way or bloody tiger bait in the arena. I'm your only hope for getting out of this jam you've put yourself in."

"I've put myself in?"

"Let's go, Quintus."

A sorrowful moan came from the darkness. Finally, the thief emerged.

"You're an evil little girl."

"This way."

I led him through the corridor to our extensive kitchen, an assortment of large pots littering the floor, set out in preparation for the Julian stew Quintus's theft attempt had interrupted. Fortunately, there wasn't a servant in sight. I ran to the window overlooking the garden, threw back the curtain.

Iron bars covered every inch of the opening.

"Heavenly Jupiter, isn't that just wonderful?" said Quintus. "Why did I expect anything else?"

"Oh, I forgot, Mother had a grate put on last month." I shrugged, looked at him. "It's logical, if you think about it. We've a nice house. Many thieves would like to break in."

"This one would like to break out."

Masculine voices arose from the house's interior.

"Tell me that's your uncle."

"The *vigils* are here." I grabbed the edge of the largest pot, wobbled it over. "In this!"

"No. By Mercury, no."

"There isn't much water. You've plenty room to breathe."

"Never."

Footsteps echoed up from the hall.

"I'll tell them you fled. Send them away. Hurry!"

"No. I can see where this is going."

"Need I remind you 'tiger bait'? Have you ever seen what their claws do to human flesh? You think you're scrawny now..."

He sighed. Closed his eyes. "I'm going to regret this."

"Shhh."

Quintus climbed inside. I set the lid just in time.

The heavy masculine voices in the atrium continued, but the approaching footsteps weren't from them. Instead, Camilla Secunda and two servants entered the kitchen.

My sister scowled. "Why do you have my ring, Tertia?"

"Oh, this…I…I found it on the floor. You should be more careful, Secunda, with that unscrupulous thief about."

"Yes," she said suspiciously, taking it from me and placing it on her finger. "I would hate to lose this…"

"Really? You would *really* hate to lose it?"

"Of course, Tertia." She motioned for Belus and the old servant, Abas, to place the pot on the strip of hot coals in the kitchen's center. "It would be an ill omen indeed if it were to disappear."

My eyes followed the pot to the coal bed before I forced them back onto Secunda. "Then you…you…wish to marry Drusus Placidius Vopiscus after all? I overheard you tell Prima you didn't."

"That was simply to soften her pain with me, her younger sister, being married when she had no suitors. Now that we're both engaged, there's no need to pretend my wedding is a reluctant one."

"But you said Drusus had a 'frog face.'"

"I think his face is very handsome."

"You said you feared the emperor would take our estate."

"What better reason to pretend I must go ahead with the wedding than risk offending the emperor's friend? It was the perfect excuse to give Prima. And now, with the emperor moving all the way to Egypt, why worry about such things? We'll be outside his notice."

I was shocked. "You're a schemer, Secunda."

"And what of you?"

"I'm as innocent as—"

The lid of the pot began to shudder violently.

My sister's eyes widened. "I've never seen a pot boil so quickly, Tertia."

"Yes," I slid over to the edge of the coal bed, leaned out, and held down the lid. With all my strength. "That can happen with these imported pots. The things Father brings back from his travels. Really quite marvelous—"

"What's in there exactly, Tertia? That's not Julian stew."

"Some boiled carrots and a few odd ingredients, probably all those radishes Prima bought…"

The lid came firing off in my hands as a pink-skinned Quintus erupted from the pot. He danced, screaming across the coals before sprinting down the corridor shouting, "Guards! Guards! Take me! Better lions than this!"

The kitchen turned silent for a very long time.

"By Juno," I said sheepishly at last. "That's not something you see every day."

"No…no, it's not," answered Secunda with a frown. She paused. "You know, little sister, we must serve lobster at the weddings."

"Yes, Secunda. Though we should cook it most thoroughly."

XVIII

THE DUNES OF SAULKRASTI

Originally published in Ellery Queen's Mystery Magazine

The Dunes of Saulkrasti

The old man dug deep into the dunes.

Hidden by a screen of fir trees, far back from the beaches, no one disturbed his shoveling. He knew the grunts of his effort, the sound of his spade splitting the sands, and the occasional moans of the dying body beside him were too faint to be heard by the revelers along the seashore. Their laughter and singing barely carried over the white dunes that stretched inland for a quarter kilometer to this spot. If those festive celebrations remained dim and indistinct at this distance, his own solitary work must be unheard.

But the old man was realistic. This freedom could not last. Someone would blunder by eventually. It was the eve of Latvia's most important seasonal holiday, Jāņi, the summer solstice, and the beaches were full of merrymakers, drinking, jumping over bonfires, and preparing for the midnight swim, when all sins were purged for the year.

The old man was comfortable with his sins. Secretly enjoyed them. He felt no need to skinny-dip in the Baltic Sea with a hundred strangers.

He had other dues to pay.

Movement caught his eye. His captive had rallied from death's door and slipped away, crawling up the side of a ghostly white dune, seeking escape, reprieve, or an audience with the perpetual solstice sun.

Whichever. The old man pulled out his pistol fitted with an antique KGB silencer and sent three bullets through his target. The body rolled down the dune to his feet. Dead.

He tucked his gun in his trousers and went back to digging. Soon his spade struck something solid. His hands trembled with excitement. He tapped again, heard the sweet echo of a hollow compartment below.

That which they'd buried decades ago was here, undisturbed.

Riches all his own.

Then he heard it. Below, from within that sealed compartment, a voice said:

"Open up out there."

One day earlier...

I. Artūrs

Artūrs Pelšs, sixty-two and grizzled, stood in the beachfront bar he owned, watching the scene. With consecutive holidays on the calendar, *Līgo* today and *Jāņi* tomorrow, he anticipated excellent business. Enough, he hoped, to keep him solvent another season. In past years, his bar was never as full as Artūrs desired. Latvian families might stop by for a bite or to purchase water or alcohol, but they seldom lingered, heading out to the beaches or countryside to celebrate the solstice. Artūrs wanted to keep customers here, locked in his restaurant, spending money.

That's where his inspiration came this year.

The bar was filled with American servicemen—excuse him, *NATO* servicemen—as theirs was supposed to be a multinational mission, the soldiers in Latvia as a deterrent against the Russian activity buzzing along the country's eastern border. So, he dressed up his recent hire, Alise, in the tiniest American flag bikini he could order online and had her running the portable tap at the open beachfront end of the bar. Alise was stunningly beautiful, a smart charmer who spoke their language. The young Americans stayed to chat her up, bought his beer, got drunk on the high Latvian alcohol content, and bought more beer. A perfect cycle.

Artūrs had only to keep the tap open and roll the kegs out every forty minutes or so long into the night. He felt brilliant.

Until the waters came in.

One moment, everything was dry; the next Artūrs saw the tides sweep across his wooden floors, customers glancing down at the touch of cool Baltic waters on their heels.

"Not again," said Alise, her servicemen courtiers scrambling to seize the mops and aid their queen.

Artūrs cursed, called Teodors on his mobile. Cursed again. While Alise and the others attempted to dam the tides, Artūrs stormed out onto the beach for a meeting.

***

The ten-minute walk along the seaside failed to calm Artūrs. Everywhere, he saw the problem. The summer sun hanging on the horizon tonight left nothing hidden. On Artūrs's left were the sand dunes for which Saulkrasti was famous, some cresting ten meters or more, and on his right, the ever-encroaching sea, which bit by bit, clump by clump was stealing the land away. The holiday bonfires were built farther inland every year. The tides could no longer be trusted.

Ahead, he spied Teodors Šics.

Speaking of things which cannot be trusted...

Five years Artūrs's senior, with his full head of hair and trim build, Teodors looked years younger. This tall man dragged his foot through the sand, measuring the distance from the tide line to the dunes. The clinical nature of Teodors's study annoyed Artūrs. Had this no meaning to him?

"*Ligo!*" said Teodors in the traditional greeting of the holiday. "How's Alise working out?"

"Shut up!" answered Artūrs, storming up to Teodors. "The bar is flooded again. The trench we dug last night did no good."

"It's global warming. The waters rise."

"The waters rise because the government blew up the offshore shoals, so the tankers and American warships can run closer to the coast. Now, there's nothing to block the surf."

Teodors shrugged. "It could be both. Or neither. The reason matters little at this point."

His calmness enraged Artūrs. "To you, it is a joke. Your hotel sits far back among the dunes. But my livelihood is ruined. How can I sell the bar if it floods daily? I want to make a withdrawal, Teodors."

"We agreed not to touch the gold again until age seventy."

"I've had nothing in twenty years. Since I bought the bar. I'll take what's mine, with or without your help."

An unwelcome authority edged into Teodors's voice. "Who is the officer here?"

"Those days are over. We are the last two."

The tall man's eyes narrowed into a scowl. Teodors was not one to accept dissension, but Artūrs no longer cared. He was ruined without his gold.

At last, Teodors relented. "When do you want to get it?"

"Tomorrow."

"On the busiest night of the year? Madness. We'll be caught. Wait until after *Jāņi*, when the beaches empty. Then we get the gold together."

Artūrs tried to keep his blood from boiling. He hated Teodors, wished to be rid of his old captain. Forty years was long enough to serve anyone.

He took a deep breath of the salty sea air. Still, two could move gold better than one.

"The night after *Jāņi* then, Teodors. Not one day more."

* * *

When Artūrs returned to the bar, he found the premises abandoned. Only Alise remained, sitting on a wooden stool, keeping her bare ankles above the invading waters.

"Bad news," she said, a rare meekness in her voice. "Things are worse...."

Artūrs grimaced. "How could things possibly be worse?"

"During the flooding, some hooligan got at the cash register."

She was right. It was worse.

"How much?"

"Till's empty, boss. We're broke."

***

The next day, the morning of *Jāņi,* Alise recruited several smitten Americans to dig a larger trench in the sand, practically a moat crossed from the greater beach by wooden planks. Artūrs's little bar looked like a fortress....

Artūrs passed the day assembling shovels in the back and constructing a canopied sled to carry the gold bars home over the dunes. If anyone asked, as Alise often did, the sled was for his grandson, coming to visit for the holiday.

When she asked Artūrs why he now carried a pistol, he spoke of last night's burglary. Alise reminded him there was *already* a security pistol tucked behind the bookshelves in his office.

He told her to mind her own business.

She stopped asking questions.

Trouble began when Artūrs was down on his knees installing a keg beneath the portable tap. Alise stood above him, leaning over the bar and charming foreign customers impatient for their beers. A Latvian fellow shoved his way to the front, one already inebriated from holiday celebration. As Artūrs adjusted the beer valve, he heard the man above say:

"Santa, it's me. Normunds from Rīga."

"I'm not called 'Santa.' You're mistaken. I'm Alise."

"We went to school together, Santa...."

"You have the wrong girl. Everyone has a twin, they say. Oh, the tap works again. Here, have one on the house, from Alise."

The tap now opened, the din of voices demanding beer drowned out further conversation. Artūrs considered what he'd heard. Drunks often got names wrong and "Santa" was among the most common of Latvian names. Still, in the two weeks she'd worked here, other drunks sometimes called her "Santa" too. An oddly recurrent mistake that always made Alise visibly upset.

Latvia was a small country. Chance encounters frequent.

A hard place to maintain an alias.

When Alise took her cigarette break, Artūrs went out back to join her, to speak privately in the narrow valley formed by the bar's rear wall and the dunes behind.

"Alise, change of plans. I'm shutting down tonight. Go out with friends, enjoy the solstice holiday. You'll get full wages for today."

Her eyes widened at the news. "But, we have so many customers, boss...."

"Let the Americans spend the holiday as it was meant to be. With nature, not in our flooding barroom. Go on. Don't waste your youth working through the holidays. You want to end up wrinkled and lonely like me? I'll see you tomorrow. Late as you wish."

She finished her cigarette in pensive silence, retrieved her purse from inside, thanked him, and headed off over the dunes. Artūrs often watched Alise walk, as men worldwide watch women walk. But tonight was different. No leer appeared on his face, only calculation. Tonight, Artūrs wanted to see where this "Santa" goes....

***

"She is a spy, Teodors!"

"A spy? A spy for whom? For what?"

Artūrs poked Teodors in the chest. "For you! She lives at your hotel, yes? You introduced her as 'Alise,' but her name isn't 'Alise,' is it? You lied to me. And then you suggested I give her a job! What a fool I am. She is your mole."

"Why would I spy on a destitute bar owner like you?"

"To see I remain destitute. You watched Einars, Valts, and Girts the same way. All who knew of that gold truck. You're a tyrant, Teodors. Murdering your old comrades for..."

Teodors struck Artūrs with a power rare for a man his age. Artūrs went down, stunned and splashing into the surf.

"Remember your place, Sergeant." Teodors reached down and retrieved the pistol tucked in Artūrs's trousers, shoved it into his own pocket.

"I'm still commander here."

II. Teodors

An hour later, in the early evening of *Jāņi,* Teodors Šics reached his hotel, a little watermelon-colored cottage nestled among the Saulkrasti dunes. He once possessed several establishments like this, charming bed-and-breakfasts sitting on beautiful beaches throughout Latvia. But the real-estate crash of 2008 cost Teodors everything: savings, property, a wife. Artūrs Pelšs would be surprised to know they were *both* broke. Now, this hotel was his only livelihood.

He checked the register. One guest, even at the holidays: "Alise Liepa." Teodors wasn't quite sure what had gotten into Artūrs about Alise. She seemed a passive enough child to him: respectful, quiet, paid her weekly rent promptly and in cash. Still, a young woman who used her figure to sell beer could not be as sweet as she seemed.

Idiot though he was, Artūrs's instincts were occasionally correct.

Teodors retrieved the spare key to Alise's room, climbed the steps to her door. When his knocking received no reply, he turned the lock and entered the tiny bedroom. His budget hotel offered guests no maid service, yet all was tidy: the bed made, Alise's bags stacked neatly in the corner. Teodors respected order. He felt foolish for letting Artūrs engender distrust in a good tenant.

Until he opened Alise's second bag.

Inside, he found a driver's license for a Santa Ezeriņa, twenty-four, from Rīga. Alise's familiar face, adorned with shorter hair and devoid of makeup, stared back at him. The same face appeared on another photo, one affixed to a press pass.

A filthy journalist?

He gritted his teeth. This was worse than the police, worse than the government. Journalists needed little proof to ruin lives.

In her third and lowest bag, Teodors discovered books, papers, publications going back decades with one common theme: the famous Soviet gold truck that disappeared in 1982 somewhere on the Baltic coast en route to Leningrad. An international mystery, still occasionally discussed in coffeehouses and radio programs throughout the Baltics. True crime experts pegged Latvia's Vidzeme coastline as a likely hiding place for the gold. One salacious cable television show, closer than they knew, believed the truck buried in the dunes of nearby Lilaste quarry. Their camera crew stayed three days at Teodors's hotel during filming. A dicey time that luckily passed without incident.

But, no one during these years suspected five Latvian soldiers on furloughs home from the Soviet Union's Afghanistan War, never dreamed these honest "local boys" planned and executed the greatest heist in Baltic history. Even the KGB, by all accounts, never seriously considered Teodors and his men.

Yet Alise was hot on the trail. She possessed a photograph of their company in Kabul, taken two weeks before the furlough and a decade before she was born. Valts, Einars, Girts, and Artūrs all circled. As was Teodors himself, under which someone had written "Heist leader?"

Teodors's affinity for order fell away. He shoved aside furniture, ripped clothing from hangers, dumped out the contents of drawers. Behind the bed, he found a hand-sized metal detector. Inside Alise's toothbrush kit, a chemical test meant to identify real gold.

The bikini-temptress routine was an act. This journalist was a serious woman.

And a serious problem.

When Alise came home, Teodors was waiting behind her bedroom door. She never saw the butt of the pistol as it struck her solidly across the back of the head.

Problem solved.

THE DUNES OF SAULKRASTI

* * *

Shovel strapped across his back, Teodors dragged the unconscious Alise across the sands, keeping far from the beaches and footpaths. He knew the dunes well, living here thirty years. It might never grow truly dark at solstice, but this lonely route should keep them unseen. Teodors long ago mapped the least trafficked way to reach his gold.

In a trough between two great dunes, he at last began to dig. The girl did not stir, and he briefly wondered if she might have died. No matter. One way or another, she'd soon be below ground.

Teodors made good time in his digging. Soon, he came upon the hard surface of the old truck's top. He cleared an area of sand, found the wooden hatch he'd constructed in the cargo-body's roof, slid it open.

Below was the near-empty cargo zone of the truck. Sand covered the flooring, the skeleton of a nosy Swede he'd killed in 2003 sticking out, his long black metal detector at his side. No gold, of course. Teodors had spent much of it on investments after Latvia's independence in 1991 and the rest paying his debts during the real-estate crisis seventeen years later. He wished to reimburse his comrades, but when repayment became impossible, Teodors chose to eliminate his men before they asked for their gold. Only Artūrs, an unambitious man satisfied to run a bar, remained passive enough to stay his execution.

That had changed tonight.

Teodors tossed Alise's body through the hatch. She landed in the soft sand near the Swede, arm across his skeletal shoulder. They appeared contented, like a slumbering couple on the beach.

Rest in peace, Alise. Or Santa. Artūrs's corpse will be joining you soon.

He closed the hatch and began the arduous task of reburying the truck's roof. When it was finally hidden beneath the Saulkrasti sands, Teodors retreated to his hotel, plotting his gambit to entrap Artūrs.

A shadow waited for him inside, and the flash of gunfire lit up hotel windows.

III. Santa

Santa Ezeriņa awoke in darkness, the back of her head throbbing without mercy. The air impossibly dry, her throat parched, it took fifty, even a hundred slow breaths before she found the strength to move. When she did stir, electric pain shot up her spine to pool in the back of her neck. She relented briefly to these agonies, tried to recover inside the womblike blackness.

Slowly, Santa's perception expanded out beyond the pulsating pain. Her arm rested across something dry, bowing, and porous.

A human ribcage. A skeleton.

She recoiled. Fear, shock, and adrenaline dampening her pains, Santa pushed herself away from the corpse over a sandy, wooden floor, until her back and shoulders rested against a metal wall. What sort of prison...?

For the first time, she realized this was not some room or basement in Teodors Šics's hotel. Her bare arms and legs burned, scrapes over the skin. She'd been dragged somewhere....

Santa forced herself to explore her environment. On her knees, she swept her hands out over the floor. Near the skeleton, she discovered a metal pole ending in a disk, like a flag stand tipped on its side. Wires crisscrossed about it, a rubber grip on the pole's end with buttons and a switch. Some sort of lamp? A vacuum? No,... an industrial metal detector. Her fellow prisoner, the corpse, a victim of Captain Šics and his men, likely caught searching Saulkrasti for the old truck....

The truck! The truck that had been missing thirty-five years. Could it be? All these years searching...was she now inside that Leningrad gold truck? And her chauvinistic coworkers said she'd never succeed....

She calmed herself. *Think logically, Santa.* She couldn't go stumbling around in the dark, tripping over corpses. With effort, Santa unscrewed the extended handle from the metal detector's disc. It was a hollow pole, open on the bottom end. Like a blind woman with a cane, she used it to probe the room. She quickly judged the distance to the other three walls. The dimensions matched. It *was* the truck. No sign of the forty gold bars that disappeared with it. On her tiptoes, she poked up into darkness, tapped the ceiling with the handle-pole.

A recess above! The sound different. Not metal-on-metal, but metal-on-wood. It could only be a hatch. Groping about, Santa managed to wedge the pole inside the aperture, push the hatch open a sliver.

A flood of cascading sand knocked her down. Choking, coughing, she only just managed to regain her footing, to stab that pole into the incoming avalanche, and somehow slide the hatch shut.

She stood there for many moments, regaining her breath, leaning on the pole. Buried alive inside a useless Soviet truck wearing a skimpy American flag bikini. What an obituary. Both sides of the new Cold War would be insulted...

If she got an obituary.

Probably, no one would know her fate. Another mystery for Vidzeme lore. She thought of her parents, of Aunt Ieva. The sadness she'd bring them... always brought them with her journalistic ambitions. Obsessions.

She shook this off. No time for pity. Act now while there's still air.

How to get out of here? *Kur acs, tur ceļš.* Where there's an eye, there's a path. What did she have to work with? A pole. A deteriorating truck interior. And sand. An endless supply of sand.

She thought of last year's assignment in Cairo. The ancient Egyptians used sand as a tool. With little wood to waste on scaffolding, their scribes and artisans filled their temples nearly to the ceilings with Sahara sands, sat on mat-rafts atop the mounds painting the walls, draining the levels slowly as they worked their way downwards.

She'd reverse that. If she had the air.

Santa groped around on the truck's disintegrating wooden bottom, found a floorboard with a knothole gap, used the metal pole to pry free a meter-square section. She set this "raft" atop the dirt, then sat upon it cross-legged. Keeping her equilibrium as best she could, Santa reached up and over with the pole, opened the hatch at a distance.

The sands flowed in beside her, forming a conical dune like grains in the bottom of an hourglass.

She closed the hatch. Used the handle to smooth out the sands. Then pressed the handle down like a gondola pole to push herself towards the opposite side, riding up the remnants of the dune beneath the hatch. She and her raft were now a meter higher than before.

She repeated this again. And again. Opening the hatch. Surmounting the dune. Leveling the sands around her. Higher and higher she rose as the truck's payload filled. She kept her weight even, legs ever crossed and used the pole to maneuver her raft, first by pushing off the floor, then later, at higher levels, by pushing off the ceiling and walls.

At last, Santa reached the ceiling, but there was no longer room to maneuver and little air left to breathe. Panting, dizzy, if she was going to escape, she must go through that hatch soon. A dicey proposition. If she fell off or unbalanced her raft, she'd sink into the sand below and smother. Her only hope was to fight her way out against the incoming torrent to the truck's roof, find firm footing, and pray she either cleared the surface or this hollow pole could be used somehow as a snorkel to breathe, shout for help.

Likely as not, the inrushing sand would carry her down into the truck's interior, burying her forever. Go now, and she'd probably die. Stay, and she surely would.

Santa was preparing to remove her bikini top, to tie it across her face to protect eyes, nose, and mouth during the ascent, when she heard shoveling above. Then a tapping on the truck's roof and scraping as someone cleared earth away overhead.

She felt a moment of elation before cold reason tamed her emotions. Anyone digging for this truck was surely a criminal. Teodors returning to dump some new victim inside? Maybe he'd finally killed Artūrs. The boys at her newspaper predicted it weeks ago.

Santa tucked the metal pole beneath her arm and held out the opened protruding end like a gun barrel. Aimed it squarely in the center of that hatch. In the shadows of the truck's interior, her "rescuer" might think she held a rifle.

A long shot. But her best chance.

It's been a nice life.

"Open up out there," she shouted.

There was a pause in the shoveling. Then the hatch flew open, an old man standing above in the comparative brightness of a solstice night.

It was Artūrs Pelšs, his bar's emergency pistol in his hands, now fitted with a silencer and pointed directly at her.

His eyes widened in shock. "Alise!? You found the gold?"

Santa held that metal handle steady as she could, willed her bluff to work. "Yeah. I got here first. If you want those treasures, throw down the pistol. I just want to leave."

"I've got a clear shot too, Alise. I wish it were different. But you can't go. I'm sorry."

"A pistol's no match for a rifle. You want a hole through your belly? Throw the gun to me!"

Please God, please...

Artūrs swallowed hard. Somewhere, revelers were singing for the holiday.

"Well?" She raised the pole higher....

He tossed down the pistol.

She almost swooned with relief. A real gun in her hands, Santa abandoned the detector handle, pulled herself out through the truck hatch, eyes on Artūrs.

Out of the corner of her vision, she saw Teodors Šics, his bullet-ridden body dead at the base of a nearby dune.

"You guys just couldn't get along, could you?"

"He was going to kill me like he killed the others. I had to strike first." Artūrs dropped to his knees in the sand. "Alise... the gold? Thirty-five years. I must see it. You don't know the dreams...."

Santa almost felt sorry for Artūrs, though her gun never wavered.

"Sorry, boss, till's empty. Again."

XIX

FAST FORWARD

Originally published in Mystery Weekly Magazine

Fast Forward

I am a time-jumper.

Whoa! Stay with me, friends. I don't mean a *time traveler* or any such Doctor Who nonsense. This isn't a science fiction story bound for *Analog* or *Asimov's*. You're in the right book. Everything I tell you is not only possible but absolute truth. All will be explained.

Let me ask you this: Have you ever wished to fast forward through the difficult times in life? To avoid the drudgery of an arduous task by skipping ahead on the calendar until it is completed? Or spare yourself pain after heartbreak or a loved one's death by jumping in an instant to a day when the wounds have healed?

This is what I mean by "time-jumping." I can do this. Have done it. Many times. Call me a coward but I often opt-out of the unpleasant moments in life. Doing so has never harmed me.

I first remember "fast forwarding" at five years of age when sentenced to stand twenty minutes with my face in the corner for some offense against our strict military family. Such incarcerations are death to a boisterous boy, and as I stared with undiluted hatred into the cracked corner plaster, a sensation previously unknown in my young life arrived without warning. A warmth along the spine, a tingling in the extremities, and a haze of indescribable color began to cloud my vision. I grew dizzy and fell against the wall. And then, somehow, it was over. My sight was clear, the penalty minutes evaporated, and Mother told me I was free again to play. To my surprise, and later, to my advantage, this experience repeated every time I was sentenced to the corner as punishment: the dizziness, the unknowable color, and time lost to instant freedom.

I soon learned to control the ability and broadened its application. Fast-forwarding was a useful tool for the dreary days of adolescence, speeding through boring school lectures, yard work, long trips to Grandma's in Bristol. Of course, no one knew I was doing it. Time passed normally for the rest of the world, and during these interludes I remained conscious to the eyes of outsiders, apparently functioning and acting as usual. In fact, during a "fast forward," I must enter a more focused state, for in most endeavors I remain substantially more successful during these times than otherwise. Take an exam myself, and I might get a C or C+. Fast-forward through it, and my alternate consciousness inevitably earned a solid A, often with distinction.

Upon reaching age thirty, however, when the signs of mortality find their first footholds, I became less keen to use up my life, to hand off the dreary hours to someone else no matter how capable. I viewed fast forwarding as destructive, an addiction, and vowed to savor every minute that remained.

This required new discipline. I endured sitting in traffic on I-95 in East Providence going into the city, doing taxes, or watching a "chick flick" to please a girlfriend. All things I would escape before. I was proud of my new endurance, viewed it as a form of maturity, even overdue penance. For nearly a year my more-focused alter ego lay buried beneath my subconscious, uncalled upon and unused. Ignored. Penned. Seething.

I almost forgot about him. Things went well enough in my one-man event-planning business, that there was no inkling to use his abilities. It didn't last, however. In September of 2019, I was engaged by the esteemed Oswald Overvold to organize a gala exhibition at his Newport estate. The previous planner unexpectedly quit, leaving an enormous amount of work to be done at short notice. I drank copious amounts of coffee, downed handfuls of amphetamines, stayed awake two full days slogging through before my resolve failed.

Why suffer if one need not?

Just once more...

So, on a warm Saturday morning, with a cup of steaming tea in my hands, I lay back on my balcony chair, listened to the honks and shouts from the busy Providence streets below, and discarded my cares. I let the still-nameless color descend over my vision and jumped ahead to a day when the work was done, my bank account full, and life moved at a playful pace again.

I awoke on my living room couch, sweaty, sore, and naked, except for the bath towel wrapped about my waist. A glance at the date on the digital clock nearby told me it was two weeks to the minute since I started my jump. I reclosed my eyes, endured the usual brief headache after fast-forwarding, breathed slowly, willed the pain to recede. Dreamed of all the work the other me had completed...

Soft lips clasped mine in a kiss.

My eyes opened. An olive-skinned beauty in a black dress worthy of a Hollies song leaned over me. She applied another kiss. The pains melted away.

"Feeling better, James?" asked this stranger.

I was usually adept at faking my way along until the sped-through memories seeped in. But this time, I only managed to mumble:

"A little."

"Good." A third kiss, this one briefer, more serious somehow. "I gotta leave, honey. Keep this secure, will you?"

She set a cool steel revolver in my hands.

Eros jumped out the window. "I...I'm not sure ...I..."

The woman read my horror. "The safety's on, honey. Don't want any mistakes like last night." She rose, shouldered a golden Gucci purse, and stepped to the door. "I'll be home by nine. It's 'Bubble Bath Saturday'. Be sure to buy champagne."

Before I could say anything more, she exited. I heard a key lock the door from outside.

I sat there trying to make sense of it all, that pistol resting in my palms. I hated guns. Feared guns. Wanted this thing far away from me.

Double-checking that the safety was indeed on, I took the pistol to the iron safe below the bedroom desk. Fortunately, my alternate consciousness hadn't changed the combo during his time at the wheel. The other James often did cruel things to spite me.

The safe's door came open easily. A man's head rested inside.

I screamed, and despite my aversion to guns it was lucky the safety was set, because I pulled the trigger as I scampered back.

No, it wasn't a human head. Only a weathered-looking bronze sculpture, slightly larger than life-sized, like something torn off a Greek or Roman statue from antiquity.

I cursed. What the Hell had *he* been up to while I was out?

Fate gave me no time to consider. A fierce knocking erupted at my front door.

I placed the gun beside the head, locked the safe. After checking the security of my towel, I went to the front room, opened the door.

A tough-looking man in his late forties stood in the hall. Wearing a frayed brown suit, yellow tie, and overcoat, he resembled something out of a colorized Howard Hawks film. His eyes looked me over.

"Did I get you out of the shower, James?"

He knew me. Or at least the other me.

"Just taking a nap," I said.

His eyes jumped past me into the apartment. "She here?"

"Who's here?"

"Dido Voutira. We know she's been shacked up at your place at least a week."

"I can't recall ever hearing that name before." Which was true. "What's she look like?"

"Tall, honey-colored hair, Hellenic figure. A Greek-American art thief wanted in the civilized world for uncivilized doings. You know her, James. Probably Biblically." He clicked his teeth, and there was something like envy in his eyes. "Harboring a criminal is a felony, my friend. But we're not after you, so play nice, and there'll be minimal trouble."

Was he a cop? He talked like a cop. A TV cop from the 50s.

"Before we go any further, I want to see some I.D."

"You never needed it before."

"I'm skeptical in my old age."

"Old age? Our files say you're thirty-one."

"I feel like I'm living two or three lives these days. That I.D., please."

He withdrew identification from his overcoat pocket. It read: "Lieutenant Callixtus F. Hood, Rhode Island State Police Department, Detective Bureau," which meant he could be dealing with cases from white-collar crime to fugitives to homicide. In short, anything or anyone that caused trouble statewide.

"Okay. So, what exactly do you need, Hood?"

"I wanna come in and look around. See if Dido is in the bedroom. And, if not, what she might have left behind. There are several very valuable works of art your lady friend may have stolen."

"You have a warrant?"

"No. But your cooperation or lack thereof will be noted when everything goes down."

"Listen, *Dragnet,* no warrant. No entry."

"You'd save me a lot of leg work, James …"

"Good day, Lieutenant."

"Okay. I'll be back with a warrant." He stepped back into the hall. "Put some pants on when I do."

I closed the door.

For a moment, I thought maybe this was all some confused dream. But I never dream after jumps. Not for days …

I went to my laptop intending to Google "Dido Voutira," but when it booted up, the computer's desktop was cleared except for one MPEG file prominently in the center named: "For Jimmy."

My other life always called me "Jimmy." This was new. He'd left notes before but never a video. I clicked on the file.

A window popped up on the screen, a video of my other self sitting at the bedroom window seat, my hair flattened in place like Clark Kent after a rainstorm, wearing khaki jeans and an Ascot sweater that nobody tolerated but our old Aunt Ethel. From the low quality of the video it was clearly a selfie taken by my ancient camera phone. The timestamp on the file indicated a recording two-hours old.

"Jimmy," he said as the video came to life. "The headaches tell me you'll soon take control. I beseech you, as always, leave a note with the date and time you plan to resume command. I've many irons in the fire that simply can't be left to the likes of you."

The bizarre novelty of me leaving a video for me was quickly lost to the familiar patronizing tone known from his letters and emails. The medium of communication changed nothing. James simply felt no respect for "Jimmy."

"I don't expect you to listen," he continued, "You never do. But this time it is a matter of life and death, Jimmy. Yes, you heard that right." He looked away briefly from the camera, then lowered his voice. "The night before the Overvold party was to occur, a known art thief was found shot dead in the exhibition hall at the Overvold manor. As I had impressed Oswald Overvold with my knowledge of art during our preparations, he asked me to assess which piece in his collection the thief, Theodore Friel, might have been trying to steal, if any, when murdered. I have thus become informally involved in the investigation. Oswald trusts my counsel more than that idiot Lieutenant Hood, a bumbling fool even you could outwit."

A woman's voice called from somewhere.

"James, why are you dressed so early? Come back to bed."

"I popped out to make you *kagianas* for breakfast, my dear," he said. "One moment."

"Please hurry. I need another back rub ..."

The selfie video showed him walking to our kitchen, presumably out of earshot of the woman. His voice resumed in a whisper. "To increase my knowledge of the seedier side of the art market, I went onto the Dark Web. Under the guise of purchasing a head of Augustus Caesar, I met with Dido Voutira, seduced her, now she resides in our apartment."

He was frighteningly proficient at seduction. In his letters, he'd bragged at a sexual partner count that would make porn stars blush. I, despite being at the helm most our life, had been stuck at two since college.

"You will have met Dido by now, I suspect. Try not to screw it up. Her presence is advantageous for all, Jimmy. She gives us access to the underworld. We provide her with another sanctuary and the occasional alibi. Dido is being hounded by the police for allegedly stealing a two-million-dollar Pergo painting from the RISD Museum of Art. Hood has raised her name in connection to the Friel murder. I believe her innocent of both crimes."

The fingers of his free hand picked at something resembling a bullet hole in the kitchen wall. "I'll need control of our body at least three weeks more, Jimmy. This is beyond your abilities. Remember when we took that I.Q. test? You earned 114. My score was perfect. The first 200 in the test's history. And you needed me to even pass your driver's exam."

Yeah, yeah. Piss off...

"Consider what I have said, Jimmy. Lives are in the balance. And be sure to delete this message, people will think us schizophrenic."

I closed my laptop.

His arrogance annoyed me. We had the same DNA and the same experiences generally. Why couldn't I solve this crime? Hadn't I functioned well enough this last year without him? Okay, if I'm "Jimmy," so be it. Jimmy, from now on.

Jimmy could do anything James had.

I found a clean blue suit crowded to one side of a closet now filled with Dido's expensive-looking things. I had just finished tying the knot in my tie when the phone rang. The caller I.D. read "Undisclosed Number."

I answered. "Hello."

A smooth, aristocratic-sounding female voice said: "Hello, James. Victoria Blossomgate."

I remembered Victoria from before the jump. She was the Overvold Collection curator. "What can I do for you, Ms. Blossomgate?"

"Mr. Overvold wants to see you at five. He needs an update on the Theodore Friel murder. Can you make it, James?"

"Yes. But call me 'Jimmy.'"

My informality changed her tone. "Why 'Jimmy'?"

"Cause, when it's over, I want everyone to know Jimmy Gothe solved this case. Not a word about anyone named 'James'..."

*　*　*

During the drive along Route 138 and over the bridges spanning Narragansett Bay to Aquidneck Island, some of James's memories began to seep in piecemeal as they always do: images of a body in a small exhibition room, each wall adorned with a single large painting. A number appeared in my mind too, a value: $1,499. As if James had long considered it.

What did that bastard know?

Soon I reached Newport with its splendid beaches and great mansions from the Gilded Age. Oswald Overvold's was one of the largest manors overlooking the coast, a palace even by Bellevue Avenue standards.

After being buzzed in through an automatic gate, I drove my sputtering Chevy over a long, graveled drive, past high hedges and gardens turning autumn colors, and at last parked before a neo-gothic stone manor that would put Hill House to shame.

A thin woman in her eighties appeared on the mansion's portico. Smartly dressed in an emerald green wool crepe suit, diamond broach at her breast, and long silver hair pulled back into a Dutch braid, there was something luminous about Victoria Blossomgate. She must have been a true beauty in her prime.

Still was a beauty, really.

"You're early, Mr. Gothe," Victoria said, waiting on the portico steps as I exited the car. "I didn't expect you for nearly three hours."

"I wanted to do some research before meeting your boss. I hope that's okay, Ms. Blossomgate?"

She smiled. "Of course. But, need I remind you again? Please, say '*Mrs.* Blossomgate.' Or 'Victoria.' At my age if you use 'Ms' they think you a spinster, not a widow. My husband should not be so easily forgotten."

Yes, her husband was the original curator before some mugger in Boston took his life. Though I could not recall if my knowledge of that fact was

James's or my own.

"An appropriate honor, Mrs. Blossomgate," I said. "You're continuing his work. Everyone who attends the exhibition realizes it, certainly."

"Thank you," She ushered me into a great entrance hall of modern décor, another world from the nineteenth century façade, yet every bit as opulent.

A butler took my coat and I asked Victoria for somewhere to review documents related to the case. She left me alone in her private office off the exhibition hall, copies of artwork purchase receipts and insurance records in my hands, a police photo of Theodore Friel's corpse on the desk, and a porcelain cup of steaming mint tea at my elbow.

I couldn't afford to wait for James's memories to crystalize, so I spent the hours making up for lost time, commuting between Victoria's office, the adjacent exhibition halls, and the lavender-colored corridor where Friel broke into the manor. All the while taking mental notes.

The other me tugged as my subconscious, wanted out.

But James could wait.

I lingered longest in the main exhibition hall, the place of Theodore Friel's demise, the four paintings from my vision on the walls. I observed them carefully.

On the north wall hung a still-life painting of a nineteenth-century kitchen table adorned with baskets of fruit, a swine leg and roasted poultry on serving plates, and in the shadows, a gleaming-eyed house cat ready to pounce. The author's signature in the corner read: "C. Montoya. 1885."

On the east wall was an urban watercolor showing a bustling dockyard at dusk, two burly workers engaged in fisticuffs on the pier as their fellows try to separate the combatants. The work dated August 1934 by Woodrow Feinstein.

On the south hung a traditional oil by an E. H. Van Pelt and dated 1741 depicting a wealthy colonial gentleman standing with his hounds on the banks of a pond, a paddling of white ducks gathered on the waters behind.

Lastly, on the west, an anonymous and undated portrait of a melancholy girl peering out her window at the snow-covered woods beyond, her lonely eyes fixed on the smoke of a distant chimney rising just beyond the trees.

I took my notes. When finished, I returned to the curator's office, scanned the pages of the visitors' comment books. Very few attended these halls. Only wealthy Bellevue neighbors at the discretion of the curator or owner.

At five o'clock precisely, Victoria popped her silver-haired head into the office. "They're assembled. Are you ready?"

"Absolutely."

Showtime.

I followed her into the main exhibition hall. Standing inside was Oswald Overvold, sixty-ish, balding with a bulldog face and a Cuban cigar clenched between his teeth. Next to him stood Lieutenant Hood, clearly disgusted at having to listen to my opinion on *his* case.

But Overvold called the shots here. Even to the police.

"I believe everyone knows each other," said Victoria promptly. "James, please make your presentation."

"It's 'Jimmy.'" I corrected. "We're all friends here."

"Hardly," scoffed Hood.

I ignored him. Cracked my knuckles. Then, in my best Hercule Poirot manner, I said: "Let us review the basic facts. Theodore Friel was found, shot in the back, lying before this painting on the south wall eleven days ago. A utility knife remained in his hand, as if he planned to cut down the canvas. It is conjectured by some he was attempting to steal the painting when murdered."

I approached the painting of the gentleman with his dogs at the pond. "Anything I've missed so far, Lieutenant Hood?"

"No," he said tersely. "Those facts are indisputable."

"Then let's dispute them. My friends, after much contemplation, I know the body was moved."

"Moved?" asked Victoria, glancing at the others.

"Moved?" echoed Hood.

"Moved," I repeated. "And Friel did not intend to steal *this* painting.

Why? Because this is the least valuable in the collection insured for less than fifteen hundred dollars. A pittance compared to the others. Ten thousand for the west wall painting, sixteen thousand for the east, and …" I pointed theatrically at the remaining painting: "one-hundred-thirty-thousand for the work on the north wall, the kitchen still-life by the Spanish master Custodio Montoya. An experienced art thief like Theodore Friel would know the value of a Montoya original. He would not waste his time with paintings of lesser value."

"Possibly," said Overvold nodding. "Just possibly."

"Observe, please, sir," I said. "If we theorize Friel was shot in the back while approaching the Montoya painting instead, the angle of gunfire matches up with the entrance to the Lavender Hall. The same hall where Friel and possibly others broke in through the skylight that night."

Their eyes lighted, the proposition well-received by all but Hood. *Ha! Let's see James do that!* "The clouds part, friends. We are nearer our answer. As I see it, the essential questions of the case are One: 'Who killed Friel?' Two: 'Why did they kill him?' And Three: 'Who moved the body and why?'"

"Malarkey," said Hood.

I ignored him. "I think our first supposition is that the killer was an accomplice of Friel's, one who entered the house with him and used the solitude of a late-night heist to do away with Theodore for reasons unknown. Having committed the murder, the killer was attempting to hide the body, hence dragging it across the room, when fear of discovery took his nerve, and he fled the manor."

"There is no evidence Friel was moved," said Hood. "We can't trust a word this man speaks. I remind you all, Mr. Gothe is suspected of sheltering an infamous art thief himself."

"Do you have any evidence to support that accusation, Hood?" growled Overvold.

"Not yet. Not firm."

"Seems to me you don't have much evidence of anything. What good are you?"

"I…I just began the investigation, sir…"

"Mr. Gothe has given us a start, Lieutenant. A theory. It's more than your police have provided in a week." Overvold walked over to me, pressed a hundred-dollar bill into my breast pocket. "Good work, James. Keep it up, my boy. Let's crack this case wide open."

"It's 'Jimmy', sir."

* * *

"So, you think the body was moved?" asked Dido, nibbling on a garlic stick at *Capriccio*, an elegant Italian restaurant in the cellar of the old Owen Building near my apartment.

"Without a doubt," I said, shoveling in the last of my tortellini. "And the mover is almost certainly the murderer. Next step is to narrow down the list of those who might have been with Theodore Friel during the break-in. An accomplice, a gang member…"

I could see the wheels turning behind her dark, intelligent eyes. Good to have a professional art thief as my Watson. And bedmate. Wish I had *those* memories. Well, tonight I'd make my own…

"What was Friel's profile?" she asked.

"Primarily antiquities out of downtown, the Jewelry District, and across the river in Fox Point," I said. "Twice arrested for stolen goods, but no significant time served."

"You talk to the MacGregor Boys yet?"

"MacGregor Boys?" That sounded like somebody she'd recommended before, likely to James in a conversation that hadn't quite returned to me.

"No, not yet…" I said off-handedly.

"What's the delay?"

"Overvold has me running about. You know."

She shrugged, dipped her garlic stick in the cream sauce cup between us. "If Friel was moving antiquities along the riverfront, he had to interact with Arch MacGregor one way or another. Friel might even have been part of the outfit." She whistled. "Rough fellows, over there. Wouldn't meet them at night."

"You know the address of this MacGregor gang?"

"By heart, Honey." She stuck the end of her garlic stick in the pesto cream sauce, used it to scribble the street and number on a napkin. I slipped it into my breast pocket near Overvold's hundred-dollar bill.

Her eyes lingered on the money's crinkled end sticking out of the pocket.

"You ever consider giving that Benjamin to Lieutenant Hood, Honey. Get him to lay off me a little?"

"A hundred wouldn't do it."

"Tell him, it's just a start." She chomped on the garlic stick aggressively. "He can't be very bright. He's still after me for the Pergo painting. Three years now. It's worth nearly two million dollars. If I'd stolen that masterpiece, I wouldn't be sitting around Providence waiting for someone to arrest me. You and I would be in Europe, on the French Rivera, living it up."

"If you had stolen it, would you tell me?"

"Of course."

There was a pause I didn't quite like. Somewhere, down deep, James was pushing words up to me. Conversational offerings. He knew Dido better than I did. Maybe I should follow his lead. Just this once.

"Why do you do it?" I asked at last.

"Do what?"

"Steal."

"It's a living." She leaned an elbow on the tabletop. "A girl with my looks from a poor family? One who can't afford education? You either become a trophy wife or a secret mistress. Ugh. I wanted a life on my own, not dependent on any man." She reached out, caressed my hand. "I only live with you because I like you, James."

"'Jimmy.' You could get legit work."

"Like what?"

James was pushing up answers. "A waitress. A maid…"

"Hardly the thrills of international art theft."

Another word bubbled up. I let it come out.

"A stripper?"

"Did you really just suggest that? You want me to make a living shaking my naked ass for men's amusement? This is 2019! Women are no longer sex slaves to men."

He was sabotaging me. The bastard.

"Well, no…but, stripping's not illegal…I mean, there's less stigma than a thief, right?"

Dido scowled, pulled away her hand. "I think I'm suddenly very tired, *Jimmy*." She motioned for the check. "No bubble bath tonight."

* * *

My back aching from two nights sleeping on the couch, I climbed the rickety wooden steps to a weathered warehouse door overlooking the Providence River. The head of Augustus Caesar tucked under one arm, I used my free hand to pound aggressively on the weather-warped door. To my surprise, the force of my knocking swung it open, revealing a deep, low-ceiling room of stacked crates and gray shapes covered in tarps and sheets. Among the clutter sat five men counting money over an electric lamp set on a trunk top. They looked up in unison, identical scowls on each face.

"Which one of you is Arch MacGregor?" I asked, pooling my courage and stepping into the room. There was a smell of weed in the air, and as the gloom receded, I noticed other men present just outside the lamplight. Two more "MacGregor Boys" were in the back, crowbars in hand, tearing up a crate with Italian words across its exterior.

I didn't like those crowbars.

A reedy, bearded man gripping the most money and standing nearest the lamp said: "I'm MacGregor. You need something, buddy?"

"I'm trying to move this piece." I held up the Caesar head. "It's first century AD, should fetch a good price, right? And seeing as you guys clearly have cash to spare…"

His scowl deepened. "What is this, a sting for stolen goods?"

"Just hoping to make a sale."

MacGregor glanced back at his men, gave a subtle nod. The crowbar twins crept around the boxes to join the meeting.

His eyes returned to me. "If you're looking to move something stolen, you wanna go over to the Edward Reed Art Emporium on Thayer Street, fellah. Us, we're an honest lot."

"Theodore Friel sent me."

MacGregor raised an eyebrow. "Theodore sent you?"

"He's with your group, right?"

"We ain't seen Teddy in months," shouted one of the monied men.

"Shut up." MacGregor flashed him a burning glare. The man shrank before it.

"Go on, stranger."

I set the head on a crate by the door. "Theodore gave me this Roman piece for safekeeping. Said if he were ever long absent, I should see you guys about it."

"Teddy's dead. Two weeks now. You know that?"

"I do. Dead qualifies as absent in my book."

"What do you really want?"

"His killer."

MacGregor looked me over. "Well, you won't find him here. We all liked Teddy before his 'retirement.'" His voice turned icy. "Why don't you ask old man Overvold? It was his house Teddy was found in. Sometimes, the simplest answer is the right one."

"Sometimes. But maybe not this time."

"I don't like this guy," muttered one of the crowbar men.

"Neither do I," agreed the other. "Hey, Arch, let's introduce him to Billy."

"Sure, introduce me to Billy. I need more friends."

MacGregor smiled. "You wouldn't enjoy Billy's company, fellah. He plays with dead things."

"So...he's into taxidermy?"

They laughed.

"Vivisection?"

"Vivisection is on living things."

"Oh."

The men started chanting, "Billy. Billy. Billy."

"No," said MacGregor with a self-pleased chuckle. He nodded to the crowbar men. "Not yet. I'm feeling merciful today, boys. Get this joker outta here."

I didn't resist, didn't give them any excuse to use the crowbars. They grabbed me and tossed me down the steps outside, a tumble worthy of the end of *The Exorcist*. But I didn't skip it, didn't fast forward. Took my lumps.

Wouldn't give James the satisfaction.

As I lay there on the pavement, skin scraped and burning, MacGregor appeared in the door next to his two ruffians. "You come back, it's straight to Billy. Understand?" He threw the Roman head down onto the pavement, a horrible metallic clang as it hit. "And keep your stolen crap. Dido Voutira's been trying to move that thing for years. We ain't suckers, buddy."

* * *

"Two thousand years old and *you* put a dent in it," said Dido with disgust as we walked up Thayer Street towards the Edward Reed Art Emporium, the damaged Roman head in a pillowcase swung over my shoulder.

"Arch MacGregor dented it, dear. I was an innocent bystander. And *you* were the one who suggested I see him."

"Your masculine disagreements probably cost me several thousand dollars."

"It's not my fault."

"It never is. I don't know what's happened to you this past week, but you're definitely off your game, James."

"Jimmy."

"Whatever."

Dido relieved me of the encumbering pillowcase, swung it over her shoulder, and quickened her pace to send a message of defiance. As she pulled ahead, I noticed an impression under her coat, something tucked into the back of her jeans.

I scampered to catch up. "That's a gun. You're packing heat!"

"Shh!" She glanced around, then lowered her voice to a whisper. "Of course. Don't think we're safe on College Hill for a second, Jimmy. The art emporium is just a glossy façade for the public. A way to make sales look legitimate. High society customers without scruples come here knowing the goods are hot, while the lowlifes like me who stole them work out of the back. White collar, blue collar, local, foreign, we'd meet less scoundrels in Howard prison. I know. I've friends there."

"I don't care. A gun makes me nervous."

"Man up, Jimmy."

We entered through the revolving glass doors of the emporium, stepping into a display room populated with sculptures and ceramic figures atop waist-high pedestals, paintings of every known artistic movement hanging on the walls, and a partition of glass cases filled with antiquities worthy of the finest museums. The crowd looked wealthy and old for College Hill. Here and there were exceptions, students in Brown University and RISD shirts casually shopping with their parents. Other patrons carried the looks of professional art buyers, intense concentration on their faces as they examined each detail on some favored piece or haggled with emporium sales reps over price.

Not really my crowd. I expected to know no one.

I was wrong.

"Those two are from the MacGregor gang," I whispered to Dido.

"Who?"

I nodded towards a pair of burly men carrying a creepy-looking Kipchak warrior statue from the backrooms to set upright in the front window.

"MacGregor's infiltrated the place."

"Unsurprising," whispered Dido. "It's easier to move artwork in and out if they have night access as official employees. I worked here myself one summer three years ago. Most profitable days of my life."

"Well, I don't like it."

"What do you like, Jimmy?"

"To find a lead or two, *he* could never find."

"'He?' He who?"

"No one you know."

I watched the men. That ugly statue in its place, the two MacGregor thugs retreated towards the doors to the back, whispering to each other as they walked, a few telling glances in our direction.

They knew me. They knew her.

I felt sick.

"This again?" asked a masculine voice.

I turned to see that Dido had removed the Caesar head from the pillowcase and handed it to a thin, sad-eyed man in a beige three-piece suit. His demeanor worn, exhausted, he looked like he belonged among the antiquities himself.

"Yes. Again. I'm sorry, Anton, but I wish to get the Roman head reappraised," Dido said quietly. "It was recently damaged by posturing macho fools." She glanced at me.

I shrugged. "Who says I'm the macho one?"

"We'll take the head to the appraiser, Madam," said the emporium man. "This way. Your gentleman friend can come if he wishes."

"I do wish," I said.

We followed Anton into the back. The rear "rooms" were really a single warehouse hall stacked with art-world junk, the path a winding and confusing maze. Above, an impressive network of curtain-rod-rails allowed thick, gray drapes to be pulled about to partition sections of the greater hall, separating artwork of different materials or origins, as well as creating privacy for meetings around a table or the occasional desk.

It was a mess, but a calculated one. Someone clearly knew what he was doing. As we snaked our way through the clutter and around hanging draperies, I kept my eyes out for the MacGregor boys.

Slowly, I dropped behind.

Dido noticed. Anton did not.

Good.

We passed a fine-looking desk, penned in by file cabinets, and surrounded on three sides by hanging partitions.

Dido slipped a hand behind her back, subtly pointed that way.

The accounting desk.

Bingo.

"The valuation should take about twenty minutes," said Anton as if to assure himself more than Dido. "Our appraiser is usually somewhere in the back at this hour. If we can ever find Ivan, that is."

"Oh, we have time," said Dido. "But please stay close, Anton, in case there are disagreements on the pricing like last time. What a row we had!"

"Of course, Madam. Don't worry. Simply a bad day for Ivan."

"A bad day for all of us."

"He was intimidated perhaps by your beauty, Madam."

She laughed, took his hand.

I dropped back further, returned to the desk we'd passed, pulled one of the sliding curtains to give me privacy, and went to work. I soon found the official sales records. I doubted their honesty or accuracy, but it was a start. I flipped through the pages, skimming over printed names and written signatures, looking for anything that triggered my instincts.

No sign of a purchase or sale by a Theodore Friel.

Or Victoria Blossomgate.

Or Arch MacGregor.

Or Dido Voutira.

But there were eleven…no twelve…Jesus, thirteen sales…by Oswald Overvold himself. Sometimes, two or three on the same day.

Something looked off about those signatures. Too loopy, too light. I pulled a letter from my wallet, unfolded it, and matched Overvold's sig for these thirteen sales against the one penned when he commissioned my assistance weeks ago.

Not even close.

I was considering this discovery when the partition curtain was suddenly pulled aside.

Lieutenant Hood stood staring at me.

"What are you doing, Gothe?"

Despite my surprise, I played it routine. "A little accounting for Oswald Overvold. Making sure his records match the emporium's here."

"You get anyone's permission to look at those?"

"I don't think Anton will mind."

"Where's Dido Voutira?"

"This again, Lieutenant? You're becoming a bore."

"Two sales clerks saw her here. With you."

I shrugged. "She might be somewhere at the emporium, but hardly with …"

My voice trailed off as Dido walked up behind Hood, her eyes wide with surprise. She flashed me an accusative look, glanced about, then stepped silently back across the aisle, nearly bumping into a Chinese dragon statue. With clenched teeth, she pulled a partition curtain slowly, cutting off the view.

Hood heard something, looked over his shoulder.

I spat out, "Theodore Friel was a suicide."

"What? Friel was shot in the back. How could it be a suicide?"

"Yes, that's what troubles me too. What say we discuss it over coffee on Benefit—"

Anton returned, Roman head in his hands. "We have the valuation. Where is Ms. Voutira?"

Hood groaned. "She is here! Where is she, Gothe? I'll have—"

A scream. A gunshot. A crash.

Hood shoved Anton aside, pulled back Dido's curtain. A fresh glare emitted from an opened street door in the warehouse wall, outside a van screeching away. The Chinese statue lay on its side, still wobbling. Smoke rose from Dido's pistol on the floor.

"Sweet Mother McGillicutty," said Hood. "Gone as fast as she came!"

My mind reeled as I watched that van disappear into the city gloom.

"Nothing sweet about it, Lieutenant. Not now. Not ever."

FAST FORWARD

* * *

The note was waiting for me by the time I got home:

"ABANDON THE FRIEL CASE OR IT'S BILLY-TIME FOR YOUR GIRLFRIEND."

I sat on the couch, head in hands, emotions whelming, mind reeling. Dido's predicament was my fault. I'd insisted she go to the art emporium with me. I'd angered the MacGregor mob. And I ignored their warnings. Me and my foolish ego.

Now, she was in murderous hands.

I turned to *him*. With Dido's life endangered, there was no room for error. The tasks ahead required a cooler head, surer nerves. Much as I hated the thought of it, I handed the reigns to James. One last time.

Damn him. Damn me.

Before fast forwarding, I set down everything on paper, all the facts I'd gathered these past days ending with three conclusions:

1. Theodore Friel's body was moved at the murder site.
2. Someone forged Oswald Overvold's signatures at the Edward Reed Art Emporium.
3. Friel was a member of the MacGregor gang.

I left these notes in an envelope on the bedroom desk labeled "For James," then stretched out across the mattress, eyes on the ceiling, waiting for that odd-colored shroud. I said a prayer for Dido, cursed my own stupidity, then fast forwarded a week ahead.

Let everything turn out all right, please, God.

* * *

I awoke in the back of a van, the floor shuddering and jumping as we passed over rough terrain. From my low position, I could see earthen cliff faces smearing mud across side windows as we forced our way through some gulley or shallow canyon. A broad-shouldered man in a black coat at the wheel gunned the engines, whistling a Van Halen tune beneath his breath. My pulse, typically low and relaxed after a jump, rose precipitously as I realized my hands and legs were bound by rope. A cool draft at my thighs, I wore a kilt, a traditional Scottish Highlander costume. Bagpipes, a tartan cap, and a bloodstained crowbar rested on the floor nearby.

What the Hell?

"You still with me, James?" asked the driver, glancing over his shoulder.

I tried to scream but found my mouth tape-sealed.

He laughed. "Good. Don't want you sleeping through anything."

The van stopped.

"Won't be a minute."

The man exited the van. I heard his footsteps. Voices. The rear doors opened. Next to the driver stood Arch MacGregor.

MacGregor smiled. "Billy's waiting, James."

They pulled me from the van, dragged my body over a muddy yard littered with broken bricks and rusted tin toward a weathered structure set into the canyon wall. With a collection of ancient beams and planks around a cavernous opening, it was impossible to say if it were a homestead, garage, work shed, or mine entrance. A bald, yellow-whiskered man in overalls and thick gloves emerged from within. He spat an animal bone into the dirt between us.

MacGregor said: "Billy, we need your special skill."

The man nodded and disappeared inside.

"He's in a good mood today," remarked the driver.

"Yes," agreed MacGregor. "Thank God." He glanced down at me. "This'll sting a bit."

I heard an engine start. Billy emerged from the darkness, the overalls discarded, naked except for black goggles on his face and a running chainsaw in his gloved hands. A whooping howl erupted from his throat, and he charged across the yard towards me.

Fast forward! Fast forward! Fast forward!

A blink later, I stood with all limbs attached at a podium in front of an applauding crowd. A man I recognized as the Providence mayor was at my elbow, a very senior-looking uniformed policeman next to him.

"James, are you all right?" said a middle-aged woman in a suit dress, adjusting the podium's microphone. "They're waiting..."

"Yes, yes. I'm sorry."

On the podium top rested a framed award honoring James Toby Gothe for "Exceptional Efforts on Behalf of Providence's Citizens," the document signed by the mayor, the district attorney and chief of police, and dated September 25th, 2021.

September 2021! Two years had passed!

I felt dizzy, tried to steady myself at the podium, listened to a murmur grow from my audience. I gathered myself, pushed on through, made an acceptance speech in specious generalities and universal platitudes. Sentiments, I blindly repeated in the lobby reception afterwards. As near as I could fathom, the gathering was to celebrate my success in assisting criminal cases citywide. The esteem of those gathered bordered on blind reverence.

After the speech, a white-tuxedo-clad Lieutenant Hood embraced me, whispered, "We all love yeh, man," in my ear. "Thanks for everything." He teared up and excused himself to the men's room.

I stood baffled.

As the evening wound down, I feigned illness, slipped away outside. The valet ticket found in my tuxedo pocket brought a sparkling Porsche 911 instead of my beat-up Chevy. My head swum.

After a difficult ride home—I never learned to drive a stick—I was relieved to find I still lived in the same apartment, though the interior décor had changed. The furniture was now plush and stylish. My autographed sports memorabilia on the wall was replaced with abstract art, and the low table for my Xbox and PlayStation supported a waist-high stack of criminal files. One interior wall now housed a glorious fish tank, another a mammoth flat-screen television.

On the TV, a sticky note:

"Jimmy, turn on. Go to Input 3. Play."

I did so. On the screen appeared an enormous image of James sitting at the bedroom desk, his hair gelled in place, wearing the same tuxedo shirt I now wore, the collar opened, the tie draped across his shoulders.

"Jimmy," he said as the image came to life. "The headaches again. Tonight, of all nights. A city honors me, yet, you arrive to take the credit. Typical."

He sighed. "Still, we must be pragmatic. Once the headaches begin, you always steer the wheel, if only for a few days. To prevent your damaging what I've built, I give you an update. We have quit the event planning business. We now run a consulting detective agency working with the police and private citizens nationwide. We have solved nearly a dozen cases the past two years in New England alone. Some of our clients are among the richest people on Earth."

He folded his arms, looked defiant. "As such, I've accrued three million dollars in an offshore bank. Of course, the account number is given to a trustworthy friend in MENSA, who will only return it after giving us very stringent tests in his presence. I'm not going to let *you* have access to that sort of money."

I sighed. I'm still a jerk. Two years on…

His face contorted, deep in thought. "What else? You might be wondering how we're alive? The police snipers along the canyon walls took out William "Billy" Graf when he approached with that motorized saw. If you had the intestinal fortitude to stay conscious another second, you might have witnessed it. Afterwards, the authorities arrested MacGregor and his driver as accomplices for attempted murder. As usual, you left the risk and dirty work to me."

A real jerk. Was this the most literal form of self-loathing?

"I knew the best way to break up the art theft gang was to catch their leader red-handed in some crime, Jimmy. So, I took a job as a costumed greeter at *Haggis to Go*, a restaurant in Fox Point frequented by the gang. I knew they'd recognize me from your investigations and gambled they'd take action. The Massachusetts police were already staking out the gang's executioner, Billy. I alerted them that I might soon be the next victim dragged to his Berkshires mud hovel, as was the case. The GPS hidden in my sporran gave the stakeout team fair warning. Their rifles ready, the danger was minimal. Even your brief interruption failed to disrupt my plans."

A real, real jerk.

"Dido Voutira escaped the kidnappers on her own forty-five minutes after your jump. Our fiancée is a very resilient woman. No helpless damsel-in-distress would win *my* heart. If you'd taken the time to truly know Dido, you'd have little cause for alarm."

That's a relief, at least...

"And, lastly, to the murder of Theodore Friel. I have spliced in this video. It should be self-explanatory. Try and keep up."

The image turned to the interior of the Overvold Manor exhibition hall, the camera at eye level and fixed on James in a navy suit, shadows under his eyes and stubble on his chin as if he'd been working long hours. Nearby stood Oswald Overvold and Victoria Blossomgate. Hood and three uniformed state policemen loitered on the edge of the frame, lurking near the entrance to the Lavender Hall.

"Gentlemen and lady," said James. "I am going to illustrate a hypothetical situation I know to be false. No one get upset as I speak, I'm only trying to make a point."

He stepped to the painting of the colonial gentleman. "Let us pretend for a moment that Theodore Friel's body was not moved, that he was indeed trying to steal this painting when shot in the back—"

"But, as you said before, at under fifteen hundred dollars, it's the least desirable painting in the room," interrupted Victoria.

James shrugged. "Its true value is less than that, unfortunately, Mrs. Blossomgate. In fact, it is worth nothing. Notice, please, the ducks."

"Ducks?" asked Overvold.

"White ducks, sir." James glanced about, then returned his attention to the painting. "The white-feathered duck is not native to America. The two breeds of white duck we encounter today, the Aylesbury from England and the Pekin from Shanghai, were brought to this country in 1840 and 1872, respectively. The painting is dated 1741. There were no white ducks in Colonial America to depict. Thus, it is a fake, made at some later time."

James rubbed his chin stubble thoughtfully. "Likely, this was some desperate Depression Era artist, well-versed in eighteenth-century art, who tried to raise his work's value by dating it almost two centuries earlier. An experienced forger, he knew how to make his work appear older. A fair approximation in the end, but, alas, he didn't know his history of waterfowl."

"And neither would Theodore Friel," said Overvold. "He probably thought it genuine."

"Possibly, sir." James nodded. "So, if we pretend Friel was shot in front of this painting, the line of fire does not match up with the Lavender Hall after all." He turned towards Victoria. "In fact, from this position, it lines up only with the curator's office. Were you working late the night of the murder, Mrs. Blossomgate?"

"No."

"Can you prove that?"

Her face reddened in anger. "Unfortunately, not. But why would I shoot a thief over a valueless painting?"

"You wouldn't. As I said, this is a scenario I know to be false."

"I should say so," she let out a relieved breath. "You had me worried for a moment."

"I'm sorry for your discomfort." James turned to Overvold. "Sir, I would like to purchase this painting from you."

He frowned. "But you just said it was worthless?"

James pulled a thickly stuffed envelope from his coat pocket. "Would you accept three thousand for it?"

"It's yours."

"A pleasure, sir." James handed the envelope to Overvold.

Then withdrew a knife from his jacket.

The others gasped, but Hood and his men did not move.

"As it is mine, I'll go duck hunting," said James. He raised the knife to stab the colonial painting.

An elderly hand gripped his arm.

"Why, Mrs. Blossomgate, what do you care if I destroy a fake?"

"I won't see art damaged. Regardless of monetary value."

"I see. I appreciate your understanding of intrinsic worth, but alas ..."

James lowered the knife, nodded to Hood. The uniformed men went to the painting, removed the frame, tore down the canvas to reveal a cubist portrait of a woman in blazing yellows and reds behind.

James's eyes never strayed from Victoria.

"I said murdering Friel over the fake was a false scenario. The correct scenario is you killed him over *this* painting, Mrs. Blossomgate. The Pergo Virgin Mary stolen from the RISD Museum, a masterpiece worth two million dollars. The painting the police have been trying to find for three years and incorrectly suspected Dido Voutira of stealing."

"I didn't know that Pergo canvas was behind the fake!" said Victoria. "The art emporium delivered it framed, hung them together."

"Your actions say otherwise," said James coldly. "Yes, the MacGregor boys were the original thieves. Having stolen the Pergo painting and infiltrated the art emporium, they delivered both paintings simultaneously and hid their million-dollar theft behind the fake you purchased. Where better to keep it than a private collection of a powerful man like Mr. Overvold. No one, not even the police, would dare inspect his pieces. It sat here for years, undetected. But then Theodore Friel went rogue and tried to steal it for his own."

"See, the MacGregors were behind it. So, you admit I am innocent."

"You killed Friel, Victoria. Look at your involvement. As the curator, you're empowered to sign Oswald's name on purchases—hence the differences in the signatures. You, not Oswald, bought the valueless fake for little more than pennies, and you, not Oswald, insured it for fourteen-hundred ninety-nine dollars, a key number. Fourteen-hundred ninety-nine dollars is the maximum value artwork may be insured without inspection by the insurance agency. One dollar more and an appraiser would need examine it, any less and Mr. Overvold might challenge the purchase, throw it out as unworthy of his exhibition hall. You found the perfect price point."

"This is all rampant speculation," said Victoria.

"I wish it were, Mrs. Blossomgate. Alas, it isn't. Once Arch MacGregor was facing charges for my attempted murder, he gave you up. Told everything in a plea for a lighter sentence. The plan to hide the Pergo painting in this hall until a buyer was found, a buyer you'd be better able to ferret out as Mr. Overvold's curator than their spurious gang ever could. This was out of league for the art emporium, too. There are only so many who can afford both the risk and price of two-million-dollar stolen paintings. The elite of Bellevue Avenue were a good place to subtly make inquiries. MacGregor's gang needed, in effect, a sales rep. You were willing to play ball for a percentage. Unlike your late husband."

"My husband?"

James glanced towards the police. "Lieutenant Hood?"

"The ballistics match, lady," said Hood. "The nine-millimeter bullet that killed Theodore Friel was fired by the same gun that murdered your husband in 2017."

James nodded. "No one thought to check the old file on your husband's death at the hands of an anonymous Boston mugger until Arch McGruder implicated you in the plot to hide the painting. Then, intrastate records were collected, compared. Now, it is obvious. *Mr.* Blossomgate, the previous curator, wouldn't go along with MacGregor's plan, so the gang found someone who would—the curator's long-suffering wife."

Oswald Overvold cursed, half in tears. "She begged for the job when Samuel was killed. Said it was her family's legacy. That I must give the curator position to her."

"Indeed," replied James. "Who fired the fatal shot into your husband's chest on that lonely street in Boston? One of the MacGregor gang? The demented Billy Graf? Since you used the same gun two years later to kill Theodore Friel from the doorway of your office, everything points to you,

Mrs. Blossomgate. A double-murderer."

"Game's up," said Hood.

Victoria did not protest. The uniformed officers escorted her out of camera range.

After a lengthy pause, Oswald Overvold said: "I can't believe it. I've known Victoria for forty years."

"Samuel Blossomgate had no life insurance. And two million dollars was perhaps too much temptation, Mr. Overvold."

A look of painful acceptance crossed his bulldog face. "Amazing. You're really a one-man marvel, James."

"Lieutenant Hood helped a little. And Jimmy brought key details to my attention."

"Aren't you 'Jimmy'?"

"No."

"Then who?"

"Something like a brother. We are a close but strained family. Please make sure the papers say Jimmy and James Gothe solved the case. In that order."

Maybe, I wasn't such a bad guy.

The video cut back to James sitting in the bedroom. He said:

"Victoria Blossomgate is now serving two life sentences in the Gloria McDonald women's prison in Cranston, Jimmy. Arch MacGregor and his driver are doing fifteen years elsewhere." He leaned closer to the camera as if to make some point. "You can see the good we are doing and the wealth we are acquiring with me at the wheel. Here is what I'd propose. I have forty-eight weeks a year. A lot I know, but with the money I generate, the vacation during your month would exceed your wildest fanta—"

I clicked it off.

I went to a brand-new climate-controlled wine refrigerator, withdrew a 1982 Shiraz, and poured myself a drink. On the balcony, I toasted our Jekyll and Holmes personalities. And the possibilities.

A cab drew up on the avenue below. Out stepped Dido, a curious smile on her face. It unearthed fresh memories. The best memories of my life,

yet to be experienced.
Fiancée, eh?
I smiled back and glanced at the calendar on the wall inside.
Saturday night. Bubble bath night.
No fast-forwarding this evening.

XX

NIGHT TRAIN FOR BERLIN

Originally published in Alfred Hitchcock's Mystery Magazine

Night Train for Berlin

August 1939

I knew I was a dead man. Yet, still, I begged. As our train sped through the Lithuanian summer night, I pleaded once more with my captor: "I was a good communist. Loyal to the People. Please…"

"You are German. And you're going home to Germany, Comrade Möller," answered my NKVD escort without sympathy. Dressed in civilian clothes, Captain Vinogradov, a big Russian with a shaved head and granite chin, scratched his arm where the manacles that bound us chafed him through his sleeve. "Stop your whimpering. You'll be with your own kind soon enough."

"My 'kind'? I hardly know them anymore. My home is in the Soviet Union. Since its conception. Is this what the Revolution has come to? Handing Soviet citizens over to the Gestapo?"

"I'm following orders."

"Spoken like your Nazi friends. NKVD? Gestapo? Who can tell the difference these days? Secret police are secret police, it seems."

"Quiet." He jangled the chain that tethered us together. Raised his meaty fist, an ugly, scarred extremity I knew too well. That same fist struck me repeatedly when I was arrested at my Novgorod home last month, pummeled me into untrue confessions during my farcical extradition trial in Leningrad, and now kept me in line as we hurtled through the free Baltic States en route to my destruction.

Having endured the Cheka man's violence for weeks, I tolerated more than feared his reprisals now. After all, what could they do to a condemned man?

"You'd beat me on a public train, Vinogradov? This is no longer Soviet territory. The Lithuanian police would interfere…"

He grimaced. "There's always the toilet nearest the engine, Comrade Möller, where the noise drowns out any cries. Shall we go?" His eyes were impossibly cold. "I don't like Germans."

"A pity. You'll be working for them soon."

"Ten minutes at the East Prussian border to exchange prisoners and then back to Leningrad for me."

And to Berlin for me, I thought. If I'm allowed the courtesy of a show trial. More likely, I'll disappear into the "night and fog" as other victims of the Gestapo did. It was always embarrassing to the Nazi government, having a German-blooded expatriate prominent among the Soviet Union's intellectuals and political philosophers, my publications in the worldwide press damning Herr Hitler and his hideous ideology long before anyone else took them seriously.

During all these years, what could the Nazis do? I was safe in the Soviet Union, backed by my comrades.

Or so I thought.

Things changed in the last few months. A thaw in relations among ideological enemies first noted in May when Comrade Stalin dismissed the Jewish minister of foreign affairs, Maxim Litvinov, as an overture to Berlin. Now, the two governments were cementing relations by exchanging expatriates who discomforted their native countries. I wondered what sort of prisoner the NKVD was getting in return for me.

The train slowed to stop in front of a small station. Other passengers moved about, entering, exiting, stretching their legs, or smoking on the platform. The seats in front of us cleared; an elderly woman and her daughter descended to the concrete and disappeared into the crowd. I remained moored to Captain Vinogradov, an unmoving boulder of a man wedged into his seat and blocking access to the aisle.

At last the whistle sounded. As the train prepared to leave, I saw two men in dark hats and unseasonal overcoats sprinting for the steps to this car. They soon appeared in our aisle. One tall and about thirty, the other medium height and at least ten years older. They took the vacant seats in front of us. Without a word, I knew them to be German. Twenty years away from my homeland and still I sensed it.

"Captain Vinogradov?" asked the younger stranger.

"Yes," answered my guard indifferently. "Which one of you is Beltz?"

"Captain Beltz is at the Eydtkuhnen station with his captive as agreed. We are an advance team coming over from our work in Kaunas to ensure your correctness until we reach German territory." He showed the dreaded identification, a disc-shaped metal badge adorned with eagle, swastika, and the words GEHEIME STAATSPOLIZEI upon its face. The Gestapo.

Vinogradov frowned. "I talk only to Beltz. At the station."

"Talk is unnecessary presently, Captain," continued the younger German. He pulled a photograph of me from his coat pocket. The two Gestapo men glanced back and forth from my face to the picture, assessing the match.

"You don't look forty-five, Herr Möller," said the one holding the picture. "The winters in Russia have aged you prematurely."

"Worries over developments in my homeland have aged me prematurely."

"Which homeland is that? You have so many." He put away the photograph. "We hear you are quite the lothario."

"Ask my late wife."

"We prefer to ask the staff at your university." He held out an open hand toward the NKVD officer. "Möller's papers, Captain Vinogradov."

"I give nothing to mystery men," growled the Russian.

"You have seen the warrant disc. The Gestapo does not reveal agent names."

"Then I reveal no papers!"

The older German, who had been silently watching, placed a black-gloved hand on his younger companion's shoulder. "Forgive Lieutenant Fashingbauer's failure of diplomacy, Captain. He is unused to dealings outside of Prussia. I am Colonel Huff. We are here only to keep your company until Eydtkuhnen." He smiled, revealing unnaturally white teeth beneath dark lips. "The papers, Captain Vinogradov, if you please."

"Where are Polzin's papers?"

"With Captain Beltz and the prisoner. You'll have them in time. When you get Polzin."

Polzin. I knew well that surname. A Russian family of the noble class who escaped the Cheka during the Revolution and settled in Western Europe. Prominent backers of the White forces, even after their defeat in 1923, the Polzin patriarch Afanasy had remained among the loudest international voices calling for the Soviet state's destruction. I crossed paths with Afanasy and his representatives at numerous conferences over the years, debated the old man himself on stages in Paris and Stockholm. Until the rise of the Nazis, they were my most dogged opponents.

But Afanasy Polzin died in exile at his home in Britain last year. The Gestapo's prisoner must be another member of a voluminous family, which extended throughout the Russian aristocracy, even intertwining with the Romanovs along several branches. Any eminent Polzin would be a plum catch for the NKVD.

It gave me satisfaction that someone would pay for the destruction the White Armies had wrought. At least there was justice on one side of this evil bargain that sent me to my doom.

While the Gestapo and NKVD continued to dispute papers, I pulled my hat low and tried to sleep, to escape this despairing reality for a while. In dreams, at least, there might still be hope for this world.

***

When we arrived at Eydtkuhnen in East Prussia, Colonel Huff led us down to the teeming platform while Lieutenant Fashingbauer trailed behind.

"The Leningrad line was late. As always," said Huff, glancing up at the station clock. "We must hurry, gentlemen."

His use of the word "gentlemen" darkly amused me. Were we on some pleasure tour?

We pushed through the crowd. It was impossibly congested for a small station, even in summer. Here, the wide-gauge rail lines of the East ceased forever, large concrete barriers in the weeds a hundred meters beyond the station marking the termination of a network that stretched all the way back to the Sea of Japan.

Huff led us to the other side of the station, climbing one of several wooden bridges over the tracks. From atop the bridge, I spied a new set of trains sitting atop narrow-gauge tracks. All passengers who wished to continue to the West must disembark at Eydtkuhnen and board new trains. Amsterdam, Paris, Madrid, and, unfortunately, Berlin all lay ahead along those narrower tracks.

We descended a stairway off the bridge to a platform before a small train with Nazi flags decorating the engine and only two cars behind. Wealthy-looking civilians speaking numerous languages—Polish, German, Dutch, English, even Russian—casually boarded the train while uniformed German soldiers watched from the platform. This then would be my transport within the East Prussian exclave, then briefly through the Polish Corridor and into the heart of mainland Germany.

I felt a tightening in my stomach, a slight dizziness. This was really happening. It might as well have been my funeral train.

"Where is the captive?" asked Vinogradov, clearly uncomfortable surrounded by so many German soldiers.

"Fetch Vadim Polzin," said Huff to Fashingbauer. The lieutenant climbed the steps of the car nearest the engine and vanished inside.

Vadim, Vadim.... Of all their politically active family, I couldn't recall one named "Vadim."

While we waited, Huff extended Vinogradov a cigarette. They smoked in silence. Some of the German soldiers nearby talked of football.

Lieutenant Fashingbauer reappeared in the doorway of the car, an odd expression on his face. He descended to the platform, asked some question of a senior-looking soldier, who replied with a negative shake of his head.

Curious.

Fashingbauer returned to us. "Can I see you inside the train a moment, Colonel?" Something unspoken passed between them.

"One moment, Captain," said Huff to Vinogradov. The two Gestapo men disappeared inside the car.

"What do you make of that?" I said to my NKVD guardian. I could see his instincts were already aroused.

"I'll find out," replied Vinogradov, and he pulled me across the platform to the car. The swiftness of his movement surprised me, and a panic took hold as we neared the door, my composure crumbling away at last. Vinogradov climbed two steps before I resisted, the chain that tethered our arms pulled tight between us.

"I won't go!" I shouted. "Let them kill me here where all can see the atrocity; better than disappearing into the night forever!"

Without change of expression, Vinogradov leaned down and struck me hard on the jaw. I collapsed to the platform, one elbow on the car's bottom step, a leg against the wheels. I sat stunned, feeling blood seep into my mouth. He dragged me over the steps, up into the corridor.

"Was that on behalf of the People or Comrade Stalin?" I said, trying to shake off the pain from the aisle floor.

"From me. No one else. Get up."

My jaw throbbing, hand against the wall, I regained my footing and was pulled deeper inside the train. Ahead, Huff and Fashingbauer conferred in front of a private cabin's opened door, worry on both men's faces. As we arrived, I peered into the compartment. It stood empty save for a small pool of blood on a seat cushion and a similar crimson smear across the cabin floor.

"What's happened?" demanded Vinogradov.

"Captain Beltz and Vadim Polzin are missing," answered Huff flatly.

"What?"

"They will be found."

Fashingbauer spoke to his superior with an air of one continuing an interrupted conversation. "I have checked the engine and the passenger car. He's not there, Colonel. Our guards assure us neither Beltz nor anyone else left the train."

"Keep everyone in their seats in the next car. At gunpoint."

"Yes, Colonel." The lieutenant slipped by us, disappearing through the door to the other car.

"What do you propose to do?" asked my guard.

"We search the train, Captain Vinogradov. Your prize captive is here. As is our man. If you want to assist, we can chain Herr Möller to a soldier outside."

"He remains with me until I have Polzin."

"As you wish."

Colonel Huff withdrew a pistol from his coat and threw open the next cabin door. This berth, too, was unoccupied. We moved to the next.

"See what incompetence you've allied yourself with," I whispered to Vinogradov in Russian. "They've lost your man, yet *you'll* be the one punished at home."

He said nothing, but a flicker in his eyes told me my point hit its mark. I enjoyed the victory.

I was tugged along as they finished checking the cabins. All were empty, without blood or signs of recent occupancy. We moved this strange alliance to the storage compartment, searching through trunks and forcing open larger crates.

I began to admire Vadim Polzin and the trouble he caused the fascists.

The light was poor here, with a single overtaxed lamp and no windows to illuminate the interior. Darkness inhabited each corner, shadows pooling behind stacked boxes and mounds of baggage. It was I who saw the shoulder of a man in the gloom, a figure hiding behind the fruit crates in an overhead bin.

My heart froze. I lifted my arm to point, to alert my captors.

The train lurched forward. The crate, with little room to hide the man behind, slipped off the shelf, crashing to the floor.

"Beltz," cried Colonel Huff between clenched teeth. *"Mein Gott."*

They cleared away the other crates, lowered the lifeless body of a uniformed SS officer to the floor. The prisoner's end of the manacles attached to his arm was opened and empty, a woman's stickpin wedged deep into his throat.

While Vinogradov cursed and threatened all of Germany about the missing Polzin, Colonel Huff kneeled, examined the man, and went through his pockets.

"His gun, identification, and all Polzin's papers are gone." Huff pulled the pin from the dead man's neck. The dreaded secret police of two nations stared at each other helplessly.

Absorbed as we were in the murder, no one initially noticed the shuddering of the car.

"We've left the station," I said as the vibrations increased.

Vinogradov's eyes widened. "Stop the train. Polzin has escaped—"

"Our men on the platform would have seen him," answered Huff. "A moving train is to our advantage."

The Gestapo colonel rose, stormed out the opposite end of the luggage compartment to the locomotive. The door was not fully closed, and even over the engines, I heard him shout at the conductors:

"This train proceeds directly to Berlin at maximum speed. No other stations. If it stops, you will be shot!"

Huff remerged in the doorway and pushed past us, his face purplish with rage. "No one gets off this train until I have Beltz's killer, Captain."

"And I have Polzin."

"If they are the same, you'll carry his corpse back to Russia."

We entered the next car, an open passenger cabin, rows of moderately populated wooden benches on either side of the aisle. I counted twenty-five passengers. Only nine adult males, including a petrified-looking porter held at gunpoint by Lieutenant Fashingbauer.

Colonel Huff, too, was counting men. "Any of them could be Vadim Polzin," he said.

This sparked a new rage in Vinogradov. "Can't you identify him?"

"I've never seen Polzin," answered Huff. "Lieutenant Fashingbauer and I were in Kaunas. Don't you have a photograph of the man you're supposed to retrieve, Captain Vinogradov?"

"No. His papers would be enough."

"Typical Russian inefficiency."

"I'm not the one who lost a prisoner, Colonel."

They glared at each other.

"Lieutenant Fashingbauer," said Huff finally, "Check the passengers' documents."

"*I'll* check! You've bungled procedures enough," shouted Captain Vinogradov, dragging me to the first row of terrified passengers.

One by one he took their identification documents: passports, visas, tickets. He matched faces, asked questions in ugly, accented German. More than once Vinogradov ordered me to clarify some point where his linguistic skills failed. It was all a farce. I could hear the two Gestapo officers muttering derisively behind us at the car door.

We were two-thirds of the way through the car, Captain Vinogradov busy interrogating some Cologne chemist, when my eyes fell upon a familiar visage. In the next row sat a young man of nineteen or twenty who wore the aristocratic nose and the same close-together eyes of Afanasy Polzin. It was like looking at a photograph of my old opponent in his youth. I would recognize those family features anywhere. Vadim could only be a son or grandson of that infamous patriarch himself.

He caught my stare, and, with calculated casualness, turned his face to the windowpane. Next to him, I spied a woman, perhaps five or six years older, with darker eyes but otherwise the same facial characteristics. A likely sister or cousin. The Gestapo hadn't mentioned a female prisoner. Was she some family conspirator planted on this train to aid his escape? The murderer of Beltz?

I wondered who else in the crowd were Polzin allies...

Vinogradov finished interrogating the chemist, moved to the next row, and demanded documents of this man and woman. They answered his questions calmly, claimed to be a married couple from Bavaria. Their

German was perfect.

Of course it was. Had a boy this young ever lived in Russia? He couldn't have. And the woman only a child when they fled the Cheka.

"Have you found something?" asked Huff from across the car.

"I'm not sure," said Vinogradov. He, too, was staring at the boy. His superiors must have shown him a photograph of Vadim Polzin at some point.

"It could be him," mumbled the NKVD captain. He ordered the boy to remove his hat, revealing a head of closely shorn red hair.

Afanasy Polzin was a redhead in his prime. I'd seen the famous painting of the attendees at Tsar Nicholas's wedding ball. There was no doubt in my mind now. I could confirm the identification for my captors. But what gratitude to expect from the NKVD? Wouldn't Vinogradov still follow orders and give me over to the Gestapo wolves?

I felt unexpected pity for the boy and his sister. Who knew better than I the terror and pain of being whisked away by the secret police? In their case, for the crimes of their fathers.

My next words surprised me.

"You'd better choose correctly, Captain," I whispered in Vinogradov's ear. "What will be your punishment if you bring the wrong man home to Leningrad? You won't live long in the Gulag once it gets out you were Cheka. A million inmates have scores to settle with your kind."

"Quiet," he said, shrugging me away. But I scored another mark. He stood too long, muttering obscenities beneath his breath. At last, he handed back their papers.

"It could be another."

We moved on, interviewing the rest of the passengers. When Vinogradov finished, Colonel Huff said: "Well, Captain?"

"All documents are correct," he replied, a hint of defeat in the NKVD officer's voice.

Huff nodded, walked down the aisle to the car's center. "Then let us proceed properly. Attention, ladies and gentlemen. The state policeman Gernot Beltz was murdered on this train by a Russian fugitive Beltz was delivering to justice. As such, this car is now sealed. When this train reaches Berlin, all aboard will be arrested as accomplices to murder, tried, and hanged within three days."

A horrified buzz filled the cabin as Huff let his proclamation sink into their collective consciousness. Those who stood or shouted dissension quickly turned reticent when Lieutenant Fashingbauer pointed his pistol in their direction.

Huff continued: "Anyone who wishes to appeal for a lesser sentence will prove their goodwill on the journey. Let us begin." He held up the bloody stickpin from Beltz's body. "Tell me, who owns this pin?"

Without hesitance the woman next to Vadim said: "It's mine. I use it to keep scarves in place during bicycling."

"How did it come to be lodged in Captain Beltz's throat?"

"I don't know. I lost it in the crowd on the Eydtkuhnen bridges. I believed it stolen. I told the porter upon boarding. Ask him."

The trembling, pale-faced porter nodded in agreement.

Colonel Huff approached the young woman. I was so fixated on her face, her resemblance to Afanasy Polzin, that I failed to notice the large canvas bag she held in her lap.

Its potential as a source of evidence was not lost on Huff.

"Dump your bag on the floor," he said.

I worried that Vadim's prisoner clothes stained with Beltz's blood would tumble out. Or the missing gun. Or the papers with Vadim's photograph. But these conspirators were better prepared than that.

A woman's scarf, perfume bottle, and various toiletries fell to the floor, along with a porcelain dog figurine, which promptly shattered, and two thick books by Nazi theorist Alfred Rosenberg.

Odd. Despite their numerous sins, the Polzin family had never possessed National Socialist connections, never affiliated themselves with a "workers' party" of any political stripe. This was a game. A disguise.

Huff rotated a book with his boot toe so he might read the title: *Der Mythus des zwanzigsten Jahrhunderts.* The Myths of the Twentieth Century.

"These are yours?" he asked. "You are *Parteigenossin*?"

"Of course. We're from Munich. My father was party member number 553. Two before the Führer."

It was a good ruse, if overplayed. I'm not sure Colonel Huff completely bought it. Still, he seemed satisfied for now.

"All will be confirmed, my dear. You can pick up your things," he said, walking back to the front. "If anyone else has information to provide, I am waiting. It is a long ride to Berlin, a short time until hanging. Think about your future and those of your families."

He took a seat near the compartment's door, elbow resting on his knee, chin propped on a fist. Watching all.

* * *

Time passed. The car fell into a tense silence, the Gestapo at one end of the cabin, Vinogradov and I sitting against the wall at the other. Every few minutes some poor passenger would rise from his seat, approach Colonel Huff to give whispered information on his fellows in a desperate bid for clemency. Huff would nod, occasionally take notes in a book he kept tucked in his coat's inner pocket. The conversations were always brief. Huff knew the game was his when we reached Berlin. Vadim Polzin would be identified from photos at the Gestapo's Prinz Albrecht Street headquarters. He was a dead man. The fate of the rest of the car only marginally less certain.

The train sped through the town of Osterode, barely slowing at the station. I believed we were approaching the strip of Polish land that ran up to the Baltic Sea and separated East Prussia from the rest of Germany. A suspicion confirmed when Huff sent Lieutenant Fashingbauer on some errand to the engine, likely to ensure the conductors did not tarry at the border.

For a brief time, we would once again be out of German territory.

How could I use that?

I glanced over at Vinogradov beside me. His hat low, arms crossed, he appeared to be asleep. An old Cheka trick. Like Huff, Vinogradov had his own ways of collecting information.

Or misinformation. I decided to throw a spanner in the works.

I leaned forward as far as the manacles allowed. Whispered into the ear of a passenger in the last row.

"If we reach the Polish Corridor, we are safe. Tell your neighbor."

I glanced back at Vinogradov. He did not stir.

I moved to a passenger on the opposite side of the aisle, straining my chains just enough to wake my captor if he indeed slept.

"When we arrive inside the Polish Corridor, we'll be rescued," I said. "Pass it on."

I returned to my seat. Vinogradov pushed up his hat.

"What did you say to them?"

"I complained about the heat in the car."

"You mentioned the Polish Corridor."

"I said nothing about the Corridor."

"What will happen there? Answer me."

"You're hearing things, you suspicious oaf."

Again, that thunderous fist struck me. Blows that birthed confessions in heartbeats. A month as my guard and master, he knew he could extract any information at will. Vinogradov never failed to break me. I counted on that.

"What is going on?" demanded Huff from his seat across the car.

"It is a Russian concern, Colonel."

The blows rained down, black spots spreading across my eyes. When I had endured enough punishment to be convincing, I pleaded: "No more. I beg of you. I'll tell you anything."

"What happens at the Corridor?"

"There will be an escape."

He snorted. "We'll shoot anyone who tries."

"If you believe so…"

"And?" He shook me like a rag doll.

"Isn't it obvious? *Polzin*. No matter how ancient that Russian surname, there is a Polish root in it. They have allies in Poland. Family." I wiped the blood from my face, willed myself not to black out. "You think the Revolution robbed them of their wealth? They are millionaires, even in exile. Hired brigands wait in the Corridor, logs across the tracks. Armed with rifles and dynamite. They'll free Vadim and his accomplices. The whole car knows it!"

"Impossible. Why should the rich pigs tell you?"

"Solidarity among the condemned. I am meant to distract you when the gunfire starts."

"It can't be true."

"I'll be free as bird when those mercenaries shoot you. The Poles have no love of the Cheka. You know this."

He stared at me for an impossibly long time, face contorted, teeth gritted.

"If you lie, Möller…"

"You'll do what, Captain? I'm a dead man walking. You lost your power over me long ago."

Vinogradov cursed, cast me to the floor. He dragged my limp, bloody body to the aisle where Colonel Huff awaited. I could barely hear the Russian's words over the growing alarm among the passengers.

"We must halt this train, Colonel. Or divert it to Königsberg or back to Eydtkuhnen."

"We go on to Berlin."

"The Polzin family has laid a trap for us in Polish territory."

"Nonsense." Huff gestured with his pistol toward me on the floor. "Möller told you this?"

"I beat it out of him. This whole car is a conspiracy. Even Möller. Halt the train!"

"This train stops for no one. Fashingbauer has a gun at the engineer this instant."

"This exchange was agreed to be at Eydtkuhnen! I go no farther!" Vinogradov reached up to pull the emergency brake. "We stop—"

Huff shot him twice in the chest.

Screams erupted around us. The NKVD officer's mammoth body lurched to one side, a ghastly gurgle in his throat. Vinogradov gripped the brake lever, pulled it hard, before he collapsed atop of me on the floor. My breath rushed out.

The shrieks of passengers were eclipsed by the screech of metal as the wheels of the top-speed train suddenly locked. The car shuddered like a ship tossed about in a gale storm. Huff was thrown to the floor, his pistol jarred free of his hand. The gun landed at the feet of the Polzin woman. She raised it, might have shot Huff, but passengers swarmed the colonel first, impeding a clear target. The vengeful mob burying the Nazi beneath their kicking, pummeling attack.

A fitting end for the Gestapo.

As the train rolled to a stop, I pushed Vinogradov's lifeless body off me, searched his pockets for the manacle keys. People stepped over and around me, a mass exodus from the car led by the Polzin siblings.

Somewhere upfront Fashingbauer was shouting, threatening the engineers, demanding the train move. By the time I unlocked the chains and threw them to the floor, the car was accelerating again, the remaining passengers scrambling to get off in time, jumping into trackside ponds and grasslands as we gained speed.

My brains still addled from Vinogradov's assault, I was the last to exit. I stumbled to the door, trying to find the mix of courage and balance to leap from the step as the ground whizzed by below me.

The boy, Vadim Polzin, was running alongside, trying to catch the step to the car, shouting something, pointing...

Why was he trying to reboard the train?

Then I couldn't breathe, something cold and metallic thrown around my throat choking the air from me. I turned just enough to see my assailant. A battered Colonel Huff stood behind, garroting me with my old manacle chains.

"You are a prisoner of the *Deutsches Reich*, Möller. You will pay for your treachery against the Fatherland."

I fought him in that doorway, pulling at the chain about my throat, fingers digging into my own flesh to try and pry it loose. If Huff himself weren't so injured, he might have finished me in an instant. As it was, I had enough fading strength to resist.

Vadim was somehow at the step, hand stretched out. I took my fingers from the chain, grabbed his arm. He cleared the step, onto the train. With the strength of his youth, he forced Huff back. The stranglehold slackened, air rushed into my lungs. I nearly toppled off the step, caught the handrail just in time.

As my wits returned, I became aware of two things simultaneously: that Polzin still struggled with Huff, and the manacles now hung loosely about my neck. I removed them, clasped one manacle around Huff's upper arm, the other to the handrail above the step.

Vadim understood my actions. We read each other's thoughts. Jumped. Landed in the dust beside the tracks.

Huff made one last lunge for me, missed, and slipped from the step. The last we saw of the Gestapo colonel, he was being dragged alongside the train, trying to avoid falling under the deadly wheels, shrieking through the East Prussian darkness.

The screams did not last long.

* * *

On a hillside far from any railroad, we paused for formalities and introductions.

"Vadim Vitaliyevich Polzin. Grandson of Afanasy Ivanovich Polzin, Third Count of Karelia," said the youth proudly, standing among his accomplices from the train.

"Eduard Möller," I answered. "An academic. From Dortmund long ago."

The sister frowned at "Eduard Möller," but there was no recognition in Vadim's face.

"We have an escape plan, Eduard." He spoke with the earnestness of the young. "North, safehouse to safehouse until Danzig, then overseas to London."

"Danzig is a free city in name only. The Nazis run things there. It will be crawling with Gestapo spies."

"It is the route the family has set down. There is room for one more. Come with us."

"I cannot."

"Where are you going?"

"Mexico City."

The young man's eyes widened in the moonlight. "You'll never make it."

"I was thinking the same about you."

A pause. Then we laughed for the truth and absurdity in the statement. Vadim held out his hand. "Good luck, Eduard."

"*Shest liva*," I said.

We shook hands on that hill, this last son of the Polzin aristocracy and I, a committed lifelong communist. We parted without backward glances. Never to meet again.

XXI

TWO TAXIS

Originally published in Mystery Weekly Magazine

Two Taxis

"Tell the gentleman his taxi is here, Jean-Paul."

"Which gentleman, Monsieur Rault?"

"The fellow in the black pinstriped suit with a red tie."

Jean-Paul scanned the hotel lobby. To his astonishment, two men matched Monsieur Rault's description.

"Do you mean the gentleman at the coffee bar or the one sitting near the elevator, Monsieur Rault?"

"Figure it out for yourself, Jean-Paul. For once."

After such censure, Jean-Paul bothered Monsieur Rault no more. He left the concierge desk and trekked over to the man at the bar.

"Did you order a taxi, Monsieur?"

"Yes," answered the man in the tone of an entitled foreigner. Jean-Paul could not place the accent.

"It is here."

The man adjusted his fedora's brim over a wide, sweaty forehead, rose from his seat, and allowed Jean-Paul to direct him through the lobby exit to a taxi waiting in the street. Jean-Paul got the cab's door, received no gratuity for his efforts, and watched the car pull out onto the *Promenade des Anglais*.

As the taxi sped away, a woman on the walkway performed a double-take. She stood for moments afterwards in the hot Mediterranean sun, contemplating what she'd seen. Then, with a determined expression, she marched past Jean-Paul into the hotel entrance.

He followed her through the glass revolving doors and found the woman standing just inside, appraising the lobby. When her eyes discovered the remaining man in a black pinstriped suit, a possessive smile emerged on her face. She quickly took a seat beyond the fountain, straightened her yellow sundress carefully and ordered coffee from the waitress. Jean-Paul observed her glancing through the dancing fountain waters towards the man in the suit, he apparently ignorant of her attention.

Odd, but after eleven years working in the resort cities of the *Côte d'Azur*, Jean-Paul had seen far odder things. Perhaps, the woman was the sort who lounges in the opulent hotels of Nice looking to meet wealthy gentlemen. Little harm if no one makes a fuss.

He returned to the concierge desk.

Monsieur Rault was now on duty at the check-in counter and Jean-Paul worked alone until an American voice called his attention up from his notes.

"Where is my taxi?" demanded the pinstriped man. "I ordered the damned thing fifty minutes ago."

"Fifty minutes, Monsieur?" Jean-Paul rifled through his papers, his preferred ruse to buy time. "There must be some mistake."

"I'll say there is."

"One moment, please."

Jean-Paul walked over to confer with Monsieur Rault.

His response was predictable: "Why can you never handle any matter yourself, Jean-Paul?"

"I did not order the taxi. It is not my responsibility, I can only—"

Shouting called their attention.

Near the revolving door, the American stood gripping the woman in the sundress by the wrist, shaking her vigorously as she tried to pull away.

"Give it to me!" he shouted.

"I've taken nothing," she answered in English with a British accent.

"Hand it back. Or I'll break your arm."

"You're mad!"

"What exactly is the difficulty?" asked Monsieur Rault as he walked over to the fighting guests, Jean-Paul trailing behind.

"This woman picked my pocket, stole something priceless to me."

"He's a liar. I simply was waiting my turn for a concierge. I never touched the man's pocket. He's a looney."

"What exactly do you allege stolen?" asked Monsieur Rault patiently.

"A silver cat broach with gemstones for eyes. Worth a fortune. And this thief knows that."

"An odd thing to keep in one's pocket," said Monsieur Rault. "And unwise."

The man stood silent, face turning purple with anger.

"The woman was, as they say, 'casing' the man, Monsieur Rault," said Jean-Paul, hoping to seem relevant to his superior. "She watched him constantly since setting foot in the door."

"Are either of you guests at our hotel?" asked Rault.

Neither was.

Monsieur Rault sighed, as if the incident were taxing to his soul, then said: "This is most inappropriate, two non-guests making a ruckus in our lobby. And in-season, too."

"Just search her," said the American. "There are few pockets in that little summer dress of hers."

"We have no authority, Monsieur," answered Rault. He turned to Jean-Paul. "Let us curtail any disturbance to authentic guests, Jean-Paul. Take these two idlers to the police station on *Avenue Maréchal Foch*." He glanced through the lobby window. "A new taxi is outside. Use that cab."

"Must *I* go?" asked Jean-Paul.

"Only if you wish to remain employed."

"The police station?!" shouted the American as if the idea stung him. "This vixen won't agree to—"

"I'll gladly go," said the woman stepping forward. "Because I'm innocent."

"Jean-Paul do your duty," said Monsieur Rault. "Take them away."

* * *

Jean-Paul sat in the back of the taxi, wedged between the two warring antagonists on the way to the station, wishing he were anywhere else. His brother had given up civilized life for goat-herding in the Alps. It could not be more irksome than this. Fresh air, working outdoors, ah, that's a life... Jean-Paul even liked animals.

He glanced at the two other passengers.

Most types of animals.

"Do you have any idea what will happen to me, if you get away with your little pocket-picking, lady?" said the American, leaning across Jean-Paul's lap to yell at the British woman. "No? No idea? I'm dead. Dead as a bug on a windshield."

"Oh, don't be so melodramatic," she replied.

"That broach is my last hope. And you've no right to snatch it up!"

"That's because I didn't, you ignorant colonial!"

They pressed in on Jean-Paul as they argued, crumpling his shoulders like an accordion. He thought the woman wore too much perfume and the man smelled of cheap cigars. Then he had an epiphany. He remembered they were not guests at his hotel, but strangers off the street, and he could be rude as he liked.

"Quiet! You're both idiots. *Appeler un chat un chat.*" His outburst little disturbed the two arguing foreigners but made Jean-Paul feel marginally better. If Monsieur Rault could see him being so assertive...

Jean-Paul leaned forward to peer over the driver's shoulder. Good news ahead.

"*J'arrive pas y croire!* We are here."

They pulled up to the police station. Forty minutes later Jean-Paul and the American, whose name apparently was Kenneth Hanson, stood in a waiting room with the police lieutenant, a thin, thirtyish man named Bonnard who seemed bemused by the whole situation. The British woman was taken to a private room to be searched by a female officer.

As the men waited, Hanson paced the room in growing agitation. Jean-Paul wondered if all Americans were so easily flustered.

"It has to be there. In her pockets or purse," moaned Hanson. "Jesus, it must be."

"If she really stole it, then it will be on her person, Monsieur Hanson," said Jean-Paul in a vain hope to assure the American and halt his pacing. "Don't worry."

"What if she threw it out the taxi window when we weren't looking?"

"We sat next to her the whole time, Monsieur. And the windows were closed despite the temperature. Impossible."

"Nothing's impossible for a pickpocket. They're trained in the art of distraction, get you looking one way, while their hands move another. Without that jeweled cat, I'm done for. I have debts. Grand debts to the wrong people."

"For how much?" asked Jean-Paul, glancing at a very interested Lieutenant Bonnard, then back to Hanson. "Aren't all Americans rich?"

Hanson didn't answer.

The door opened, and a female officer led the British woman into the room. In the officer's hands was a burgundy-red passport, several printed documents, and a silver broach in the form of cat with fiery gemstones for eyes.

"*C'est magnifique!*" said Jean-Paul fixating on the opulent broach. "You are a lucky man, after all, Hanson. A fortune is returned to you."

Hanson sprinted across the room, seized the cat from the officer, kissed it, cradled the broach in his arms as if a living thing. His euphoria appeared genuine if short-lived. When the joy dissipated, the American's eyes focused on the woman, a renewed rage in his voice.

"I told you she was a thief. A criminal. A liar."

"I simply wanted to take something—anything—from your pockets," said the woman, her accent different now, almost Eastern European. "I had no idea the pickings would be so valuable."

"Price doesn't matter. Only intent," replied Hanson with vindictive triumph. "I assume you're going to prosecute, Lieutenant Bonnard?"

"Madame Tanguy," said Bonnard to the other officer. "Make a courtesy call to the British consulate, inform them there is a problem with one of their citizens."

"She's not British, Lieutenant." Tanguy handed him the burgundy-red passport. "She's a Latvian citizen."

"Latvian?" Bonnard opened the passport, read the first page, then glanced at the accused woman. "Ms. Santa Ezeriņa? From Riga?"

"I am a journalist, *Monsieur l'agent,* following a vital lead," said the woman. "That man before us, calling himself Hanson, is a sociopath, a serial killer, a diseased murderer of countless women and children. The worst in Riga's eight-hundred-year history."

"What? What are you saying?" said Hanson, stunned.

Jean-Paul marveled that he'd shared a taxi with such a man.

"His real name is Edgars Dukurs. He's not American. He's Latvian like I am. A disguised identity, the so-called 'mask' of the sociopath. The police were finally getting too close in our homeland after years of searching, so he fled to France. EU laws allow for easy relocation. But my French source described him to a tee, just as I found him in the hotel today. I did everything I could, including donning a non-Latvian accent and picking his pocket, to get Dukurs into police custody."

"Are you listening to this? She's insane." Hanson glanced around to the officers, to Jean-Paul himself. "I prove her a criminal, so she accuses me of being one too. A third-world killer whose name I can't even pronounce. You saw my passport. I'm American. From New Jersey!"

"Fakes," said the Latvian journalist. "It's easy enough to obtain counterfeit passports on the black market. Especially if you're the sort who carries priceless jewelry around in your pockets as he does. Transactions are untraceable."

"She has documentation of her investigation," said Officer Tanguy to the lieutenant. "A certified letter showing submission of evidence to the *Commissaire de police* only yesterday. Looks genuine."

"This is madness," scoffed Hanson. "I'm a Latvian serial killer? That's rich. I don't even know where Latvia is on a map. I'm an expat in Nice, and I—"

"It's easy to prove his identity," said Santa Ezeriņa. "One of Dukurs's intended victims fended him off with a knife, left a deep S-shaped wound in the killer's chest. A vivid scar. It's all laid out in the documentation I provided."

"So, it is," said Tanguy.

"Monsieur Hanson," said Lieutenant Bonnard, "Would you be kind enough to remove your shirt? If only to placate—"

"No! I'm not doing another freakin' thing until we get a lawyer over—"

Before any could stop her, Santa Ezeriņa stepped across the room, seized Hanson's shirt, and tore it open, sending buttons flying everywhere. His bare chest exposed for all to see.

The skin was deathly pale.

Clean.

Without scar.

"*Velns parāvis!*" seethed Santa Ezeriņa. "*Velns parāvis! Velns parāvis!*"

Jean-Paul did not speak Latvian, but he knew blasphemy when he heard it.

* * *

On a lonely rural road, two gunmen stood over their target. He'd crawled away from the bullet-ridden taxi into the weeds before death.

"The right man?" asked the younger of the hitmen, the one who'd fired too soon.

"Right clothes. Right hotel," said the other assassin. "Strip him."

The bloody black suit was tugged away.

No broach. Not on his person. Not in the taxi. Not with their man, the driver. *Le Milieu* bosses wouldn't like this.... Kid was trigger-happy. Hanson may be dead, but his gambling debts remained unpaid. Two-hundred-thousand euros lost to the organization.

Qui sème le vent, récolte la tempête.

They kicked the corpse.

With an air of failure, the mobsters returned to Nice, left the nude body in the undergrowth.

An S-shaped scar shining in the dying sunlight.

XXII

DEMON IN THE DEPTHS

A Novella
Originally published in Ellery Queen's Mystery Magazine

I

1958

At this altitude, the sky turned violet and daytime starlight pierced the atmosphere from outer space. Cosmic wonders that Soviet test pilot Elita Priedite found enthralling, if not unexpected, as her experimental plane accelerated towards the speed of sound. Beneath her jet's small triangular wings, stretched an endless blanket of gray clouds, and kilometers below these, the cold Arctic Ocean with its crushing ice floes, abyssal trenches and locked secrets. A hostile environment at all levels, yet she traversed it with ease, hurtling with her Savior towards destiny.

"Mach zero-point-eight," reported Elita into her headset, her words steady even as the cockpit shuddered around her. "All normal."

This last remark was in truth a lie. A woman—a *Soviet* woman, a *Latvian* woman—going this fast was far from normal. In fact, it had never been done before. The sound barrier within reach, she'd be the first Soviet pilot of either gender to break it outside the USSR's borders, a Politburo-calculated event in international airspace for the world to see. An act of blunt intimidation for real and imagined enemies of the Soviet people. Elita herself cared nothing for wargames or national posturing. Let the political chatterboxes talk of messages to America and NATO, she only wished to fly.

"Begin your acceleration dive in fifteen seconds, Captain Priedite," instructed a firm Russian voice through her helmet speakers. Colonel Anton Baranov sat in safety forty kilometers away on a Soviet destroyer, yet, thought himself master of this experiment.

Elita knew who was in control. And if not she, then the Lord himself guided her hand.

"Beginning acceleration dive in fifteen seconds," she answered as if a formality.

Elita took another long breath of oxygen, watched the observation plane on her right fall away, unable to keep pace. For the first time since her girlhood when the Soviets, then the Nazis, and then the Soviets again invaded her Latvian homeland, she was untethered to an occupying government.

Unseen. Unobservable. Free.

Taking one hand from her control stick, Elita dug into the collar of her flight suit, pulled a simple Lutheran cross up through the sliver of exposed flesh at her neck beneath the helmet. She let it hang freely across her chest, the crucifix swinging with the vibrations of the cockpit.

The Communists had driven religion literally underground in Soviet Latvia, but the devout continued their worship clandestinely. Elita baptized her children in secret fruit-cellar services, sang hymns, and exchanged homemade gifts before glowing Christmas trees in a Rīga basement, lookouts at the top of the stairs to watch for KGB spies. Now, flying along the belly of Heaven, Elita was free to display her allegiance to the Lord. Let Him see whom she honored when they made history. A silent prayer from Psalm 40 as Elita returned both hands to the control stick and began her acceleration dive.

Steidzies, ak Kungs, man palīgā!
Make haste, o Lord, to help me!

"Report," interrupted Colonel Baranov, a man far from Heaven.

The airspeed climbed as fast as the altitude dropped. "Mach zero-point-nine-four," Elita replied, wondering at Baranov's reaction if she left the cross exposed when returning to the Soviet Union a hero. All the *Pravda* photographers would be horrified. Would they ban the photos or touch

I

them up to hide the truth? So, tempting to make a display of piety.

But Lord forgive her, she was not as strong as Job. She could not pay the high price for honesty. Not for her sons' sakes.

"You've deviated from the flight plan," Colonel Baranov admonished. "Correct it."

Elita's eyes flicked over to her instruments. Baranov was right. So intently was she focused on speed and altitude, she'd let the directional vector drift well off route. How long had she flown this path? At near supersonic speeds the plane could be kilometers off course.

"Correcting." Elita adjusted her rudder until the directional dials realigned. Her eyes returned to the airspeed indicator: "Zero-point-nine-nine."

So close to history...

Elita's eyes never left the indicator as it crawled higher. She knew the future. There would be no jolt, no sudden turbulence that threatened to tear the plane apart when she broke through into the supersonic. Those who'd gone through before—men like Yeager and Fyodorov, women like Cochran and Auriol—said nothing unusual happened the moment the plane crossed over. There was no barrier felt inside the cockpit. Not from the pilot's point of view. Everything dramatic happened outside...

"Captain Priedite, what is your intended destination?"

She barely heard Baranov, Elita's attention fixed on her instruments. The airspeed indicator's last digit turned smoothly, like a simple wooden gear in some quaint old-time Cēsis clock shop. The display was clear. Mach one-point-oh-one. Mach one-point-oh-two...

With the Lord's assistance, Elita travelled faster than sound.

"Mach one-point-oh-five achieved!" she shouted into the headset, girlish elation in her voice.

But there was no celebration in Baranov's reply: "Captain Priedite, divert course immediately, or we assume defection!"

"Colonel, my readings show proper—"

Elita's instruments lit up like a cellar Christmas tree.

DEEDS OF DARKNESS

***

On a bleak island beach, Norwegian lighthouse keeper Bjørn Borsheim examined the three mutilated seal carcasses washed ashore. The wounds on the animals' bodies were unlike any he'd seen. Deep gullies of torn pink flesh wrapped around the seals' dark forms in a corkscrew fashion, winding about the corpses like stripes on a barber's pole.

These were adult harbor seals, abundant in the Svalbard coastal waters, animals that were well over one hundred kilograms alive. Yet, in each carcass easily half the mass was missing. Gobbled up in these gruesome, remarkably consistent injuries.

"Could it be a boating accident?" asked his wife, Ylva, kneeling next to him.

"A boat that struck three seals in a day's time? Without us seeing anything from the house?" He shook his head, pointed to divots in the skin near the trench-like wounds. "I believe these are teeth marks, Ylva."

"Teeth marks?"

"Yes, here and here. The strangest bites I've ever seen, if bites these are."

Ylva set a gloved hand on the closest seal's snout. "The remains are warm." She stared into the creeping tides, the sea too near. "What sort of creature leaves such wounds, Bjørn?"

"Who can say? You know the old stories..."

"I still say it must be a propeller. Off a submarine, maybe." She stood, rubbed her shoulders in the driving coastal winds. "We can ask the university on the mainland to photograph the carcasses."

"They are too busy to fly to our little isle near the top of the world."

Ylva started to speak, then abandoned her reply and pointed to the sky.

"*Someone* flies here, Bjørn."

From the clouds far above emerged a black arrowhead-shaped projectile. Bjørn's keen keeper's vision, so proficient at spotting ships at sea, made it out to be a compact airplane with unusual triangular wings sloped back. It was very high but appeared to be travelling impossibly fast.

"Another marvel, Ylva. A plane like I've never—"

I

A clap a thousand times stronger than thunder struck the island, the force knocking Bjørn off his feet, shattering windows in the lighthouse tower, and sending wide ripples across the ocean's surface and through the tundra grass that stretched inland.

They were trying to recover their senses, and Bjørn his footing, when another, softer boom exploded somewhere in the skies.

Trailing white smoke that strange plane fell into the depths of the sea.

II

Present Day

Standing in the ship's bow, Santa Ezeriņa watched the black-gray billows on the horizon as a young volcano rose inexorably above the Arctic Ocean's surface. Every few seconds, geysers of lava erupted along the skyline, the accompanying gasses turning pinkish or purple as they mixed with a budding sunrise and remnants of *aurora borealis*. A mosaic of stunning colors that must be seen to be conceived. Nature's grandeur on display, a new island being born to join its eons-older mates in the Svalbard archipelago.

Yet few eyes rested upon this amazing sight. The Norwegian authorities had warned boaters of the dangers of 1,000-degree embers and lethal toxins in the volcanic smoke, restricted access to the area for tens of kilometers around and patrolled the region vigorously to enforce the ban.

But Santa and her shipmates had slipped inside the restricted zone, used the smoky air to camouflage their activities just eleven kilometers from the burning new island. Occasionally, they donned gas masks, kept fire-proof suits and flame-retardant foam at the ready. But the winds changed in this last half-hour and for now she could watch the volcanic panorama unprotected with minimal fear.

Though not quite an eased mind.

Another presence tickled her reporter's instincts, repeatedly pulled her gaze from the natural majesty. Inside the haze, not two hundred meters

II

away, sat the only other ship in view, a small scientific-looking vessel with no visible name or national markings, its heavy floodlamps searching the dark morning waters. Whoever they were, they too must be trespassers. Anyone official would have radioed the Svalbard coastguard by now and reported Santa's own ship, the *Anja*.

Curious. Santa never trusted lawbreakers even if she frequently crossed legal lines herself in her journalistic pursuits. As she did now. Hypocritical, this lack of trust? Sure. Wise tactic? Definitely. There were some ugly people out there.

"Santa!" shouted a voice from within her ship's cabin.

She left the grimy deck and went inside. Gathered around a display monitor was the *Anja's* two-man crew of old Norwegian salts, Dag and Anders. Absent were their Icelandic divers, who at this moment explored the sea below them: Daníel Rafnkelsson, a professional deep-water expert from Reykjavík, second-cousin of Iceland's prime minister, and well-known internet blogger on all subjects aquatic and occasionally political; and Páll Erlingur, the best underwater topographer willing to work illegally, at cost, and who didn't mind an erupting volcano or two nearby.

Santa was the only Latvian on this venture, the only journalist, the only female. And the only one under thirty, though in character she possessed maturity the others lacked. A woman among boys, even if the chronological ages didn't bear that out.

"What's up?" she asked in English, rising to her tiptoes to peer over Dag's and Anders's wide Nordic shoulders. "Páll find anything?"

"Look for yourself," said Dag, his voice charged with excitement.

On the screen was the sonar imaging feed transmitted live from the subsurface scanner mounted on Páll's helmet, the picture a collection of white and blue lines outlining the ocean landscape below their divers. The sea floor beneath the *Anja* was rising, driven higher by the growing volcano nearby, a subsurface ridge carried up from abyssal depths by the new island being born in the heart of the sea.

As Páll floated in place, keeping his multi-beam scanner fixed over that ridge, the sonar image clarified, sweeping scanlines tightening detail. A manmade shape rested on a jagged outcropping, the object little more than a slight yellow-orange outline on their monitor, but wing and tail sections were distinctly visible.

"Captain Priedite's plane," whispered Santa.

"Unseen in more than sixty years," confirmed Anders.

"Can it be?"

"It's what we came for!" shouted Dag, clapping hands with Anders, their motion rocking the ship and allowing Santa to squeeze between them for a closer view of the screen.

There was no doubt.

The Soviet jet lost in 1958.

She felt her pulse rising.

"Páll's done it!" shouted one of the men, Santa's attention too focused on the plane to notice which.

"*We've* done it!" replied the other.

Santa glanced at the iPad mounted on the monitor table, the open app showing the positions of their two divers against the topographical map taken by the sonar.

"If the sensor on Páll's suit is correct, he's at forty meters," said Santa. "And that plane must rest at what? Two hundred meters down? Two hundred ten?" She glanced at the men. "Too deep for scuba gear. We'll need ADS to get down there."

"None to be had," said Anders, that revelation taming the men's euphoria. "The Russians bought every deep-water suit in the Svalbard archipelago. Shipped them off to their Barentsburg settlement."

"The Russians?"

"Need the suits for deep-sea cable repair. That's what my pal at the Longyearbyen dive emporium says."

"We couldn't afford more equipment anyway," said Dag. "I hocked everything I owned just to help finance this expedition so far."

"We all did,' agreed Anders. "Those deep suits cost six hundred thousand U.S. dollars each. Worth more than the *Anja* these days."

"We'll find a way," said Santa, eyes back on the sonar imaging feed. "We

II

can sell the coordinates and sonar images for worldwide publication. And Daníel knows some rich people in Reykjavík. The plane waited six decades; it can wait—"

The monitor went black.

"We've lost the bloody feed," cursed Dag.

"Give it a minute," answered Santa. She looked to the depth meter. Páll was rising. "He's stopped scanning and coming up."

"Too quickly."

Santa frowned. Dag was right. What had gotten into Páll? Despite having plenty of oxygen, he was shooting upwards like a missile. No decompression stops. "He'll get the bends. That could kill him."

"Páll knows that. The sensors gotta be broken." Anders pulled the iPad from its mounting, glared at the readouts, shook it violently. "Daníel is rising too. Safer rate. Barely."

Santa sprinted from cabin to deck, searching the sea for her divers. Páll broke first. Away from the *Anja*, within the floodlights of that peculiar, lurking ship. He flailed about at the surface briefly, then went limp with a finality that twisted Santa's stomach.

"*Su'ds*," she whispered, cursing in her native tongue as Páll began to sink. She glanced around the cluttered deck for a wetsuit. *Where was Daníel?*

The crew of the other vessel threw Páll a line. He clung to it as they pulled him in and lifted his spent body from the water.

"It's okay," Santa said to her men. "That boat's got him."

The other ship's floodlamps dimmed, replaced by higher, focused headlights. They ignited their engines, turned heading and sped away at highest speed.

"Where are they going?" asked an astonished Dag, now standing beside Santa.

She wasn't quite sure. "Gotta be rushing Páll to the Longyearbyen hospital, right?" She turned to glance inside the cabin. "Radio and confirm that's their plan, Anders."

"We break radio silence, the harbor patrol's gonna know we're here, Santa."

A blaring alarm erupted somewhere inside the fog.

Too late.

The smoky atmosphere over the waters parted and a new ship emerged from the gloom. A Norwegian patrol boat headed their way.

"They already know, Anders," Santa said. She raised her hands. "The jig is up, boys."

III

"Santa Ezeriņa, your lawyer's here," said the guard, opening the cell door.

Exhausted from sixteen hours in the Longyearbyen jail, Santa was slow to comprehend his Norwegian. They'd been arrested this morning, even Daníel when he surfaced. As the only female, Santa was imprisoned separately from the men, locked away in a small, overheated cell on the Svalbard archipelago's largest and only permanently settled island, Spitsbergen. With virtually no crime in the dominant town of Longyearbyen, its jail and harbor patrol station consisted only of a few offices and holding cells nestled in the back of a town hall, a small complex that turned deadly quiet at night. After hours of silent solitude, deciphering a foreign language was difficult even for a polyglot like Santa.

"The court appointed me a lawyer?" she finally asked.

"Not us. He's an American but says he's your lawyer. Rather insistent about a meeting, too." The guard read her dismay. "You're not required to see him."

"Why would I have an American lawyer?"

The guard began to slide the door shut. "I'll tell him to come back during official hours."

"I'll go," she said, forcing her stiff body off the bench. "Anything to chat with a human being for ten minutes. The voices in my head grew stale hours ago."

* * *

The man waiting for Santa in the nearby interview room was trim, dressed in a navy-blue suit with red power tie, and radiated calm authority. Square jawed, peach-blond hair gelled in place, he might have been thirty-five or fifty-five, his age difficult to measure with much of his face hidden behind the wide reflective lenses of aviator glasses.

He stood when Santa entered, his height slightly less than hers, but his grip firm and masculine as he shook her hand.

"I want you to know, Ms. Ezeriņa, that we are working diligently on your behalf," he said in a strong mid-Atlantic American accent. "I can say with confidence you'll be freed on Thursday at latest."

She took a seat at the table as the guard closed the door, giving them the illusion of privacy. The man sat across from her, elbows on the tabletop, a smartphone and dogeared notebook resting before him.

"I'm appreciative," said Santa in fluent English. "But who are you? Do you work for the Norwegian authorities?"

An eyebrow arched behind those glasses. "We work *with* foreign entities, Ms. Ezeriņa. Never for them. I am Hugo Sommers. I represent a private organization concerned with America's place in the world. And we are here to assist."

"Which organization?"

"That too is private."

She frowned. "Are you connected to the ship that rescued Páll Erlingur?"

"Who is Páll Erlingur?" His eyebrows met above those lenses in a deep grimace. Sommers opened the notebook and ran his index finger down a list of the *Anja's* crew and financial backers, Santa's own name at the top. "I don't believe we've heard of him."

"He's an Iceland national. A diver of ours picked up by a ship without markings in the restricted zone. We suspect Páll may be suffering from decompression sickness and need medical care. So far, no one can tell us what became of him. We're worried."

Sommers withdrew a pen from his breast pocket and added Páll's name to his list. Santa noted he matched the Icelandic spelling perfectly.

III

"There are only two medical facilities in the archipelago," said Sommers. "The local hospital here in Longyearbyen and the miner's clinic at the Russian settlement of Barentsburg."

"The ship may have had a decompression chamber of its own."

"What makes you think so?"

"It was…well, it looked… industrially or scientifically outfitted."

"Let's hope for your friend's sake that ship remained seaworthy until he received medical attention. A patrol boat was set ablaze by shifting winds the morning of your arrest. The volcanic zone is forbidden for good reason," he said, censure in his tone. "Anyway, I'll look into Mr. Erlingur's status for you."

Santa was thankful for anyone concerned about Páll's health and location, but the rest of this unexpected assistance was too odd for her liking.

"Why are you helping us, Mr. Sommers? We're hardly affecting American interests."

"When dangling from a cliffside, never ask the motivations of those throwing you a rope, Ms. Ezeriņa." He shut the notebook. "Accept aid with silent, tasteful gratitude."

"I'm a journalist. I'm never silent. And seldom tasteful, for that matter."

"You will be out by Thursday."

"Yes…you said that before. Why wait three days?"

"The *Anja*'s presence in the restricted zone is no trivial matter. We'll need to prove it a navigational mistake. Assuming, of course, your proximity to the volcano *was* accidental, Ms. Ezeriņa?"

Santa had a hunch his "assistance" was a charade. "You know that's not the case, Mr. Sommers."

"I do," he said flatly. "What is your interest in a Soviet-era plane?"

Santa wondered how Sommers knew. Did he interview the others? Read texts and emails in seized devices? So many easy avenues. It all depended on what the Longyearbyen police would allow.

She shrugged. "It's a good a story. Reporters report."

"A journalist from a tiny European country does not mortgage her future to finance an expedition in the Arctic only to photograph a volcano and a decades-sunk plane. You'd never get a return on such an investment." Sommers pressed his glasses higher up the narrow bridge of his nose. "There's more to it than that, Ms. Ezeriņa. Do tell."

"Maybe I'm a bad businesswoman."

"Or more than a businesswoman."

She leaned forward, consciously kept her voice measured. "The plane's pilot, Captain Elita Priedite, was a countrywoman of mine, Mr. Sommers. We believe her the first Soviet woman to break the sound barrier. There were reports of an explosive noise resembling a sonic boom all over the Svalbard islands moments before her plane went down in 1958. The USSR, embarrassed by the crash and unsettled by Christian paraphernalia found in Priedite's Rīga apartment after her death, labeled her a traitor, an attempted defector, and never confirmed the top speed. They preferred to let Marina Popovich, a loyal Russian atheist, become the official record breaker six years later."

"What do you care of decades-old records?"

"Priedite's family suffered for the USSR's embarrassment. Her relatives were disenfranchised, some sent to Siberia on trumped-up charges. The harassment was so unrelenting, one son committed suicide. The attacks subsided when the Soviet Union broke up, but the family's shame lingers to this day. Latvia is a small country, Mr. Sommers. Only two million of us. We need our champions. I want to find out what happened to that plane. Discover if it was indeed pilot error that sent it to the bottom of the sea that day."

"And if it wasn't?"

"Let the chips fall where they may."

"You hardly sound impartial."

"The great-granddaughter of Elita Priedite cannot be impartial. The surviving son was my grandfather. But the truth does not take sides. Even in a new Cold War."

"Truth is subjective, Ms. Ezeriņa. The sides are not."

"We'll see what we find down there, Mr. Sommers. Mother Nature

III

is bringing the answer closer to the surface every second. And there is nothing Uncle Sam, Ivan the Bear, or anyone else can do to prevent it."

"Yes," he said with a smile. "But it won't be answered by Thursday. I promise you."

IV

Santa Ezeriņa did not have to wait until Thursday and American assistance for freedom. The other diver, Daníel Rafnkelsson, raised bail for the entire Anja expedition the next afternoon with a generous wire-transfer from wealthy friends in Reykjavík. By the time Santa rejoined the men in the townhall's front office, Daníel had completed his paperwork and headed over to the Longyearbyen hospital in search of Páll Erlingur.

As Santa, Anders, and Dag finished filling out their own release forms, the conversation turned to Hugo Sommers.

"He's an odd *faen*," said Dag, fiddling with the tip of his pen in a vain attempt to start the ink flowing. "Put me off using the English language for a while."

"How many of us met with him?" asked Santa.

"We all did. One by one," said Anders. "I saw him last. By then, Daníel already had the bail money coming. Sommers was furious that we were gettin' out of here today."

"Too bad."

"He didn't care much for you, Santa," added Dag. "Said you organized the expedition out of a family vendetta. That we'd never make a cent for our efforts and would end up in jail for crimes worse than trespassing if we kept at it. He claimed Anders and me might lose our boating licenses associating with you."

Santa felt an unexpected chill around the table.

"How could I cost *you* your licenses?"

IV

"If we went back near the volcano," answered Dag. "Come within forty kilometers of that sunken jet, Sommers told us, and we'd never captain a vessel again. Not in any sea worth sailing."

"Is the Arctic worth sailing in?"

"For us? Yes."

Anders leaned forward, his voice lowered in case the Longyearbyen police were listening. "Sommers said you're known in Latvia for getting your associates in trouble. Or killed. That the newspapers in Rīga call you 'Lady Death,' so many people die."

"Charming."

"Ugly names don't scare us," said Dag. "But...thing is, Santa...We can't afford to lose our licenses. Or the *Anja*. It's all we got to live by."

"Dag and me have families. I got four kids, a fifth coming.... You...you can take risks, Santa. The Communists destroyed your family. You got no one in this world."

"Apparently."

"I didn't mean—"

"I know exactly what you meant." She grimaced, set her hands flat on the table between them. "Let's postpone the mutiny for now, okay? We find Páll first. That's most important. Then we take a vote, all five of us. Continue after the plane or go home. Fair?"

The two Norwegians glanced at each other.

"Yeah. All right," said Dag.

"Sure," said Anders. "But what will you do if you lose the vote, Santa?"

"What my great-grandmother did. Fly solo and trust the Lord. But for now, Lady Death has a diver to find. I want to keep another soul off my conscience."

* * *

When Daníel called Santa's cellphone at noon, he sounded nearly in tears. Páll Erlingur was not at the Longyearbyen hospital. No one had heard of him. No Icelander was admitted yesterday or today, nor any diver of any nationality complaining of decompression sickness symptoms. Their lodge said Páll's bed was not slept in. The police were indifferent. Daníel was at a loss what to do next.

Santa told him to have a drink on her at the local tavern until they arrived. He agreed.

Their walk through Longyearbyen to the Amundsen Tavern was brief, uneventful, and filled with incredible vistas that might have been stirring if the mood was lighter. A town of two thousand miners, fishermen, and researchers, Longyearbyen was the most populous settlement this far north in the world. Red, blue, and green Scandinavian houses sat along snowy roads on either side of the Longyearbyen River, which flowed in warmer months into the Adventfjorden, itself a bay in the much larger Isfjorden. The rusted towers of an abandoned aerial tramway, which once carried coal from mines to harbor, crisscrossed the town, giving Longyearbyen a faded, days-gone-by industrial atmosphere. And outside the town, looming over mankind's incursions, stood an impenetrable ring of jagged mountains, their brown-black masses walling off sheets of primordial inland glaciers. So, rugged was the landscape, so quickly did the heights ascend from the waters' edge, that awe-struck, first-time arrivals at the harbor often asked Longyearbyen's elevation.

Sea level, you idiot. You just got off a boat.

Even with her insular focus on Páll and the coming mutiny, Santa's journalistic ear noted a varied range of dialects spoken on these icy streets. Norwegian was the dominant language in Longyearbyen, a logical enough state since Norway politically controlled the whole archipelago. But there were others present. The treaty of 1920 guaranteed the rights of forty countries to exploit the resources on these islands unimpeded. The Russians, here since the whaling days of the seventeenth century, never left, and still operated mines throughout Svalbard. This occasionally brought conflict. The whole island chain was supposedly a demilitarized zone, and during the Cold War, the Soviets and NATO frequently accused each other of storing weapons under those towering mountains or hiding spy submarines in the misty fjords of the archipelago's remotest isles.

IV

Accusations revived in recent years with renewed tensions between the West and Moscow.

Accusations that interested Santa Ezeriņa deeply.

* * *

The interior of the Amundsen Tavern reeked of male sweat, wet fur, and burnt cooking fat drifting in from the kitchen. Gangly, red-bearded Daníel Rafnkelsson waited at the back, sitting alone by a dark wooden table below paintings of whaling ships and sepia-tone photographs from Longyearbyen's centuries of grim habitation. While Dag and Anders stopped at the bar, leaning on its whalebone rail to order drinks from a sleepy, whiskered barkeep, Santa went immediately to Daníel.

"Any new developments?" She asked, taking a seat next to him at the tiny scarred table.

"He's still gone," said Daníel forlornly. Santa was amazed how hard the disappearance had hit him, though she shouldn't have been, truthfully. Páll was something of an older brother to Daníel, had mentored him from trainee to experienced Dive Master and eventual business partner. Though they came from different economic strata in their native Iceland, the two men found a common bond in their love of the sea.

Santa was unsure what to say. A solitary operator by nature, she was leader in this endeavor by necessity, not inclination. Questioning others was easy, a product of years of investigative journalism, but despite her shattered family, consoling the despondent remained uncomfortable guesswork.

"Páll's only missing, Daníel. Not gone," she finally said. Her words felt trite. Insufficient.

"Páll would call if he could. He knows my mobile number by heart. Eighteen years together. His silence means he's sick or dead."

She thought of Hugo Sommers spelling Icelandic surnames perfectly. "Or a prisoner."

"Is that supposed to be better? I have to call his wife tonight."

"Better than dead, sure."

"None of those options suit me." Daníel looked at her fiercely. "How about you, get anyone else arrested today? Or killed?"

"I see Sommers was at you, too."

Born of frustration, Daníel's rage faded as quickly as it'd come, replaced by a mild embarrassment. "Yeah. Sorry. He's an ass. So am I." He finished his beer, smiled wearily. "How does Sommers know so much about you anyway?"

"I'm wondering that too. He seems to have a lot on all of us—except perhaps Páll."

They said nothing a long while. Even when Anders and Dag joined them, little alleviated the silence.

"Páll needs to be in a hospital," Daníel said finally. "The bends can take a day or two to manifest the worst…the potentially fatal…signs."

"Any idea why he came to the surface so quickly? Without decompression stops?"

"Something mythic, maybe. Some *skrímsli*…a terrible *sæskrímsli*."

"Say again?"

His mind returned from somewhere. "We're a superstitious race, Santa. Ten percent of Icelandic people still believe in elves, ghosts and faeries. That's a fact. And old rural boys like Páll are worst of all. I think he saw something which triggered a…a primal reaction in him. Sent Páll Hellbent for the surface, uncaring of the repercussions other than immediate escape."

"What could override years of training and experience?"

"I've been his diving partner for nearly two decades. Never seen a hint of panic in Páll. Barracuda. Moray Eels. Ruptured tanks. We lost our dive boat once, treaded water for a full day and night. Nothing fazed Páll." His eyes looked to Dag, Anders, then back to Santa. "You know…. Look, I'm among the non-elf-believing ninety percent…I'm educated…"

"But…"

"I saw something, too. Not as closely as Páll, and…Well, I'm not sure what it was. Only a glimpse at a distance. But I know what it looked like."

IV

"What?"

"You won't hold it against me, boss lady?"

"Never."

"A serpent, Santa. A serpent as long as a city bus with burning fire for eyes."

V

Santa Ezeriṇa stood alone on the ferry deck as it cruised through the icy waters of Isfjorden. Deep in concentration, she leaned on the sea rail, little seeing the magnificent scenery around her. As the only member of the Anja expedition fluent in Russian, she was best suited to take transport to Bartensburg, the Russian settlement, three hours by ferry from Longyearbyen, and look for Páll. She preferred company, but a comprehensive search of the archipelago necessitated splitting her team. Dag and Anders headed to isolated Norwegian towns in the North, while Daníel stayed in Longyearbyen going ship-to-ship in the harbor asking about Páll.

Two days now. It wasn't looking good.

Santa's eyes flicked down to the ferry's wake, a trail of white foam stretching across the fjord's black surface. Her mind returned to Daníel's peculiar sighting. Santa didn't believe in flame-eyed sea serpents, but clearly her divers had seen something more substantial than the denizen of an Icelandic fable. Something real haunted the depths of these waters.

She felt a chill unconnected with the northern latitude. Had her great-grandmother looked out her plane window in the last moments of her life and seen the same creature? As she sank forever into the abyss?

She fought off her melancholy. No. Not forever, Santa reminded herself. She glanced up to the ever-present column of volcanic smoke on the northern horizon. Somehow it comforted her. The truth was getting closer to the surface each day.

Through the sea fog she spied a great five-pointed star outlined in white

V

on a shore hillcrest with the Communist slogan "Peace to the World" in bold Cyrillic letters beneath. The ferry soon arrived at Bartensburg, a collection of small houses on a ridge above the fjord, the whole village less than a quarter the size of Longyearbyen. Unlike the larger settlement, there was no array of languages in the air. Santa heard only Russian on the docks and as she made her way up the steps of a slushy hillside towards a drab, square building that held the coal miner's medical clinic. During the phone call from Longyearbyen, the staff told Santa that Páll was not admitted here, but she wanted to see with her own eyes. Santa trusted no one, least of all a community that still sported hammers and sickles on government building facades, thirty years after the destruction of the Soviet Union. Several of Santa's own relatives perished in similarly ill-equipped clinics in the wilds of Siberia.

The investigation turned out to be a waste of time. The infirmary was a solitary open room, all patients visible with a single glance from the doorway. Three miners. A fisherman. Two young children.

No Páll.

After clinic records revealed nothing, Santa left without answers, yet, not quite alone. A man dressed in a gold and black Pittsburgh Penguins ski jacket trailed her along Bartensburg's only street *Ivana Starostina*, refusing to pass when she tested him by tarrying egregiously at the miner's chapel and then again outside the souvenir-filled windows of the Polar Star community center.

"Penguins are *Antarctic*, you know," she finally said in English. "You're at the wrong end of the world, buddy."

He made no reply, continued to linger.

By the time Santa reached the Bartensburg Port Sea Office, she had a measure of the man, certain he was an agent of Hugo Sommers's investigating her activities in a Russian town. Likely some Pennsylvania native tapped to play spy for the "private" organization protecting American interests abroad.

Santa went inside the port offices. So did her pursuer.

The interior was as empty as the street outside, with only a heavy-set guard, a woman behind the ticket window, and Santa's new shadow for company. The chamber's decor was dominated by a Soviet-era map of the Svalbard archipelago painted over the entirety of one wall. As her watcher took a seat on a nearby bench, Santa scanned the community names on the map, hoping for some magical insight that would lead her to Páll. Nothing triggered her instincts.

She reasoned through alternate scenarios. Who had a motive to keep Páll? Who were the players in this drama? Santa looked at the Pittsburgh man, his eyes on the ceiling, humming a tune she didn't recognize. The Americans had no settlements in Svalbard. No official ones, at least.

What about the Russians?

Her eyes spied a plaque near the door honoring soldiers from the archipelago who had fallen in the Soviet Union's Afghanistan War, the listing broken up by settlement, effectively cataloging Soviet towns here circa 1982. Only two.

Bartensburg. Four dead.

Pyramiden. Two.

Why had she never heard of Pyramiden?

"What is Pyramiden?" Santa asked in fluent Russian, stepping to the ticket window. "The prominence of the lettering indicates a sizable settlement."

"An abandoned mining town," answered the woman with a tired indifference.

"Russian town?"

"It was."

"Can you still buy a ferry ticket there?"

The woman sighed. "Pyramiden closed in 1998. Private charters sometimes overnight in summer for hikers and tourists who like ghost towns or bear watching. Never this early in the year. It's too rough."

"How would I get there out of season?"

"Snowmobile. Around the fjord. But I wouldn't advise it. Too far."

Santa considered this. She presented her passport and bought a return ticket to Longyearbyen. A glance at the American sports fan still sitting

V

casually on his bench, brought a new stratagem.

She returned her eyes to the clerk, nodded towards the exit. "I'm going out that door. Sometime in the next three minutes, that man on the bench will come to your window. He'll want to know what I asked about. Tell him only I wanted to know the schedule for Longyearbyen, okay?" Santa pushed forward a two-hundred-*kroner* bill. "I understand private citizens accept Norwegian currency here?"

The clerk's eyes widened. "I don't comprehend."

"You don't need to. Just do as I ask. If that man wants a ticket, ask to see his passport. Get his name and confirm nationality. There'll be more bills in it for you."

"I don't think so." She began to close the window.

Santa shoved forward five additional two-hundred *kroner* bills. "Have it all. I trust you."

"Don't trust me. I beg you."

"Too late. I'm trusting again. Happens all the time. Ask my last three boyfriends."

The woman paused, clearly conflicted, then finally took the money, slipped into her breast pocket. "If our guard asks...you wanted to buy a seasonal ferry pass. I went to check on their availability during my smoking break. I told you to come back."

"Good idea."

Santa left through the exit, walked casually through the slush outside, slowly circumnavigating the building. Down on the pier, a crowd was gathering around a seal carcass pulled from the waters by a fishing boat. Santa could see little at this distance, but the din of voices and the alarmist body language of those near the dead animal were puzzling.

She had more immediate concerns. When five minutes passed, Santa re-entered the pier offices through the same door. The ski-jacketed man was coming out as she came in.

"Miss me?" Santa said in English as they passed. "Or should I say, 'Missed me?'"

Silence. The door swung closed behind.

Santa returned to the clerk. "He was American, wasn't he?" she asked. "Did he have a U.S. State Department passport? The CIA uses those."

"He's a policeman."

"A policeman? Local police? Of what nationality?"

"If he tells the guard about your bribes, I'm jobless." The clerk slammed down the window. "I'm a law-abiding citizen. I don't want any part of your schemes. You're trouble, young lady! I knew it!"

"That seems to be the consensus."

"I told you not to trust me."

"That's what the boyfriends said. What about my money?"

The clerk disappeared into the offices behind the glass.

Law-abiding citizen....

Santa exited the building.

The mysterious policeman was nowhere in sight. She circled the building again but found nothing but snow tracks leading deeper into Bartensburg. A trail that could have been left by anyone.

Santa went down to the pier to await the return ferry to Longyearbyen. The crowd had grown to a dozen or so, and she pushed her way to the front to get a better view of the seal hanging from a line. The body was in tatters, deep gully-like wounds wrapping about the corpse-like ribbons around a maypole. She'd never seen anything like it.

"What makes such twisting wounds?" She asked a fisherman standing nearby.

"Don't know," he said. "But the man from Hornsund will soon be here to tell us."

Santa well knew Hornsund, a Polish research community on the south side of the island. Every science applicable to the northern latitudes was studied there.

"How soon?" she asked.

The fisherman smiled as the crowd parted. "Here he comes, now."

VI

The scientist from Hornsund emerged from the crowd to examine the mauled seal hanging on the line. The narrow, weathered face under a knit hat hinted at a man of about sixty. He withdrew from his jacket a tape measurer and medical caliper to take measurements of the wounds on the animal. When finished, he spoke in Russian with a heavy Polish accent to the fisherman standing in the boat:

"This carcass has research value. Thirteen thousand rubles for the seal and for transporting it to our facilities. Agreed? Good. We pay upon delivery. I'll be in the café when you're ready to depart." He turned and marched up the hill stairs towards the one visible restaurant.

Santa was not far behind.

"Mister!" she shouted, catching her breath after quickly climbing the stairs. "I'm a journalist. I'd like to ask you a question."

"About what?" his tone, while curt, was not disagreeable.

She handed him a business card to prove herself an actual journalist. "This will sound idiotic, I know, especially for educated professionals in the twenty-first century, but…" Santa forced out the ridiculous question. "Look, my friend claims he saw a sea serpent the size of a fishing boat two days ago. A creature with magical fiery eyes forty meters below the surface. Silly, of course, and we'd dismiss it as a depth hallucination, but another diver reacted to something similar at the same moment. Can there be any scientific basis for what they encountered?"

To Santa's surprise, the researcher did not dismiss her query outright. Instead, he calmly asked:

"In the local waters?"

"Arctic Ocean, northwest of the island. Near that young volcano."

He considered this, then said: "I would guess your friends saw a Greenland shark; they inhabit the deeper waters here." He pointed back towards the pier. "One killed that seal out in the fjord."

"Greenland shark?"

"It is a large, lank shark with narrow fins. From the right angle they may look serpentine. The species is prone to eye infections from deep-sea parasites, some of whom are bio-luminescent. In low light, it gives the impression the shark's eyes are glowing. With a diver's mind under the 'Martini effect' of scuba gasses at forty meters, one could rather poetically see fire."

Maybe, those bloody divers weren't mad....

"When you say large, sir, how large do they get?"

"Six meters or more. They are neck-to-gilled-neck with the great white as the largest predatory fish in the world."

"Oh, good."

He smiled. "Fortunately, Greenland sharks live in waters too deep and too cold to encounter humans frequently. Unless you go down there...I wouldn't recommend it, a big one could swallow a man whole. The Inuit peoples fear them greatly, claim on rare trips to the surface these fish attack kayaks, take walrus, even elk and other large land animals when they cross open sea. Examination of stomach contents confirm this. I personally removed the body of a reindeer from the belly of a Greenland shark caught off Edge Island last year. Several beaks of giant squid, too."

"Yikes." She gestured back at the seal on the line. "And if they don't swallow you whole, they leave wounds like that?"

"These fish are stealth predators. They catch seals sleeping underwater. The shark grabs ahold and twirls its body, unraveling the living flesh off the prey in a distinctive spiral fashion. Hellish way to die. Nature can be cruel."

He produced a card from the Hornsund Center. "I'm Doctor Abel Mazurk, the director at the facilities. We've all the sciences working

VI

there—geologists, meteorologists, oceanographers. Call, if you have additional questions." His tone lightened. "We don't get journalists up here often. To have a non-academic writer interested in our work...It is all rather flattering."

Santa promised a full interview published in her newspaper. As soon as she found Páll Erlingur.

* * *

The first hour of Santa's return journey to Longyearbyen was a tranquil affair, the afternoon mists eclipsing the mountains on either side of Isfjorden. Despite a colder turn in the weather, Santa was dressed warmly enough to endure the open air. She leaned on the ferry's sea-rail, listening to the engines churn the water, her mind wondering what sort of creatures swam in the depths below her.

This tranquility was disturbed by the sounds of a second engine approaching in the fog. Santa's eyes found the black shape of a ship in the mists, some small vessel passing along the north side of the fjord. As it came nearer, details emerged.

A ship with floodlamps in the fog.

A scientific ship.

The ship. Páll's ship.

Her pulse rising, Santa pulled her smartphone from her jacket's pocket, took photo after photo of the vessel as it passed within two hundred meters...

A figure just visible on its deck. A man in a yellow and black ski jacket.

It couldn't be. How many Penguin fans are there at this latitude?

Yet, the figure seemed to recognize her. It *was* the same man. Binoculars in his hand, the ski-jacketed man gave a mocking wave as the distance between the ships grew again.

He's no policeman. Some sort of gangster, local mob, maybe...

Santa rushed along the sea-rail to the ferry's bridge, tugged at the door, found it firmly locked.

"Call the harbor patrol," she shouted, pounding on the door's window to get the captain's attention. "That ship we passed, they're kidnappers!"

Without taking a hand from the controls, the captain glanced over his shoulder. "Kidnappers? Did they somehow take a passenger off this ferry?"

"No…Days before…It's them. I know it."

"I see." He returned his gaze to the waters ahead. "Take it up with port authority at the harbor."

"But…they'll be gone. We need to arrest them!"

"Continue this disturbance, and you'll be the one arrested. You're a dangerous distraction. Want us to ram an iceberg? Run aground in the fog?"

"Sometimes, I wonder."

"That statement can be used against you if needed."

Santa returned to the deck, watched the ship until it disappeared into the fjord's mists. Not a marking or flag to be seen…

"So close, Páll," she said when it was at last out of sight. Santa returned to the passenger cabin, took a seat on a hard-wooden bench, fighting to tame the frustration at her helplessness. Counted the minutes until they reached the harbor.

Time passed impossibly slowly. When the ferry was within an hour of Longyearbyen, the internet connection returned to Santa's smartphone. She sent out the foggy pictures of the offending ship to every contact she could trust and a few she couldn't.

She waited for responses. None came.

With an exhausted resignation and nothing to pass the minutes until docking, Santa Googled "Greenland shark." The fish that appeared on her screen lacked the familiar torpedo shape of most sharks, instead its body resembled a great brown-black cigar, the tubular mass propelled by comparatively small fins, and its face—if it could be called a face—featured a mouth brimming with countless saw-like teeth. It was the ugliest creature she'd ever seen, roaches, slugs, and drunken barflies included.

VI

The associated text said they were the longest-living vertebrates on Earth, some individuals living over five hundred years.

Five hundred years. A fish that swam in these waters this very moment may have been living before Svalbard was settled, as the New World was only just discovered, when Martin Luther was nailing his demands to the cathedral door.

Better to meet an actual sea serpent, she thought, then encounter that near-immortal *thing* in the cold, black depths of the sea.

VII

Daníel Rafnkelsson was waiting for Santa at the Longyearbyen harbor, leaning on his rented snowmobile, the vehicle parked off to one side on an industrial access road. After the briefest wave to gain her attention, he resumed an unmoving, arms-crossed posture while she exited the ferry and trudged through the slush to him. As Santa neared, she grew apprehensive of Daníel's grim countenance. The reason was soon evident.

"They've denied all access to money, Santa," said Daníel the moment she reached his snowmobile. "Anders, Dag, and I, we can't get a penny out of any bank machine on this island. Credit cards, too. Even PayPal and Skrill. My Reykjavík connection did another wire, and it was blocked locally. Everything's shut down."

"Who would do this?"

"Better to ask who *could* do this. Either the Norwegian authorities or someone working with them. The bank manager claims ignorance, says it'll take a week to straighten out."

"Someone wants to scuttle our expedition." She glanced at the two American ships in the harbor. "Someone who knows all our names."

"It gets worse. Dag and Anders were up in Ny-Ålesund looking for Páll when their credit cards were cut off. They can't rent transportation. They're stranded until the next public ferry back to Longyearbyen."

"Don't tell me…. The next ferry is Thursday?"

"Saturday night. We're on our own till then. I only hope they can find shelter. At least we got our lodge."

VII

If that, she thought.

They took the snowmobile in search of cash, Daníel driving, Santa on the seat behind, hands around his waist. There were two ATMs in Longyearbyen: one at the town's only bank, the other at the airport three kilometers away.

To no one's shock Santa's debit and credit cards failed. Since Páll's wallet was stuffed away in the same pack as Daníel's before that disastrous final dive, they tried his bank card too. Three wrong guesses at a pin number and the machine ate the card.

Santa hoped she'd see Páll again to apologize.

They decided to return to their lodge, use the WIFI and internet call services to raise hell at every bank and credit company connected to their expedition. Instead, they found their bags packed and stacked neatly in the tiny lobby.

"We were informed of illegalities by the port police," said the girl at the desk. "We don't harbor criminals here."

Santa bit her lip, demanded to speak with someone in authority.

The girl called an authority.

Hugo Sommers.

"Ms. Ezeriņa, Mr. Rafnkelsson, this is all a regrettable mistake," said Sommers, stepping into the lobby from the street five minutes later.

"Were you involved in this?" asked Daníel.

"If you mean working for a solution, Mr. Rafnkelsson, then yes. In Longyearbyen news gets around quickly. I understand, in addition to this unfortunate eviction, you've lost access to funds. A terrible situation in this Arctic place. But don't worry. We've worked diligently on your behalf and I think arrived at an acceptable resolution."

Neither Santa nor Daníel said a word.

Sommers pulled two envelopes from his coat pocket. "My organization, at our own expense, has purchased plane tickets for you both to Oslo tonight, with connecting flights onto Rīga and Reykjavík respectively. There you may rectify your financial and legal problems from the safety of your own homes. As opposed to out here in this wild country, where missteps can prove fatal."

"You're trying to run us out of town on a rail," said Santa. "And do so under the guise of assistance."

"Ms. Ezeriṇa, please listen to—"

"You couldn't keep us in jail, so now you want us off the island." Santa shoved a finger into Sommers's breast. "What are you up to, Hugo? Why are you in Longyearbyen? Why are the authorities kowtowing to you?"

"You misunderstand my intentions, Ms. Ezeriṇa. Our presence is benign. We've a car waiting outside to take you both to the airport. I'll explain on the way."

"We're not going."

"They can't stay here," said the desk clerk to Sommers. "You deal with them. Or I'm calling the police."

"Listen to her uncaring tone…. Such indifference to your plight," said Sommers. "I'm your best hope, Ms. Ezeriṇa. Let me help you, please. It will be a frigid night to sleep on the streets."

"We'll manage."

"And you, Mr. Rafnkelsson?"

"I'm with her."

A grimace behind those glasses. "As you wish. My organization cannot interfere on your behalf in the future. Even if enemies come visiting in the night."

"Thanks for letting us know," said Santa. "You've interfered enough."

"I am truly sorry for your interpretation of events," said Sommers sullenly. He opened the door to the street, a blast of Arctic air flowing in to chill all souls. "If you're still in the Svalbard islands by Thursday, we take no responsibility. Goodnight and goodbye."

Sommers stepped outside. A few seconds later, they heard the growl of an engine as a car took him away.

Santa looked at Daníel. "If I hear 'Thursday' once more, I'll vomit."

"I wonder who 'we' is exactly?"

The clerk picked up the telephone receiver. "Unless you are both out of our lobby in thirty seconds, I'm calling the police. Understand? Thirty,

VII

twenty-nine, twenty-eight…."

*　*　*

They wrapped their luggage in a polyethylene tarpaulin found among Daníel's things and placed the bundle in an alley with enough of an overhanging roof to partially block snowfall, withdrawing only important items: passports, smartphones, and binoculars.

"We can find a café' to stay warm in until closing time," said Daníel.

"Not with ten *kroner* between us," answered Santa, sitting on their bag-bundle in the alley. She rubbed her arms and shoulder in a vain effort to keep warm. And she thought Latvia was cold…

"Some kind heart will give us a break, Santa."

Her mind turned. "You ever heard of Pyramiden?"

"Yeah. A ghost town on the other side of the fjord."

"A woman in Barentsburg said they have excursions out there that sometimes stay over a few days. Which means they must have kept a few buildings habitable. Maybe we can break in, start the furnaces…"

"And, if not, we freeze to death a long way from help. Better to start a fistfight in the local pub and spend the night in a warm jail."

"We go to jail, Sommers will find a way to keep us there. At least until he gets what he wants in Svalbard." Her legs were already freezing. She stood up, walked in circles to restore the circulation. "Is there any way to look at Pyramiden from this side of the fjord?"

"The higher hills along the Longyearbyen Valley should have a nice view. I reckon the snowmobile can get us up the slopes easily enough. The effort ought to keep the blood flowin' too."

A minute later they'd mounted the snowmobile. As Daníel started the engine, he said: "You understand we're breaking the law again?"

"How so?"

"Anyone venturing outside of a settlement is required to carry a rifle for protection."

"Why?"

"Polar bears."

"I didn't want to know that."

"I thought journalists wanted to know everything." He started to accelerate, and they pulled out of the alley onto the snowy street. "Relax. You know the old proverb. Give a monster a name, it's not a monster anymore. Just an animal."

"Like the *sæskrímsli*?"

"*Sæskrímsli* means 'sea monster.' But you get the idea."

Any further words spoken fell hostage to the wind, the cold, and the rumbling of the engine. In muted silence, they sped past the edge of town and down into the Longyearbyen Valley, grim dark mountains looming above.

* * *

Huddled together for warmth, Santa and Daníel sat on a thermal blanket stretched over the snow of a valley hilltop, field glasses in their gloved hands. Above, two-thirds of the sky was lost to the smoke of the volcano erupting north of the island. But the south-east skies remained clear, and that sliver of the celestial canopy revealed more stars than Santa had seen on any night of her twenty-nine years. Heaven viewed through the encircling billows of terrestrial, volcanic Hell. Like Lucifer's last glimpse upwards as he fell.

Below this cosmic war, stretched the waters of wide Isfjorden. On the opposite bank among the mountains and glaciers was an inlet, the smaller but still substantial Billefjorden on whose western shore sat Pyramiden. Dark and brooding, the buildings were only tiny boxes at this distance, rows of gray cubes starting at the water's edge then stretching back towards the base of the pyramidal mountain that surely gave the town its name.

Along Pyramiden's pier sat a ship as still and dark as the town itself. From across the fjord, Santa couldn't be certain it was *the* ship, though by the silhouette she guessed it likely. Its presence guaranteed life in a ghost

VII

town, though neither living nor dead had materialized so far.

After twenty minutes watching, with the unrelenting cold seeping into their bones, Daníel exclaimed: "I found one."

"A ghost or sailor?"

"A bear. Three, in fact." Daníel pulled his eyes back enough to wink at her. "No worries. They're kilometers away. A mama and her cubs swimming across Isfjorden."

Santa scanned the fjord until she found three white bodies churning through the black waters, the mother ahead, one cub just behind, another twenty meters or so back, swimming steadily towards the nearside shore.

"That means bears are out and about tonight, Daníel. You still got the keys to the snowmobile, right?"

"I think I dropped them in the snow somewhere."

"Not funny."

She returned her attention to the Pyramiden pier. "That ship could be Páll's abductors. It looks the proper size, but I can hardly tell at night...Wait!" Santa felt her pulse jump. Two silhouettes emerged from a shadowed doorway in Pyramiden. "We got people moving between the houses."

"I see 'em."

The figures walked from a central building up the sloping streets to a large brick structure nearer the base of the pyramidal mountain. They were clearly dressed for the weather, and by their size Santa presumed them male, but all other details were lost to night and distance. A moment after they disappeared into the brick building, lamps lighted in windows on the ground floor. The glow steady. Not a trace of flicker.

"Electric lights mean power," said Daníel. "Power means heat."

Indeed, it did. "I'd be interested to hear what they've got to say. Can that snowmobile get us there?"

"Long way around the fjord." Daníel pulled down his glasses, thought for a moment. "We should just make it. But we're not coming back without refueling. And the reports say a snowstorm's coming..."

"What's a little bad weather? Adds to the challenge. I want to see a ghost town at the top of the world close up. You?"

"Where better to become a ghost?"

"Do all Icelanders have such macabre senses of humor?"

"I'm cheery. Talk to Páll after a few beers."

"That's the idea. Talk to Páll in person. Promptly."

"Yeah."

They stood, packed up the blanket. Before starting the snowmobile, Daníel took one last glance with his binoculars at the fjord waters. He frowned.

"What is it?" Santa asked.

"Didn't that mama bear have two cubs?"

"Yes."

"Sad. She lost one crossing the fjord."

VIII

By the time they approached Pyramiden, morning had come to the Arctic, drifting volcanic smoke transforming the sun to an angry red orb low in the southeastern sky. Bathed in this blood-red light, the town ahead looked even more desolate than it had across the nighttime fjord.

They stopped at a small lighthouse on the outskirts of town, a structure whose abandonment appeared more seasonal than permanent to Santa. Though the lighthouse door was secure, the boarded-up ground-floor windows fell prey to a crowbar Daniel found in the snowmobile's storage compartment. They were both soon inside.

The living quarters in the adjacent house were quaint, clearly occupied within the last year with assorted canned goods, a newspaper from July, and a well-maintained bear skin rug complete with head and foreclaws. In a cabinet, Santa discovered the keys for basement, lamp room and roof. All were soon explored.

From the lighthouse's top floor, they scanned the snowy streets that stretched out before them. The town consisted of several long gable-roofed brick dormitories, each four stories high, with groupings of smaller, weather-worn wooden houses, barns and workshops on the margins. A ruined coal factory dug into the base of the mountain. A pyramidal collection of painted iron bars, the Bolshevik red now faded to a feminine pink, served as a monument at settlement's edge, welcoming all to Pyramiden.

Nothing stirred at this hour, but smoke emanating from two chimneys near the pier revealed the location of habitation. That ship remained moored at the same spot. Seen in the light of day, it was clearly Páll's ship.

Santa focused her binoculars. "That boat's really something else, Daníel. The deck's got a crane, a lift built into the starboard side, and what looks like some type of radio-controlled submersible drone thingy under a cover."

"An ROV. Remote operated vehicle."

"That's what I said. Drone thingy."

"Think Páll's still onboard?"

"Only one way to find out." Santa moved her binocular focus down the coast, searching for the best approach to the ship. Her glasses spied a corpse on the beach. Another seal, this one untouched by the characteristic attack of a Greenland shark.

Probably died of sickness. Or fright, poor thing.

She moved her binocular view inland.

"Well, hello, old friend," she said. Among the buildings at the base of the mountain, walked the man in the Pittsburgh Penguins jacket. "You see this, Daníel? That's the 'policeman' from Bartensburg. The worst penguin since Wallace and Gromit."

"I see him. What should we do about Mr. Penguin?"

"Grab him. Have a chat."

"What if he doesn't want to chat?"

She glanced back at the seal on the shore. Smiled.

"He'll talk. I'm very persuasive."

* * *

In a narrow valley outside of Pyramiden, Santa sat on her haunches in ankle-deep snow. Through the eye holes of a ski mask, she gazed intently at the captive directly ahead of her.

As he had for twenty minutes, their ski-jacked friend sat in the ice, hands tied behind him to an old post capped with a sign warning trespassers of avalanches.

VIII

And bears.

Across his knees lay the seal carcass from the beach.

"They'll be coming soon," she said. "The scents up and down the whole valley by now. Time to fess up. Now, who are you?"

"I already told you."

"Russian secret service?"

"I never denied being FSB, but I'm an analyst. A desk jockey. My superiors ordered me to follow you on arrival in Bartensburg and see what you were doing in our town. Simple."

"If you're not a field officer, why are you disguised in American clothes?"

"You mean the jacket? I'm a fan of Evgeni Malkin, the great Pittsburgh center." He snorted. "Any real Russian roots for the mighty Malkin. Nations are one thing, but hockey quite another."

"Rooting for American teams? What's happened to the KGB?"

"FSB."

"Whatever. Where is Páll Erlingur?"

"Never heard of him."

"You were on the ship that kidnapped him."

"I was on a ship to come to Pyramiden. There are no ferries this time of year."

"Why come to a ghost town?"

He fidgeted against the pole. "Can you move this rotting seal? And untie these binds? My circulation is failing. There will be repercussions if I lose a limb."

Tired of a circular conversation, Santa stood, shook the blood into her own legs, tried to reason the next step.

She glanced pensively over the valley floor, her eyes falling on a high snowdrift half-eclipsed by the mists, as the coming snowstorm clashed with volcanic drift in the sky, lightning branching everywhere, a gray powder slowly descending to Earth.

Behind that snowdrift appeared at first the ears, then snout and finally the whole rising head of a mammoth white predator.

"By thunder, a polar bear!" shouted Santa, taking a dramatic step back.

She scrambled towards the snowmobile. "I'll have to leave you...unless you talk."

"It's not a real bear."

"It is! A man-mauling giant carnivore is bearing down on us!"

The man shrugged. "The bear's mouth is fixed, the eyes dead, and I can see your friend's hands moving beneath the fur."

"It's real."

"Let him come out from behind the snow then."

Santa's shoulders slumped.

"You'd be a terrible spy—or actress," he said.

"So said my guidance counselor."

She motioned for Daniel to stand. He rose behind the drift, bear head cradled in his arms, the lighthouse's rug still draped over one shoulder. His face looked as dejected as Santa felt.

Stupid idea.

Too bad it was hers. She hoped the storm would be camouflage enough...

Their captive began to struggle violently against his bonds with renewed strength, a sudden, almost desperate energy. His eyes fixed on Daniel.

Had the ruse worked after all?

No, his gaze was past Daniel.

Father down the valley, something huge and white lumbered in their direction.

Oh, Jesus...

Santa's first thought was to signal Daniel, but the bear was still very distant, moving at a slow, disinterested gait. Despite their size, these were notoriously wary animals. But, if Daniel looked back, he'd run.

And the animal's hunting instincts would kick in.

She'd get to Daniel first. Santa mounted the snowmobile.

"You're not going to leave me," shouted the FSB man. "I'll talk. I'll talk."

She calculated the intersection of bear and Icelander...

He'd do the same for her, right?

"Okay, come in—slowly. Very, very slowly," she shouted to Daniel. "Our man here's going to talk."

VIII

"Why slowly?" Daníel replied, voice echoing through the canyon.

"Potential avalanches. Just keep a nice, steady motion towards me. A stroll in Laugardalur Park."

She turned her eyes back to the captive. "Where's Páll Erlingur?"

He was lost, mesmerized at the size of the bear.

"Hey! You hear me?"

The man swallowed. "He's in the abandoned Pyramiden *banya*. The only place we could leave him without a guard."

"How do we get in there?"

"I...I had a key. On my keychain."

A keychain that now rested in Santa's hip pocket.

She started the snowmobile.

"Aren't you going to untie me? With the seal stench on my clothes, I've no cha—"

"What is this all about? The ship? Hiding out in a ghost town at the top of the world?"

"The Americans are going to salvage that plane Thursday—tomorrow morning—assuming the volcano winds hold. We're planning to get it first. Tonight. Our ship's full of equipment. Dive suits. Drones."

"Why salvage a plane? Why do the Americans care? Why do you care?"

"They don't tell me. We're just supposed to beat them to it."

A scream echoed through the valley.

Daníel had looked over his shoulder. The bear began to trot quicker, its interest growing.

"Hurry!" said Santa to her prisoner. "How do we get out of Pyramiden today?"

"The ship. The same keychain allows access to bridge, ignition, cabin. Don't abandon me and I'll show you everything."

"You've keys for prisoner and ship, yet you're a desk jockey dragged in last minute? Right." She pulled away to rescue Daníel, who was now sprinting for his life.

"I'll be back soon. Lucky for you, Teodors Bļugers plays for the Penguins too."

***

After Santa picked up Daníel, returned for the FSB man, and all bears were left behind, their captive refused to provide additional information. With time short until he'd be missed—if he wasn't already—they locked him in the lighthouse and headed into Pyramiden. When their fuel finally ran out on the outskirts, they hid the snowmobile under the ruins of a barn collapsed against the mountainside and proceeded on foot as the storm moved in over the ruined town.

It was not difficult to find the abandoned bathhouse, the Russian word "BANYA" painted prominently in weather-scarred letters across the wall of one brick building, tracks in the snow indicating recent visitation.

Santa found the proper key and they made entry into a heated complex of decaying, wooden-walled foyers, rooms and sub-rooms before emerging into the main bathing chamber.

There, at the bottom of a two-meter deep, waterless dipping pool, lay Páll Erlingur, his wrists raised above and handcuffed to the bottom rung of a rusted entry ladder. Maybe fifty-five, he looked a decade older than when Santa last saw him three days ago. His eyes were shadowed, his face puffy and pale, saliva running from his mouth to collect on the tiles below. The pool both prison and toilet, his clothes reeked of sweat and human waste.

Daníel dropped down and in an instant was cradling his friend, the two exchanging words in their native language which Santa did not understand. Even so, she could tell Páll's words were slurred, slow in coming. She threw Daníel the keychain. He found the correct member, removed the handcuffs. Their mysterious conversation resumed.

"How about some English for the spectators," Santa finally said. "What's he saying, Daníel?"

"No signs of the bends, so far," said Daníel. "Thank God."

"I can speak for myself," interrupted Páll with a slow-spoken defiance. "They kept me here the whole the time. The Russians think I work for the Americans. Wanted to know what I saw of Priedite's plane, what I knew

VIII

about the events of '58. There are a few FSB among them, but engineers and divers, mainly. They drugged me often. I'm drugged now. Truth serum, I think."

"Truth serum? Really?" asked Santa incredulously. "Did *you* take the last beer from the *Anja's* 'fridge?"

"Yes."

"And my onion soup?"

"Santa…" said Daníel.

"Yes, to everything," continued Páll. "The FSB has the best-equipped ship I've ever seen. Deepwater suits with every gadget a diver could want. And the exact coordinates of the wreck. They'll get at that plane with ease."

"Not if we get there first. And not if we take their ship," said Santa, motioning for him to throw back the keys. "Let's go, boys. This is about to get deep. Pun intended."

* * *

The blizzard was in full force now, at war with the volcanic smoke in the atmosphere. Webs of lightning stretched horizon to horizon, the accompanying tides of thunder drowning out even thought. Visibility was only meters, and the snowflakes raining down onto Santa's boots and jacket were infused with specs of burning ash.

"Listen up, boys," she said to the Icelanders. "The bad guys won't be out in this. The ship's there for the taking."

"If the ship doesn't catch fire from falling ash," said Páll, his observation unwelcome even to himself.

Damn, truth serum, thought Santa. "It's still snow. Mostly. We'll count on the blizzard to keep things cool for now."

Santa offered Páll her ski mask, brushed away his chivalry until he took it. They went together, jacket hoods over their heads, moving building to building in the downpour. Half-blind, Santa seized upon a rope chain the FSB had set out between the buildings, and hand over hand, they followed it down a slight slope to the water's edge.

Ahead was the rectangular shape of the pier extending out over black waters. They rushed over the icy planks as hotter ash began to land, wisps of smoke rising off the boards. Santa found the key to the cabin, ushered the men inside. As some blaring alarm went off, she pulled the door shut behind, tossed the keychain to Daníel. He headed to the bridge.

In seconds, they were moving. As the ship accelerated towards deeper waters, Santa heard gunfire over the engine's roar.

And her eyes caught flames aft.

She seized an extinguisher and rushed out of the cabin to the stern's decking. An exposed wooden compartment burned at one end, several smoldering pits in its top where ash particles had fallen. Careful to stay under the metal roof's overhang, she smothered these fires under foamy extinguishing agent, as gunshots from the shore echoed through the deadly downpour. On the pier, a man risked the storm, some type of pistol in his hands. Santa knew him blind or near-blind in the snow, the fire the greater danger.

Fear rose up her spine as she exposed herself to the falling ash-snow, climbed a little ladder, extinguished embers lodged in the roof.

A bullet hit the extinguisher canister.

And all exploded.

IX

As the fire extinguisher burst, the force threw Santa Ezeriņa from the ladder, her body crashing hard to the ship deck below. She lay stunned, eyes open, but unseeing, uncomprehending, as snowflakes pregnant with smoldering ash drifted down around her.

The sound of gunfire continued from the shore.

"Páll," she whispered as some of her wits returned. "Help me."

Sitting in the cabin, he stared at her wordlessly.

"Páll…please…"

At last, he moved, grabbed Santa's jacketed arm, brushing away the smoldering ash-flakes burrowing into the fabric, pulled her inside.

On the wet cabin floor, she breathed slowly, regaining her strength as Páll kneeled beside her.

"*Takk fyrir,*" she said, thanking him in Icelandic, one of the few phrases she knew.

No response, his eyes adrift. Santa wondered how much of his mind the FSB interrogators had taken.

They sat in silence, listening to Daníel strain the ship's engines to the limits, the deadly gunfire fading away behind.

* * *

Later, moored kilometers south in the open waters of *Bellsund*, where the snowfall remained pure and untouched by ash, Santa made her point for a next course of action:

"We have the boat and equipment, let's go find the plane."

The divers looked at each other.

"It's a hijacked *ship,* Santa," said Daníel. "We are now pirates."

"What can the Russians do? This vessel has no name, no colors, no markings. It's a spy boat. They can't report it stolen. If they do, we bring up the kidnapping of Páll. Tit for tat."

"They can find *unofficial* ways of dealing with us." Daníel paced around the cabin, throwing his hands up in frustration. "We've made enemies of the Norwegians, Americans, and now Russians."

"It's good for international relations. Nothing unites people like a common enemy."

"I don't want that common enemy to be me!"

Páll spoke in that slow drawl he'd adopted since rescue. "Down an extinguisher, it's risky to go out near the volcano. There's not enough fire retardant on this ship. No foam at all. They must have been storing it in Pyramiden."

"Not a problem, if the winds are with us."

"And if they're not?"

"We need to be forewarned." Santa snapped her fingers. "I know just the guy." She dug her mobile out of her burn-marked jacket, made a call.

"Dr. Muzark? Santa Ezeriņa… Yes, you'd be surprised… Listen, the Hornsund Center has a meteorological department, right? Great. Ask them when the winds should clear east of the volcano. Tomorrow between 6 and 6:40 A.M.? That's a mighty prompt answer…. Oh, I see…Hugo Sommers called about tomorrow's winds, too."

She raised an eyebrow, looked at her divers. "Can you keep us updated on any changes, Dr. Muzark? Say at least twenty minutes before Sommers? We're kinda rivals, he and I… Yes…thanks, Doc, you're a dear."

She clicked off, smiled, looked at the men, a queen surveying her court.

"So, we dive down to the plane as soon as the winds allow. Before the Americans get it and before the Russians get us."

Daníel nodded. "Those ROVs—the drone thingys, Santa—are locked

IX

on the deck. No keys to free them. Took some fire damage, too." He took a deep breath. "We're gonna have to dive ourselves."

Páll seemed almost bemused: "We'll need to get both deep-water suits prepped, show Santa how to operate the lifts to lower them into—"

"Can you dive, Páll?" interrupted Santa. "I don't want to seem ungrateful…but what was the delay pulling me off the deck after the extinguisher blew? Are you sure you're healthy?"

A shadow passed across his face. "I'm sorry," he said softly. "My thinking was somehow slow…I'm all right now."

Daníel stepped in front of Páll. "Touch your nose."

"Why?"

"Do it, please."

Páll relented, extended his arms, and closed his eyes. He bent his arms inwards, index fingers out, trying to reach his nose. He missed, hitting his chin with both hands.

Daníel shook his head. "All those drugs the FSB pumped into you."

The older diver's embarrassment ebbed towards anger. "They'll wear off."

"We can't put you in a dive suit anytime soon, Páll."

"I'll go," said Santa.

The idea of being replaced crushed Páll. "You don't know how to operate an ADS. It's as complicated as a space suit."

"You can show me. We got all night."

"Absolutely not…not some young girl barely with an Open Water."

Daníel said something rude-sounding in Icelandic. Páll responded in an even harsher tone.

"I'm going," she said, raising her voice.

They ignored her, continued arguing in their native tongue.

"Is any of this Icelandic for 'She's the boss'?" Santa forced herself between them. "We've no time to waste. After tomorrow, our target is going to be out of reach, one way or another." She set a calming hand on each man's shoulder, trying to be the bridge between them all. "The logical thing to do is spend tonight waiting for Dr. Muzark's 'all-clear' call and teaching me how to operate a deep-water suit." She appealed to pride. "Páll here will captain the ship when we dive. It's as important a job as any other. We lose our ride in arctic waters, and we're dead."

Silence.

"Well?"

Daníel nodded.

With a sigh, so did Páll.

"Good. We've got a plan." Santa grinned. "Come on, boys, it's not such a surprise. Did anyone think I would *not* be going on this dive? You're smarter than that…"

X

Santa could barely hear Páll's words over the volcanic storm churning the surface, as he used the ship's crane to lower her exosuit-clad body into the sea. She caught a last glimpse of the surface world, then felt a jolt and heard a metallic clank as her ADS was unhooked from the winch, and Santa was free to sink or swim in the depths of the Arctic Ocean.

"All okay, Santa?" asked Páll through the suit's intercom. "We'll be with you the whole time."

"Did I really say I wanted to do this?"

"Davey Jones's last words."

"I warned her about your humor, Páll," came Daníel's voice into her headset. "But she still wanted to rescue you from the Russians. I said, 'let 'em keep you, you old *asni*.'"

Santa spied Daníel in his own ADS floating near a guiding line that descended to the shattered ocean floor, his bulky equipment, like hers, resembling a bulbous red robot with thruster-capped fins spreading out like small bat wings from the back. This state-of-the-art FSB gear was equipped with sonar, searchlights, telecoms with each other and the Mother ship, and a rotatable hand device fitted with a gripper, collection receptacle, camera, and underwater blow torch. All movement was controlled by pedals in the boots. As Daníel sank along the line before her, Santa pressed down her left toe and descended with him.

It was slowing going, sinking down the diving shot line. Santa, unfamiliar with these suits, had difficulty adjusting her thrust to a gentle drift downwards. Daníel extended a clamped cord from his suit to hers, tethering them. They resumed descent. Everywhere fish and small squid flashed in and out of their chest searchlight beams, so effortless and swift in their natural environment, Santa felt impossibly sluggish and awkward.

Despite these troubles, meter by meter, minute by minute, they lowered themselves closer to…well, somewhere. The Russian coordinates for the wreck differed some six hundred meters from those recorded with the *Anja's* equipment four days ago. They'd finally split the difference and dove between the two points. There was little time to waste. American salvage ships had been spotted in the gloom.

In the end, their judgment was off. The line brought them not to the precipice harboring the plane, but into the center of an extensive kelp forest forty meters down, the hearty marine algae thriving even in Arctic waters. Surrounded by green, wide-leafed stipes meters high and swaying in the currents, Daníel untethered their umbilical cord to keep from becoming entangled.

"Well, what now?" Santa asked into her microphone.

No reply.

"Guys? Is this thing on?"

Santa glanced at Daníel. She could see through the lighted glass of his faceplate, that he was speaking, yet no words came through her speakers. Somehow, the channel settings changed during the jostling on the way down. She used the buttons inside her metal glove to toggle preset channels until she heard him or Páll.

Silence.

Silence.

Silence.

"Twelve minutes, Roger that, St. Louis," said an American voice.

Santa gasped, clouding the lower glass of her faceplate. Hugo Sommers whispered like the Devil in Santa's ear.

"Drones three and five in position. ROV two is having some trouble with the Arctic conditions," answered another American voice. "We'll have her up and running shortly, Boss."

X

It took Santa only seconds to understand. The Russian spies had tuned these suits to listen in on American transmissions, to learn all about their salvage operations in a gambit to preempt them.

Those cunning FSB bastards. Santa wanted to monitor this channel as well.

But if she could spy, she could be spied upon. She toggled the settings again, risked one more communique on their own channel. "Páll, Daníel, we gotta go silent. Sommers is here. Switch off."

She glanced at Daníel. His eyes wide with excitement.

Men....

She waited until he mouthed a clear "okay," followed by a half-mystified smile. Santa toggled back to Sommers's channel. He was still speaking calmly, giving GPS directions to the underling.

"Eleven minutes," said Sommers.

No time. They needed to be at that plane.

Santa pressed down with her right foot's toes and glided forward through the kelp forest, stipes, and fronds tugging at their suits, the only light emanating from their suit lamps and the bioluminescence of countless plankton and tiny fish, living willow wisps flitting in and out of view. Often glimpsed but seldom fully seen.

When they cleared the kelp-forested ridge, they descended again, deeper and deeper into the inky depths two hundred meters down. Soon, a steady constellation of electric lights appeared ahead, like a glowing string of Christmas bulbs strung along an elevated subsurface ridge, the greatest concentration circling the ruins of a jet plane at the apex.

Santa's emotions welled at the sight of her great-grandmother's final resting place, yet, she kept focus in this treacherous environment. The American ROVs hovered about the ruined plane like bees about a flowerbed, their extended mechanical arms poking and adjusting instruments set within the wreckage and the cliffside below it.

Santa knew those drones were mounted with cameras and they risked discovery going nearer. When Daníel shut off his suit's lights to avoid detection, she did as well.

They waited in darkness. Save for the lights at the wreckage, there was absolute blackness at this depth. Santa could not see her own steel-clad limbs or even a hint of the glass faceplate just centimeters beyond her nose. She floated in a void of nothingness.

Her sonar pinged.

Something large glided thirty meters below her.

She tipped forward and peered into the abyss. Nothing visible, save a slight, roughly spherical phosphorescence that merged with the darkness as it passed.

It looked rather like an eye.

Her sonar went silent.

Santa was still looking for the source of that sonar ping when new light and motion pulled her attention forward. The American ROVs glided upwards and away in one coordinated movement, their work at the jet apparently finished.

Daníel reignited his lights. So did Santa.

"All equipment clear," said the Sommers voice. "Six minutes, mark one."

As the ROVs disappeared above, Santa and Daníel descended towards the precipice. Flashes from an indicator light on Daníel's suit-camera told Santa he was taking photographs. While he continued to hover five meters above the cliff photographing the plane, she lowered herself down within the wreckage itself, her suit's fin thrusters kicking up dust along the ridgetop.

The state of the plane itself was telling. Six large sections lay strewn across the precipice, each surprisingly well-preserved by the Arctic waters, much of the silt shaken free by the land's volcanic rising. She wondered what pieces had been lost in the ridge's many crevices and into the far deeper trenches on either side of the outcropping, and if what she suspected was here.

As Sommers said: "Five minutes," Santa found, to her horror, exactly what she was looking for.

XI

Hovering within the plane's wreckage, Santa adjusted the lenses on her suit's automatic camera and photographed the most damning evidence yet.

The entry wound.

It *was* a missile that destroyed this plane. The impact hole rested in a large tail section sticking out of the silt at an angle, a perfectly round puncture in the fuselage metal. But whose missile?

Her stomach twisted. Soviet factories in the 1950s produced munitions that released their explosive blast in a single concentrated direction, leaving downed planes with an entry hole and a massive rupture on the opposite fuselage, but otherwise intact. Especially with a comparatively soft water landing.

This jet was in pieces. A higher production value in the warhead. A better dispersal of force. One the USSR had a hard time matching. It could not be the Russians.

She took the hole's dimensions.

Thirty-four centimeters. Or thirteen-and-half inches.

The diameter of a Terrier B T-3 missile, brand new to American submarines in '58 and freshly modified to take out supersonic targets. A NATO missile fired either by error or poor-enough judgment that military and political decision-makers covered it up for decades, unwilling to spark a potential war with the Soviet Union.

Until the volcano awakened the past.

She wished to her soul's core the Soviets were the ones to destroy this plane. After what they'd done to her family, her country, she always sided with the West against Moscow.

But truth was truth. This would have to come out.

A journalist's duty. To ring the bell for all the world to hear.

More immediate thoughts came to her. Why hadn't Sommers's drones taken or destroyed this key piece of evidence? The ROVs had clearly been to this spot. Stray equipment fumbled away by their clumsy claws littered the area, the shiny newness of recently lost items contrasting with the sea-worn wreckage. Among them, the long black-blue cylinders of blasting caps.

Blasting caps...

"Four minutes," said Sommers in her ear, the countdown pregnant with new meaning. Santa rotated her glove piece to the gripper, gingerly picked up the nearest cap. It was an empty shell devoid of trigger wiring or primary explosive, likely discarded for some flaw, but its presence implied others less benign.

Engraved on the cap's side was a manufacturer number. Everything she needed to find about those behind Sommers. She'd broken stories with less.

Santa dropped the cap into her suit's storage receptacle, followed a series of wires over the edge of the ridgetop. Beneath, the cliff face receded quickly into a cavernous inlet. Inside, shoved into every crevice within lamp range, were pressure-resistant canisters, each half-the-size of man. With abundant blast caps and wiring there was little doubt what the canisters contained.

This was no salvage operation. Sommers was here to rebury the mistakes of the 50s. To blow this ridge to Hell and send its secrets back into the abyss. To prevent an American blackeye in the current propaganda war with Moscow. To keep NATO from admitting weapons were in Svalbard archipelago in 1958. To preempt anyone asking if weapons remained today.

Her pulse rising in her ears, she followed the explosives network until its end, then rose again to an unexplored region of ridge. Here Santa

XI

spied a conical structure just within sight, a piece of the jet's hull resting twenty meters from the rest of wreckage.

The cockpit.

"Three minutes," said Sommers.

She and Daniel should be off this ridgetop.

But her demons got the best of her. She was too near the *grave* to turn back now. As Santa's thrusters pushed her forward, the lights of Daniel's lamp and camera rose on the other side of the cockpit, like some morning constellation over the horizon. His presence reassured her. *Plenty of time.*

She knew it a lie.

Santa settled herself just outside the cockpit's window. The canopy glass long cleared away by water pressure, she forced her encumbered body inside. Santa knew that after sixty years, there'd no sign of her great-grandmother's remains, thank God. Still, she had a burning desire to see the chair Elita Priedite sat in when she flew so high, so fast during the last moments of life.

The interior of the cockpit was covered in accumulated silt from decades on the ocean's floor. Half-buried in the buildup, the pilot's chair sat intact. At its base, the fractured dome of a helmet protruded from the sludge.

Santa hesitated, heart racing. Might there be remains after all? She preferred not to see a skull. Yet, Santa couldn't resist examining the helmet. As her gripper sunk inside the silt to clutch the helmet's edge, the metallic tongs entangled with something else buried alongside.

A crucifix.

Astonishment shook Santa's soul. As devout as her great-grandmother was said to be, uncovering a Lutheran cross inside a Soviet wreck was as unexpected as discovering one on the moon.

"Two minutes."

She barely heard it.

Santa slipped the crucifix into the storage compartment. She'd wear it soon enough.

Something pinged on her sonar. Santa's gaze turned upwards.

Through the ruptured canopy, she saw an immense black shape with eyes of green fire glide over the plane's remaining wing. A great fish, easily seven meters long, turned slowly, silently, passing away from the cockpit until a last motion of the tail took it away over the apex of the clifftop.

Directly towards Daníel.

Oh God....

Not necessarily an attack, she prayed, *curiosity a hallmark of predators.*

Santa forced herself out of the cockpit.

Daníel saw the fish approaching, the bulk of his gear making his movements slow and valueless in defense. The shark took a nipping test bite at his shoulder, found the suit not to its liking, and veered off. As it turned, the massive tail struck Daníel full force, crushing him hard against a rise of rock behind. He toppled forward, grasping at a bent thruster wing and disappeared down into a nearby ravine, much of the sludge wall he'd struck falling with him.

In seconds, Santa was above the ravine.

No sign of Daníel, the gorge's depth too great for her lamp to illuminate. Sonar mapping said it dropped another two hundred meters.

Was he already dead?

Santa descended into the blackness. The atmosphere inside the ravine absorbed light itself, her chest beam revealing a gray-brown cliffside and little more. Down and down, she went, eyes flipping from lamplight to the depth readings.

"One minute," declared Sommers's voice.

At four hundred twenty meters below the Arctic Ocean's surface, she spied the narrow, V-shaped bottom below her boots. Buried beneath the avalanche was an unmoving Daníel.

Santa struggled in these black confines, removing stones and sludge as fast she could. His suit remained intact, the atmosphere stable, and as she moved aside a slab of stone, Santa could see through his facemask—Daníel unconscious, but breathing. She grabbed an arm in grippers, set her suit thruster's in full reverse, her body rising slightly off the ravine floor. But Daníel remained unmoving.

XI

She cursed, descended, went back to moving stones.

"Thirty seconds."

The ravine offered no shelter from a blast. The shock waves would tear open their suits, eviscerate them. And even if the forces didn't quite reach, the displaced ridge could bury them forever.

She clasped the gripper onto his torso clasps, full thrusters upwards, her body rose slightly off the ravine floor. But Daníel didn't budge.

"Ten seconds."

A meter-long squid sped through her lamplight.

Brown-tinted blackness engulfed light an instant later, a wall of mass rushing past Santa, like standing near a subway train barreling by the platform. She pressed herself to the canyon side as a toothy open maw, shining electric eye, and an endless fishy body charged through in pursuit of the squid.

The prey was lucky. The ravine narrowed ahead before opening into the wider sea. The squid escaped through the straight, but the shark's inertia wedged it into the narrowing, stopped it cold. Too constricted to pass, the fish's great tail slammed the canyon walls birthing small avalanches and jostling currents until it tired and grew still. Stuck in the ravine not three meters from Santa.

"5 seconds….4…3…."

Santa threw her body over Daníel's to shield him, thoughts on the crucifix so close.

"2…1…Detonation."

XII

Blackness.
　　Cold.
　　　Pain.
Pressure. Unyielding pressure and immobility.

Santa was aware of only these. No sight, no sound. Outside the cracked glass of her facemask was the mud and earth of the eternal avalanche, a sticky sludge enveloping her armored body, an inelastic morass through which she could only move infinitesimally with greatest of will.

Measured by breaths, her confinement went on forever. A stint in purgatory.

And yet, this mire was thinning, her suit's few functioning sensors showed an undulating current drifting in from her left, slowly pushing the shackling slime away. Millimeters of freedom edged to centimeters, then tens of centimeters, and finally allowed Santa motion enough to press down her toe, to force the ADS thrusters into action. The suit lurched, the engines growling, but little more. The thrusters frozen or crushed by the explosion's landside, little worked inside or out of her suit. If the flickering digits on her monitor display could be trusted, the heat was dwindling, the carbon dioxide levels rising. Eight minutes had passed. She never lost consciousness, but time was gone. Eight minutes lost to shock and shockwaves before her wits returned.

Somehow, despite water pressure, explosion and avalanche, her suit's integrity held. The designers should get some sort of award. A medal, if she lived to congratulate them.

XII

Santa continued to press with all her limbs' strength and to floor the toe pedals attempting to take the suit in any navigable direction. She listened to her suit's tortured metal skin groan under the strain. The limb joints or faceplate would be first to go. No pain, her life in milliseconds if they did. Yet, she found the loathsome hold loosening at last, that strange current continuing to clear a gap, a flow pocket forming around her. She groped through her softening atmosphere, explored the canyon's stony recesses and sucking pockets with her clumsy mechanical gripper of a hand. Her chest lantern shattered, she blindly slung through the mud, until the gripper clanked against something hard and bulbous nearby.

Daníel's form buried beside hers.

She cleared the mud between them, managed to get her interior lights on, used the limited glow emanating out through her faceplate to examine Daníel. His suit unruptured, she could just see his face. Eyes closed, blood smeared across his forehead, yet he breathed. Breathed too rapidly, perhaps, but alive, thank God. Half the mountain had slid down into this ravine, but they lived.

Santa shoved a slab of stone off Daníel's torso, a glow emerging. His chest lamp functioned, the uncovered beam illuminating their environment. They were wedged into a horizontal seam in the mud-packed ravine, the recess little more than a meter high at their position but rising another meter or two where the source of that miraculous current became shockingly visible.

The shark, alive and still stuck in the narrows, gently moved its tail side-to-side, exhausted from straining to free itself, trying to push forward, force water over its gills. The tail's undulations clearing the water behind it, the motion creating the pocket they were marooned in.

She marveled. Trapped under a landslide on the Arctic Ocean's floor with a Greenland shark.

Be a journalist, Mother said. *Such interesting work. It'll take you places, Santa.*

Despair overcame Santa. They could never climb up through the morass above and their thrusters would clog or freeze even if functional.

Lady Death. She'd earned that nickname at last.

She toggled through the intercom channels, trying to communicate a valedictory to Páll or even Sommers. An epitaph worthy of a journalist. But Santa found only silence.

Alone.

She lay back and waited to die.

Yet, her eyes never left that shark, its undulating tale casting shadows in Daníel's beam. She felt empathy with it. Sympathy. Santa thought to kill the animal, to put the doomed fish out of its misery.

Then another idea came.

That squid had escaped before the avalanche. Her last functional sonar reading had shown the open sea was close by at the end of this ravine, just beyond the narrowing that constrained the fish. A path to freedom. Not upwards, but horizontally. All she had to do was go through meters of shark and countless kiloliters of displaced mud.

She watched the fish's tail move side-to-side. The shark itself breathed, its gills unclogged by mud. The water must be clear at the animal's head. Maybe even sooner.

Only seven meters away.

Santa turned to her fellow diver. She found the coupling to Daníel's suit, used the fumbling gripper to hook her own tow line to his fastener, linking their bodies as they had in descent. She extended the line to maximum length, and without thruster aid, used all her strength to crawl towards the great fish.

I must be insane.

The shark seemed to sense her presence. The tail grew still. From the triangular anal fins, she knew it female. Faceup, Santa slid her armored body beneath the fish's tonnage, looped the tow line around the tail. Once, twice, thrice.

She pulled the line tight, until it pressed into the fish's flesh, moored herself to the shark.

Absolutely insane.

Santa checked that the tethering to Daníel was unobstructed. She

XII

rotated the hand piece from gripper to blow torch. Lit it.

Insane.

Make haste, o Lord, to help me.

She set the torch close to the animal's skin. The powerful tail came to life, thrashing side-to-side, hammering against the canyon walls. Mud splattering across the glass of Santa's faceplate, clipping her vision. The suit's alarms sounding at impact.

Yet, the fish inched forward in the ravine.

Santa moved the torch nearer,

Come on girl.

She pricked a fin. *Nothing too bad. PETA will never know.*

The tail thrashed, the shark lurched forward, scraping through rock, out—

Suddenly, clear water.

Santa glanced backwards. The line pulled Daníel free of the morass, bouncing like a rebellious yoyo against the straight's sides, chest lamp flickering.

Then he, too, was out. The crumbled ridge-side dropping away behind, lost within the gloom.

Santa took a slow breath, released the line from the shark, watched the great fish swim away, its motion agitated, but otherwise unharmed.

Those spectral green eyes faded into the darkness.

Santa turned off the blow torch, retracted the line, and pulled Daníel to her. Her thrusters nonfunctioning, it was all she could to keep them buoyant and floating at depth.

His engines were their only chance.

She toggled through the channels again, hoped to hear Páll's voice calling for them, offering information.

Nothing.

"Daníel!" she shouted into their shared channel. "Daníel, please! Wake up!"

She felt them drifting downwards.

Santa shook him ferociously.

"Daníel!"

His eyes opened.

"Up!" she shouted.

He looked at her groggily.

"Your toe pedals. Floor it up! Rise!"

Bubbles emerged at his thrusters.

They began to climb slowly as she held onto him. He said nothing, eyes still half-closed, acting more on instinct than reason. Judging by the coordinates on Santa's GPS their ship's original location was near.

She tried Páll again. Still no response.

Relief came with the sight of the ship's floodlights above. Páll had set a beacon for them.

But why was the beacon flickering?

They surfaced. The answer became obvious.

The volcanic winds had shifted again.

Their ship in flames.

XIII.

As the surface currents pushed them slowly towards the burning pyre that had once been their ship, Santa's ears detected the sound of an outboard motor approaching. A ripple appeared in the gloom, then the low shape of an inflatable dinghy emerged, a flame-resistant tarp draped over the raft's surface. At short intervals, a gloved hand would emerge near the motor, push aside the covering, and the raft's captain clad in a silver fire-proof suit, would peek out and correct course.

The motor shut off, the tarp undulating as the dinghy's captain crawled to the bow. A hooded face popped up, peering over the raft edge.

Páll.

"About time, I returned the favor of a rescue, isn't it?"

They ditched the ADS into the ocean, and Páll pulled them into the dinghy under the tarp. In the cramped quarters beneath were two rolled fire suits. As Páll gunned the engine and steered the raft away from the burning ship, Santa and a woozy Daníel exchanged their diving suits for flame-resistant ones. Santa slipped the ADS camera memory cards and all collected items into her thigh pocket.

"The ship went up ten minutes ago," said Páll, crouching near the motor. "Dr. Muzark called with warning the winds would turn and I had the raft ready. Gas masks, suits, emergency beacon, fresh water, life jackets. We still won't last out here. One of those volcanic embers finds the raft skin, and we're sunk. Fortunately, I found a shield."

"A shield?" asked Santa, pulling on her own fire mask, then helping Daníel with his.

"Hold on." Páll pushed up the tarp to take another peek. "Almost there."

A minute later, Santa felt the edge of the dinghy strike something solid, as a cold flooring rose under the bow. Páll slid back the tarp, cautiously at first, then with more resolve. They were half-aground on the lower slope of an endless iceberg, fifty meters high, its ice-wall enormity stretching away unbroken into the mists. Resting downwind, the volcano's smoke passed high in the sky over them, leaving the immediate area sheltered and breathable.

"Muzark warned me about this drifting ice sheet even before the change of winds," said Páll. "I spent half your dive here watching the sensors, waiting for you to surface."

They pulled the raft to higher position, huddled together under that tarp for hours. Trying not to freeze, praying not to burn, listening to a symphony of hisses as those embers struck the far side of the 'berg, weathering away their protection.

Exhausted, Santa fell asleep calculating the shifting volumes in a war of fire and ice.

* * *

She awoke to shouts in English.

American calls nearby.

The first to stir, she gingerly pushed back the tarp, found late afternoon light, clear and still air without the scent of smoke. The winds had shifted again.

Santa sat up, pulled off her mask, as the men, too, awakened.

An American cruiser lingered at a safe distance from the iceberg. A familiar man on the bow with a bullhorn.

"Good afternoon," said Hugo Sommers. "Need a lift?"

* * *

Soon their dinghy was moored against the ship, a ladder lowered so they

XIII.

may board.

As Páll climbed first, Sommers leaned on the sea rail, looking down into the raft. Even through his glasses Santa read his smugness, his triumph.

"Mother Nature is not as kind as you thought, Ms. Ezeriņa," he said. "A tremor early this morning sent Priedite's plane back to the depths. Sensors show the wreckage is now at six thousand meters and under several thousand tons of rubble."

He removed those glasses, revealing piercing blue eyes. "The truth will never resurface. Your Quixotesque quest is at an end. I'll buy you a consoling beer in Longyearbyen."

She grabbed the ladder's first rung. "No jail? This is a restricted zone."

"I won't tell the Norwegians if you won't."

Santa smiled. Said nothing. Felt the bulk of the photo memory card and blasting cap in her suit's pocket. For the future. The very near future.

And the crucifix. She paused on the ladder to don it. Forever.

As Daníel reached the ladder's top ahead of her, he cast his gaze across that iceberg scarred and shrunken in only a few hours exposure to the billows, and then beyond to the blood-red sky over the Svalbard archipelago's newest island.

"The volcano burns everything," he muttered.

Just below, Santa heard.

"Sometimes a phoenix rises from the flames, Daníel," she whispered and climbed aboard.

XXIII

MYRNA LOY VERSUS THE THIRD REICH

Originally published in Ellery Queen's Mystery Magazine

Myrna Loy Versus The Third Reich

1938, Berlin

Irma Sauer could not sleep. Speaker-amplified Russian voices penetrated her apartment's walls, the Slavic words slipping under the door and through the vents to disturb her modest dreams. Four o'clock in the morning, and Irma had been tossing and turning all night, listening to those gathered in the next room watch an advance copy of Sergei Eisenstein's historical epic *Alexander Nevsky* on the Cinema Club's projector. Irma had given up and gone to bed after the second showing. Asked her husband Otto, the organizer and projectionist, to turn down the volume for safety's sake. Yes, Eisenstein was a genius. The world acknowledged that brilliance after *Battleship Potemkin*. But Eisenstein was also a communist. And it was risky to watch the films of communists too loudly in Berlin.

Or anywhere in Germany.

Or at all.

Irma's husband remained defiant. To Otto, film was film. Eisenstein was Eisenstein. Otto and his friends would analyze this print for days. Rewind and replay each scene until the film strip snapped. Then they'd mend it and start again. So Irma buried her head in the pillow and wished she were home in Bavaria. Or on a Mediterranean island. Or somewhere, anywhere that was peaceful and still...

Most in the club can't even understand Russian. Why have it so loud, Otto?

Are you so foolish in your enthusiasm? Tomorrow, I'm buying ear—

A knocking! A full-bodied thumping without the tinny compression of the projector's speakers. Irma sat up in bed. The knocking repeated louder, more violently, followed by the shouts of angry men outside on the landing. These cold calls of doom were answered by a click of the projector's Off switch, a sudden silencing of the film speakers, and a fearful utterance from her husband.

"*Mein Gott. They heard!*"

The knocking grew to a hammering even as the voices of the Cinema Club members lowered, panic in every hushed whisper. Someone dropped a glass, its shattering joining the din.

The bedroom door slid open. Otto's forlorn face poked inside. Irma had never seen such naked terror in her man.

"Irma. Get rid of anything objectionable," he whispered. "They're coming in."

"Who?"

"The police. Dump everything over the railing. Hurry!" He slid the door shut.

Irma did not move. Did not follow her husband's orders, sitting on the bed in shock. She heard bodies shuffling about in the next room, then the aggressive commands of raiding policemen flowing into their apartment. Otto's words turned pleading.

"It is only a private showing for film enthusiasts. Foreign films, yes…it won an award. No…. The Stalin Prize in Moscow. I—"

A metallic crash.

A masculine shriek.

These horrific sounds roused Irma to action. Her pulse drumming in her ears, she pulled every film cannister from the shelves, ran to the bedroom's balcony, cast them over the rail, heard the metallic clangs as they struck the street far below.

The shouting increased in the next room. Gurgles, clicks, crashes. Pleas, threats, and mangled unintelligible sounds.

Irma's mind raced. Her body cold in the autumn winds, gasping from panic and exertion, she pulled the balcony door shut from the outside, crept along the apartment's exterior to peak into the window of the main room.

Chaos.

Chaos and evil.

Uniformed policemen beat the room's occupants with clubs, blood and brain matter spilling out onto her Persian rug. One baton struck Otto with such force that his eyes rolled up, and he fell into a seizure on the floor. Despite his convulsions, the assault continued unabated.

"Otto!" Irma gasped. "Please...!"

Her exclamation caught the attention of a little officer with an "SS" collar. In an instant, he was into her bedroom, his shoulder slamming against the locked balcony door.

"Open this door, woman!" he demanded. The panel bowed violently as he rammed it a second time. "It'll be worse for you if you disobey. I won't ask again!"

Irma hesitated. There was no place to go. Nowhere to run. She reigned in her emotions, willed herself calm to these horrors. If she capitulated quickly, she might save Otto. *Yes... save her husband...* Irma reached for the latch, to let the aggressor, the monster, out...

As she touched the knob, the door burst open, the policeman's body barreling through, slamming against hers.

Irma stumbled backwards over the balcony rail.

A fatal fall. Three stories to the pavement.

Irma Sauer died seconds after her husband. Alone, on the Berlin street, her head against a discarded reel of *City Lights*.

* * *

Three weeks later...

Nick and Nora Charles burned in the pyre.

As did Nora alone. And Ann Barton. And Gertie Waxted. So too burned exotics like Ursula Georgi, Fah Lo See, and Morgan le Fay. Every role played by Myrna Loy that Willy Dittmar knew, every persona felt the fire's touch tonight. Her image on posters, in magazines, and most especially celluloid film consumed.

All forbidden. All fed to the flames.

Standing in the shadows off the Opernplatz, Willy watched the multitudes toss the works of the American actress into the square's bonfire. Bodies filed in carrying newspapers, show-business periodicals, canisters of film, and autographed photographs from when Loy and the "King of Hollywood" Clark Gable had visited Germany earlier this year to promote their film *Test Pilot*. The rally's organizers, uniformed fascists standing on the steps of the State Opera House, had only one goal: eliminate any shred of Loy's existence in Germany.

Wipe her out of the collective memory.

To Willy, the scene was an abomination. He detested the Nazis. Loved cinema and cinema's stars. Surely, his countrymen couldn't hate the popular Loy, always a box-office hit here? This must be a show orchestrated by Propaganda Minister Goebbels out to make a nefarious point. To fan the flames of hatred against any high-profile foreigner who criticized the Reich. Most of the rally participants, Willy prayed, acted out of fear rather than outrage. Fear of punishment by the government. Fear of ostracism in a changing society. Fear of the diabolical mentality that now gripped much of the country.

These emotions were not new to Willy. He was weaned on such fears, had been an outcast all of his nineteen years. God had punished him with a runtish body and legs that barely walked in a nation that worshiped athletic, idealized supermen. A lifetime devotion to motion pictures was his only avenue of escape. As a film student, Willy could recreate the world as he liked in his work: kinder, more beautiful, and more tolerant.

Or illuminate its evils, if he could evade the Nazi censors.

And now he was watching films burn. Destroyed because a foreign actress had publicly and correctly condemned Germany for its treatment of Jews and its occupation of the Sudetenland. When her studio tried to muzzle Loy, she only became more vocal. Yesterday, she cabled a letter of support to Jan Masaryk, the beleaguered foreign minister of Czechoslovakia. German officials knew the contents before Masaryk did, and it was the final straw. Loy earned a spot on Minister Goebbels's Enemies List above even Nazi-loathed filmmakers like Charlie Chaplin or Soviet director Sergei Eisenstein. Rumors persisted the Gestapo had put a price on Loy's head.

Bonfires burned throughout Germany.

Madness.

A young man passed on his way to the fires, a film canister in each hand, a third tucked under one arm. Willy knew him from the Cinema Club, one of the few members who hadn't vanished in the last month or so....

"Elias!" Willy shouted. "What are you doing? What have you got there?"

"A motion picture bound for the pyre. The second *Thin Man* film."

"An original-language print?"

"Yes. Pristine condition. I got it off a Hamburg sailor just back from Liverpool. Didn't have a chance to watch it before the ban came down. Real shame."

"I'll give you five Reichsmark for all three reels."

"Willy, the rally is our last chance to dispose of these. If you're found to possess a Myrna Loy film past midnight tonight, you'll—"

"You can hand it to the fires for nothing. Or hand it to me for five Reichsmark. What's it gonna be, Elias?"

Always a businessman, Elias made the exchange. "I'm going to regret not seeing that picture."

"Don't worry. I'll organize a showing." He nodded towards the fascists on the stairs. "But keep it under your hat. I don't want to end up like Otto Sauer."

"Not sure I've the nerve to attend, Willy."

"Suit yourself, Elias. *Auf Wiedersehen.*" Willy slipped the canisters into his shoulder pack, tightened the straps on his leg braces, and struggled through the chaotic Berlin crowd for home.

Elias smiled as they parted.

* * *

Willy fought his way up the stairs to his third-floor apartment, the coolness in the late autumn air making his brace joints stick, hindering his climb. But enthusiasm carried the day and gave him tunnel vision. He passed their den mother, old Frau Buchholz, on the landing with barely a salutation and hurried into his flat.

"I saved one!" he shouted, throwing his jacket to the floor and propping himself on the door-side stool to remove the braces. "Plucked it from the flames myself."

"Which film?" asked his roommate, Arnold, pulling his nose from an American book on moving-picture sound design. "I hope it's the *Thin Man.*"

"The sequel. *After the Thin Man.*"

"Better still. I've never seen it."

The braces off, Willy withdrew the reels from his pack. The first canister had a slightly torn poster label on the front adorned with the faces of Loy, her costar William Powell, the terrier Asta, and a newcomer Willy had never heard of named James Stewart.

"I bet this Stewart fellow is the killer," said Arnold. "They always put the murderer on the cover in whodunits. He's got a fiendish look to him."

"Probably typecast as the villain."

"Let's find out tonight. I oiled the projector this morning."

"We've got film class tonight," replied Willy with an unfortunate truth. Classes were usually very late at UFA-Lehrschau Studios out in Babelsberg. As UFA was a functioning studio by day, Hans Traub's new film institute had to slip its lessons into the gaps in production, leaving meetings and classes at the oddest hours. Not that either student minded.

"What if we make a grand showing of it later this week? Find a larger place and invite the other film students. And the Sherlock Holmes Reading Group. And…" Willy's eyes flared. "And Gertraud. Sweet, curvaceous Gertraud."

"Oh yes," said Arnold, smiling. "Especially Gertraud. She'll sit right next to me."

"We'll see about that."

"What about Lambert?"

"His papa is in the Party, Arnold."

"And? Lambert is the black sheep of that family. They exclude him, and he excludes back. Would I bring a Nazi? Lambert loves mysteries… and Miss Myrna Loy…more than his wretched family, Willy. I think he'll keep his kinfolk in the dark."

"He's your friend, Arnold.…"

"Good. We invite Lambert. Gertraud. Anyone and everyone. Just as long as they can keep a secret. I don't want to share the fate of the Cinema Club members.…"

"We do it *because* of the Cinema Club, Arnold. Let the fascists try and stop us. As Otto Sauer said, 'Art trumps politics.' Always."

* * *

"Tell me everything," said *Kriminal-inspektor* Kurt Glass to his informant on the telephone. "Wilhelm Dittmar. Arnold Enns… Yes, I have their files… When is the exhibition?… I see. Good work. Let me know when you know."

Kurt hung up the phone, continued to take notes at his Breite Straße police station bureau desk. Without a glance upwards, he could feel the watchful eyes of the young man at the desk next to his. It would not be long until ambitious *Kriminalsekretär* Hartwin Vieth had to know what was up. He was so desperate to impress…

Let the little Nazi wait.

"You've found something, Inspector Glass?" asked Vieth seconds later.

"Your hidden man among the film students caught us a fly?"

"I have a mole to prevent pornography. This is nothing of interest to a real lawman."

"It interests me."

"You prove my point, Vieth."

A pause. He could feel the tension grow. Kurt was fifty-eight and waiting for retirement. Vieth was half his age, two grades lower, and thus in theory his subordinate, though the twin thunderbolt 'S's on his colleague's collar closed the gap considerably. It was getting so you couldn't tell the local *Kriminalpolizei,* or Kripo, from the national Gestapo. The *Gleichschaltung*, or Nazifying of all facets of life, had continued unabated for five years now. Every time a Kripo man retired, resigned, or died, his replacement came with a double-S collar, a sneer, and a healthy disrespect for "old-fashioned" things like human rights and due process. Kurt had so few old friends left....

Devils. He'd retire today if weren't for the wait for a full pension, the needs of an invalid wife, and a daughter he could never refuse any trifle.

"Two students are trying to organize an exhibition of a harmless mystery comedy, Vieth. Nothing to concern us. No communist propaganda this time. No one for you to push off balconies."

"Is the film banned, Inspector?"

"It's a Loy picture. Minister Goebbels's latest adversary. Not high priority to me."

"But it is a priority to Director Foth. He is running stings all over Berlin. I know he wants a successful Loy sting to curb the American influence. Will you tell him?"

"Not likely. Much bigger fish to fry."

Vieth sprang up, plucked the notepad from the desk before Kurt's aging body could react. "Then I will."

"Secretary Vieth! I order you to—"

The younger man sped into Director Foth's office, out of Kurt's sight. *This will be trouble, Kurt thought.*

***

"She fell three stories," said Willy, peering up at the apartment balcony across the street. "Pushed, the neighbors say."

"At least we know what happened to Irma Sauer," replied Arnold. "Everyone else has vanished."

"Night and fog. They want to make examples."

"If they wanted examples, they'd put them on trial. Hang the culprits in the square down the road."

"Give them time."

Willy and Arnold stood on a residential corner in the Dorotheenstadt neighborhood, waiting for their film school classmate Lambert Meyer. The trees were filled with golden autumn leaves, and early frost decorated the countless windows. It seemed impossible that murder had occurred so near, the Sauer family tragedy hidden under nature's veil.

But there were many murders hidden these days in Berlin.

"I was invited to attend that Cinema Club showing but wouldn't skip class," said Arnold distantly, his cigarette smoke rising in the cool air. "Otto knew my admiration for Eisenstein."

"I wouldn't say that loudly," replied Willy.

"It doesn't mean I'm a communist, just a film student…an artist…"

"The Kripo equate them all."

"There are still good men among them."

"The good men are in camps. Or dead."

"You sound so bitter, Willy."

He did not reply. A new silence fell over them. Arnold smoked his cigarette while Willy wondered if it would be painful to fall off a balcony or if Irma Sauer's death was instantaneous. There must be a second or two of fear during the fall. Or perhaps it was a release…

"Where is Lambert?" moaned Arnold at last. "He's twenty minutes late."

Willy did not hear his friend's complaint. His eyes were on a group of brownshirts marching along the avenue under the golden tree canopy. A few of these fascists spied Arnold's cigarette, three of them peeling away from the others to approach.

"I see you flaunt your filthy habits," said a tall, tough-looking brownshirt, waving away the cigarette smoke with a thick hand. "Tobacco is disgusting. Why aren't you in the army?"

"My mother is Polish," replied Arnold, continuing to puff on his cigarette, though Willy detected the subtlest tremor in his friend's hand. "I'm forbidden to serve."

The brownshirt grimaced, turned his hostile blue eyes on Willy. "And you? Why are you idle? Why not lend a hand to the nation?"

Without a word, Willy unbuttoned his long overcoat, revealing his braces.

The brownshirted thugs smiled.

Willy expected a beating.

He got one.

"Look, a cripple!" shouted the delighted brownshirt leader as if he'd made some great discovery, the Nazi shoving Willy to the ground. Willy's pack sprang open on impact, his lunch, books, and film canisters spilled out onto the street. He reached out to grab them.

Two swift kicks changed his mind.

As other brownshirts seized Arnold, the first fascist plucked up a reel, unwound the film to have a look in the autumn sunlight.

"What sort of film is this, cripple?" He extended the film tape in the light. "A sex film, maybe? Do you dream of mating? Passing on your unhealthy seed to the nation?"

"It's a mystery film…" said Willy on the ground. Another kick silenced him.

The brownshirt laughed, then crumpled the filmstrip. "Well, nobody will watch it now, whatever it was, you little degenerate,"

"Stop!" shouted a young man in a plaid cap and waistcoat hurrying up the avenue. "Leave him alone!"

The brownshirts laughed, balled their fists. "What is this little cripple to you? A lover? Are you sissies?"

"I am Lambert Meyer," said the new arrival. "My father is Fritz Meyer.

Do you know who that is? Publisher of *Völkischer Beobachter*."

The laughter died away.

Lambert produced his Aryan identity card from inside his vest pocket "Can you read this, thug? What are your names? Well? I'll have them in Father's newspaper tomorrow. Give them to me. All of you! If you refuse, I'll have you out of the party at once."

"You don't know…"

"I will." Lambert stepped closer. "I have only to ask your leader!" He pointed up the road to where the other brownshirts stood watching. "Your names!"

They fled.

When the assailants were out of sight, Lambert returned his Aryan card to his pocket, offered Willy a hand on the ground.

He refused.

"I can get up on my own." Willy struggled to his feet. "I'm used to it. Five years this has been going on."

"You took a good kick to the ribs," said Arnold.

"Yes," Willy grimaced. "And you wonder why I'm bitter."

"Brutes," said Lambert. "Fascists only fear bigger fascists. Like my father."

"Your words, not mine," said Willy, grimly looking over the ground at his spilled things. "They really crumpled our film."

"Creased it badly," said Arnold, picking up the twisted film strip.

"Maybe I can help…" said Lambert softly. "I know people at—"

"If you *really* want to help, Lambert," said Willy tersely, "have your papa find the Cinema Club's members. And free them."

"I'm afraid that's impossible," said Lambert grimly. "Father made a toast to their fate at dinner last night. Minister Goebbels gave him a standing ovation.…"

* * *

In the evening, a weary Kurt Glass opened the door to his Fischerinsel apartment. Inside, the lights were off, the hearth fire dead. The only sound was his wife's rasping from the bedroom.

"Hello, *meine süsse*. I am home!"

The distant breathing continued. Without waiting for a response, Kurt set the groceries down and went into their bedroom. Orlantha lay buried under the blankets, only her pale, wrinkled face visible, eyes closed. Did she sleep? Or would this be another of the bad days?

Kurt kissed her on the cheek. "Is our *Mäuschen* here?"

"Out," she said without opening her eyes.

A response. The first this week. Good.

"Don't worry, *süsse*. *Mäuschen* is the busy kind."

Kurt pulled up a stool beside Orlantha's bed, sat holding her hand. Before making dinner, before the sponge bath and changing bedpans, he would languish at her side and tell of his day, of the world outside that Orlantha had not visited in six years. On responsive days, if their talks didn't quite rekindle love—the ailment had gone on too long for that—it at least reminded of affection, of matrimonial commitment.

He caressed her hands, began his update: "Today I was assigned a very serious case, Orlantha. To lead a raid on a banned motion-picture exhibition and arrest the attendees. Like my colleagues did last month against the communist propaganda film, remember, I told you? They want more control this time. A defter hand. The prisoners alive. A show trial for treason." He watched her features for a reaction.

None.

"They're mere boys, Orlantha, too sickly for the army. They know not what they do. Unfortunately, Foth asks this of me. I wish he didn't. But I have you and *Mäuschen*... A man must persevere."

The words felt confessional. He sought strength. Kurt's eyes found the portrait of his company from the last year of the Great War. He was so young and hardy then. Surrounded by men of his generation.

Eight killed by the French.

Eleven by disease.

And more recent tragedies.

Two executed by the new government.

Three dissenters in camps somewhere in the countryside.

And six Jewish veterans vanished, including the officer who awarded Kurt the Iron Cross. A medal he sold for food during runaway inflation and the crisis that brought a demagogue to power.

The photograph failed him.

"The arrests are inevitable, Orlantha. We're only waiting for when and where. It is a film from Hollywood. A sinful place—Perhaps they deserve some sort of punishment... I don't know..."

She squeezed his hand.

"Proud of you," she whispered. "*Mäuschen* too."

Understood without understanding.

"There is no reason for pride, *meine süsse*. Not yet. The test is before us."

* * *

To Willy's and Arnold's horror, the entire third reel of *After the Thin Man* was now damaged and without sound. Emergency measures were taken. They wrote and recorded English dialogue for the final reel themselves. Invited the best actors from their film-school classmates to speak the new words: "Husband, I think that vile gangster James Stewart hath murdered three suffering innocents. Release our terrible hound upon him!"

Gertraud stopped, lowered the sheet from which she read. "Is that really something Nora Charles would say?"

Arnold shut off the tape recorder. "Stay to the script, please. I have to sync all this by hand!"

Willy tried diplomacy. "You're just not comfortable with theatrical English, Gertraud. We've given Nora affectations. The *Thin Man* is about style."

"It sounds more like Shakespeare's brain-dead son than Dashiell Hammett."

"I spent hours writing this dialogue."

"I can doctor the script if you'd like, Willy," interrupted Lambert, their Nick Charles for these recordings. "I *did* live in the United States."

"For three months when you were nine."

"I absorbed the American mentality, Willy." Lambert gathered the dialogue sheets from Gertraud and Arnold. "For example, modern San Franciscans seldom say 'hath.'"

It convinced Arnold. "Let's take a break while Lambert looks at the screenplay," he said, going to the window for another cigarette.

As Lambert sat at the table, pen in hand, to make his edits, Willy languished dejected on the floor. His body still ached from yesterday's beating.

But his pride hurt more.

Let Lambert try to write a script in English just by watching a silent reel. Reading pantomime, making up plot. Loy and Powell couldn't do better themselves....

"Don't take my complaints to heart, Willy." Gertraud plopped down next to him, the end of her Havelock jacket fanning out on the floor behind them. "You're a good writer... Maybe not for female roles, so much...Nora has to be clever...."

"I'm not clever?"

"Not as clever as Nora. Or Nick," she teased. "Maybe Asta..."

Willy grimaced. Gertraud knew her stuff. She was older than the others, twenty-two or three, had spent years as a traveling theater actress before being accepted to Germany's first film school. Gertraud carried the wisdom of experience with her. That, plus beauty, made her entrancing to sheltered teenage boys with polio legs.

"I shouldn't be writing, really. Especially a foreign language," said Willy. "I want to direct. Jean Vigo did it from a wheelchair when his consumption got too bad. Why not me?"

"You will. Someday." Gertraud picked up a film canister lying on the floor nearby, perused the cover. "Why not just pass these around to friends? Why have an exhibition?"

Willy shrugged. "Most of our friends don't have projectors. And I want to show it because the government says we can't. They can't silence everyone. Understand?"

"Understood."

She lay back, looking at the ceiling, blond "Gretchen" braids strewn out over his floor, a hint of a tattoo peaking up from her collar.

What kind of woman has a tattoo? A professional thespian who's traveled. Lived.

He wanted a tattoo now.

"How strong can the Führer be if he fears an actress a million miles away?" she mused.

"I think that's the point of the ban."

"Actors over politicians any day."

"Some are the same."

"Now who's clever, Willy?"

"It's almost eleven!" shouted Lambert, suddenly over at the table. "I must be home before state curfew. Papa would make an example of me." He shoved the script pages into his jacket's pocket. "I'll work on this tonight. Get them back to you tomorrow."

"Remember, we're still looking for a place for the showing," said Arnold. "Big enough for at least twenty people."

"I'll check around. *Gute Nacht!*" He bolted out of the apartment, slamming the door behind, his footsteps echoing on the stairs outside.

"Without the script, what can we do now?" asked Gertraud.

"Rehearse the Charleses' flirtation scenes?" Willy suggested.

"But Lambert is Nick…"

"I'll be his stand-in." He puckered his lips.

"You *are* a student of Hollywood. Does the script actually call for kissing sounds?"

"We'll do other effects," replied Arnold with a smile. He went to the projector, forwarded the film to a new scene, a shootout between William Powell and some deadly thug. "Watch this."

Arnold pulled a small horsewhip from his box of sound-effects equipment, lowered a pillow from the couch, and, in perfect timing, struck the pillow with the whip. The crack sounded just like a gunshot.

"Impressive."

"Thanks, Gertie. Okay, quiet. I'm recording." Arnold switched on the tape recorder. Repeated whipping the pillow. *Crack, crack, crack, crack, crack* in time with the gunfight projected on the wall.

Perfectly realistic, thought Willy. Best he ever heard.

* * *

Ilsa Buchholz was awakened by the slam of a door above and hurried footsteps racing down the stairwell outside her apartment.

Those kids upstairs again, she thought. A glance at the clock. Nearly eleven. *Will they never sleep?*

She pushed aside the blanket and sat on the edge of her bed. *Was that a feminine voice above? Had those boys smuggled a girl in again? Probably that tramp Gertraud Glass... Tattoos! Disgusting!*

Ilsa rose from her bed, went to her kitchen where sound carried best. Listened.

Yes, a girl's voice among the others.

A sudden, explosive sound shocked Ilsa's consciousness, sent fear throughout her aged body.

The terrible noise repeated.

Again. And again.

Ilsa hurried to her telephone, dialed the operator. "Patch me through to the police! There's a gun battle upstairs!"

* * *

A fierce pounding erupted on Willy's door.

"Kripo! Open up!"

Willy, Gertraud, and Arnold all exchanged horrified glances. Arnold plucked the reel off the projector, scooped up the other canisters, and opened a dresser drawer.

"Not there…" whispered Gertraud. "That's the first place they'll look."
"The hearth," said Willy. "The chimney flue."
The pounding repeated. One matched by Willy's heart.
"Open immediately! Or we break it down!"
"One moment," said Willy. "I don't move swiftly without my braces."
Arnold shoved the films up the chimney, pulled the damper lever back to secure them. Nodded.

With a last glance at the others, Willy took a long breath, opened the door.

A tall, sixtyish plainclothes detective entered, a smaller, younger officer behind him, an "SS" insignia on the latter's collar. Both men wore hard stares that turned Willy's blood cold.

Gertraud tried to slip out the door.

These probing eyes assessed every detail of the room and its occupants before the older policeman said: "Just where are you going, *Fräulein?*"

"It's late to be in boys' rooms. My family has a good reputation."

"No doubt. Sit down!"

She sat.

The tall officer reset his gaze on the boys. "We have received reports of gunfire in this apartment. What do you misfits have to say about that?"

Realization dawned on Arnold's face. "It was simply an effect.…" He grabbed the stick, struck the cushion again. The gunshot noise repeated. "An old trick I learned on Radio Warschau as an apprentice."

"A sound effect?"

"We're UFA students," added Willy. "Practicing our craft."

"Sorry, sir… sirs," said Arnold with a nervous smile. "We'll keep it down."

"They're lying," barked the younger officer. "They know firearms are forbidden to civilians." He tugged the whip from Arnold's hand, flogged the pillow himself, his *whumps* unlike gunshots. "See, Inspector? This would not fool the crone downstairs."

"It takes a certain skill," said Arnold.

"Pathetic!"

"Enough," said the older lawman. "Secretary Vieth, go to *Frau* Buchholz's room and take a formal statement."

"Inspector, I prefer to help search—"

"You have my orders, Secretary. Obey them."

"Yes, Inspector."

When Vieth was gone and the door shut, the remaining officer said: "What are you hiding in this room? Out with it."

The three students again exchanged glances.

"We've nothing," said Willy.

"I heard you bustling about before we entered," said the inspector coldly. "I've been a policeman too long to be fooled by children. What is hidden? And where?" He moved deeper into the apartment. "You're not foolish enough for the drawers or wardrobe...."

"Are you looking for narcotics?" asked Gertraud. "I don't even smoke."

"Quiet."

The inspector's dark eyes focused on one spot. "Perhaps the hearth. The inexperienced's favorite hiding spot." He walked to the fireplace, bent to a knee, then reached up and grabbed the damper handle.

Willy felt dizzy. Arnold and Gertraud both grew pale.

The inspector grunted as he tugged at the handle in the chimney. "The lever resists. Is something hidden up there?"

"No," said Arnold. "It... it just sticks sometimes. Can never get it free."

"There's fresh ash in the hearth. You had it open recently."

He jiggled the lever, the metallic rattle of the canisters above clearly heard.

The policeman cocked his head. "What's this? Do you hear it?"

No one said a word.

The officer watched them awhile, hand on that lever. Then, to Willy's surprise, the inspector pulled his arm back, stood. His face remained expressionless as he said:

"Do you wish to throw away your lives?"

"No," said Willy meekly.

"No, sir," echoed Arnold.

"*Fräulein?*"

"Of course not," said Gertraud.

"Whatever's up there, I want it burned as soon as I leave. If it will not burn, throw it in the river tonight. Better to be arrested for curfew than possession of that item. Understood?"

"It's empty!" shouted Arnold.

"Then I'll open the flue now."

"Understood," interrupted Willy. "Clearly, sir. Every word. Thank you."

"Good. This is no time to joke around in Germany. Be smarter."

The door opened, and the younger officer reentered. "Inspector, Frau Buchholz won't give the statement. For some reason, she doesn't wish to be alone with me."

"An astute woman, *Frau* Buchholz. We'll take the complaint together."

"And the search, sir?"

"There is nothing here. Idiot children making noise. Let us go."

At the door, the inspector paused.

"I wash my hands of you all."

The door shut.

All let out long sighs of relief before Arnold said:

"I'm too good at sound effects."

* * *

The next afternoon, the three students sat at a picnic table on the shores of Lake Griebnitzsee, waiting for their nightly classes to begin. Nearby stood the gleaming gates to the Babelsberg Film Complex, by far the largest film studio in Germany and the birthplace of German Expressionism. In better days, these lots produced *The Cabinet of Dr. Caligari, Metropolis, The Blue Angel,* and other masterpieces. Since Minister Goebbels purchased it, effectively nationalizing UFA, he'd turned artistry and free expression into propaganda with reprehensible dreck like *Triumph of the Will*.

Dotted around the lake were mansions once owned by studio heads, directors, and major actors, now infested with the Nazi elite. The old tenants forced to sell while Jewish owners simply had their property seized.

Ugly times.

But the declining quality of Babelsberg residents was not the topic of discussion among Willy, Arnold, and Gertraud. Yesterday's visit by the police was.

"So strange that an inspector came at a noise violation," said Willy. "Especially so late. Why not a uniformed officer?"

"Maybe with gunshots, they go straight to detectives?" asked Gertraud, sitting next to him. "Hard to know with the government changing the rules daily."

"Maybe. But he knew we had something."

"Probably thought it was pills," muttered Arnold, an odd distance in his manner, his eyes out over the lake.

"Or pornography," said Gertraud. "Film students. With a girl in the room..."

"I'm not so sure," said Willy. "I wonder if our project has reached untrustworthy ears...."

"That's how it unraveled for Otto Sauer, I'm sure," said Arnold. "A traitor in the Cinema Club. You know I never trusted Elias Bremer...."

"He sold me *After the Thin Man*."

"I thought you pulled it off the pyre?"

"I fibbed... a little."

Lambert came running up the trail from the main road, excitement on his face.

"I've found a place for our exhibition," said he upon arrival. Lambert pointed to a manor on the far side of Griebnitzsee. "That house on the lake's edge. It's got a huge windowless cellar, dark and perfect for projection. We can fit everyone in without danger of some policeman peeking in from outside."

Willy gazed at the stony walls of the mansion, half-eclipsed by the lake mist. "Who owns that house?"

Lambert smiled proudly. "We do. My father acquired it just yesterday. The family won't move in for weeks but I already got a key." He slammed a keychain down on the picnic table. "How about Saturday?"

Willy and Gertraud exchanged glances.

"How many ways into that cellar, Lambert?" she asked.

"Two. One from the yard, one down the back stairs. Why?"

"Just want a lay of the land. In case we're raided."

"No policeman would dare raid a house owned by *my* father. He'd be ruined!"

"Let's put it to a vote," said Willy. "We do this showing on Saturday?"

"Okay," agreed Gertraud. "Lambert?"

"Absolutely!"

"I'm in too," said Willy, despite his reservations about Lambert. "Arnold?"

Arnold came back from wherever he was. "I keep thinking what that inspector said about washing his hands of us."

"He's just trying to scare you," said Gertraud.

"It worked. Do you think he washed his hands of the Sauer family the same way?"

"Well, what's it gonna be, Arnold?" asked Willy. "It's your beloved Myrna Loy versus the Third Reich."

A dreamy look came to Arnold's face. "Myrna. Always."

"We're unanimous. Saturday's gonna be the big show."

* * *

Kurt Glass hung up the telephone receiver.

"My source has the time and location of the Loy showing."

"Really?" asked Vieth, beaming from his desk. "When and where, Inspector?"

"Saturday at four o'clock in the afternoon." He scribbled the address on a note page and handed it across to Vieth. "You know where this is?"

The junior officer clicked his teeth as he read. "One of the mansions on Griebnitzsee Lake. Wealthy patrons supporting the film. More proof of an agenda."

"It'll be held in the cellar. Clandestinely. The house is otherwise unoccupied." Kurt sat back in his chair, staring through Vieth into the void of life. Saturday was his off day. He could use that as the flimsiest of excuses to not attend this raid.

Of course, Director Foth had ordered him to handle it. But Foth would be away on Saturday, meeting with Minister Goebbels.

Which left only…

"Secretary Vieth," he finally said, "do you remember when Director Foth said if I were not up to my duties, you should attend them? I want you to do me the honor of leading this sting. I have no stomach for it. It's time for a younger man to take over. Will you grant me this favor? Take us forward to the next generation. Into your era."

Vieth's eyes shone like beacons.

"With pleasure, sir. Thank you. Thank you with all my heart."

Glass wondered if Vieth had a heart.

"You're welcome, son. But remember to temper the violence. They must be fit to stand trial."

"No balconies in the cellar, my friend Inspector. Accidents will not happen. They'll stand trial. For treason."

Glass smiled. "Yes, friend. Do the Führer proud."

* * *

Lambert's cellar was packed with thirty or more bodies. Willy was overjoyed at the turnout even if Arnold worried constantly about leaks. It was a low, wide chamber that reminded Willy of the factory basement where Peter Lorre gave his impassioned speech against the mob in *M*. Before the Nazis drove Lorre and director Lang from the country, back when Germany made the finest films in the world. Then Hollywood had its turn.

Now Hollywood was being denied them, too.

Gertraud handed Willy the first reel, which he carefully threaded through the projector feed. At his hip, resting on a small table, was the tape recorder with their third-reel dub ready to be synced with the projector. When all was ready, Willy stood with a finger on the projector switch. All he had to do was press, and the magic would begin.

But first, he and everyone else had to endure Arnold's speech. He paced before the brick wall that would serve as their screen, talking about the challenges he'd faced in the dubbing, his great respect for Dashiell Hammett, and his eternal and very earthly love for Myrna Loy, whose husband surely never read the letters Arnold sent to her in passionate German.

The crowd turned from appreciative to bored to restless. The cellar door slammed shut as someone exited. More might follow.

Arnold, seeing this, changed the tone of the speech. Dedicating the showing to the Cinema Club. To Irma and Otto Sauer. And Sergei Eisenstein. Applause replaced jeers and Willy started the show. The projector beam bathed Arnold, drove him off to the side, allowing Willy to focus the image.

But the image he'd focused on that wall was shockingly unexpected.

What was happening?

Groans erupted from the crowd. Moans of complaint that silenced immediately as the cellar door opened, a horde of policemen standing outside.

In shock, Willy stumbled back, tipping over the recorder's table, tripping over the projector's power cord, the force of his fall to the floor pulling it from the wall.

The police invaded the already packed cellar, forcing all bodies to the walls with such brutality Willy feared for his friends. Arnold was shoved into the corner with several others, Lambert tackled to the ground near the door, shouting out: "Do you know who my father is? I'll have you all in Spandau!" Willy could not spy Gertraud in the chaos.

She must be here...

"We don't mean to interrupt your display of American propaganda," said the young SS officer Willy recognized from the night *Frau* Buchholz reported sound-prop gunshots. "Are you the projectionist?"

"I don't understand."

"Plug in that projector. Let's see what filth you revolutionaries have been watching."

Still lying on the ground, Willy followed orders. The machine came to life, the projector beam shining over the wall, over the bricks, and across bodies forced by the police to stand unmoving.

The officer's face softened as he watched, changing from a countenance of controlled rage to one of absolute bewilderment at what he saw.

A confusion shared by everyone in the room.

* * *

Kurt Glass waited for his spy deep in Babelsberg Park beside the Havel River. When Gertraud appeared at last, canisters of film in her hands, it was already growing dark and especially cold down on the bank.

She handed him the film.

"What did you switch it with?" he asked without glancing at her.

"Cartoons. Nice, legal cartoons."

"Mickey Mouse?"

"Felix the Cat."

"Vieth's favorite, I'm sure." He opened the canisters one by one and dumped the film into the river. When the strips had disappeared into the waters, he threw the canisters in as well.

"What sort of world is it when throwing a can of film in the river saves lives?"

"Did we save lives today, Papa?"

"I think so. Your classmates would not survive long in Plötzensee or Spandau. Not with the Nazis marking them as conspirators. Now, Vieth has nothing to hold them. I'll make sure of it tomorrow. He'll be quite contrite after breaking into a Nazi official's house to interrupt a cartoon show. Might cost him his career."

"I hope so, Papa. I miss Irma Sauer."

Kurt's eyes found the lights of Berlin in the darkening sky. "I took a bullet for my country at Ypres. We lost that war. I fear we will soon be dragged into another."

Gertraud was silent a long time. Then she changed the language to English and said:

"I read you were shot in the tabloids."

He looked at her slyly, mood lightening against his will. Kurt Glass put his arm around his daughter and they headed for home.

"They were nowhere near my tabloids, *Mäuschen*."

XXIV

HOUSE OF TIGERS

A Novella
Originally Published in Black Cat Weekly

I

The mosquito swarms, black, undulating, and infinite, stretched horizon to horizon over the Siberian wilderness. No instrument forged by man or God penetrated this terrible dark living fog. Not the headlamps of the police car on a lonely road, not the keen vision of the man at the wheel, and not the golden rays of a late summer sun.

The parasitic clouds were ravenous. Murderous. A man exposed would die in half an hour from blood loss, be driven mad by ten thousand bites well before.

Inspector Ilya Dudnyk, with a career on both sides of the law, was familiar with exposure, death, and madness in all their myriad forms. He was a cautious man, successful in sheltering the citizens of his oblast from violence and the oligarchs who employed him from justice. This afternoon, his most generous patron, Konstantin Aristov, he of the fashionable "lap tigers," had summoned Dudnyk to Aristov Manor. The old man wanted to make some family announcement and needed Dudnyk as muscle in case things got out of hand.

Things often got out of hand at Aristov Manor.

Out here law was an import.

The drive to Aristov Manor was three hours from town through forests, tundra, and semi-swampland, but Dudnyk went alone without hesitation. The pay was worth the journey, even with the eleventh plague of Moses in the air. Truthfully, he'd come at half the price. One afternoon out here earned him as much as a month of casework in the city. And the work was usually simpler.

If not safer.

Dudnyk's police car rumbled through a flooded section of road, the mosquito haze rising like a mushroom cloud as the tires cut through the waters. God help him if the car floundered. The vehicle interior was sealed like a spacecraft and just as limited in air. The vents couldn't be opened, or those tiny monsters would be inside in seconds. All that global warming, the newspapers said, brought longer summers, more melted ice, and left limitless still water for their breeding grounds. In one measly hectare were as many mosquitos as people on Earth. And there were 1.3 billion hectares in Siberia. Do the math. Like something out of the apocalypse.

The car cleared the water, the tires back on firm ground. Through the rearview mirror, Dudnyk watched the amorphous black shroud resettle behind.

Damn creepy.

His mobile rang. *The office.* "Yes, Ludmilla?"

"Just checkin' on you, Inspector. How's the drive?"

"Air conditioning went out, but almost there. Konstantin Aristov call again?"

"No…though I did want to alert you. There was a prison break at Kapitsa. A little after two p.m."

"Well, the escapees won't make it a hundred meters with these conditions."

"Just one got away, stole thick clothes, fireman's gear, and several cans of repellant. It's only thirty kilometers from Kapitsa to Aristov Manor. Survival's not *impossible*."

"Might as well be three thousand with this plague. My money's on the mosquitos."

"Should I call the manor?"

"No. I'll handle it. Take the rest of the day off, Ludmilla. I don't want anyone disturbing us out here. Let the sewing circle know I'm off grid."

"Yes, Inspector. Thank you. Good day."

"Good day, Ludmilla." Dudnyk hung up.

I

Curious. An hour into the journey, Konstantin Aristov's lawyer had called Dudnyk's mobile, said they'd captured an intruder in the manor. A woman. Insisted that Dudnyk arrive as soon as possible. Which he was, but this was still Siberia after all. Nothing is near.

He clicked his teeth in thought. This intruder couldn't be the escaped prisoner. The timetables didn't match up. And Kapitsa was an all-male penitentiary.

Two people were out in this blight. Two who shouldn't be. Three, if he included himself.

The mosquito clouds briefly parted to reveal an eerie array of jumping firelight and steady electric lamps ahead. The electric source radiated from the windows of the three-story manor complete with rotunda, Doric columns, and a second-floor veranda overlooking a gated courtyard.

Aristov Manor. As expected.

But it was the substantial firelight that surprised Dudnyk. An earthen moat had been dug around the estate's perimeter, a deep trough filled with combustible material that sent flames and smoke into the air, the burning billows meant to drive off the insects in a swirling war of gas and swarm above.

With its flaming pits, gilded manor, and rising billows, the Aristov estate was like a narcotic dream of Hellish opulence, reminding Dudnyk of a painting he'd seen in the Hermitage called "Beelzebub's Palace."

Fitting. After all, wasn't Beelzebub "The Lord of Flies"?

But mosquitos would do.

The road wound around the estate margin towards the opened front gates, where an earthen bridge bisected the vaporous moat. Dudnyk's car penetrated this smokey barrier, crossed the bridge into a yard populated with numerous buildings including an astronomical observatory, bathhouse, greenhouse, and what he knew to be animal pens. Here a private cell tower rose high into the smokey night, an antenna of sorts that allowed Konstantin Aristov to communicate with his vast empire from any point on the estate. The car then passed into the courtyard where an array of fiery mosquito-killing cauldrons lay as near to the manor as possible without risk of gusting winds setting it ablaze.

A compact three-wheeler with rent-a-car plates was parked along one side of the courtyard. A visitor. Or intruder. Either way out of place. The expensive cars of the Aristov family were housed in the main garage while the humbler vehicles of the staff were confined to another garage to the rear.

He took a photo of the plates with his mobile.

Dudnyk switched off the police car engine and emptied his last can of mosquito repellant, covering his exposed skin and applying a layer along collar and cuffs. Then he slipped on his gloves, donned a riot helmet brought for the occasion, and pulled his face shield down.

Just like the space-walking cosmonaut Dudnyk dreamed to become as a boy.

He stepped out of the vehicle into a hostile, alien environment and made his way past the burning cauldrons towards the hall's front doors.

Let us see what adventure awaits in Aristov Manor.

II

As Inspector Dudnyk reached the manor steps, a familiar woman's voice came over the house intercom. "Welcome, Ilya," said Ninel Safronova, the Aristov attorney and Dudnyk's occasional bedmate during sojourns here. "Basking in our fine summer weather, I see."

"I'm going skinny dipping in the river later. Want to join me?"

"Sorry. I'm using my blood today." One of the twin doors opened. "Quickly, Ilya. Quickly."

He stepped inside. Ninel, a tall woman with a pinkish pixie cut that rebelled against her conservative gray suit dress, pressed the door shut with one hand. In her other hand, she held the nozzle of a vacuum, sucking up the insectile invaders at the door seam, counting aloud at her mosquito victims.

"Eleven…twelve…oh, you too, bloodsucker…that's thirteen, isn't it, Ilya?"

"At least."

Ninel thumbed off the switch. "And then there were none." She bolted the door lock, turned on the house alarm, set the vacuum against the wall, then pushed up Dudnyk's face shield and kissed him fully on the lips.

"You taste like insect repellant," mewed Ninel when the lengthy kiss ended.

"Do you say that to all the visitors?"

"Only the handsome ones." She kissed him again. "I'd say 'Insecta-Guard' brand. My favorite."

"You're the connoisseur. A man has no secrets around you, Ninel."

"Konstantin does. But I want to stay alive."

"Me too."

He set the helmet on a table at the door, then arm-and-arm Ninel led him through the foyer to an expansive chamber dominated by an ornately carved spiral staircase descending from the rotunda above. No staff arrived to greet them.

"Where are Gleb and Inna?" asked Dudnyk.

"Konstantin sent all staff home on private autobus yesterday. His announcement tonight is to be absolutely secret. Family only."

He nudged Ninel. "And his best lawyer."

She nudged back. "With his best soldier."

"Yes."

"And that intruder, unfortunately."

Dudnyk was about to ask about this intruder when movement caught his eye and a deep, baritone meowing registered in his ear. From some back room behind the stairwell emerged an ambush of small tigers. Slightly larger than a husky housecat, the tigers had been selectively bred down from the comparatively small Sumatran tigers and then genetically altered by Konstantin's now-deceased son Rurik for temperament and sterility. The "Aristov Lap Tigers" were the rage of the jet set throughout the world. Kim Kardashian Instagram-ed nude with hers while David Beckham often kicked a football around to his cats, and the three owned by Harrison Ford actually made the eternally stoic actor smile. Melania Trump possessed five, all tax-free gifts from Moscow. This breed made the family name famous beyond Russia's borders. And since those sold were infertile, one had to pay a hefty fee and import them from the Aristov's centers in Moscow, St. Petersburg, and Vladivostok. It was Konstantin's most lucrative "100 percent" legal business and highly effective at money laundering, as Ninel perhaps unwisely told Dudnyk over pillow talk.

"*Privet*, Olga!" said Dudnyk, scratching the head of the first tiger to arrive, the cat rubbing against his leg with a guttural purr several octaves lower than a housecat's.

II

"I'm always amazed you can tell them apart."

"The inspector's eye, Ninel. I miss nothing," he said pointing to the cats. "That's Anton, here's Galina, over there is chubby Dmitry, and on the steps is proud Valeria. Am I correct?"

"You'll have to ask Konstantin. They all look the same to me."

He gave a final pat to Olga, then rose. "Now, who is this intruder then?"

"It's best if I show you. We have her in the 'priest's cupboard' below ground."

"Lead on, my sweet."

"No handholding around the guests."

"It's our secret."

They walked into the library, which Dudnyk privately referred to as "The Shrine" since there were prominent pictures of Konstantin's dead son Rurik at various stages of life. He looked much like his father in the later pictures, same burning eyes, same furled brow, just younger and with more hair. Whichever direction one looked in the library, Rurik was glaring back, the haunting ghost of Aristov Manor.

Though why he was the ghost exactly remained a mystery. Rurik and his common-law wife Anna died when their Porsche went off the road and through the ice of a lake some thirty months ago. Both managed to get out of the car but succumbed to the freezing waters before help arrived. Dudnyk always found the deaths suspicious, wondered if some rival oligarch had done in the heir to the Aristov fortune. Or perhaps a foreign animal breeder, as the lap tigers were just taking off then. But Konstantin refused to let him investigate. Or anyone investigate. So, Dudnyk let the matter drop. Yet, his inspector's instincts remained unsatisfied....

Sitting on the library couch were two strangers. A handsome, redheaded man in his early forties dressed in a polo shirt and khaki pants, and a dark-haired woman a little younger, pretty but plump, with one of the tigers—Vlad, Dudnyk thought—purring in her lap, its paws reaching up to bat at her turquoise Native American pendant.

Ninel switched the language to English, glanced between all parties. "This is Konstantin's American cousin Pyotr and his wife Nancy. Here for a short visit. May I introduce, Inspector Dudnyk. He'll attend our meeting."

"Peter Pashin," said the man, rising and offering his hand. "From Palo Alto. Near San Francisco."

"I'm aware of the location. Nice to meet you both," replied Dudnyk, shaking his hand and giving the woman a formal nod. "You'll excuse us. Ms. Safronova and I have a matter to attend in the basement. We will chat later."

"Of course."

On their way out, Dudnyk's attentive ears caught mutterings behind.

"Not very friendly," whispered the woman.

"He speaks English well," replied her husband indifferently.

"The less we communicate with police, the better. I don't like them here."

"There's only one."

"One's enough in Russia."

Dudnyk and Ninel descended a narrow backroom staircase into the brick tunnels that ran beneath the entire estate. Designed to allow access to various locations without the necessity of going outside in the harsh Siberian winter, they functioned now as safe burrows beneath the mosquito apocalypse above. The sections at the stairs' base formed a perfect four-way intersection. To the south ran the tunnel to the main garage and the bathhouse. To the east went the passage to the staff garage and the astronomical observatory. The north held the entrances to the greenhouse and underground sports court. And to the west lay the storerooms and the animal pen. This pen held only one type of animal. Tigers. Not the Aristov pet tigers nor even their Sumatran ancestors, but adult Siberian tigers, amongst the largest cats on Earth, and a symbol of Konstantin's strength. They were quite convincing animals, useful in negotiating deals and breaking whistleblowers. Dudnyk had witnessed the hardest of men recant at the threshold of those pens.

The priest's cupboard was closer, only a few steps down the south passage. The original tenants of the manor, long before the Aristovs, had

II

sheltered clergy and nobility here when the Reds were scouring the lands for their perceived enemies. A secret door of brick, invisible in the olden days, was even now revealed only by a lock keypad on the wall. Dudnyk rather liked the idea of the hidden passage in the old castle, like something out of ghost and pirate stories from his youth. Or *Young Frankenstein*. Such adventure. He was too much a dreamer for law enforcement really.

Ninel tapped in a code, and a wall of bricks on invisible hinges swung open.

"Your show," she said, motioning for him to go first. "Inspector Dudnyk is entering, captive!"

He stepped into a room he knew well. Three walls of bare brick, a fourth covered in plumbing pipes from the manor above. A bare mattress bed, a couch that folded out into a second bed, old-fashioned brass bathtub, a toilet and sink on the wall near the pipes. It could be as plush or sparse as needed, depending on if the room were sheltering a friend or holding an enemy. Dudnyk had seen both. Presently, the décor tended towards the latter.

The room's occupant, sitting on the bed, back against the brick wall, was a woman in her late twenties, scowling beneath dark bangs with hints of a reddish cast, and dressed in a cat-burglar black jumpsuit zipped to the collar. Next to her on the mattress was an opened animal carrier. A housecat—and it was definitely a *true* housecat—dyed in tiger-colored stripes lay curled beside the woman's hip.

"We've had her here four hours," said Ninel. "She used that pathetic painted animal to talk her way into the foyer. Claimed she was friend of the family and her Aristov tiger was wasting away. While I was fetching Konstantin, she slipped away from the door and went gallivanting through the house unsupervised. I finally found her outside one of the bedrooms. Armed with this." She pulled a miniature pistol from her suit dress pocket, handed it to Dudnyk.

"A Llama Micro-Max?" He laughed. "I thought they discontinued these nasty little things."

"Our occupant is a nasty little thing herself. She fought tooth and nail to stop me putting her in this cell. Finally, it took Bogdan to get her inside, and she bit him along the way."

"Bit him?"

The woman shrugged. "I didn't bite him. It was my cat."

Perfect Russian, thought Dudnyk, but just a trace of an accent. Where was she from?

As if reading her lover's mind, Ninel produced a burgundy-colored booklet from her pocket. "Her passport, Inspector Dudnyk."

He took the passport. Read it.

"Santa Ezeriņa. From Rīga."

"Present."

"A Baltic girl. You're a long way from Latvia, Ms. Ezeriņa."

"Duty calls. I'm a journalist. The whole world wants to know who'll be heir to the Aristov fortune. Especially given the fate of the last heir, Rurik. Those little tigers have made your employers international celebrities. And—"

"I'm employed by the Russian state, Ms. Ezeriņa."

"As a hobby?"

"As you can see, Inspector," said Ninel, "Konstantin is concerned about her presence. If the staff can't even know what is said tonight, well, we don't want a foreign journalist—"

"Oh, Latvians aren't really foreigners, Ms. Safronova," mused Dudnyk. "Baltic or not, they will be reunited with Russia someday soon. I have faith in Mr. Putin."

Ezeriņa glared at him, slipped off the bed, and stood in the middle of the room. "I think the least the Aristov family can do is grant a few interviews. I came six thousand kilometers, braved a plague, and dyed a cat. That's dedication."

"We should call PETA," said Ninel.

"It'll wash out."

"You'll be taken to town," said Dudnyk, "and charged with assault and trespassing, possibly illegal possession of a firearm. And count yourself lucky. Mr. Aristov's trespassers sometimes get lost in these tunnels. Open

II

the wrong door and accidents happen."

"That's why I carry the pistol. Now let me talk to Konstantin Aristov."

"Has she been searched, Ms. Safronova?"

"No. Just the gun, her cellphone, passport, and the keys to her three-wheeler. Bogdan went to attend his bite and never came back. I wasn't going in alone."

"Strip," said Dudnyk.

Without flinching, she unzipped her jumpsuit, let it fall to the ground. Underneath Ezeriņa wore thigh-high boots and a white dress of low cut and exceedingly high hem.

Dudnyk smiled wolfishly. Ninel nudged him disapprovingly.

"I don't like this getup," said Ezeriņa, "but Konstantin and his grandsons are known to appreciate a lady's figure. Whatever gets me an interview."

"You could have more weapons. Take the rest off."

"This is as far as I go without an interview and a thousand Euros in the garter."

Ninel's mobile rang. She took the call, listened for a few seconds, hung up.

"Konstantin is ready to start the meeting, Inspector."

He nodded. "We'll deal with you later, Santa Ezeriņa."

They stepped into the passage. Ninel shut the door, locked it with another code.

Dudnyk handed the Llama pistol back to Ninel. "Put this in your safe." He took her arm. "She's a brave one to invade the house of the most feared oligarch this side of the Urals while carrying a weapon."

"Foolish."

"And rather good looking too."

"I hadn't noticed."

"Ninel…you're cute when you're jealous." He kissed her on the cheek. "Did I ever tell you that?"

III

Dudnyk and Ninel let their arm-in-arm intimacy drop, then stepped into the library. Assembled were all current occupants of Aristov Manor excepting the salacious journalist trapped in the priest's cupboard far below.

The waifish, blond Maksim, in his white suit and vest, sat cross-legged on a chair beneath a painting of his father, Rurik, the figure above in much the same pose. Maksim's older brother, Bogdan, leaned against the bookshelves nearby. Grim, with a stubbly shaved head and muscular tattooed arms, Bogdan stood well over two meters, an imposing presence tempered only by the dainty cloth bandage tied on the finger of one hand.

Peter and Nancy Pashin remained on the same couch as before, the couple appearing anxious and old compared to the calm, twenty-something Aristov brothers across the room. Between these twosomes, on a Persian rug decorated with symbols of decadence and fertility, lounged the eight resident lap tigers, the pack looking sleepy and bored, except feisty Vlad who played with Valeria's tempting tail.

"Ninel, put all these cats away. They are distracting," boomed a voice like God's on the mountain. Konstantin Aristov entered from a far door, dressed in a black suit with a blood-red shirt and tie. Bald, thick-browed, and broad-shouldered, in his hand he held a walking stick capped with an obsidian skull, a cane carried like a king's scepter and wielded at times like a weapon. Dudnyk had seen it knock out the teeth of an unsympathetic policeman in this very room, cave in the face of a would-be assassin on the veranda. The old man still had power in those limbs. Even hulking

III

Bogdan feared his grandfather.

While Ninel herded the eight little tigers into an adjacent reading room, the Aristov patriarch stopped before the library window. Behind him, through the glass, the black clouds of mosquitos spiraled through courtyard lights and retreated before burning cauldron smoke, denser swarms waiting beyond the moat of fire, the insectile enemy stretching away into the endless night.

Three hours from anywhere, thought Dudnyk. Shatter one window and the house would be invaded in seconds, fires or no.

"Greetings," said the oligarch standing before this nightmare vision. "We will speak in English for the benefit of Pyotr and his wife."

"Hassle," complained Maksim, puffing on his ever-present cigarette.

"You know English, Maks," chided Bogdan. "You attended Oxford."

"Only one term. They won't let you smoke in the dormitory."

"That's not why you got expelled." Bogdan sniffed suggestively.

"Quiet, boys," said Ninel. "Konstantin has the floor."

"The floor is indeed mine, dear Ninel. As is the house, the estate, and all businesses, legitimate and otherwise. But they will soon belong to one of you. That's what we're here to discuss." He leaned forward on his skull cane. "The doctors number my days in months. I want to appoint an heir while lucid enough to take comfort in the decision. I will not repeat the mistakes of the Khans or Alexander. The empire must not be divided. To the strongest and most loyal alone goes the spoils."

"So, who gets the money, Grandpapa?" asked Maksim with a yawn. "It's almost cocktail hour."

"Patience, Maksim. We—" A creaking from above interrupted. Konstantin's deep-set eyes turned to the ceiling. "What's that noise?"

"The house moaning under the winds," offered Peter, glancing at his wife for confirmation. "Siberia and its vastness."

"Or the weight of ten billion insects on the roof," said Bogdan with a rare smile. "All about to suck us dry."

"I should be sucking a cocktail dry," replied Maksim. "Why did you send the servants home, Grandpapa? Hassle to find the vermouth myself."

"Sounds like someone upstairs," said Konstantin. "Ninel, check if that journalist is still inside her cell."

Ninel left the room, returned promptly. "She's there, sir. Locked safely in."

"Then we continue. The fortune will go to the winner of a contest among the Aristov males: Bogdan, Maksim, and Pyotr. Only a man can be king. A test of loyalty is required! Who will remain by my side in my ailing days? Who will prioritize family and shun the outside world? The victor is the last to leave this estate henceforward. By estate I mean the grounds within the moat at furthest. Emergencies, commitments, acts of Man or God provide no excuse. The last Aristov male remaining with me gets eighty percent of the money immediately and the house, remaining monies, and all businesses on my passing."

A din of surprise filled the library air, voices bantering about in Russian and English. Dudnyk used the ruckus to whisper "Are we *loyal* retainers allowed in this game, Ninel?"

She shook her head "no."

"Silly thing, then."

"Our visas only last four more days," objected Peter. "We have a plane back to America on Monday."

"Peter, think of the opportunity," said Nancy, cuffing him across the back of the head. "I want furs and pearls. Oysters in Sausalito. My own lap tigers!"

"How can I run a Russian criminal empire? I'm a database programmer! I don't even use pirate software."

"You are welcome to leave, Pyotr," replied Konstantin, "But of course, then you'll forfeit."

"I think any issues you'd have for overstaying your visas would be worth billions," offered Ninel. "I can assist should the government try deportation or imprisonment."

"Listen to the lady with pink hair," said Nancy. "Don't be foolish, Pete!"

"We have a prenup, Nancy. Remember? Won't do you any good to be greedy."

III

"Aren't you supposed to start training camp in Moscow soon, Bogdan?" asked Maksim of his brother. "Got a contract, don't you?"

"More than one, actually. I—"

"I'll get you out of the CSKA Moscow contract, if needed, Bogdan," offered Ninel. "I've dealt with sports and entertainment law on behalf of Mr. Konstantin before."

"My, she is a helpful one," mused Maksim with a touch of sarcasm. "Happy to play kingmaker. What's your price, sweetie?"

"*We* play this game," said the oligarch, "Because I won't have what I built in the shadows of communism reduced by idiot family. As none of you have proven anything, a loyalty contest is a better filter than rolling dice to find an heir. Ninel has prepared contracts—in English for you, Pyotr Pashin. All participants must sign, agreeing that they will stand by the outcome and not contest the results in court. Our Inspector Dudnyk will find you—even in America—if you break this agreement."

Dudnyk tapped his gun handle. The Americans turned pale.

"Seems an enormous hassle, Grandpapa," moaned Maksim. "It—you—could last months. And us fending for ourselves without the staff."

"You'll have to fend for yourself, Maksim. Now or forever depending on the results of this challenge. If you love me—and love money—you'll outlast Bogdan and Pyotr."

Ninel pulled a folder from the library shelves, opened it, and distributed contracts to the participants. "There are pens on the table. Sign."

After dispirited arguments, they all signed. When Ninel had collected the documents, the great patriarch announced: "One last detail. This contest remains among the seven of us until resolved. Any family member who leaks this is out of the game. Any employee is terminated." He pointed with the terrible cane to Dudnyk, his enforcer. "The secret stays in this room on pain of death."

Rīga, Latvia

Journalist Alberts Krūmiņš was sitting in the oppressive heat of the *Baltic Beacon* newspaper offices watching the football highlights for his overdue sports report when he received a text from Santa Ezeriņa off on some longshot freelance assignment as usual. (No wonder she was always broke. Alberts was tired of lending her money.)

The text read:

> *News Flash. Konstantin Aristov to bequeath fortune to winner of family contest. Last male relative remaining on estate grounds from this moment forward is deemed heir. No exceptions. Leave and you're out! The contenders:*
>
> *Bogdan Aristov, grandson. Pro basketball player, CSKA Moscow.*
> *Maksim Aristov, grandson. Unemployed. Oxford dropout.*
> *Peter Pashin, cousin(?) from CA, USA. Occupation software engineer. Wife Nancy also present.*
>
> *Class 62 insect outbreak complicates matters. A police inspector and attorney referee proceedings. My prime mobile seized. Assume will lose backup and go out of contact. I am restrained but plan to rectify. 2 web-linked microphones planted on premises. FTTP into the microphones directly and listen in. Record everything on the internet stream but don't publish unless I give OK. Links below.*
>
> *DON'T STEAL MY STORY, ALBERTS! OR THERE'LL BE MURDER WHEN I RETURN!*

Alberts yawned and went back to watching football.

IV

"Ilya, come to the greenhouse," said Konstantin, the baritone voice little diminished by the intercom speakers. "Alone."

Dudnyk obeyed the familiar command, walking down the north tunnel as he had a hundred times before. The house above normally would be bustling with activity at this hour, servants making dinner, Konstantin or Maksim hosting some luxurious events, Ninel and Dudnyk sneaking away to make love. But everything was quiet tonight, the manor's tenants retreating to their rooms to absorb Konstantin's bizarre announcement.

Dudnyk thought he detected footsteps behind. He glanced back into the tunnel, saw no one.

"Who goes there?" he shouted, his voice echoing down the passage. Nothing. Just to be certain, he retreated to the intersection at the base of the stairs, glancing down each of the four dimly lighted tunnels. No one. He checked the priest's cupboard. Still locked.

"You in there, Ezeriņa?" he shouted through the hidden door.

"No. I'm off golfing in the Ladies Open at Edinburgh," responded a feminine voice. "Three over par, so far."

"The ninth green tilts to the left. Good luck, my dear."

He continued to the greenhouse, climbed stone steps, and opened a door into a humid, lighted world. A comparatively small structure given the grandiosity of everything else at Aristov Manor, the inside garden showed a tamer, more reflective side of the master. Few outside the family saw this aspect of the feared oligarch.

But tameness and domesticity had limits. Terrible orders were often uttered among the orchids. Dudnyk the executor of those commands.

"Ilya, why the delay?" asked Konstantin, dressed in gardening clothes and leaning over some viny plant at the end of the row.

"I had to play through at Edinburgh."

"Meaning?"

"I was double-checking our privacy."

"Good. Come closer."

Dudnyk walked down the aisle passing exotic vegetation, labels affixed to each planter with scientific name, common name, and the plant's indigenous land: *Crassula umbella* (wine cup, South Africa); *Nerium oleander* (oleander, Libya); *Nepeta cataria* (catnip, Bulgaria). He always laughed at the last. In a house full of tigers, big and small, one had to have catnip. The drug worked on all members of the feline family. Little Vlad and Valeria needed their fixes just as Konstantin's addict grandson Maksim craved his own narcotics. A private joke. One never spoken aloud.

When he reached his boss, Konstantin whispered in his ear as soft as a lullaby:

"When you take that journalist into town tonight for arrest, I want you to bring Fyodor Zharkov back." He reached into his gardening apron pocket and withdrew a thick roll of US one-hundred-dollar bills. "Have him bring whatever Maksim normally buys. Enough for a month." Konstantin handed him the money.

This was surprising. Though Konstantin had his fingers in the drug trade coming up from China and Afghanistan, he was adamant against the use of narcotics in his own family. He'd taken drugs *away* from Maksim many times in the past.

"I want to test if Maksim's clean, Ilya."

A month's supply was quite a test. Or temptation. But Dudnyk didn't ask questions. His predecessor among Konstantin's police lackeys had been a gabber and disappeared suddenly. Dudnyk discovered his badge in the greenhouse fertilizer bin his first day here and tossed it in the river.

"Ilya, if Fyodor refuses to come because of the plague…"

"He'll come. Have I ever failed you?"

IV

"No...but...Well, Azrail is active today. I found him stalking through the rosemary and lavender. A bad sign. Death is coming."

Konstantin nodded towards the wall. Constructed in the nineteenth century, many of the greenhouse's canopy windowpanes were made from the discarded glass photographic plates that predated film. Among the top-hatted gentlemen and elegant ladies was a truly terrifying figure. On a single pane near the sink was affixed the negative image of something sinister emerging from the woods nearby, the house rotunda clearly seen in the background. The foreground figure, skeletal, and wrapped in a funeral shroud was frightening for its very realism and proximity. Dudnyk had stood in that very spot. One long bony arm of the specter dragged on the ground, in the other it clutched a puppet. Or doll.

Or child.

Surely, this was a costumed man, a denizen of a travelling freakshow or the ritualistic garb of backwoods peasants, customs gone strange in the solitude of Siberia. There was some myth about a son of the manor's tenants disappearing. A story not quite dispelled by the atheistic communists in their time. And now, with its gaunt body suffused with crawling mosquitos on the pane's outside, the insects appearing gigantic atop the bony figure, sucking blood from it and the child, well, the composite was even more revolting.

Konstantin named it Azrail. When the sun shone through the glass, he jokingly used to note where its shadow fell among his plants. The Angel of Death stalking among his crops. Truly medieval.

But as Konstantin's illness set in and his mind began to slip, these musings were taken as omens. Azrail had predicted Rurik's demise. Now, Death walked among his medicinal plants. And forecasted trouble on Dudnyk's way to town.

Konstantin, the king, was mad. Narcissistic, monomaniacal, paranoid...

But still the king.

"Fyodor will come, sir," said Dudnyk at last. "Azrail never stopped us before."

***

Dudnyk was retreating down the underground passage towards the stairs to the manor, when he saw Ninel walking towards him.

"Where have you been, Ilya?"

"Konstantin wanted help with his gardening."

"You've a trigger finger, not a green thumb. Azrail didn't order you to shoot anyone again? Maybe, Santa Ezeriņa?"

He laughed. "Not her."

She took his arm and they walked silently. They heard the drumming of something hitting the ground repeatedly, passed the open door to the sports court. Bogdan was dribbling a basketball, pensively working on his craft. Surely, thinking of other matters.

They left him undisturbed. As they approached the stairs, Ninel said:

"If he asked you to target me, what would you do?"

"If Konstantin asked, I'd refuse. If Azrail, well, I'd mourn you."

"Good. Wait, that means—"

He kissed her on the cheek.

Gunshots erupted above.

They scaled the stairs into the house. The gunfire came from the courtyard. Near the main door, they found Peter and Nancy staring out a window in horror.

Outside, among the swirling smoke from the cauldrons near the door stood a bare-chested Maksim, wearing a maniacal, euphoric expression as he tossed repellant into the fires, the canisters bursting like gunshots.

"This will make Grandpapa's game a little more fun," Maksim shouted watching a canister explode, shrapnel bouncing off the windowpane. "Who goes anywhere without repellant?"

Bogdan arrived behind Dudnyk, he too called by the din. "Maks's on the dust again."

As the last canister burst, Maksim pulled something sharp and glinting from his pocket and sped across the courtyard towards the police car.

A knife! He'll puncture the tires! Dudnyk was out the door instantly, felt

IV

the bite of a dozen mosquitos before he tackled Maksim from behind.

"Leave me alone!" He kicked at Dudnyk but dropped the blade. Bogdan, too, was outside now and together they dragged Maksim into the house, Ninel slamming the door.

"I must have forty bites," complained Dudnyk, rubbing his stinging skin. "In ten seconds. Idiot boy."

"If you'd gone beyond the fires, Ilya, it'd be forty thousand," said Ninel, massaging his shoulders. "Those things hate smoke."

"Spoil sports!" cried Maksim, kicking and screaming in Bogdan's massive, tattooed arms. "Grandpapa wants his entertainment. We're all puppets in a bigger game!"

"Downstairs into the priest's cupboard," said Dudnyk.

"We're running a full prison tonight," mused Bogdan, dragging his brother along. Peter joined the other men, and they forced Maksim down the back stairs and into the tunnels.

Konstantin was waiting, still in his gardening garb. "You swore you were clean, Maksim."

"Sorry, Grandpapa. But this house is so dreary. What's a cultured man to do?"

Konstantin tapped in the code, and the door opened.

Santa Ezeriņa, back in her black jumpsuit, was sitting on the cell mattress, petting her painted housecat, a perpetual scowl on her face.

"A roommate?" she asked.

"A replacement," said Dudnyk as they forced Maksim down onto the couch inside.

"We can't leave her with him in that state," said Ninel from the doorway. "She's a reporter. He could tell every family secret he knows!"

"Oh, yes," smiled Maksim as the men released him. "We'll have a lot of fun, won't we deary?"

"If you consider castration fun."

"Never tried it. Might be. Will you use your teeth?"

"Baltic girl, out!" shouted Dudnyk.

"What about my cat?"

"He keeps secrets. You don't. Go!"

Ezeriņa exited. They shut the door. Konstantin punched in the code, Dudnyk watched the journalist's eyes taking note.

"You were heroic, Peter," said Nancy, hugging her man.

"Sweating like a pig. Need a bath."

"What about the journalist?" asked Konstantin. "I don't want this paparazzi out of your sight, Ilya."

"I'll give you two choices, Ezeriņa." Dudnyk pulled the handcuffs from his belt. "Either you stay with me until we leave for town, or I manacle you to the front gate, out with the insect storm."

"A trillion mosquitos versus your company? Can I have more time to consider?"

"No." He manacled them together at the wrists.

"You can't lead her around like that," complained Ninel. "I don't like her…proximity."

"It won't be long, Ninel A quick meal then I'll take her in my car to town." Dudnyk looked to his boss. "I'll work on that other task, sir. From the greenhouse. Assuming, you still want me to do it?"

Konstantin nodded.

"What's that other task?" asked Ezeriņa. "Oppress the peasantry?"

"Not on an empty stomach. Let's get some food."

* * *

Food was slow coming without staff. In the kitchen nearly an hour later, Dudnyk shifted the sink faucet handle side-to-side, but no flow. "Maksim is playing with the water again," he said to his prisoner, Ezeriņa forced to stand nearby as he tried in vain to make them borsch. "The pipes in that cell have a valve controlling water to the whole house. Plumbing mistake. It allows Maksim's little game when stoned and angry. On and off to gain attention."

"He's been imprisoned there before, then?"

Questions, questions… "Maksim detoxes in there. His drug problems are

IV

well known, Ezeriņa. If you're looking for a story, it's old news."

"I know about his shooting up that club in Ekaterinburg. Miracle no one was hurt."

Several were hurt, one killed, but we managed to pay off the families. Not such a good reporter, after all, are you? "I didn't mention Ekaterinburg, did I?" Dudnyk gave a final twist of the faucet handle. "No flow. It's beer and crackers, then."

"I expected lobster salad in the House of Aristov."

Dudnyk pulled a box of wheat crackers from the cupboard and a bottle of Czech beer from the fridge and directed Ezeriņa over to a table near the window. They sat at a right angle to each other, the maximum distance the handcuff chain allowed.

After a few sips of beer and two brittle crackers, he made conversation, tried to learn more about his charge.

"Why are you a journalist? Hard life."

"Because I'd be a lousy Queen of the World."

"Say again?"

"I was a finalist in the Miss Latvia contest a decade ago. One of the last ten. They asked one of those inane beauty pageant questions. 'What would you do if you were Queen of the World for a day?' So, I told 'em the truth, and they booted me out. Booed me right off stage and disqualified me."

"What did you say?"

"It's on record in Rīga. Look it up. Anyway, I decided I'd rather ask inane questions than answer them, so I became a journalist."

"Is that story true?"

"Some of it. You ever tell the truth and damn the consequences, Ilya?"

"Prisoners don't usually question officers, Ezeriņa. You're an enigma." She raised her manacled arm. "Handcuffed to a riddle?"

He took a long swig of beer. "Me? Hardly."

The intercom buzzed. Konstantin's voice asked: "Ilya?"

"Yes."

"We've been all over the house. No repellant left after Maksim's little show. Bring copious amounts back from town."

That'll cost a fortune with this outbreak. "I'll put it on the expenses."

"Do. The official one. Leave the cash for *that other thing*."

This amused his dinner partner. "You seem bright to be hired muscle, Ilya. Why do you do it?"

Money and Ninel. In that order. "Because I'd make a lousy King of the World."

"That's your boss's job. Or so he believes." With a wry smile, she bit into a cracker. Somehow, he found it sexy.

"He ever order you to kill someone?"

Dudnyk didn't find *that* sexy. *Why do women keep asking variations of that question tonight?* "No. You're reckless with your questions, Ezeriṇa. A male would be on the floor with a split lip."

"I figure if I'm going to jail, I'd better get a story out of it."

"I'll tell Konstantin you accused him of ordering killings."

"Well, if he and you don't kill, I've nothing to worry about, right? But tell him, I want to hear his response. Admission or denial, the quote will be good copy."

This girl was trouble. The sooner he got her in a city cellblock and away from the Aristovs, the better.

"Eat your crackers. We've a long ride ahead."

Bogdan appeared in the entrance from the hall, his usually stoic face a mask of worry. "Ilya, come quickly to the south window."

Dudnyk rose, and with Ezeriṇa tethered behind, they trailed Bogdan into the parlor. Ninel stood at the great window, peering over the south lawn towards the distant bathhouse. The *banya* door was ajar and its retractable roof elevated to a crack, not wide enough to let a man climb out, but enough to let *them* in. An endless black swarm, like some terrible tornado just outside, descended from the sky into those bathhouse openings.

"Ilya," said Ninel in a little girl voice. "Pyotr and Nancy are inside the *banya*."

V

As all eyes stared in horror at the thickening insect cloud flowing into the bathhouse, Ninel shouted into the intercom for Peter and Nancy Pashin.

"They don't answer."

"Is that any surprise?" asked Ezeriṇa, who had brought the bottle of beer from the kitchen. She took a swig, swallowed hard. "Would you stop to chat with those things crawling over your skin?"

"I'm not going out in that nightmare for two idiot Americans," said Bogdan. "Even family."

"The tunnels! Quickly!" shouted Dudnyk, dragging Ezeriṇa around and heading towards the backstairs. He was met immediately by Konstantin, back in his black suit, totem walking stick in hand.

"What is happening, Ilya? Why are people shouting?"

"That's what I'm trying to discover. An incident in the *banya*," he said, sidestepping the old man and his questions. "Go to your bedroom, sir. Lock the door until I know it's safe.

"Azrail plays his hand, Ilya. I told you the trip to town would be interrupted."

"Hold my beer," said Ezeriṇa, handing the bottle to the oligarch as she was dragged past.

Dudnyk led a procession of Ninel, Bogdan, and Ezeriṇa down into the south tunnel towards the bathhouse's underground entrance.

"Why were they alone?" Dudnyk asked. "The *banya* is a social place."

"American shyness," replied Ninel, huffing to keep up the brisk pace.

"They wanted to bathe by themselves."

"Foolish."

They came to the bathhouse entrance, an iron door at the top of a short stairwell. The door was padlocked shut.

"The lock's new," said Bogdan, scaling the steps and tugging at the padlock. "I used the *banya* only yesterday. Maksim, too."

"This is no accident!" shouted Ninel, pounding on the door. "Nancy! Pyotr! Answer me!"

"The wires to the bathhouse are severed," said Ezeriņa, staring at two exposed nodes off a metal box on the wall near the *banya* controls. "Someone opened the roof, then cut the electricity so the occupants couldn't reclose it. Shut down the intercom too."

"We have to get in there," said Dudnyk.

"Not without smoke or repellant," replied the journalist.

"There are bolt cutters in the storeroom, Ilya," offered Bogdan. "And maybe I can rig some torches."

"Help him, Ninel. We stay in pairs until the situation is secured."

"Ilya, I want—"

"Go!"

With a despairing mumble, she followed Bogdan down the passage towards the storeroom.

"That could be unwise, sending her with him," said Ezeriņa, watching the pair disappear into the tunnel gloom. "If Bogdan rigged this accident to help win—"

"Win what?"

"Nothing."

"Bogdan is an Aristov. And Ninel is not a threat to anyone."

"You don't sound impartial, Inspector."

"Quiet."

Dudnyk spent the next minutes listening at the door for sounds inside the *banya*, then examining the stairs and controls for evidence, annoyed by the constant tugging on his arm as his prisoner searched the same ground in her own way. Their shoulders bumped, and they repeatedly stepped in each other's path. Soon, he had enough and reached to his belt for the handcuff keys. Not there. Had he put them in his pockets? They were so tiny, smaller than a twenty-five-kopek coin...

"Lose something?" asked Ezeriņa.

"No." He dug his hands deep into his trouser pockets. "You're going into the cell with Maksim. Whatever gossip he'll tell you is not my concern. Getting ahold of a dire situation is. I can investigate far better with you off my arm and mind."

"Getting to you already, am I? The seven-minute-itch?"

"Just being efficient."

"Efficient men don't lose their keys."

"I did not lose—"

Flickering lights appeared in the tunnel. Bogdan and Ninel returned with burning broomsticks, the ends wrapped in flaming-oil-infused rags. Bogdan handed his broomsticktorch to Dudnyk, then produced a pair of bolt cutters from a pack slung over his shoulder. With a grunt, he cut the padlock from the door.

"Well done, Bogdan," said Dudnyk, asserting his command.

"I put tar on the torch rags to increase smoke."

From the same pack, Bogdan withdrew a blowtorch. Ignited it. He smiled, face blue-white behind the shooting flame. "Ready to kill those bugs?"

"We're here for a rescue. Not a hunt. Keep your violent urges in check."

"Don't I get anything burning to play with?" asked Ezeriņa.

"No," said Dudnyk. "Stay close to me."

"How things change...Have I a choice?"

Bogdan opened the door to Hades. Inside lurked a thick, living atmosphere, which retreated before their torch smoke. The blackness itself undulated, the air buzzing, and they were several steps inside before Dudnyk spied two humanoid shapes, one curled on the bathhouse bench, another, the female, lying prone on the floor near the drain. Their forms were black as any pantomime silhouette, every centimeter swathed with parasites, and it was only when Ninel swung her torch, and the feeding mosquitos rose in a continuous cloud, that the victim's deathly pale skin below became visible. The bodies were nude, towels wrapped around their heads in a vain attempt to protect the face. And sanity.

The absolute whiteness of the bodies left no doubt. Dead.

Tugging Dudnyk to the side, Ezeriņa kicked at the *banya's* ground level garden door. The violent impact opening it a crack further, the expansion halted with a metallic jingle.

"It's chained on the outside," she said.

He barely heard her, hoisting Nancy's nude form over his shoulder. Bogdan was already carrying Peter down the steps into the tunnels.

"We go, Ezeriņa."

"It's Santa."

Waving the smoking torch, they retreated down into the tunnels. Slammed the door, let the swarms that had followed them underground thin in the smokey atmosphere.

"Horrible," said Ninel, coughing from the smoke, as the men set the bloodless bodies on the tunnel floor. "What sort of person would do this?"

"Persons, possibly," said Ezeriņa. "Someone had to brave the outside to lock that second chain around the bathhouse garden door. And take a circuitous route to avoid being seen from the house. Either a lone killer did it quietly, so Pyotr and Nancy didn't notice, and then the assassin headed down here to open the roof, cut the wires, and chain the tunnel door, too." She sighed. "Or there are accomplices. One in the tunnel, one who went outside."

"Two makes a conspiracy," said Dudnyk.

"Outside?" asked Ninel. "But Maksim destroyed the supply of repellant!"

"Not all of it, apparently," replied Dudnyk, waving away the amassing smoke with his free hand. "Bogdan, put these torches out before we burn the house down around us."

Bogdan collected the broomsticks. "I'll douse them in the greenhouse water troughs."

"Come back. We'll carry the bodies to the long-term freezer. Go with

V

him, Ninel. Pairs, always."

She gave Ezeriņa a dark glance. "Yes. *Pairs, again.*"

"If looks could kill," said the reporter, watching the twosome head away down the passage.

Dudnyk patted down his breast pockets. "Where are those damn keys?"

"I swallowed them. With your beer."

He looked at her, amazed. "You ate my handcuff keys?"

"After picking your pocket. Foolish of you not to reattach them to your belt. That's 'Policing Day One.' You should be more careful. Someday, someone will go for your gun."

"Are you insane?"

"If there's a murderer, the best place for a reporter is handcuffed to the inspector."

He pulled his pistol, pressed the muzzle to her forehead. "I could shoot you, pin the murders on your corpse, and call it a day."

She didn't flinch. "That wouldn't eliminate the killer in the house. Or killers. The only one with an airtight alibi is me, Ilya. I was handcuffed to you. Beer and crackers in the kitchen."

"I'll get a saw. When Maksim sobers, into the cell you go."

"You sure you want to do that? I'm another pair of eyes. They're all suspects except us, Ilya. Konstantin, Ninel, Bogdan, Maksim. We're innocent lambs in a house of hungry tigers."

VI

"I will not cower behind a locked door in my room, Ilya," seethed Konstantin, leaning on his walking stick at the head of the great central staircase. "No one threatens a king in his own palace."

"It's for safety, sir," said Dudnyk standing a step below, with his cuffmate, Santa Ezeriņa, sitting on the handrail looking impatient. If she decided to slide down the banister like some boisterous child, it would send him tumbling down the staircase in front of his boss.

He suspected she knew that.

"Catch the killer, Ilya, and we're all safe," continued the oligarch. "There's nowhere to run, not with this plague. If he reached a car, we'd have heard an engine, seen the headlights. Search the estate, Ilya, every dark corner. Have this case wrapped up before midnight."

"And I thought newspaper deadlines were tight," Ezeriņa quipped. "You'd make a good editor, King Lear."

"Can't you stick her somewhere, Ilya?"

"You people talk like I'm an ugly piece of furniture."

"Ilya, whatever you conclude in this investigation make sure she's implicated. We rid ourselves of all troubles at dawn."

"I'll keep her in sight, every second." Dudnyk tugged his captive off the banister onto the stairs. "At least until backup is called…"

"No, other police. What do I pay you for?"

Dudnyk felt himself swimming upstream. "I should at least inform the American consulate of deaths. This'll bring international attention."

"Later," said Konstantin, pointing with the death's head cane. "I want

VI

that killer, tonight, Ilya. No excuses." He marched away towards his suite of rooms off the second-floor hall.

"So, we're going to search every 'dark corner'?" asked Ezeriṇa. "Except that suite, of course?"

Dudnyk waited until Konstantin shut his door, then quietly said, "First, I talk to the suspects."

"Interviews?" she raised an eyebrow. "Now, we're talking, Ilya. It's what I came six thousand kilometers for."

* * *

Dudnyk and Ezeriṇa entered the underground sports facilities off the north tunnel, weight machines and yoga mats on one side, a hybrid tennis-basketball court under fluorescent lights on the other. The tennis net had been shoved aside, so Bogdan Aristov could shoot baskets into a hoop on the wall.

Perfect form. *Woosh* through the basket.

"Can I talk to you, Bogdan?" asked Dudnyk, walking onto the court with Ezeriṇa.

"Sure." Bogdan retrieved his ball, continued shooting. "What do you need to know, Ilya?"

Another make. *Woosh!*

"Were you in or near the *banya* today?"

"Only with you, dragging out corpses."

Woosh!

"Not before?"

"No."

Woosh!

"Did you kill Pyotr and Nancy Pashin?" asked Ezeriṇa.

Clank!

"Mosquitos did that." Bogdan glared menacingly at the reporter as he retrieved his miss. "I don't like accusations, Ilya. Why'd you bring the paparazzi?"

"I'm writing a story on Ilya's broken nose."

"My nose isn't broken."

"It will be if you keep tugging on these cuffs."

"She's feisty," said Dudnyk, laughing off the remark to maintain authority.

"I can attest," Bogdan held up his bandaged finger. "This is my shooting hand."

"I had my rabies shot. No worries."

Dudnyk continued, aware that Bogdan someday could be his boss and hold the power of life and death over him. "Sorry, I have to ask, your grandad's orders, but where were you during the hour Peter and Nancy were in the bathhouse?"

"Here. Then up in the house for water."

Woosh!

"Was the water working then?"

"Bottled water."

"You got those bolt cutters pretty quickly when we were 'dragging out corpses,'" said Ezeriṇa with a bravery towards the Aristov family Dudnyk envied. "Did you expect to need them today?"

Bogdan laughed. "I'm sure when the staff returns, they'll confirm we've had those shears for years. The keepers use 'em to trim claws on the big tigers next tunnel over."

"And you had broom torches ready. Maybe to go outside and chain the *banya* door?"

"The torchlight would be seen from the house. Call off your watchdog, Ilya." He tossed up a hook shot.

Clank!

As Bogdan went up to rebound the miss, his extension revealed a hideous image on his shoulder usually hidden by his jersey.

"Is that an Azrail tattoo?" asked Dudnyk.

"Yep," said Bogdan, propping the ball against his hip and walking closer to let Dudnyk appraise the ink. "I've loved that creepy photo plate since I was a kid. Only one who could look at it." His eyes turned to Ezeriṇa.

VI

"Got a lot of gothic ink on my body in some *very* interesting places. You tatted, honey?"

"No graffiti on this temple. What's the fresh scar on your forearm?"

"CSKA Moscow logo. Had it removed. That club is behind me." He smiled triumphantly. "I signed with the NBA, the San Antonio Spurs yesterday. That's in Texas, honey, if you don't follow basketball. Three years, thirty-six-million-dollar contract. Guaranteed. I'm set for life, Ilya."

"You kept pretty silent about such big news."

"It's on the internet now. Coach Gregg Popovich welcomed me on the Spurs website. In Russian. Nice, eh? I was going to announce the signing in the library, but Grandad stole the show. And now we got troubles here...."

He tossed up a blind flip shot.

Woosh!

"Or maybe you're reconsidering the NBA? Millions aren't billions," said Ezerina. "You're willing to leave Konstantin's inheritance to Maksim?"

"Why to Maksim?" Dudnyk asked her.

"Maksim mentioned a contest when you were switching out my prison cell. It's logical it'd go to one of his grandsons. Big sportsman like Konstantin...He likes competition."

"Yes...I may need to mention that to Konstantin..."

"I don't need Grandad's riches," shouted Bogdan, looming over them. "I made it on my own. Respect that."

Ezerina said flatly: "Maybe you eliminated Pyotr to help Maksim win. A brotherly favor."

"We're not on good terms, Maks and I." Bogdan shrugged away her accusations, spoke directly to Dudnyk. "Wouldn't bother me, Ilya, if Maks....well...if you want to bother anyone, bother my brother. I heard voices down near his pen earlier."

"When?"

"Twenty minutes before we discovered the *banya* roof open. I was leaving this court to head up to my bedroom. Voices down there. Maybe inside the cell, maybe someone standing outside in the darkness. Not sure. Tunnel lights were off that way."

"You hear the speaker, Bogdan?" asked Dudnyk. "Man or woman? Multiple voices?"

"That's all I'm saying. Could be anyone. Could be Azrail here haunting the grounds. Go chat up my brother. I don't need the drama anymore. I'm rich on my own."

Woosh!

VII

Dudnyk used his body to shield the lock code from Ezeriṇa and opened the door to the priest's cupboard.

Maksim lay reposed on the mattress, the painted cat curled on his bare chest, the animal purring as he scratched it beneath the collar.

"Well, it's Inspector Ilya and his pet newshound. Not the couple I expected."

Dudnyk locked the door behind them. "Would you be more surprised if Peter and Nancy walked in, Maksim?"

A dark smile appeared on Maksim's lips. "I expected Ninel on your arm, Ilya. But you always were a ladies' man. Remember the nightclubs in Ekaterinburg? How many girls did we bed before the trouble started?"

The trouble you started, Maksim. "Good times, long ago," Dudnyk said. "Are you aware of events of the last two hours?"

"What could I know? Locked in a cell like Hannibal Lecter."

"Word is you had visitors," said Ezeriṇa.

"Who does she mean, Ilya?"

"Bogdan heard chatting down here."

"No one since you criminals put me here. If anyone, I was talking to the cat. Promising this little faux tiger catnip when I get out. I'm kind to animals. Like them more than people sometimes."

"Pyotr and Nancy are no longer with us, Maksim."

"They left for America?"

"They're dead."

Maksim removed the cat, sat up on the mattress. "Was it the mosquitos,

Ilya?"

"Why do you think so?"

"Well, if they're both dead, it must be something terrible…It stands to reason that the swarms will get inside eventually. Have you never seen *The Birds?* Or *Night of the Living Dead?* Barricades fail." He shrugged. "If the deaths were from fire, the alarms would have gone off…. Or maybe you shot them, Ilya? At Grandpapa's request? It's happened before…Or shouldn't I have said that in front of your journalistic S&M partner here?"

"Were you in the *banya* today?"

"No. Is that where they died? In the bathhouse?" A frown appeared on his youthful face. "Odd. I only turned the estate water on minutes ago. They must have died in a dry sauna."

"With a few million unexpected guests."

"Ilya, can I have my cat back?" asked Ezeriņa.

"Later."

"Everything is 'later' in this house."

"Yes, and we'll chat with Maksim more 'later.' I want to consider a hunch." He opened the door and pulled her quickly through into the tunnels.

"I meant what I said about the 'broken nose' story, Ilya."

"If you're not more respectful, there'll be no more stories of any kind." He locked the door, caught her watching.

"Don't make me change the code…." He set the lock. "Maksim sobered quickly, didn't he?"

"Remarkably lucid. Skin was clean. Without the beads of sweat or self-inflicted fingernail scrapes of an addict forced into cold turkey. Relaxed and calm."

"Course, this an old game for Maksim. He's good at faking sobriety to be let out," said Dudnyk, dragging her back down the tunnel. "Clean or stoned? Who can really tell with him? He's practiced in the art. But I've an idea."

"Get him stoned again?"

"Better. Get baked. Or baking…"

VII

They climbed the stairs to the house, headed to the kitchen. Dudnyk seized two bags of flour, and they returned to the tunnel depths, sprinkling the flour in front of the priest's cupboard's door, and several meters in all directions.

He went to an iron control box at the tunnel intersection, opened it, and turned off the light for the south tunnel.

"We'll check back later," he said to Ezeriṇa. "See what our trap has caught."

"Your secret's safe with me."

"Said no journalist. Ever. Come on." He tugged her down the east tunnel towards the observatory.

VIII

In the observatory, Dudnyk watched Ninel stare into the eyepiece of the room-filling telescope that extended through the domed roof, a fitted rubber skirt about the great cylinder, stretching over any gaps in the curved ceiling, sealing the room from invasive weather or deadly swarm. They'd often spent time here early in their affair, staring up at the night sky, imagining the universe beyond this blue marble.

He wondered what the heavens revealed tonight.

"Can you really see Kapitsa prison from here?" asked Ezeriņa. "Through smoke and swarms? Does the scope even tilt so low?"

"No," answered Ninel. "But Kapitsa light pollution will be obvious in that direction."

"And is there light pollution?"

"Yes. The prison searchlights are on." Ninel pulled her eye from the lens, scooted around in the observation chair to face them. "The escaped inmate is still at large."

"I'd feel sorry for him if he ends up with our motley lot," mused Ezeriņa.

"Trillions of mosquitos between him and us and anything," said Dudnyk, helping Ninel down from the chair."

"It's like we're under siege," said Ninel with a shudder. "Like Leningrad. Eight hundred-seventy days my great-grandmother endured there."

"I had ancestors on either side of that siege," said Ezeriņa distantly. "Both the Nazis and Soviets conscripted Latvians to fight their wars. What's a small nation to do under such oppression?"

Ninel frowned. "I see you're duplicitous by heritage, Ms. Ezeriņa."

VIII

Dudnyk felt the tremor of Ezeriņ's agitation through the handcuffs. "Let's not cast stones. With a name like 'Ninel,' I guess your family was hardline communist? How do they feel, with you as chief counsel, to the worst sort of capitalist, an oligarch?"

Ninel, as Dudnyk well-knew, was *Lenin* backwards. A common girl's name in the Soviet era, a name given by parents who wanted to honor—or appease—the communist party. But Ninel was born three years after the Soviet Union collapsed. She had taken the name of her own accord. To make a statement.

Ninel—the opposite of Lenin in every way save the attorney vocation. But why patronize the journalist with such information?

"Mother has no objections," said Ninel fiercely. "Communists needed to eat, too, in the chaotic first days of the free market when fortunes were made. She worked for Platon Elenin, Artyom Tarasov, and on their recommendation briefly Konstantin Aristov before I was born. Her toil helped get me this position."

"So, cronyism replaces communism."

"You fascist."

"Russians always call any who oppose them fascists."

"Ladies…stop this bickering. We have a killer in our midst."

"'We?'" asked Ninel. "Is she part of the investigation now?"

"No. She's not. But you are, Ninel. And I want your opinion as a trained attorney. Maksim seems too sober for a man who drugged himself to madness less than two hours ago. Can you come with me to the priest's—"

The intercom interrupted him.

"Ilya," said Konstantin's imperious voice. "Is Santa Ezeriņa still with you?"

"Yes."

"Shoot her. Immediately."

IX

"Shoot her, sir?" Dudnyk was uncomfortable resisting Konstantin's orders, but the suddenness of the fatal proclamation surprised him. "Why?" He regretted asking the question. The endless silence on the other end of the intercom felt threatening, like a gathering storm. Finally: "Come into the library, Ilya. I'll show you the wickedness our spy has wrought."

Dudnyk tugged the journalist down through the tunnels and up the stairs into the manor, Ninel trailing behind. As they entered the library, Konstantin seethed.

"She put a microphone behind a picture," he said, gesturing to a framed painting taken down from the wall and lying face down on the couch, a metallic spherical device hooked to the inside frame. "On the portrait of baby Rurik on the Volga. Sacrilegious. Do you know what we do to spies in Siberia, girl?"

"Send them home first class with travel expenses covered?"

"Send them home in a box. Or several." Konstantin pulled the microphone from the picture, slammed it down on the library table, then shattered the device with one blow of his walking stick. "Shoot her at once, Ilya."

"Words clearly and unequivocally said in jest, of course," interrupted Ninel with a theatrical laugh, her eyes darting around. "As anyone present can see by your humorous expression, Mr. Aristov. However, it might cause confusion to those who cannot see your face. Someone listening in on other microphones, for instance, may get an erroneous impression

IX

that you are serious. As your attorney, I suggest we all watch our language. Even the fascist girl."

"Oh, I see. Well done, Ninel," said Konstantin. "Ilya, take this journalist somewhere private. Gently and legally find out if there are more surveillance devices on the property. Then…well, you know what to do."

He did.

* * *

Minutes later, Dudnyk was tapping in the code to the Siberian tiger pen, his other hand holding Santa Ezeriņa by the scruff of her neck, trying to keep her still. Konstantin and Ninel did not accompany them, the attorney recommending the boss not expose himself again to the journalist's shenanigans. Or be present at potentially compromising situations.

Standard protocol.

"I want to thank you again for resisting Konstantin's order to shoot me," said Ezeriņa. "I'll remember that when everything goes down."

"I'm not saving you, Ezeriņa. I'm feeding you to the tigers."

"Little sweet tigers?"

"A bit bigger, these."

"If we have to play that game."

The doors slid open to a darkened room, bestial growls somewhere below. Dudnyk flipped on the slow-to-activate fluorescent lights and frog-marched the journalist inside until he pressed her against a balcony over the pen.

As the lights slowly illuminated, he could just see the shapes of three mammoth cats five meters below. Artem, Boris, and the female Kamilla.

Artem and Boris had eaten reporters before. Kamilla was picky.

"You're going over, Santa. Tiger food."

"Not while we're handcuffed. You didn't think this bluff through, Ilya."

"I'll hang you down and let them nibble your legs and work upwards.

Then slide what's left of you through the cuff afterwards."

"Okay, okay…. There is one more microphone, the last, in an upstairs toilet off the main hall."

"Why there?"

"You can learn a lot in the toilet. People step in for private conversations. Or to make mobile calls. Or talk themselves up in front of a mirror. Even to make love. Like I heard your Ninel doing earlier."

"*My* Ninel?"

"You think I didn't notice the nudges and glances between you? She's attractive. And clearly another man thinks so, too. It was someone else, wasn't it, Ilya? You don't have trysts on duty? I'm asking for a friend."

"She couldn't."

"She could, and she did. Went on for twenty minutes. It wasn't Pyotr with her, the Russian was too fluent. But any other male in the house… Maksim, Bogdan, even Konstantin. Do you want to know his pet name for 'your' Ninel? It's quite creative. Six syllables, first letter starts with—"

"No."

"Too bad. I wonder if it was more than just sex. Has your communist lover aligned herself with another man in the house? With all the secrets she knows? Hard to keep the loyalties straight…familial, sexual, financial…well, no sense wondering, now. I'm ready. Hang me over the tiger pit. Send my boots back to Mother in Latvia. We wear the same size, and she always liked these boots. I think she's too old for thigh-highs, but who am I—"

"Quiet. I'm thinking."

As the last lamps finally illuminated and the room brightened, Dudnyk pulled her back. "We're going up to that toilet. And if we don't find a microphone, there *will* be a body in the tiger pit. I promise."

"Ilya…there's already a body in the tiger pit."

X

They leaned over the pit's rail, peering down into a landscape of horrors. A human torso remained near the water pool, scattered pieces throughout the pen, little more. By the familiar tattoos and bandage affixed to a dismembered hand that now rested between the tiger Boris's paws, the identity of the victim was obvious.

Bogdan.

"The San Antonio Spurs are going to be pissed," said Ezeriņa. "No chance he fell in there?"

"There's a possibility," replied Dudnyk, not believing his own words. Bogdan was too athletic, too familiar with the big cats and their pen to just stumble in. And that was before considering recent events…

No, this was murder.

"If the staff were here," he said at last, "this couldn't have happened. The cats would be well-fed, the keeper alerted whenever the door to the pen is opened. I've swum with these tigers unharmed."

"Well, who got rid of the staff?"

"Better to ask, who benefits? Only Maksim, way I see it."

"Maksim has an alibi. Behind iron doors."

"Yes," he double-checked his gun. "Let's confirm that alibi."

***

The footprints left in the flour were exceedingly thin and bony. They passed from the tunnel's depths to the very edge of the priest's cupboard door, then changed direction and headed towards the stairs to the house, petering out before reaching the steps themselves. There were no prints exiting the priest's cupboard itself, but a clear space at the door hinted that the visitor may have lingered to listen or converse with the prisoner inside. Or maybe the clear area was just a spot they'd missed when sprinkling the flour earlier.

Hard to know.

"Our visitor must be a child, waif of a woman, or very emaciated man," whispered Ezeriņa, looking at the print. "Who does that match? No one."

Dudnyk raised a finger to his lips to silence her. He'd prefer the prisoner not know of these footprints. If he didn't already...

"Maksim," he shouted through the portal. "It's Ilya. Did you have any guests recently?"

"No," replied a weak voice within. "You were the last."

"No one since us? Even outside?"

"None."

"Hear any noises in the hall?"

A long pause. Finally: "Only you two creeping around out there. That's the journalist girl with you? Or Ninel?"

He could hear us, but not whoever left these footprints.

Ezeriņa read Dudnyk's thoughts. "He's lying," she quietly mouthed.

One mind. The two of them. Conjoined twins.

And he was going to feed her to tigers.

"Can you let me out now, Ilya?" said Maksim's voice behind the door, contrite and strangely fearful. "I'm going a little crazy down here alone... this dungeon isn't meant to be tolerated sober. The underbelly of the world. Please, I'll be good."

"That's up to Konstantin." He thought to mention Bogdan, maybe to console Maksim, maybe to test and interrogate him. Somehow, Dudnyk didn't know his own intentions. This was like nothing in his experience. Three dead in hours...

Better to break the news to Konstantin first. Let him decide what Maksim should know and what should be done with him.

X

Dudnyk flicked off the tunnel light.

"I'm going to talk to your grandad now, Maksim."

"Don't leave me alone…please. There's something not right here!"

An understatement. "Sorry. No time."

"Leave the girl, at least. To chat through the door. I need to hear a living voice a while longer. Reengage with humanity."

Dudnyk didn't reply. Grim thoughts in his mind, he tugged Ezeriņa towards the stairwell to the house above. Looking for Konstantin.

And truth in a house of tigers.

XI

They entered Konstantin's personal rooms on the second floor, found them unoccupied.

"I told him to stay inside," said Ilya, glancing into the bedroom, the expansive closet, the trophy and cigar rooms, then the office. "He never listens…"

"Yes," said Ezeriņa softly, perusing the scene.

"Neither do you."

"Yes. Never listen."

"We'd better look for him elsewhere."

"No, let's stay here, Ilya." She kneeled at a wastepaper basket and with her free hand began rummaging through the refuse inside, tossing out everything from cigar wrappers to chocolate packets.

"I'm employed to stop such snooping. Get up." He tugged upwards.

She did not move. "Ilya, we're down to three suspects," she said without glancing up. "You really want to turn a blind eye to Konstantin? Even if you cover up his crimes for a living, don't you want to know the truth for your own self-preservation? If he'll murder his grandson, he'll murder you."

He gave her ten seconds…

It went on twenty. Longer.

"Do you frequently search bins for papers?"

"Better than searching dumpsters for food…Here we go!" She lifted a printed envelope from the bin. "'CHARITÉ BERLIN' Did Konstantin take a trip recently to Germany?"

XI

"Yes. For treatment."

Her perpetual scowl returned. "The envelope's intact, but the letter itself shredded. Interesting." She dumped out the rest of the trash, gathered the strips of shredded letter, shoved them into her jumpsuit pocket.

'You can't take those."

"I just did. You're going to have to choose Ilya. Investigator or hired thug. Right now, you're getting in my way."

"Your way?"

They heard heavy footsteps climbing the stars. Ezeriṇa righted the basket, stuffed the remaining refuse inside, stood by Dudnyk.

Konstantin appeared in the doorway.

"Ilya, what are you doing in here?"

"Searching for you. Terrible news." He summoned his courage. "Bogdan is dead."

The words transformed the old man. The wrinkled face paled, the cane dropped from his hand, and Konstantin fell into the chair nearby. The unassailable body suddenly helpless and frail.

"Murdered?"

"Likely. We found his remains mauled in the tiger pen. I want your permission to shoot the cats and examine the body."

Konstantin looked impossibly ancient and forlorn. "No...those cats are all the family I've left. Nearly. Except useless Maksim..." He gathered himself. "Secure the grounds, Ilya. Another Aristov death on your watch. Find that killer before we're all corpses." He pointed to the hall. "Get out. I've nothing more to say to you. Don't you dare slip up again."

They went.

"Spoken like my publisher," said Ezeriṇa as they passed away down the hall. "After every libel suit."

"Come on."

He pulled her into a comparatively small bedroom at the end of the hall. Chocolate mints with a happy-face card signed by Ninel on the pillow. Dudnyk brushed them aside, sat on the bed, forced his captive down next to him.

"These are your quarters?"

"I sleep here, yes. Or at Ninel's." At least, when she's not with other men, apparently. *Focus.* "Let's see what you found."

Ezeriṇa spread out the letter strips on the bed before them, the sections too narrow to read the characters. "We're in luck," she said, flipping over a few pieces. "All text is on one side. Give me your mobile, Ilya."

He pulled it from his pocket. Hesitated. "Whom do you mean to call?"

"No one. I want to go to Unshred.net."

"I'll do it." A few taps and he had the website up. Looked dubious, virus warnings from his security software.

"I've a lifetime account," she said, leaning the softness of her body close to look at the screen. "Enter name 'StocktonF' Password: 'DoorOnTheLeft' We in? Good. Now take a photo of the strips and upload it. They got the best character recognition software on the Dark Web."

He did so. After a few seconds processing, the website returned an image of all pieces aligned and readable.

Well, readable for some. "German. Konstantin knows it from his days in East Berlin. I don't."

"I do." She translated aloud: "At your request, as confirmed in our examinations of June 17, July 14, and August 3rd, due to aggressive immunotherapy and chemotherapy, we assess a state of full remission of your intestinal cancer. In addition, as results of the physicals and test on.... Blah, blah, and blah...lung and heart capacity of a man ten years younger. We find you in full health. Full copies of this letter have been sent to the appropriate parties."

"Long live the king," Dudnyk said.

"Fascinating. See what searching bins does for you?"

"Puts you in perilous positions."

"That's what all the guys I'm handcuffed to in bed say."

"Yes." He smiled. *Two can play the lothario game, Ninel.* Dudnyk grabbed the metal gripper at the end of Ezeriṇ's jumpsuit zipper, dragged it down, revealing cleavage. "Maybe you stole more things from Konstantin. I should do a security check."

XI

"That's creepy, Ilya." She pulled the zipper back up, shook free his hand. "If you're doing this because Ninel betrayed you, I need to fess up. I made up the whole story. There was no microphone. No tryst in the toilet."

Eros evaporated. "You lied to me?"

"Does that surprise you? You were feeding me to bloody tigers. Now, check the hormones and tell me why a perfectly healthy man like Konstantin holds a dangerous contest to resolve his will now? This letter is dated a week ago. Why not host a gala party to announce his remission instead? A Prince Prospero orgy with the Red Death outside. The family should be thrilled. He didn't say a word. Why?"

Dudnyk sat confused, relieved about Ninel, angry and embarrassed all at once. Seeking energy for his whirling mind, he plucked one of the mints from the bed, popped it towards his mouth.

She intercepted it. Crushed the candy.

"No, Ilya."

"What?"

"Trust no one."

Someone darted across the hall doorway. A motion glimpsed. Gone in an instant.

"Ninel!?" he shouted.

"Or worse."

Dudnyk hopped off the bed, dragged his captive into the hallway. "Ninel, we were just talking!" He lurched one way, Ezeriṇa the other, the recoil sending them both tumbling to the hall floor.

"I'm in a Marx Brothers film."

"Karl Marx, Ilya."

Even from their low position, they could see the hall was empty. Somewhere a distant noise. Like a door or window slamming.

Then silence returned to Aristov Manor.

XII

They stepped up into the humidity of the greenhouse. A flick of a switch at the door and the specialized garden lamps came to life above with a hum and whiff of ozone. Dudnyk watched the journalist take in the exotic greenery around them.

"Pretty place," she said with understatement, eyes scanning across the rows of plants. "Easy to forget the catastrophe outside, isn't it?"

"I'm more worried about the catastrophe inside, Santa…. You're a stranger in a strange land. Few beyond the Aristov family are allowed here. Not even the servants disturb Konstantin's Eden."

"And did the Serpent of Eden tempt you with the marijuana and poppy plants along the rear wall?" she asked with a disapproving stare as they walked deeper into the greenhouse.

She misses nothing, Dudnyk mused. He'd never even noticed the poppies. How long had they been there?

"Konstantin disapproves of narcotics. But as his pains grew worse… well."

"And now that he's healthy, Ilya?"

"He'll get rid of those plants. Surely to Maksim's chagrin."

"I see he has poisonous Oleanders. Might consider destroying these with a killer about, Ilya."

"A wise suggestion. I'll ask Konstantin."

"I wouldn't ask. Do."

"An unwise suggestion."

She ran a finger along the edge of three empty planters. "What was

XII

here?"

"Catnip. All the lap tigers love it. And I believe at least one of the Siberians. It was here earlier."

"Better restock." She leaned over a wash basin near the glass canopy, staring at a whitish paste about the drain. "What was this?"

He leaned close, hand on her shoulder, hip against her hip. A pleasing proximity. And view. "I don't know. Something Konstantin was mashing up."

"Making poison for the next—My God! What an ugly creature!" she exclaimed, eyes on the terrible figure in the pane just above the wash bin.

"Azrail. Our local spook. A window for Death."

She wrinkled her nose in distaste, leaned closer to the glass.

"Is it real?"

"Who knows? The Aristovs say it still haunts the land."

"As if we didn't have enough trouble." She laughed, returned to examining the basin. "Whatever this muck is, it's fresh. You think Konstantin came down here to do garden work in the past few hours? With a murderer in his house?"

"He might garden to clear his head. Or before the trouble started." He tried to remember what Konstantin was doing when last he met him inside. Pruning some vine, wasn't it? Which plant? He couldn't recall.

Ezerina forced his attention, tugging his arm downward as she leaned in to stick a finger down the basin drain.

"Something in here..."

The canopy glass above her head imploded, Death's Angel blown away as a gunshot rang out from somewhere near the tunnel stairs. Ezerina screamed, clutched the side of her face. The canopy shattered under three more shots, the higher panes falling to open an immense gap in the glass wall.

They came flowing in.

Attracted by humidity and sweet garden scents, the mosquito scourge invaded more swiftly than imaginable. A denser swarm even then the bathhouse was inside in a heartbeat, the living black cloud filling the room, the air unrelenting and ravenous.

Dudnyk acted on instinct, pulling Ezeriņa towards the exit stairs, knocking over planters, and down the steps along the very escape route the gunman must have taken seconds before. Despite the voluminous buzzing of insect wings behind, he could just hear footfalls on the steps ahead and taste the gun smoke in the air as they fled.

Mercifully, no one waited to ambush them at the tunnel entrance, some silhouette sprinting away into the passage gloom. Dudnyk and Ezeriņa together slammed shut the door, damming the insect storm, but the door draft was high, a flow of mosquitos coming in from underneath to assault their unprotected flesh.

"This way," Dudnyk shouted. His gun drawn, suspicious of every shadow, they rushed to the sports hall, returned with yoga mats, and stuffed them beneath the draft to halt invasion. Swatted away the hundreds that already infested the hallway air. He tried not to think of the tens of millions on the other side of the door.

Ezeriņa leaned hard against that door, as if unsure the panel would hold. She huffed for oxygen, spitting out mosquitos sucked in with every breath.

"You see the shooter, Ilya?"

"No," he whispered, bent over, hands on knees, trying to find clear air for his burning lungs.

"Me neither. I'll try not to take those shots personally." She smirked. "Any chance they were trying to kill Azrail instead? No?"

"'And with strange aeons even death may die.'"

"Pushkin?"

"Lovecraft."

"Figures, you'd prefer the pulps. Next time, handcuff me to a literary type." She slid down the iron door to the comfort of a mat stuffed at the base. As she slid, Ezeriņa left a bloody smear on the pane.

"You're hit."

"I'm okay."

Dudnyk kneeled, gently moved her head to one side. Her right cheek

XII

and ear were covered in crimson, hungry mosquitos flying to the wound.

He swatted them away. "Just a nick of the earlobe. A shard of canopy glass."

"I better not have lost an earring."

"Better earring than ear." He pulled a handkerchief from his pocket, wiped clean her face, brushed away the glass. "Press this close for a few minutes."

She smiled weakly, took the cloth. "Why, Ilya, I believe you care? Are you developing a conscience?"

"Not if I can help it…Just don't want you leaving a trail of blood. More paperwork to file if someone confuses you for a murder victim."

"We'll all be victims if this continues." Her smile faded. "I've got bad news, Ilya. I recognized the sound of that gun. Not on the first shot. I was too surprised. But the second, third, and fourth confirmed it. A Llama Micro-Max. A distinctive ring." She tied the handkerchief around her ear. "Someone tried to kill me with my own gun."

XIII

"Ninel?" shouted Dudnyk as he and Ezeriņa entered her second-floor quarters, three rooms that formed a lavish suite surpassed only by Konstantin's. Not even Maksim and the late Bogdan had such nice lodgings.

Ninel was not in the sitting room or bedroom, and they discovered the office also uninhabited. Dudnyk was about to call Ninel on his mobile when Ezeriņa said:

"Hold off on that a minute, Ilya. Look." She nodded to the safe in the corner, its door ajar. "Wasn't this vault supposed to contain my Llama?"

"Yeah."

She kneeled, dragging him down next to her. Ezeriņa opened the door fully, searched the safe's interior with her un-manacled hand. "No gun. And conveniently, left open."

"Why convenient?"

"You know the drill, Ilya. Experienced thieves close the door to delay discovery of the theft." She squinted, reading the manufacture plate affixed inside the door. "I know this brand. A common model of safe in the former USSR."

"How do you know so much about safes?"

"I infiltrated a safecracking ring in Tallinn a few years ago. Spent two months with the gang before exposing them. Learned a lot."

"Like what?"

"Like safecracking rings get really, really angry when you expose them. And, secondly, this model of safe has a false bottom." She pulled up the

XIII

safe's lining, the cloth secured by Velcro snaps at the corners. Underneath was a small compartment door in the safe's floor secured by a combo pad.

"We should ask Ninel before proceeding," he said.

"Ilya, be brave. Give it a try. What would be her combo?"

He shouldn't. He should call Ninel and have her punch it in. Still...

He keyed in a series of numbers. A key date in Ninel's life. The lock released.

"Opened! Well done, Ilya!" Ezeriṇa exclaimed with glee, kissing him on the cheek. In the compartment was an unlabeled envelope. She plucked it out, opened the envelope, slid out two pages paperclipped together.

"What is it?"

Ezeriṇa ignored him, frowning in concentration as she read.

"Well?"

"Two medical tests. Only patient numbers, otherwise anonymous. A DNA test for a male proving him a close relative of Konstantin Aristov.... One or two generations." She flipped to the second document. "And this other page is a blood test on a woman. Can't fathom the reason at a glance."

"Pyotr and Nancy? The American relatives proving their connection to the Aristovs?"

"Likely. Or another couple somewhere. Nancy have a child, Ilya?"

"I don't think so. Ask Konstantin. Why?"

"Just looking at the estrogen levels on this woman's test. Maybe this couple are another twosome with links to Konstantin...but we're running out of bodies."

"They'll turn up, Santa. That's how these things go."

Dudnyk's mobile rang. Ninel. "Hi tigress."

"Where are you, Ilya?"

He glanced at Ezeriṇa, her eyes down, still considering the documents. "In your office."

Ninel's voice turned icy. "I'll be there in thirty seconds."

Ezeriṇa slipped the documents into the envelope, placed the packet into the compartment, and reset the safe lining. They'd just stood when Ninel entered, a dark frown on her face.

"What are you *two* doing in here?"

"Waiting for you," said Dudnyk. "Did you hear about Bogdan?"

"Konstantin told me," she said grimly, taking his un-manacled hand. "Let's get out of here, Ilya. In your police car. Forget everything." Her eyes fell upon Ezeriṇa. "What happened to her ear?"

"Ilya bit it while making passionate love to me."

"That might explain the lipstick on his cheek," Ninel didn't miss a beat. "So that's what you've been doing instead of finding this madman in the house? Sex?"

"A lie. Clearly," said Dudnyk. "Why do you goad her so, Santa?"

"Maybe she'll slip up."

"I see you two are on a first name—Wait! You suspect me?"

"Someone tried to kill us with a gun you last possessed," said Ezeriṇa. "My Llama pistol."

"It's in the safe. I placed it there hours ago."

Ezeriṇa stepped back, revealing the opened safe. "It's not here now. We found the safe door ajar and unlocked."

"It can't be." Ninel brushed her aside brutally, examined the vault. "Ilya, I was robbed."

"Obviously," said Dudnyk.

"You do believe me?"

"Of course."

"Unless you left it open yourself," said Ezeriṇa. "To give you an excuse for the missing gun…"

"Would I leave my own safe open? I'd lose all documents."

"What documents?" asked Dudnyk.

"They must have been stolen too." She shut the safe door. "Nothing terribly important."

"Then why were they kept in the safe?" asked Ezeriṇa.

"Ilya…she's terrible!"

"I know. Can you take your shoes off, Ninel?"

XIII

"My shoes?"

"Please."

Ninel leaned against him, pulled of her black dress shoes, one at a time.

"Flat feet," said Ezeriņa. "Nothing like the bony tracks in the flour."

"And I'm sure your feet are perfectly delicate works of art!"

"Ninel," said Dudnyk with a smile. "I've never been happier to see a pair of flat feet in my life. I may be developing a foot fetish."

"Such an odd statement, Ilya—"

"Everything will be fine." He kissed Ninel passionately, felt her anger and confusion dissolve as the seconds turned to minutes… He needed this. She needed it. To think Ezeriņa had him suspecting sweet Ninel…He was a fool. Their bodies melted together.

He felt the journalist nudge him at the hip. A second time. Very lightly, as if Ezeriņa were unsure she wanted his attention. He ignored the motion, the pressure. Let the kiss continue.

At last, the Latvian woman said, "I'd tell you two to get a room, but you'd probably drag me in with you."

"No threesomes with killers about," he said at last breaking from Ninel.

"I was complaining, not suggesting."

He ignored her. "Ninel, dearest darling, stay in here until I return." A last kiss. "Even if Konstantin orders you out. Or Maksim screams on the intercom for release from his cell. Or you hear bloody murder in the hall. Open it for no one. Promise?"

She nodded.

He dragged Ezeriņa out into the hall. "I'll be back soon, lover."

When they'd reached the stairs, Ezeriņa said: "Well, that was all very touching, Ilya. But I notice you didn't mention the envelope."

"You're not as clever as you seem, Santa. Did you watch my embrace with Ninel?"

"Yes, your hands were all over her. Thanks to the handcuffs, so were mine."

"Exactly. A subtle frisk disguised as a lover's caress. Your gun was not on her person."

She smiled as they descended the steps. "I'm impressed."

"Good. Now it's time we took a closer look at Bogdan. Before the tigers finish their meal."

XIV

Far below the safety of the observation balcony, Dudnyk led Ezeriṇa through the keeper's corridor to the door to the tiger enclosure. He peered through the door's one-way window, watching the cats.

"What can you see, Ilya?"

"Not much." *Here it goes.* "Ready?"

"We're not actually going inside?"

"You wanted a story, Santa." He pressed the door release and dragged her with him into the pen. The smells of enclosure vegetation, tiger fur, tiger urine, and human blood tickled his nostrils. The three great cats watched them curiously. None made aggressive moves, though the twitching of annoyance in Kamilla's tail suggested dangerous surplus energy that may be released at any moment.

"Ilya, I have something to tell you…"

"Not now."

They crept cautiously away from the door. What was left of Bogdan was now dispersed throughout the pen, though a mostly intact torso rested at a short distance from the water pool's edge.

"Look at this mess," whispered Ezeriṇa. "And he complained when I bit him."

Boris rose, the big male batting Bogdan's hand around like a house kitten with a ball. A swipe of a paw sent it to Ezeriṇa's feet.

"Ick," she said, inching backwards.

"Nice of him to share."

"Maybe he expects me to return the honor?"

"Not with my limbs, you don't."

They reached Bogdan's torso, knelt to examine the remains.

Kamilla rose on the other side of the pool, tail twitching quicker.

"Don't worry, she can't stand the taste of reporters."

"How does she know I'm a reporter?"

"Show her your press pass." Dudnyk turned over the corpse. Among the mauling and claw marks was a different sort of wound. A gunshot with powder burn right in the shoulder tattoo of Azrail.

"Rough day for the ole Reaper," said Ezeriņa. "What do you people have against the Angel of Death?"

He ignored her, glancing quickly about to ascertain the tiger positions, then pulled a utility knife from his belt and dug into the wound to retrieve the slug.

"I'm fairly good with ballistics…looks like a seven millimeter. Could be from many guns. A Mauser…a host of Remingtons."

"Not my Llama. It's a nine-millimeter."

Kamilla was fording the pool, head just above the water.

"Ilya…I don't like how she's looking at me."

"Stay steady." He put the slug in his breast pocket, pulled his gun. "Konstantin's pets or not, I'll fire if they charge us."

"Should I mention now I unloaded your gun?"

"What!? When!?"

"When you were kissing Ninel in the office. You're a very attentive lover. Focused. A good quality in a man, if not a *police*man." Ezeriņa smiled apologetically. "I didn't want to risk being fed to tigers at gunpoint again, Ilya. Ironic."

That was the bumping he'd felt. "Where are my cartridges?"

"In her office. I didn't know you'd drag us inside the pen. I thought we'd look from the balcony."

Boris was now pacing. Kamila, emerging from the near side of the pool. His pulse was racing. This was not how he envisioned death…

"Don't panic, Ilya. I've dealt with large carnivores before. I once almost

XIV

fed an FSB man to a polar bear—"

"Quiet. Retreat slowly to the exit." They stood. Edged backwards, almost stumbling over each other. As they passed Bogdan's hand, he kicked it away. Boris pounced on the limb playfully. Kamilla kept her attention strictly on them.

They reached the enclosure wall, found the door. Eyes never leaving Kamilla, Dudnyk pulled the release, felt his arm tugged violently as Ezeriņa rushed out. He followed, stepping into the keeper's corridor and slamming home the door just as the tiger charged, heard her body impact against the panel as he set the triple bolts. A glance through the window. Kamilla was stretched out, pawing at the door, claws scraping on metal.

"Missed your chance to get me, girl."

"You talking to her or me?"

"Both."

A paw the size of his head slammed the windowpane, rattling the glass. He knew it tiger-proof.

Still...

"Yeah, don't taunt her," Ezeriņa said.

They watched until Kamilla grew frustrated, then slinked off to a dark corner near the third tiger, Artem, who'd barely moved the whole adventure.

"Maybe her pen mate will mellow her out, Ilya."

"Artem? He's usually the fiercest," said Dudnyk as they hurried away towards the main tunnels. "Someone must have given him catnip."

XV

They heard creaks as soon as they reached the top of the second-floor stairs. Footfalls hurrying away.

Dudnyk peered down the hall. "Can't tell which room…"

"They're not coming from a room," said Ezeriņa, turning him around and pointing to a panel in the wall at the end of the passage. "But that dumbwaiter door just closed. Maybe Konstantin ordered a snack."

"From whom? No staff to operate it or make the meal."

Dudnyk edged closer to the closed dumbwaiter panel, his empty gun drawn as a tool of intimidation. He held his pistol steady over the panel, then pressed the CALL button with his manacled hand. With a grinding old-fashioned gear noise, the panel retracted, revealing a terrified girl in her late teens balled up on the dumbwaiter platform. She wore a staff maid's uniform, but Dudnyk did not recognize her.

The girl screamed at the sight of the gun, threw her hands up to protect face and body.

"Easy," said Dudnyk, pressing the LOCK button on the controls to keep the dumbwaiter in place. "We're not going to harm you. Not unless you harm us first. Climb out."

The trembling girl stepped down into the hall. Her uniform was creased and sweat-stained as if she'd worn it a long while and under duress or strain.

"What is your name?"

"Eva, sir," she answered in a whisper.

"Are you staff? Why were you in there? Why are you still in the manor?"

XV

"One question at a time, Ilya. She's terrified," said Ezeriṇa. "We're friends, Eva. The guns and handcuffs are just late-night adult fun."

"Late-night fun?" she looked at Ezeriṇa quizzically, then back to Dudnyk. "I'm staff, sir. Four months now…As for being still here, I had no place to go. Family disowned me." She seemed on the edge of tears. "Mr. Konstantin said the staff would return in a few days—plague and God willing—so I thought I'd wait it out in my room. He was most insistent that staff should leave, but I've been having the most terrible dreams. Premonitions, I think they call them. Of the autobus breaking down in the wilderness with nowhere to go and those things getting inside. Millions of them…and I'm always naked in the dreams with no protection…Maybe it was cowardly to stay and hide, but I didn't want to risk my baby."

"Baby?"

"She's at least three months pregnant, you idiot," said Ezeriṇa. "Can't you see the bump?"

He hadn't noticed. She was so thin.

"Who is the father?"

"I can't say."

"Can't or won't."

"Better if I don't."

"Ilya…," said Ezeriṇa. "Later."

"Let me see your feet, Eva. Pick 'em up. One at a time."

"If she picked them up at the same time, she'd fall down, Ilya."

Eva obeyed. Her bare feet were small, thin, bony, though clean of any grime or flour.

"You don't wear shoes?"

"I…I can walk around quieter without them, sir."

"Why were you in the dumbwaiter?"

"I was trying to sneak down to the kitchen for some food, the stairs are risky, but then I heard the two of you coming. You bicker awfully loudly—"

"I never raise my voice."

"Ha!" said Ezeriņa.

"So, I hid in the dumbwaiter. If the Aristov family finds me…."

"Yes, you told us. You been in the tunnels lately, Eva?"

"No, sir."

"The greenhouse? The tiger pit?"

"Never."

"The banya?"

"Staff aren't allowed its use. And I was never assigned to clean it by the butler."

"Are you aware of the killings tonight, Eva?"

Her eyes widened and face turned ghastly pale. "No…You don't think I…I wouldn't…"

"The natural first question is who died, not denial."

"Don't be so harsh, Ilya."

"I thought you were the tough journalist, Santa."

"Not if you scare the girl into a miscarriage."

"Well, who died, sir? I hope it wasn't Mr. Bogdan. Only one who was nice to me…"

"We'll fill you in, but you're spending the rest of the evening in the company of a lawyer. No more running around unsupervised. You know Ninel Safronova?"

"All too well."

Dudnyk took her arm, Santa followed suit, and they escorted her to Ninel's door. He knocked.

She answered. "Ilya, I was—"

"Ninel, we've a guest," he directed Eva into the room. "A maid. You're acquainted? Good. Watch her for an hour, my love. Have her dust. Dust for fingerprints."

"I don't—"

"That's a joke, Eva."

He retrieved the cartridges Ezeriņa had unloaded, rearmed his pistol, and they went to Konstantin's door to report on Eva and many other matters.

XV

As usual, the boss was missing.

XVI

Looking for a gun that matched the one that killed Bogdan, they wound their way through the maze of Konstantin's private suite towards the trophy room on the far northwest corner of the house. Here, amongst the cigar humidors and plush furniture, were the prizes of a bold life. Animal heads and skins from Africa and the Americas, clothing and artwork crafted by Indigenous people worldwide, photographs of Konstantin and son Rurik trekking through the wastes of Antarctica and cloud-shrouded peaks of Nepal. Most interesting to Dudnyk were the assorted weapons mounted on the walls, ancient and modern armaments from every corner of the globe.

At first glance, nothing was amiss. The weapons were dusty, the maids forbidden in this room, and no firearm seemed likely to match the bullet that slew Bogdan.

Out of the corner of his eye, he saw Ezeriņa reaching up towards a nineteenth-century British elephant gun. He nudged her.

"Ah, no. No weapons for you. Stay close. "

"Spoilsport."

Dudnyk examined two comparatively modern pistols: a Berretta Tomcat and a Walther PPK. The wrong calibers and not recently fired. He set them back.

"Some lovely pieces here," he said. Dudnyk took down an old flint musket, admiring the antiquity of the weapon. Seventeenth century or so. "Most of these couldn't possibly fire, of course." His finger caressed the trigger. It blew a hole in Konstantin's couch, stuffing flying to the ceiling,

XVI

the residue and smoke coating everything.

"The forensics teams must love working with you, Clouseau," Ezeriņa mused, shaking the dust and stuffing out of her hair. "Just blame Eva. Konstantin will be firing her anyway."

"With all this old gunpowder, I'll need a shower."

"Well, don't expect me to take it with…Yes, what about that gun?" She pointed enthusiastically with their linked arm to a revolver mounted high on the wall. "That could be the one! I know it!"

"That? It's an eleven-point-four-millimeter Magnum. Nothing like the gun that killed—"

"Get it anyway."

He tried to reach up, on his tiptoes, then felt a violent tugging on his arm. Glanced back at Ezeriņa.

She'd seized a Japanese polearm ax from the wall, in an instant forced their arms against a bare spot in the display, slammed home the blade severing the handcuff chain.

"What the Hell are you doing?"

"No time to talk to a duma." She charged away, polearm in hand.

"I am not a duma!"

He sped after her, out of Konstantin's suite, into the hall towards the stairwell.

A scream!

On the stairs Ninel and Eva stood, pale faced, the younger woman clinging to the banister.

"She has an ax!" shouted Eva. "Is this more adult fun?"

"Where?"

"Down the stairs?"

"She's after Maksim!" said Ninel. "The last heir! She's a fascist assassin. I told you!"

Dudnyk sped down the levels into the tunnels. Caught just a glimpse as Ezeriņa pounded in the code, and fled into the priest's cupboard, polearm in hand.

A masculine scream. Then a metallic crash.

The last Aristov? Dead?

He pulled his gun, confirmed it loaded, and stepped cautiously into the cell.

Maksim crouched on the floor, the hissing cat near him. Ezeriņa stood near the pipes, hands behind her head, the ax polearm resting at her feet. Nearby, lay the main waterflow handwheel, severed from its pipal position.

"Back against the wall!" he shouted.

"Easy, Ilya," she said, raising her hands higher to emphasize her surrender. "All I did was cut the water supply. Literally."

"I'll never trust you again."

"That makes me sad, Ilya. Without water, these proceedings will be forced to move elsewhere. With less biased policing. And responsible judges."

"Responsible judges?"

"Konstantin rules here."

"Shoot her!" said Ninel coming in from the tunnels, Eva meekly peeking over her shoulder.

"He won't," said Ezeriņa. "Ilya wants to see this through."

Dudynk's mind reeled with indecision. A reprieve came with his ringing mobile. He retrieved the polearm from the floor before putting away his gun and answering the call.

Konstantin's voice was calm and authoritative.

"Gather everyone in the library, Ilya. I have solved the case for you."

XVII

They assembled in the library—Dudnyk, Ezeriņa, Eva, Ninel, Maksim, and Konstantin. The paintings and photographs remained on the floor from Konstantin's search for microphones, the lap tigers cried from imprisonment in the adjacent reading room, and through the window, the early summer sun was fighting its way over the horizon, red rays obscured by fading, unattended smoke and endless swarms.

"I have solved the case for you, Ilya," repeated the old oligarch, pointing with his deathly cane. "The murderer amongst us is Maksim."

"Grandpapa," replied Maksim, swigging a cocktail Eva had fetched for him. "That's not amusing."

"Agreed, Maksim. We are not amused," said Konstantin. "Let me iterate my thinking. Who had the most to benefit from the deaths of Bogdan and Pyotr? Maksim. He wins the inheritance. Who has killed before? Maksim. He murdered that clubgoer in Ekaterinburg pointlessly. Wouldn't he kill his own brother and cousin for billions? Rurik wanted you to live a straight life, Maksim, go to university, and manage the pet tiger industry. You didn't want that. You wanted to be a crime lord. But Rurik planned to legitimize us when his time came. So, you killed your father, too."

"Patricide? Never. And, as for the killings tonight, or *yesterday* as it's dawn, Grandpapa, need I remind you I was locked in that cell?!"

"You weren't in the priest's cupboard when the deaths occurred. Some accomplice let you out. Probably, this maid you hid in the house," said Konstantin, looming over his descendant in the chair. "You faked being intoxicated, so we'd lock you away and give you an alibi. Destroyed the repellant, so only you and your ally would have a supply. It's obvious." He turned to Dudnyk. "Shoot Maksim, Ilya."

"Grandpapa, I haven't finished my cocktail!"

"At least, it isn't me this time," said Ezeriņa.

"Shoot her, too, Ilya. We can't have a journalist airing our secrets to the world."

The Latvian's eyes widened. "Hey, hey, wait a minute…"

"I won't shoot anyone on your behalf, Konstantin. Not anymore," said Dudnyk in a whisper, his voice rising with resolve. "A boss bent on killing his family? No. Maybe you'll kill off loyalists like Ninel and me next? The Aristov operation is broken beyond repair. I learned that tonight."

"If you're loyal, you'll do what—"

"You're insane, sir," interrupted Dudnyk. "And our killer is not Maksim. It's you, Konstantin."

"Me?"

"You arranged this contest for the purpose of murdering your grandsons. Then an American showed up with a DNA test—yes, we found it—proving himself family, and you had to add Pyotr to the game, last minute. You're perfectly healthy. We discovered that, too. You had no need to settle the will imminently. This was a trap."

"You suggest I murdered Bogdan and Pyotr?"

"You had ample opportunity. You're the one who announced over the intercom that there was no more repellant. A lie. Catnip is a natural insect repellant, used worldwide where commercial ones aren't available. As a gardener, you knew that. You used catnip oil from the missing plants. We found the remnants in the greenhouse sink. Once protected from the swarms, you went outside and chained the *banya* door. So much for Pyotr and Nancy. Later, with Maksim trapped in his cell and me off searching the house, Bogdan was alone in the sports court. You lured or ordered him into the tiger pen, shot him in the back, and dumped the body over the rail. Scratch off, Bogdan."

"You disappoint me, Ilya."

XVII

"Maksim was to be last, so you could pin the murders on him. As you have done. Earlier, you ordered me to bring heaps of drugs for Maksim. Why? So, he'd overdose. Or you could feed him a hot dose later laced with oleander or opium toxins grown in the greenhouse. Now you order me to shoot him. A slight detour to the same destination."

"What is my motivation for killing potential heirs? I could choose anyone I wanted."

"To eliminate kin who would contest your will, divide your empire with infighting. Division of the spoils is your admitted fear. There is a new heir you want to have everything, a favored heir. A secret heir too young for the contest."

"Who?" asked Ninel.

"Eva's baby. We found a blood test for a woman, too. Konstantin, you fathered a child with a girl a quarter your age, didn't you? A chance to start again after the loss of Rurik. Why give everything to an inattentive athlete grandson bound for Texas, or a wastrel addict grandson, or a clueless foreign relative who forced his way into the game. Since you're healthy, you'll have time to mold Eva's child into whomever and whatever you want. As long as the others aren't around to interfere."

"It's a lie!" shouted Eva.

"Well, who is the father?"

"Maksim."

"If true, Eva, that changes nothing. Konstantin wouldn't let Maksim corrupt the chosen heir. Even more of a reason to eliminate him."

"You're a dead man, Ilya."

"Perhaps, Konstantin, but I'll see you in prison before I die. It'll be easy with what I know of Aristov history." He pulled his pistol. "You're under arrest, sir."

"Bravo, Ilya!" clapped Ezeriṇa. "At last, you stand up to the bully. And thanks for not shooting me. Well done. But let's change one little thing about what you said."

"What's that?"

"Your conclusion."

XVIII

Santa Ezeriṇa rose from the couch, maneuvered herself to the center of the room near Dudnyk. "Ilya's logic is essentially correct. The killer was saving Maksim for last as his drug habits made him an easy target and allowed a simple coverup. And catnip oil was used as a replacement repellant. There also is a secret heir. Isn't that right, Ninel?"

"I never had a child."

"*You* are the heir. Your mother left the Aristov service soon after you were conceived to hide the pregnancy. Konstantin is your father? Or was it Rurik? The DNA test we found in your office revealed a descendant of Konstantin's. One or two generations."

"But Ilya said that was a male DNA test," said Maksim.

"You're her lover, Ilya. Ninel is a transgender woman, isn't she?"

"Yes," he said softly.

"Perhaps that's why you consciously or unconsciously excused the obvious, Ilya. A DNA test always shows the birth gender. But the blood test of an individual taking heavy estrogen treatments would return female. Those results we discovered in Ninel's office weren't for a couple. They were for one individual. Ninel Safronova, likely born Lenin Safronov. Our secret heir."

"So, what if I'm an Aristov? It doesn't mean I killed anyone! Ilya, please…"

Ezeriṇa continued. "It was the only way to get the money. She was a bastard child. Her mother a communist, an ideology hated by the criminal tycoon who fathered her. And there are few countries more transphobic

XVIII

on Earth than Russia, especially to an old patriarch of Konstantin's generation. I'm guessing he didn't know his lady attorney was once the son he fathered...but with the other heirs eliminated and DNA evidence available, the state couldn't deny Ninel her legal birthright. As an attorney, she knew this.... So, she kills Rurik, Bogdan, and Peter. Later, she'll rub out the easily disposable Maksim. Then Ninel lets Konstantin die of old age. Everyone thought he was terminally ill. And, best of all, her lover was the investigator. Ninel could manipulate Ilya, manage the evidence. Bribe him with sex, money, or love, if needed. Even if you found out, could you go against Ninel, Ilya? Did she ever ask who you would choose between your loyalty to her or Konstantin?"

Dudnyk did not answer.

"A matter for another time, I see," said Ezeriṇa. "So, we all have our suspects. Konstantin has Maksim. Ilya has Konstantin. I have Ninel. We'll let the judges decide. I told you I wanted fairer judges, Ilya."

"No judge would dare rule against me," said Konstantin.

"These might." Ezeriṇa opened the door to the reading room, eight tiny tigers spurting out, happy to be free. "They'll find the killer for us."

It was only a few seconds before little Vlad began rubbing against Ninel's leg. Then Valeria. Then Anton and Galina.

"Get off me," Ninel said as the other cats joined in, mobbing her. "Not now."

"They smell the catnip oil on your skin, Ninel. I cut the water to prevent our murderer from washing off the natural repellant." Ezeriṇa glanced at Dudnyk, who still held his gun aloft. "I'm sorry, Ilya, with your feelings for Ninel, I thought it best to not reveal my suspicions. It wasn't jealousy that caused her to take a shot at me in the greenhouse, but our investigation of the missing plants. Of the leaves she smashed to oil in the greenhouse wash bin. I found the plant's stem in the drain right before the shots came in."

"You betrayed me, Ninel!" Konstantin charged at her, swinging his skull cane, scattering the miniature tigers. "I'll kill you!"

Dudnyk shot him dead.

"Well, that's a lucky turn," said Maksim with a sigh, and lighting the cigarette Eva extended to him. "I guess I get everything in the end. Who's up for vodka and strip Scrabble?"

Epilogue

Under orders from his new boss, Maksim Aristov, Dudnyk placed Peter's and Nancy's bodies in the police car trunk next to a garbage bag that contained the remains of Bogdan. There was no room for Konstantin, so he put the oligarch's corpse in the passenger seat.

As he pulled the car out of the courtyard, he spied Maksim dancing in one of the upstairs windows, the victor clearly stoned out of his mind. Poor Eva served him drinks. The servant who feared leaving, who had premonitions of death, was now marooned with a billionaire addict. Well, they said it was his kid anyway…At least they can be together. How long until he overdoses, and it is all for naught?

Dudnyk glanced at the corpse next to him. "You throw a hell of a party, old man."

"Let me go, Ilya," said Ninel through the security glass from the backseat. "That reporter framed me."

"Quiet, Ninel."

"I embezzled millions. We can run away like we always planned. Konstantin can't touch us now. Maksim won't care. I'll convince you. I always do."

"Quiet, Ninel."

She sighed. "Well, I hope you're not going play that pop music all the way into town."

"You smell of catnip, Ninel."

"Better than Insecta-Guard, Ilya."

***

Santa Ezeriņa, having rubbed *Nepeta cataria* leaves over her exposed skin, darted out to her rental vehicle, opened the passenger door, and threw the animal carrier into the seat before too many mosquitos descended on her cat.

Just like Sigourney Weaver at the end of Alien, she thought. *She should really have named him Jonesy.*

She slammed the door, noticing the side mirror glass was missing.

Great, I'm gonna have to pay for that too.

Well, she could soon afford it. This story was going to be big news.

Santa went around and climbed into the driver's seat, slamming the door with satisfaction and starting the engine. She unhooked the bulbous gripper from the end of her jumpsuit zipper, set it in the arm rest.

The final microphone hanging right in front of Dudnyk the whole time, and he never noticed. Amazing given how often he'd stared at her chest.

She withdrew her spare mobile from the pillow inside the cat carrier, checked the *Baltic Beacon* website to see if there were any teasers of her coming story. What she saw made her gasp.

TIGER OLIGARCH KONSTANTIN ARISTOV MURDERED IN POLICE SHOOTOUT
3 OTHER FAMILY VICTIMS. GRANDSON INHERITS ALL
AN EXCLUSIVE BY ALBERTS KRŪMIŅŠ

An anonymous source confirmed tonight that Russian oligarch Konstantin Aristov was gunned down in his Siberian home by...

What? Oh, no....

Alberts was listening the whole time. Stole it all. No, no, no....I'll kill him. Sue him.

Santa pressed her face into her hands, pounded her forehead against the steering wheel.

EPILOGUE

Sue him with what money?
It was all for naught.

Her cat hissed. Then she felt something sharp press against her jugular vein. Her eyes went to the rearview mirror. A wild-eyed man, head and body wrapped in sweaty rags leaned over from the backseat, holding a shard of side mirror glass against her throat. He reeked of insect repellant. Under the rags at his collar was the vivid orange of a prison uniform.

"Drive on, lady. Slowly. Try and signal that police car ahead and I'll cut you. We're going our own way. A million kilometers of Siberia to get lost in."

"Oh, thank God," said Santa with a relieved smile, easing forward, and shifting the car into gear. "I thought I was going to leave here without a tale to sell."

* * *

Naked as the lovers they were, Maksim and Eva descended the steps into the tunnels beneath Aristov Manor.

"Have you never been to the north tunnel, Eva?" asked Maksim in the slurred voice of an alcoholic stupor.

"I was forbidden."

"Well, housemaid transformed into house mistress, you can go wherever you will. We will sleep in Grandpapa's bed tonight. You will never sleep in a better bed. A luxurious life awaits."

"Freedom."

"Yes...we are free." Maksim's cloudy brain tried to grasp how close it all came to crumbling. Razor's edge. "I feared Grandpapa had us until Ilya and that reporter started babbling. Then, I knew we had a chance. Luckily, we washed off the catnip—unlike Ninel. Who knew she was a man?"

"Once a man. And your relative."

"Well, aunt or uncle, I gave her millions to assist. Ninel will trouble us no more..."

In their naked drunkenness, they moved slowly, lurching along, supporting each other. At last, they reached the entrance to the greenhouse. Some fool had stuffed yoga mats underneath the door. In their stupor, they thought these mats served no purpose.

Hassel.

"Grandpapa kept the best marijuana plants here, Eva. And I grew poppies." Maksim tugged away the mats, scrapped his bare feet upon them. "Did I ever tell you of Azrail? No? He's a haunting figure in the canopy glass. Ghastly. A terror called up from opioid dreams…an Angel of Death."

"I'm not sure I want to meet Azrail."

He laughed, pulling on the handle. "Trust me, my love, the most terrible Death imaginable awaits us behind this door."

About the Author

William Burton McCormick is an Edgar-award nominated writer of crime and thriller fiction set mainly in Eastern Europe. He is a regular contributor to *Alfred Hitchcock's Mystery Magazine, Ellery Queen's Mystery Magazine, The Saturday Evening Post, Mystery Magazine, Black Mask*, and elsewhere. He is the author of the award-winning thriller novels *A Stranger from the Storm, Lenin's Harem,* and *KGB Banker*, the last co-written with whistle-blower John Christmas. His forthcoming Western novel *Ghost* was a finalist for a Claymore Award for best unpublished novel. A native of Nevada, William earned his MA in Novel Writing from the University of Manchester in the UK. He has lived in seven countries for writing purposes, including Ukraine, Latvia, Estonia, and Russia. Learn more about his writing at williamburtonmccormick.com

SOCIAL MEDIA HANDLES:
   https://www.facebook.com/bill.mccormick.73345
   https://www.facebook.com/William-Burton-McCormick-365316520150776/

Twitter: @WBMCAuthor

Goodreads: https://www.goodreads.com/author/show/5447401.William_Burton_McCormick

Instagram @williamburtonmccormickauthor

AUTHOR WEBSITE:

www.williamburtonmccormick.com

Also by William Burton McCormick

Lenin's Harem (novel) 2012

KGB Banker (with John Christmas) (novel) 2021

A Stranger from the Storm (novella) 2021

Printed in the USA
CPSIA information can be obtained
at www.ICGtesting.com
LVHW090611201124
797034LV00001B/10